THE

LONG

GUEST

JENNIFER MUGRAGE

OUT OF
BABEL

OUT OF
BABEL

ISBN: 978-1-7358354-0-2

First Edition Printing
Cover Illustration Copyright © 2020 by Jennifer Mugrage
VTC Goblin Hand font by Larry E. Yerkes, licensed under the
1001 Fonts Free For Commercial Use License (FFC).

https://outofbabel.com

To all our grandfathers and grandmothers

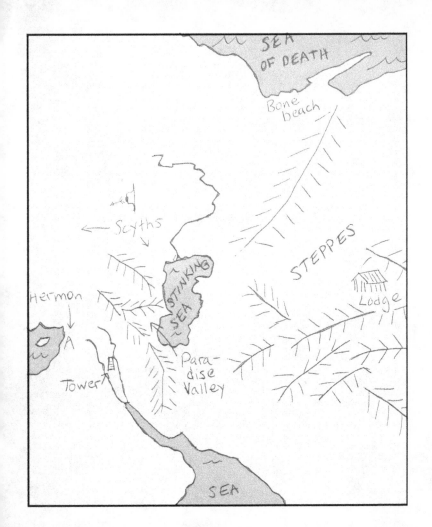

Prologue

Long ago, thousands of years before human civilization is now thought to have arisen, there was already a mighty civilization that encompassed all of humankind. An ancient record tells us how that civilization came to an end:

> Now the whole world had one language and a common speech. As men moved eastward, they found a plain in Shinar and settled there. They said to each other …
> "Come, let us build ourselves a city, with a tower that reaches to the heavens, so that we may make a name for ourselves and not be scattered over the face of the whole earth."
> But the LORD … said, "If as one people speaking the same language they have begun to do this, then nothing they plan to do will be impossible for them. Come, let us go down and confuse their language so they will not be able to understand each other."
> So the LORD scattered them from there over all the earth.
>
> GENESIS 11:1 – 8

This ancient, catastrophic collapse of a civilization instantly produced many small family groups, now strangers to one another, each of which was forced to make their own journey as they scattered over the face of the earth.

This book tells one such family's story.

The Family of Golgal at the Time of the Tower's Fall

Golgal was descended from Noah:

Noah
↓
Japheth
↓
Tiras
↓
Golgal

Golgal married his cousin Zillah and had four children. His household also included servants. Family members in bold, servants in Roman:

Golgal	*married to* **Zillah**
	Shufer, *Zillah's maidservant*
Enmer	*married to* **Ninshi**
	child: **Angki**
	Gia, *Ninshi's maidservant*
	Gia's child by Enmer: unnamed
Endu	*unmarried at the time of the Tower's fall*
Sut	*unmarried at the time of the Tower's fall*
Ninna	*unmarried at the time of the Tower's fall*
Hur, *Golgal's slave, same age as Enmer*	*married to* Shulgi
	child: Hur-kar
"The Cushite," *a foreigner, not a member of the family*	

CHAPTER 1

THE FALL

Nimri

I never imagined I would fall so low. Here I lie – carrion, looking up at the Tower – I, who only days ago used to ascend it every morning. I would look down and see the city, the storerooms, workshops and barracks, but the people were too small to be seen. I could watch the sun rise from the tower an hour before it would reach the roofs. Below me, the eagles wheeling … eagles that now are coming after *my* flesh.

There was still scaffolding, of course. The drawback was that there would be scaffolding until the whole tower was done. It had taken much longer than we had expected, to build a tower high enough to reach the heavens. The empty air had gone up and up, and the tower had grown taller and finally had begun to get out of balance, and we'd had to tear it down and begin another. I still remembered the heated discussions surrounding that decision, one taken twenty years ago. Some men, weaker men, had said we should finish it there and be content. But finally the stronger and braver had come out on top, as we always must. I myself had arranged not a few assassinations, all so that the decision should come out right, all for the sake of the tower. No, not of the tower – for the sake of humankind. Truly there is nothing in the earth or the heavens greater than man. This tower alone was proof of it – we had built it up in only twenty years, practically as quickly as a flower grows, yet taller than a mountain and as deep in the ground as it was tall. Surely nothing can compare to man, especially a man who lives long and learns much. Whatever we set our hands to we are able to accomplish.

I set this down now so that it will not be forgotten. I don't know if there is one real human being left still in the world, one who understands this tongue and who when I am gone will be able to read and understand this writing. These fools who have now taken charge of me with my broken body, these barbarians … I am sure that they knew nothing of letters, even before. They must have been the lowest kind of slaves. But perhaps this account will one day be found by one who can read it.

And so, let him who reads understand: I am Nimri the Great.

We were the first people and the greatest and best people. We chose clay for the tower because though it may be unsightly, clay is a material that never runs out. And it is eternal. It gets harder and stronger as it gets older, just as it was supposed to have been with mankind. Just like humankind, it draws its strength from the sun. Its only enemy is water.

We had writing – *of course.* We were the first and best people. Our writing system was the most elegant the world has ever seen, but now it has vanished and I am the only one who remembers. With it we planned the towers, the first and the second, and aligned them with the stars.

The tower was to be covered in gold when finished. But it never happened.

I was at the top of the tower that morning. I had run up before dawn. I never grew tired. We first people were the strongest. I looked out over the emerald green plain, patched in blue shadows, and thought to myself that an enemy could never surprise a people who had such a tower. I could see farther than an army could move in a day. I could see the blue mountains to the north; and to the south, the sparkling sea.

A slave approached from my left, walking slowly up the ramp through the scaffolding, a tower of bricks on his back.

"What level have they reached today?" I asked.

"*Kura?*" he said.

At first I did not realize what was going on.

"What?" I said.

"*Kura?*"

"What?"

"*Kura?*"

Fear began to seize me.

"What's wrong with you, man?"

He too looked afraid. And he said, "*Aku aroko pahapm,*" – or some such gibberish as that.

That was when panic set in. I began running back down the ramp. All around me, others were doing the same. Everyone was yelling. I couldn't understand any of it, but I knew that we were all saying the same things: "What?" "What?" "I can't understand you!"

We were terrified. None of us had had an experience like this before. We had always been able to accomplish anything we set our hands to.

A man ran up to me, grabbed my shoulders. He was doing what all were doing now – searching the faces of the people we passed, looking for someone we thought would still understand us.

"*Vee os lees*?" he said.

I shoved him away roughly and yelled at the top of my voice, "Can't anyone here speak normally? Can anyone hear me? Answer!"

It was impossible that anyone should hear above the cacophony.

Behind me, the slave had dropped his bricks in the middle of the ramp. I heard a rattle, looked down, and saw a pulley falling free, carrying a huge raft of bricks with it. It would be minutes before it reached the bottom.

Some people were fighting, clearly even murdering each other. Others were running and falling. Screams were coming up from the bottom. The eagles were wheeling excitedly.

"Nimri!" called someone. On the scaffolding two levels below me I saw Zira. When our eyes met, his face relaxed in relief. He didn't bother to run, but grabbed the scaffolding and swung himself up easily by the arms. He grabbed my shoulders and kissed my cheek. A sign of brotherhood.

"Nimri," he said. Relief washed over me. But then he opened his mouth to greet me, and relief dissolved into horror. For his greeting was gibberish, just like the others'. I couldn't understand it, sounded something like "*Rachangkupancha?*"

I did not try to decipher it. The sound of his words filled me with loathing.

"You are demon possessed!" I shouted. I broke away from him and ran again, and then I felt myself falling.

I woke. Not in pain, but knowing that I would vomit. I was beneath the tower – of course I was, for was not the whole world beneath the tower? The eagles were busy, not wheeling but popping into the sky again and again like water on a hot cooking stone, fighting one another, tearing at carrion all around me.

But not tearing at me.

Why?

I was not on the ground at all.

I was moving. Slowly, painfully, moving. I smelled horse.

I was being dragged along on a sort of litter. Behind a horse.

Away from the tower.

I told my body to move; my head and shoulders obeyed.
I leaned over the side of the litter and then I did vomit.

CHAPTER 2
THE AFTERMATH

Enmer

My name is Enmer son of Golgal. I am a Japhethite descended from Tiras. I was thirty-one years old when the tower fell and the world changed. This is the account of how I survived with my family and with a few others.

I was a mid-level engineer on the tower when the God came down and confused the languages of men. On that morning I had just arrived and was about to start work; I had not yet gone up the tower. Like everyone else, I was fortunate to survive, for many things were dropped from the tower, and almost immediately riots began among the slaves.

When I saw that the city was thrown into confusion, I made my way back home as quickly as I could. I found the house barricaded and I had to pound and shout to be let in. At last my wife, Ninshi, unbarred the door and quickly barred it again after me.

Imagine, if you will, the confusion that I found there. The women – my wife Ninshi; my mother Zillah; and my sister Ninna – were wailing and sprinkling themselves with ash from the fire. My father lay dead on the floor. He had been killed defending our house against rioters.

Everyone in the household were able to understand one another. No one had been struck with another tongue, thankfully, except my wife's maidservant Gia, who was not able to make herself understood. She cowered in a corner, terrified of all of us.

My father's slave, a young man about my age whose name was Hur, had been wounded as he fought beside my father. His wife Shulgi was tending him.

My younger brothers, Endu and Sut, had not yet returned to the house since that morning. They had been out working the family gardens. My mother and sister were terribly worried that they had already been killed.

I took stock as best I could and we began to take action. My sister and mother and my mother's maidservant Shufer laid out my father's body on a table and began to dress it as best they could with the materials we had to hand. Hur I stationed at the door, armed with a makeshift club and with a bucket of water lest the house should be set afire. Outside, the riots were still raging and seemed likely to go all day and into the night.

Ninshi tended to the little ones. There was Angki, my infant son, who was not yet weaned, and Shulgi had just borne Hur a son whom they called Hur-kar. Also, Gia had a child, mine, to whom she had not yet given a name. It looked likely to me that his name would now be called Sorrow.

I sat near Gia and tried to communicate with her. She did not seem to want to stay with us, and it seemed to me that she might want to go to her own people. Seeing this, I brought her a shawl, a flask of oil, and a sling for her baby. She took them eagerly and made ready to go out.I offered (without words) to accompany her, but she rejected the offer. Perhaps she thought a lone woman with a baby would be safer than one accompanied by an armed man. I shed a tear as I watched her go, scurrying down our narrow, peaceful for the moment, brick street.

I never found out what happened to her, or to our son.

In the evening there was a lull in the noise of the city. The rioters had all been killed, perhaps, or found others who spoke their own tongue, or were resting and waiting for confusion of night. In this lull came our first good news … Endu and Sut, leading four horses.

My brothers had been in the fields when they heard a great noise arising from the city. They crept nearer and tried to discern what was happening. Though unable to do so, they did make out that there was rioting and danger, as when an army breaks through a city wall, and that our family would likely have to flee. They returned to the farm and made safe the livestock (we have goats, sheep and cattle). With admirable foresight they sheared the sheep (leaving the wool dirty for the sake of time), harvested such herbs and vegetables as they could, though unfortunately no grain, and loaded these onto my father's two horses.

It took them some time to bring these goods safely to my father's city house. They managed it by dint of much hiding and waiting, and only one fight. For the last stretch they waited for the lull that they cannily guessed would come. In the process, they picked up two more horses that they found running wild, frightened and only too glad of the company of fellow horses and of a firm, gentle, guiding hand. To our great good luck, one of the two horses they captured was a stallion, one a mare.

We spent the night resting, preparing, and planning our next move. My brothers grieved for my father, but we put off the formal grieving until we should come safely to our farmstead outside the city. Our plan was now to make for the farm, as quickly as possible, just before light the next day. At last, well into the night, I made them all lie down and sleep, for I knew they would need it. I was now the leader of our little family. I had never dreamed that I would so soon need to take over from my father.

The next morning, we put our plan into action. One of our horses carried Ninshi (with Angki) and Ninna, both of whom could ride. Two were loaded down with the provisions my brothers had brought and many additional articles from our house. The fourth, the mare we had found, dragged a litter, bearing the body of my father. In the back walked my mother, accompanying my father's body as if this were his funeral procession, Shulgi with her baby, and my mother's old maidservant Shufer. Hur and my brothers and I stationed ourselves around this procession, and in this way, we came safely out of the city just before dawn.

When we came to the fields, the rising sun showed us similar processions all around us, some poor, some well-equipped, heading in every possible direction.

We spent two days camped at the farm. The first day, we buried the body of my father. We mourned him through the night, except the little ones and their mothers, who slept. My mother wanted to do a proper mourning, but we had not the time or wealth for such a thing. War had returned to the city, and the looting was spreading to the countryside.

We slaughtered the sheep (which were few), cooked the meat, and began to dry it. We wanted to flee quickly, more quickly than would be possible with sheep, and we thought the chances were good that we could obtain sheep elsewhere. The wheat had already been harvested and was in the storehouses. We fashioned sacks to carry as much of it as could be. The olives were not ripe; nonetheless we tried to pick them and squeeze from them such oil as we could. We also brought cuttings.

The whole earth was rich in those days. It was only two hundred years since the Great Flood, and if you dug, you could still find all manner of sea creatures, land creatures and even human bones. Seeds grew as soon as they were planted and always did well.

We made our plans. Most people were moving west, so we would go east. We knew there was much land yet to the east of the Tower.

Various parties passed us throughout the day. Some of the groups were so large we could not tell one from the next, an unbroken stream of people. So many people in this world. We always called out to them, or sometimes I myself went to greet them, always hoping to find others who spoke as we did. So far, there were none. Some only stared, some answered with jeers, others with arrows. These were people we had lived alongside. Until two days ago, we had passed them in the street, perhaps done business in the markets. Some of them were even Japhethites like ourselves. Blood brothers. Yet because of this small change of language, they were already beginning to look different to my eyes. Their faces no longer looked as human as they had done. There was, as it were, a shade of evil, their eyes either too dark or too bright; like giants, like demons. I saw no one I recognized, although for all I know, my eyes might have passed over the faces of a dozen of my former friends.

Hur found a war bow and brought it to me eagerly. He told me that he had come from a family of archers himself, before they fell in to slavery. He boasted of his skill. I was not inclined to believe him, but then he demonstrated that he could shoot a leaf from a tree and even shoot while riding horseback. I was impressed. Who knew that my father had acquired such a treasure? But my father was gone, and Hur was my slave now. I let him keep the bow and set him to making arrows from some of the trees on our property.

By the morning of the third day we were ready to go. We had our four horses, a donkey, and a cow. The cow and donkey would slow our progress, but we might have need of them later. The cow was a milk cow. The women could make cheese. I hoped that at some point we could acquire a bull.

We wanted to get away as fast as might be. We managed to get all our gear on our backs, and on three horses, the donkey, and a litter with poles that could be easily replaced. The mothers with their infants we put on the gentle mare. The two older women walked.

I saw the tears sliding down my mother's face as we left our family farm, and I took her hand.

Our farm was to the west of the tower. We had to approach the city and pass it, then pass the tower, as we made our way toward the sun that had now risen and was climbing overhead.

The city was a bad place to be. In the countryside people had organized themselves and had begun their journeys, but in the city, they were still looting. The best had left, like ourselves; the worst had stayed. We did not enter the city.

As we passed to the north of it, we came upon three master-less men stripping a body. They looked up at us, with our rich booty, smiled and began to approach. All three were armed. Then one of them fell, with an arrow in his throat, almost before I heard Hur's bow sing. I looked over at him; he was small, square and brown. He had set down the load from his back and was already stringing a second arrow. He grinned at me and loosed the arrow at the second man. The third fled.

Endu and Sut cheered for Hur. I clapped him on his shoulder. We retrieved the arrows and looted the looters. They did not carry much of value, but one of them had on him a fine iron axe that ended up serving us well for many years to come.

We passed under the very tower. Its shadow did not fall on us; that was streaming westward, over the city. Passing under the tower was a terrifying feeling, even to me, though I had worked on it nearly every day of my life. We felt safe when up on its sides, but to be under it was to feel its threat.

The tower was not silent. Many people were up on it, tearing apart the scaffolding for their use, yelling to or at one another.

Below, there were bodies.

The fields below the tower were littered with carrion. People had fallen on the ground, they had fallen into the tar-mixing pits and onto the great stacks of bricks; they had been impaled on the bits of scaffolding. We had heard of scenes like this from the great battles and massacres before the Flood, but we had never seen anything like it, not with our own eyes.

Wild dogs had come out, and hyenas, vultures, and even pigs were eating the bodies. Those that were not yet eaten presented even greater horror. Three days in the sun, they had begun to become grotesque. Some were already blackened, swollen, start-eyed and staring. Ninshi and Shulgi hid their faces. Ninna, and my brothers and I stared.

My mother was looking ahead. Suddenly she said, "That one is alive."

Ninna ran up beside her. "Where? Where?"

Mother pointed. Then the two of them ran to the body that was alive.

The rest of us caught up to them a few moments later. We were now due east of the tower. Mother and Ninna were kneeling on either side of a great, black-haired, richly dressed man.

"He's asleep again now," said Mother. "But I saw him move. He raised his head and opened his eyes. He spoke to me."

Ninna was nodding, her dark eyes enormous. "I saw it too."

"Well," I said, my heart sinking, "Did he speak our tongue?"

"I cannot tell," said Mother. "I did not understand what he said. But he was clearly dazed. It may be that with care, he will speak properly."

"But it is more likely," said Sut impatiently, "that he speaks only gibberish like the rest of them."

Endu, who until now had looked at the man in silence, spoke and said, "I think he may be one of the Great Ones."

He was right. The man was large, with a great fine nose, well-drawn features, and long, curly black beard and hair. His skin, now of an awful pallor, had once been burnished bronze. Gold rings stood in his ears. It was not hard to imagine a crown. He must have been of the family of Cush. Cush's sons were mighty on the earth and they had been leaders when it came to the tower.

I put this to the party.

"If he is Cushite," said Hur, "He will not speak our tongue."

I nodded. Gia had been Cushite, and she had parted from us when the tongues were confused.

"That does not matter," said my mother firmly. "We have found him alive, and since it is in our power to save his life, we must save it." And then she spoke from the covenant made by God with our father Noah, "*From each man I will demand an accounting for the life of his fellow man. Whoever sheds the blood of man, by man shall his blood be shed; for in the image of God has God made man.*"

"We are not shedding his blood if we leave him," said Hur. "We need not lay a hand on him."

"Slave," I said, "this discussion is finished. My lady mother has said we must save this man's life, and so if we can save it, it will be saved."

Hur flushed and hung his head.

Perhaps my mother felt she had been given a replacement for my father. I myself saw no great harm in bringing the man with us. From the blood and stench beneath his body, I thought that he had suffered damage to his inner parts, and would probably die within a day or two.

We tore apart some scaffolding and fashioned a litter for him. We four young men lifted him onto it, Hur helping willingly enough, although he had been against the decision. The Great One screamed in his sleep as we moved him, but he did not wake.

We had a drink and then we were on our way again. We had lost less than an hour on our Cushite. My mother and Ninna walked beside him, half besotted. Shulgi and Shufer were less enchanted. Ninshi did not care; she had eyes only for her child, and was half mad with impatience over the delay in this dangerous place. Indeed, I agreed with her that we must not linger here. Worse things than hyenas might soon come to ravage the bodies.

Well, he was our guest now, and come what might, if he lived, we would have to care for him.

Then he woke up.

The women tell me that he vomited, which any man might do who had been grievously injured and then found himself being dragged ignominiously on a litter, behind the back of a horse and among strangers. They offered him some water. He took it, as far as he was able, having little use of his hands at that time. They offered beer; he took that. Then as his strength came back, he began to speak to them, loudly and imperiously, but in gibberish of course. They tried to tell him what had happened. It seemed to enrage him. By this time, I had come to that part of the line, and I tried to speak with him as well. I tapped my nose, saying my name. He laughed, I thought, with scorn; then he began again to make his incomprehensible demands. With his eyes and head he indicated the Tower, now far behind us but still starkly visible, for the morning mist had all burned off the plain.

His voice rose more and more. He began to shout.

Our Cushite was a strong, vigorous man. He shouted and screamed all afternoon, speaking now to us (it seemed), now to the tower, now, perhaps, to God.

We did not stop for a meal. People were strong in those days, and even women could walk for up to three days without food.

The Great One screamed through the heat of the day. He continued to scream as the sun began westering and the afternoon turned golden. Hour after hour. The horses were frightened at first, but we patted and soothed them and they grew used to it. Only near sunset, when we stopped to make camp, did his voice grow hoarse and he fell into a sulky silence, eyes turned in the direction of the tower, which was now a thin spear of red in the darkness of the middle distance.

"He is like a child," said my mother, amused, as we walked. "Except if he were my child, I would have beaten him long ago."

"How on earth," said Sut with a laugh, falling in beside me, "did he manage to fall from the tower and still stay strong enough to shout like this?"

"I think he must have tumbled, not fallen," I replied. "Tumbled down the tower in stages, that is. There is a puncture on his thigh that looks as if it came from the scaffolding."

I shuddered as I continued. I had climbed the tower daily. What had seemed to me no more than simple daily conditions of my work now seemed pregnant with death. I said, "It would have been difficult to take a clear fall from the tower, because of all the works. A clear fall would have killed anyone, even a Great One. Besides, for a clear fall he would have to have been – thrown out."

Sut stopped laughing.

Only Ninna remained true to our inconvenient guest.

"He is grieving," she said gently, sitting in the twilight of our cooking fire with her eyes fixed on his face, which in turn was turned stubbornly to the west. "Some men shout when they grieve, don't they?"

"We have all lost a great deal," my mother agreed.

"Here," said Endu dryly, scooping up a handful of ash from a long-dead part of the fire. "Perhaps I can help him grieve in a more conventional way." Before I realized it, he walked over to our guest and sprinkled the ash on his head.

The Great One snarled and whipped his head around, snapping at Endu's hand with his teeth as if to bite it. Endu, thank God, did not hit him, but jumped back and exploded into dismayed and angry laughter.

"This is quite a guest you've brought us, Mother, Sister," he said to them; and then to me, "Are you sure you want to keep him?"

"It's too late," I said. "He is with us now. He is our guest; we are obligated not to harm him."

"*In the image of God has God made man,*" my mother murmured.

"Hunh," muttered Endu. "Perhaps so, but it seems to me he's more of an animal."

"Do *you* think he's an animal?" Ninna whispered to me as Endu stalked away.

"Of course not," I said. "He has the power of speech. He is – I hate to say it – a brother. He is descended from our father Noah. Probably via Ham and Cush."

"Well, even if he is – like – an animal," she said, still in a low voice, "I feel a connection to him. I cannot understand his speech, but I feel as if I could tell what he is thinking."

"Oh, really? What is he thinking just now?"

We both looked at the Cushite, who was glaring at us with his great black eyes.

"He's just watching us and wondering what we are saying."

I could only laugh.

"Perhaps you are right, little sister," I told her.

We had examined his injuries (and by *we*, I mean mostly my mother, though I took some professional interest). He had the puncture wound from the scaffolding, which miraculously did not seem to be infected, even after his three days on the ground. It was nearly as clean as if a spear had gone right through his leg and emerged on the other side, taking of course because of its great diameter a good bit of leg with it. To suffer such a wound and not grow sick from it would be even more of a wonder nowadays; but again, in those early days of the world, people's bodies were strong. The other leg was broken, and this we straightened, more for appearance's sake than because we thought he would ever need it. We knew a little about medicine, having only occasionally seen falling or crushing injuries that were incurred in the course of the work on the Tower.

The Great One's legs were long, bronze and muscular, and I could imagine that only a few days ago they had often been employed in things like delivering kicks to slaves, and even to mid-level engineers like myself, whenever mistakes were made. Touching his lower extremities, even his feet, would always cause a great deal of indignant screaming. At first, we thought this was the screaming any patient might do, from pain; but then we discovered that he could not actually feel his legs. This was proved because he did not react if we touched him when he was not paying attention. The thing that was screaming, therefore, was his pride. This discovery had made our job in setting the bone in his left leg infinitely easier.

So somehow, we got him cared for, although with his stubbornness it was rather like caring for an injured camel or donkey. If we had followed strict reason, of course, we wouldn't have tried to mend him. But I suppose it was human instinct, just as my mother had said: When you have a human being in your care, it is natural to try to heal as much as possible. To refrain from doing this, you must actively fight the impulse, and so do violence to something human in yourself.

But that night, as I lay bedded down with Ninshi and Angki sleeping beside me, I thought grim thoughts to myself. No, our guest was no animal. Worse in some ways, a person. A guest, whom we could not harm. And he was showing signs of becoming strong, yet no signs of regaining the use of his limbs. He could live for years, vigorous and demanding, and we would have to doctor and feed him. Yet of work, or even comfort, he could contribute nothing.

That very night, however, he proved me wrong, at least partly. We had set a watch, consisting of Hur, but perhaps I had expected too much from my slave, asking him to walk through the day, carrying a burden, and then sit up through the night as well. Hur had fallen asleep at his post, sitting upright but with his head slumped over. So it was that all of us (Hur included) were wakened by the Cushite shouting loudly and imperiously as usual, but with a note of urgency we had not heard before, in his garbled tongue.

I sat up in anger, intending to chide him for interrupting our sleep, but Hur, quicker on the mark, sprang to his feet and shouted,

"It's an attack!"

So it was. The Cushite, who apparently was sitting up all night for reasons known only to himself, had seen a few dark figures approaching and had begun calling out, as we later concluded, to them.

I do not think he was trying to warn *us* of any danger. More likely, he hoped that they were his brothers, who would rescue him and perhaps slaughter or enslave us in the process. But as it turned out, they did not share his tongue. They could have been Semites, or other Japhethites, or even Hamites like himself but from a different subfamily. There had been many languages made, far more than three, when God shattered the children of men into shards as a man shatters a pot. At any rate, all our ungrateful guest accomplished was to warn us of the danger.

The four of us men leapt to our feet, fumbling for weapons, and fortunately that was all it took. Our attackers were few in number and they must have been counting on the element of surprise. When they saw armed men silhouetted in the starlight, they did not want to engage, and scattered. Still, it made for a miserable night after that. Everyone was frightened. We set a two-man watch, rotating through the remainder of the night, and the women were hesitant to sleep. I believe the babies were the only ones who got any rest between then and the morning.

As for Ninna, nothing could convince her that her hero had not meant to save us all. I soon stopped wasting my breath, realizing that our guest would show his true character if he lived long enough to do so.

CHAPTER 3

COVENANTS

Enmer

We continued across the plain. On the third day we reached a river. There we saw a flock of dragons. They were small (about the height of a man), two-legged, and striped in green and yellow. They were drinking and playing in the water, but when they saw us, they scattered like birds.

Dragons were beasts like any other. They were classed among the wild animals rather than the creeping things or livestock. They had existed before the Flood, and had come through it, with the help of Father Noah, in young breeding pairs. The earth's climate was colder now than it had been in Noah's young days. It was something to do with the Flood, we thought, with the springs of heaven having been opened, but who could say? At any rate, the dragons had adjusted to it and thriven, though the grandfathers told us that the creatures now ran considerably smaller than they had used to, as did many beasts.

Our crossing was uneventful, but tedious. The river was low, as the autumn rains had not begun. But we had to bring across the women and children first, then the goods and animals, and then, slung between me, my brothers, and Hur, our ungrateful guest. When we had crossed, we rested. The next day, we washed the wools, our clothing, and ourselves, and dried everything in the sun.

The dragons returned – evidently this was a favorite spot of theirs – and Hur managed to shoot one. It ran quite a way before it fell, and Hur and Sut went after it. They followed it out of sight, and came back bearing it over their shoulders in triumph. They reported that they had followed it to a low hill, and that from this they had been able to see mountains drawing near.

We plucked, skinned and ate the creature. I did not relish eating dragon. Only since the flood had men been permitted to eat the living creatures, and then not with the blood in them. Quite a few people, especially of my grandfather's generation, still felt horror at the thought, but what had been passed down to me was only a slight distaste. There is certainly nothing like the meat of a once-living creature to make a person feel full and sleek.

But that night, sitting before our fire enveloped in the deep sense of well-being that comes after the body has feasted, I suddenly felt my mind give way into a pit of horror and dismay at all the things we had lost. I put my head in my hands, and was near to curling up into a ball, like a child.

We had lost my father. His name was Golgal, son of Tiras, son of Japheth. He was a very young man, only sixty-one years old when he died, vigorous and still in his prime. If he had not been killed, he might have lived hundreds of years more.

I missed his leadership. I had been living these last few days as if it were my job to keep our family together until he returned. But he would not return.

Not only had we lost my father, we had lost all the fathers.

Father Noah was still living. He did not come to the City; he stayed on his estate in the west. All of us had met him at least once, I when I was just a child. He had been a formidable man, tall for one of our kind, with iron-grey hair and beard, who radiated a sense of calm and sadness.

Then his sons, Shem, Ham and Japheth. Japheth was my great-grandfather. All of them were master builders. They had long experience of carpentry, farming, and a rich knowledge of the living creatures. They remembered the days before the Flood. We had relied on them heavily when building the city, particularly on Ham and his son Cush.

All of these were still vigorous men. No one knew when they might die. People had been used to live a span of about a thousand years, before the Flood, and even in this second age, since the earth was destroyed with water, very few had so far died, except the occasional one by violence. This had been true, that is, until seven days ago. Now, perhaps, the fathers were all dead. But whether dead or alive, we had lost their wisdom.

More than this, we had lost the City. There had been markets, fruits. There had been canals that carried water from the river, and others that carried waste water from our houses so that it might not defile the city. An army of strong slaves; of skilled craftsmen; of trained engineers like myself; of kingly planners like this Great One must once have been … all gone. I could never hope to build a city like that one, even if I lived another nine hundred years. I no longer had with me the minds, the people. My training as an engineer was not even complete. And now – I realized with a shock – it never would be.

We had no metalsmith in our group, nor anyone who knew how to extract ore.

We had – another shock – no musician. My mother and sister had some basic musical skill, but they were not professionals, not temple musicians. How would we worship?

How would we farm?

How would we live?

I felt a presence beside me and raised my head. Hur had come to sit next to me in the dark. Perhaps he had some matter to discuss with me, but the weight was so great on my heart, on my very bowels, that I burst out in a low voice,

"Why has He done this to us?"

"We were not worshipping Him."

"We were. I was. We were obeying Him."

"Were we?"

"Yes, of course. I have never killed a human being, never eaten blood. I have offered sacrifices –"

"Your tower," said the slave. His voice was curiously flat.

"*Our* tower?"

"Yes, your tower. The tower that was the pride of you, of all of you, of you high ones … Do you miss it?"

"Of *course* we do! Of course, I do. It was my life's work."

It almost broke my heart to think of it standing there, year after year, unfinished. It had been planned to be so beautiful. It would have been beautiful. We had the ability to do it, we could have done it.

"What was it meant to do?" asked Hur. Again, tonelessly.

"Why, to reach to the heavens. To show how great we were."

"Perhaps you loved your tower," he said. "But I will tell you something, Golgal's son ... I had no love for that tower of yours."

I had nothing to say. I had never imagined this.

"But I did not come here to talk about the tower," my slave said, in a more animated and yet more businesslike voice. "That is past. Things are different now. That is what I have come to talk about."

I sighed and sat up straighter. My grief could wait.

"I am here to make a covenant with you," said Hur. "I want you to set us free."

Again, I was staggered. "Set you free? You – who? We already have a covenant."

"Written on mud in your father's house, not brought with us," said Hur. "By now, it is probably destroyed. This is the new covenant I want with you. You are to make me, Shulgi, and Hur-kar free people. Make us members of your family. If you do this, I will stay with you and serve you faithfully as a brother."

"And if I don't?" I queried, hearing the threat.

"Then we will leave," he said, in deadly earnest. "But that is not what I want to do, and I do not think you want me to leave, either. You need me, son of Golgal. You need my strength, my hands, my bow."

I was silent, thinking that he was right. Already he had saved us thrice, twice from looters, and once – the day before – from a lion.

"Things are different now," said Hur, pressing his case. "There is no city. We are few in number. It no longer makes sense for one man to enslave another."

If he had approached me at another time, I could not have brought myself to free him. But this was my lowest moment. He had caught me when I was most distressed about how we were to survive. I could not lose him.

Besides, he was right. Things were different now.

"What do you want?" I asked. "Are you asking – are you asking to share my leadership?"

Hur appeared to think. "I am a Japhethite," he said. "I am your brother."

It was true, he was descended from Japheth.

"How old are you?"

"Thirty summers."

I smiled. "I am thirty-one. I am your older brother."

"Then you should have the privileges of the older brother," said Hur seriously. "I won't contest you for it. You take the inheritance, and I will be your second in command."

"We will do it," I decided. "But let it appear for a while that you are serving me. If Endu and Sut see you suddenly elevated to be their older brother, we will have war in the family."

So we agreed, and the next day we privately took some clay and made a covenant on it. It was dried in the sun, a little distance away from the skin and sinews of the dragon, which were also drying.

We stayed in that place through the winter. The soil was good. We planted our grains, keeping back almost none of them, for in those days we had scarcely heard of a harvest failing. The rains came; the river flooded, as we expected, and we irrigated our fields. The next spring, we had a good harvest.

Our complex we built out of unseasoned timber rather than of brick, as there was not much time to make and dry bricks, nor to season wood, before the rains came. We went into the hills for timber. There were many trees there, some of them too big for the four of us to fell – all manner of evergreens; willows along the rivers; and many, many different oaks. They were all young trees, having been growing only since the flood, but then we young people had never seen living trees bigger.

So we built a timber house, sinking the posts down deep into the earth, and lining the walls with reeds mats woven by the women. Many, many times we were glad of the iron axe we had salvaged. I acted as engineer for the building, with my brothers helping, and Hur distinguished himself in scouting missions. He was not trained as a builder, but his skill as a bowman grew and grew. He killed many things – lions, bears, wolves that were coming after our cow. We ate of those that could be eaten, and for all of them we used their skins, either for dress or to line the walls and floors of our complex through the cold, rainy winter.

The complex was a pitiful thing compared with the projects I had worked on in the city.

Once, we saw a party of people passing far to the south of us. They were heading east. We stood on a hill and watched them, being careful not to call attention to ourselves. They were very dark-skinned and there were a great many of them. We were relieved when they had gone.

The proudest achievement of the winter, at least of the men, was the capturing of a wild bull. Hur found it; his gift seems to be for finding things, and he is blessed with great good luck. He had gone on a jaunt among the foothills in search of something or other, and came running back reporting that he had seen the creature nestled miserably in a little valley, waiting out a rainstorm. Of course, a rainstorm is the worst time to try to capture a four-footed animal. I did not want any of our party injured, but I was equally concerned that the creature not get away. We quickly offered up a tiny sacrifice (we burned some mint, which the women had found and dried in great quantity), and then the four of us went out, following Hur, to see what might be done.

We found the bull still sheltering in the lee of the hill. He was not pleased to see us, but because of the cold and rain he could not be bothered to flee. We crept out of his sight, felled some trees, and began constructing a large paddock on two sides of him, leaving the steep part of the valley to serve for his prison on the other two sides. And all the while we worked, I was blessing our iron axe and cursing the fact that we had not more men in our party.

We had him fenced in by nightfall. Then we had to go home and rest. We hoped that our work would hold, for he was large and strong.

We walked home in the dark, very pleased with ourselves, and when we arrived, we found that our Cushite had also made a discovery.

This man had been cared for in a room of our lodge near my mother's. It was merely a corner, not large, but was by no means a prision. It had a high ceiling and an opening that let in the morning sun. Every day the women brought him food and means with which to bathe, and mint tea. Also he was brought outside to sit in the porch of the complex, within sight of the river, whenever the weather was fine. All in all, with the way we cared for him, he was the most privileged member of our household. Such care as we gave him was the kind that people give to a baby – or else to a god.

He had prospered under our care. He had gradually been getting back the use of his hands, and the women had observed him putting himself through torments to strengthen these and his arms – raising and lowering his arms; contorting them behind his head and shoulders; or lifting many times, again and again, such small articles as he could reach. He would later progress to lifting and dragging his body by his arms.

On this particular day, he had put his hands to evil use. My sister Ninna came in as usual, bearing a lamp and a bowl of barley soup, to give him his evening meal. She set the lamp on the floor beside his pallet, and was straightening with the barley in one hand, when he made a grab at her.

She screamed, dropping the bowl on the bed, and the other women rushed in to find him trapping her with a hand around her upper arm, with a strength none of them had suspected. With his other hand – I regret to write – he was fondling her breast.

As soon as we men came home from penning our bull, everyone surrounded us and began telling the tale. But Ninna cried out,

"Everyone be quiet! *I* want to be the one to tell Enmer. Alone!"

So she drew me aside and told me the tale. She was crying with shame and anger as she told it. Ninna is a proud girl.

"How could I have been so stupid?" she wept. "I feel a thousand fools that ever I admired him. He is a camel's ass."

I comforted her, telling her that she had been no more stupid than any girl her age might be when confronted with a Great One.

"Great Ones feel they are better," I told her. "They think of the rest of us as their slaves. As for this Cushite, he was humbled for a little while by his fall from the tower, but now that he is getting his strength back, he remembers his so-called privileges."

Then I said, "We are all tired and distressed, and some of us are wet and cold. Is a meal ready? Good. Let us eat and warm ourselves and only then discuss this matter."

So this was done. (We did not feed the Cushite.) Then we took counsel. Hur and Shulgi were for killing him, but this could not be done because he was our guest and had not actually succeeded in violating Ninna. Killing him would have been murder, not execution. We talked about it longer, and finally took a decision. And so that night, by the light of a lamp, I said to him in front of the entire family,

"Very well. This is how you have repaid our hospitality. We saved your life, we have cared for you as tenderly as for a child, and you have been always demanding, and never grateful. Now, you have behaved more like a wild animal than like a human guest. So we will treat you as a prisoner.

You will not leave this room to see the sun, except once a week on the seventh day. You will be given plain food, no delicacies, and it will be brought to you either by a man – or by Shufer."

Shufer smiled as I gestured toward her. She was the oldest woman in our company, although by no means a crone. In her early sixties, she was still attractive and might possibly have been able to bear children.

"You must learn," I said, speaking the words of Hur, "that the world has changed and that we are not your slaves. Ninna here is a great lady, a virgin, and a daughter of this house … not some temple prostitute for you to treat as you please."

I am sure the Cushite understood not one of my many words. I am equally sure that he understood my meaning, and he could not fail to know the reason that all the family had gathered in the doorway to his room and were now staring at him with hateful looks. He stared back with a face that was hard to read, but which might have been amused and contemptuous, and was certainly proud.

"No repentance there," muttered Endu as we filed out.

"No," I replied, "For him to repent I think you'd need a horsewhip."

After this he was no longer our guest but, for a long time, our prisoner. We grew to forget him, except as one who must be guarded and fed.

I guess I can keep my womenfolk safe from a crippled man. The day I can't do that, I should resign as head of the family.

How I long for the days before the Great Flood. Then everyone could do as he pleased. Now, I can do nothing, not one thing, without the help of these vile slaves whom Fate has made my masters. I cannot eat or drink, I cannot bathe, nor even look at the sky, unless it is their will. All I can do is piss in a pot.

"Everyone did what was right in his own eyes." I had this from my father Cush. The other old ones would say it too, Japheth, Shem and Noah; but they would say it as if this were a terrible thing. We Hamites know better. Men did amazing things in the days before the Flood, when they were free to do as they pleased. They circled the globe, they made maps, they built things as wonderful as our Tower; huge things, of all shapes, perfectly aligned with the paths of the Sun, Moon, and even the stars. Things that will probably last forever, though in these degenerate days I can never hope to

see them. They were true men, our fathers before the Flood. More intelligent than anyone today; giants, some of them; and they lived a thousand years. Really, they were more gods than men. Completely free from the hand of God. "What was right in their own eyes."

So much has been lost. Even before the curse that fell on the Tower; but now, this, this will be the end of the human race. We will never recover to what we were before.

The water was a judgment, they say. Men were corrupt and had to be destroyed. Or else they threatened the very foundations of heaven. As I still hope to do, were it not for this crippled body.

I exercise. I grow strong. But I do not think I will ever move my legs again. I cannot even feel my toes.

Did anything like this ever happen before the Flood? Surely not. Surely all men were of one language, free to move, able to do whatever they set their hands to. None of this paralysis, this powerlessness, this pissing in a pot.

Noah was not such a holy man himself. There was the incident with the vineyard – walking about naked, falling naked on his bed. Hard to believe he was the father of Great Ones. A fine man to talk of judgment.

I must end these etchings. It is time to strengthen my arms.

The next day the men of the complex returned to visit our bull. We had explained our progress to the women. We had prayed, offered sacrifices, and asked that they be standing by, ready to dress any wounds we might get from the animal.

It was a fine morning, but the grass was still wet. Our bull was awake and grazing. Already he had cropped short a large corner of his paddock. We had brought rope lassos. All four of us felt our pulses quicken when we saw his horns and thought of how we might get our lassos around them.

"Let two go into the paddock and try to lasso him one by one," I suggested. "Don't harm him, don't excite him if possible. Once he is captured, we must still get him back home. And don't try to *dance* with him."

"Why not?" whined my two younger brothers. They had wanted to make a display.

"You are not professionals," I said firmly. Oh, all three of us had dared each other to vault the cows on our father's farm at one time or another, but we did not really know what we were doing. We had heard there were amazing teams of bull-dancers before the Flood, and other kinds of dancers too. But now that lost art was just beginning to be recovered by a gifted few. The gifted few would not be us – not today.

"Please," said Sut, who was young, limber, hardly more than a boy.

"No," I replied. "We will be lucky to bring this one home today. Don't risk a goring … that is, don't risk it any more than you must."

They entered the paddock, scrambling over opposite ends of the fence. Hur and I watched silently. The bull, when he saw them, rolled his eyes a bit and moved to the far corner, near the two hills. The little valley faced east, so his corner of it was filled with winter sunlight.

He went back to grazing, switching his tail.

They approached him from opposite sides. Whenever one of them got too close, the bull would walk away, and whenever the bull felt trapped, he would make a feint at one and that one would dash out of the way.

This went on for a long time. I was not overly worried, but I was glad my mother was not there watching.

At last Endu flung his lasso out and got it over the fearsome horns. The bull tossed and tossed his head, and Endu gave him plenty of slack and let him toss. Endu's rope was long, so he was safe as long as the animal did not bolt.

Then our bull grew tired of his labors. He decreed a rest for himself, put his head down, and resumed grazing.

When he raised his head, Sut lassoed one horn from the other side, but the bull tossed it free.

Sut tried again.

The rope missed. The bull charged him, dragging Endu, and Sut barely managed to get over the fence to save himself.

Endu managed to get to his feet, staying well out at his end of the rope, and while the bull was near enough to the fence, he climbed over a few paces down. From the safety of the outside of the fence, he tethered the animal.

We had one rope around the creature's horns, but we needed two.

And so it went, for many hours that day. When my brothers tired, Hur and I would take a turn. At length we got our bull's head by two ropes. And so, at long last, we got him back to our complex and turned him out into our own cow's nighttime paddock. It was high and strong, built to repel lions and dragons. We hoped it would keep in the bull.

Soon we heard munching.

"He has found the hay, I hear," said Endu dryly.

Hur said, "Are we going to keep him after he mates with the cow, or release him?"

"We'll keep him if we can," I decided. "It will depend on his disposition."

We kept the bull. Our cow bore a calf in due season, and soon we were on our way to having a herd.

Sometime later during that first winter, Shufer came to me, very angry, but trying to conceal it with clasped hands, rigid shoulders and lowered eyes.

"I have heard," she said, "That you have made a covenant with Hur and not with me."

I was forced to admit that this was so. And so we made a covenant, that same day, with Shufer as well, making her a free woman and a sister of my mother. My mother, to my surprise, was not against this. Even so, we were able to conceal it for a long time, from Endu and Sut. When they finally found out about Hur, they were displeased, but we did not come close to bloodshed. By that time, they had realized how indispensable he was to us. In their gratitude it did not take them long to come around to treating him as a brother.

And another thing happened that winter, a thing of which I hate to write. I would almost rather die.

My mother came to me, drawing me aside privately during a break when we were building irrigation channels.

"If we are to thrive, we need to bear more children," she said.

I raised my eyebrows. "I am doing my best, Mother," I said dryly. "You must remember Angki is not yet weaned."

She smiled and said that of course she had already blessed my union with Ninshi, and also the union of Shulgi and Hur. "You young ones will have many children, I don't doubt," she said. "We will become a great tribe, a nation. But now, at this time, we must grow quickly so that we may live. This is a good place, a safe place to have children. We may well be driven from it. Now, while we are here, we should have children."

"Yes?" I said, blinking.

"I am saying," she pronounced carefully, "I myself may be able to contribute a child to our nation."

I stared at her in confusion.

Then my bowels turned to water when she added, softly, "This Cushite, he does not contribute much, but he may yet be able to help us."

My mother wanted to go in to the Cushite and have his child. I cannot describe how appalled I was by this idea.

I pleaded with her for a long time, standing there in the field. I pleaded with her to honor my father, who was not yet a year in his grave. I pointed out that the Cushite might, God forbid, think that we had decided he was entitled after all to a woman of our family. Above all, I said, we must not mix our blood with that of foreigners. We were to have children according to our kind. The Cushite, he was a descendant of Adam, but not of Japheth. He was not of our kind. Did we want the blood of Ham in our family?

I begged her, respectfully as she was my lady-mother, yet with a quiver of disgust in my voice and with tears in my eyes.

She would not hear any of my objections. About the short mourning she had given my father, she pointed out that one world had ended and another begun. This was a new age; my father died at the end of the last age, an age that was now past. It was urgent that she have a child now, while we still lived in a safe place and she was still able to bear children. She would not become the Cushite's concubine, she would go to him but once, on the day she had calculated (by her woman's knowledge) most likely to give her a child.

After that, let him long for it as he might, she was not to be his.

And about blood-mixing …

"For shame, Enmer! You know this Cushite and we are of the *same* kind. He is not an animal, after all. Nor is he a god. This is nothing like what women did – before. The … the horrors that lived before the Flood, all perished in the flood. All who survived are of pure blood, coming down through Noah. A man perfect in his generations."

"I will never consent to this, Mother," I said in a shaking voice. "I – it is repulsive. I do not like him."

"Nor do I," she said simply. "Nevertheless, I am your mother. I will go in to him. The only way you can stop me," she added, "Is to banish me from the family."

I hung my head. She knew I would not do that. The thing that gives a patriarch's authority its teeth is his ability to disinherit any of the tribe who do the unthinkable. Yet not once, but twice now, the members of my household had turned that power around on me, threatening to leave if I did not let them have their way. I wondered whether I was losing control of the family. A patriarch ruled by his tribe. Everything was upside down.

Still, she was my mother. If not the throne, then the power behind the throne.

"Ninna will never forgive you," I said.

"She will when she sees the baby," said my mother. A baby could heal all. That was what women believed.

"Mother," I said. She had already turned to go.

"Yes?" She stopped, giving me her full attention again, yet with one foot pointed back toward the house.

"Do it, then, with my blessing. I cannot rule over you, since you are my mother, but I must rule over this Cushite. He is our prisoner. Anything you do to him must come from me."

"Of course, my son," she said.

So she went in to him, and I still burn with shame to write it. But she wisely kept it very secret. I think Shufer may have guessed, but she, too, said nothing. Thus, I had no need to deal with a reaction from Ninna and my brothers. And as it turned out, my mother did not conceive. This was a relief to me, because it meant that her secret need never be known, not to mention that we should have no bastard child in the family. Yet, it still deepened my shame all the more, for it meant that it was all for nothing that my mother had crossed that terrible line.

CHAPTER 4

BROTHERS

Hur

The forest in spring.

The hills are high, folding back on either side of deep canyons, filled with mist that stays long, trapped under the trees. The trees are tall, towering over us; first ferns, pears, wild apples, figs, palms, planes, and willows; then as we rise higher, oak, elm, maple, various kinds of nut trees. And eventually, it will be pines. Their breath fills our noses and expands our chests, giving us new strength for the climb. Our limbs stop burning.

Everything drips.

I am with Sut, and he is getting cold. We are on the hunt; but really, we are just exploring. Spring is a not the best time to hunt. And though we may crave meat, we don't strictly need it, for the rivers are full of fish.

So far, we have seen only monkeys. They follow along above as we tread on the ground, quickly outpacing us in the upper story, stopping to look back over their shoulders at us and then using their little fingers to pick out a pine nut. They are useless little things, not good to eat that is. Perhaps a person could tame one, if he had the leisure. But for us, they are there only to make us laugh. Purely for ornament.

I am hoping for a wild pig or some such thing. Something that will have used its nose to dig roots, and so survived the winter with the flesh still on it.

Sut is new at this. He grew up on his family farm and in the city. Learned all the things a gentleman should learn, but not true hunting. He walks naturally light, and that helps, but he still makes plenty of noise as we move along. That's as well; we are less likely to startle a deer or a unicorn or something else that might take fright and kick or gore us.

But we are more likely to attract predators.

I look back and forth. I listen. I sniff. Sounds are harder, but smells are easier in this wet and drippy weather.

I have not always been a slave. I did not grow up in a slave family. My dad was a bowman and a hunter. He first lived in the great forests far to the north of the great city. One of those men who can't be brought indoors, or it kills them.

He loved his drink, too. Beer, wine. We made our own. We had a family farm, like everyone did.

But all human beings were called to work on the tower, so he spent part of his time in the city. No time to make all the beer he wanted. He would buy it, then, with part of his wages. He used to drink a lot, during his stints in the city. He drank less when out on the hunt, because that would interfere with his abilities.

But that tower.

He would work on it by day – another man's project, not his – and drink to relax by night. He never got angry, or violent, when drunk, but he would get lazy. When home on the farm, he'd let whole days go by without doing a thing. And – he was not being paid enough for his time on the tower. Impossible, to pay a man enough for work he hates, but I mean not paid enough to replace the farming.

I can say so, now. There's no one to hear. There is no supervisor to report to.

And drink led to debt, and debt led to slavery. It is an old story. We lost the farm, and we were split up and sold off to pay his debts. I don't blame him. I blame that tower. If not for that, then when the world ended, we would have been living in the forest, drinking beer and eating meat, and would probably not even have known what had happened.

Might never have known, unless the refugees had found us.

But that's all foolish talk. *Might have* this, *would have* that. Tower-building happened to us, as it happened to every poor fool on this earth, including the ones who thought it was to their benefit. That's why, at the age of fifteen, I was sold off, and my bowman's training cut short. Luckily, I'd been at it for ten years by then. We keep our skill up only by practice, and during the years of my slavery I had no practice, but when I picked it up again, it all began to come back.

Ended up with Golgal for a master. Enmer's father. He was a fair man, that one. I could have done worse, far worse. He fed me well. He made his wishes clear, didn't expect me to read his thoughts. Spoke to me as if I could understand. Beat me rarely, and then only for reasons he (and usually, I) considered just.

But no hunting, and no beer. Day and night, all was the tower. The city and the tower.

I took a wife (she was also a slave – we can't marry above our station), and I was pleased with her. The family of Golgal made no trouble for me over it. She had just had a child when all *this* happened. I was fairly happy with her, and with Hur-Kar, but I never dreamed that bows, and freedom, and the forest would so quickly be restored to me.

I love the forest.

Dad did not live to see the end of the tower. It killed him, it and the drinking and his master – for he was not as lucky in that way as I was – and his broken heart. I tried to keep up with him, through rumors and occasional visits, but there was never any time. I did manage to be there when he died. It wasn't pretty.

I also kept up with my sisters and Mom, after being sold. There was no way to get to them, though, when all the rioting broke out. Although we hated the tower in our family, yet we had never, never imagined that some kind of violent judgment would fall. And so we never made a plan of what we might do if it did, nor ever set a place that, in case of a siege or other disaster, all of us could go to find each other. Seeing as all the people in the world were there, in the city, we didn't expect an attack. We thought the only threats in our lives were our masters and the tower.

In the days afterward I kept my eye out for them, but never saw a trace. God, I hope they got away safely. Unlikely, though. Mom had yellow, almost white, hair. It really made her stand out. She was probably one of the first to go.

Finally, Sut and I spotted something. Up the slope, it was a flash of color, a pinkish red flower-color far too bright for this time of year. We froze, and hid, and began to creep. Whatever it was, it was likely to have a better view of the hillside than we had, and better vision as well. Probably vision for movement. If brightly colored, it was not a stalking predator, but it might be something so big that it need not fear being seen.

I thought I knew what it was, but it wasn't until we got closer that I became sure.

We moved up and forward, about an inch every thirty in-and-out breaths. Flat on our bellies, soaked to the skin. I looked at Sut, worried he might start shivering, or else grow impatient and move forward at a dangerously faster pace. But the sun was up, stabbing through the canopy, and the fog was clearing as we rose, and the ground, though still damp, was not icy. We crawl-rested on. Past tiny, brand-new, curling ferns; through cedars. Eventually the spot of bright pink, which looked like an oversized flower, resolved into a large spot on an otherwise mottled-brown crest about a tall man's height above the ground ... and there she was.

The dragon.

She was sitting, facing away from us. Her huge rump curved around gracefully, like a woman's, on top of a pine-litter nest. On one side we could catch just a glimpse of a slender neck, a long snout, a bumpy skull topped with that showy crest. She was weaving her head back and forth placidly, like a duck, closing her eyes in between.

I glanced at Sut. He looked back, with a grin. I gave a short nod in relief; it looked like he would not break and run, or try to attack her. His was no predatory grin. It was one of delight.

We lay perfectly still, staring at her a long time. She was probably brooding on her eggs. It was early spring, this, and there she sat. I had an idea that spot of color might mean that the little ones were almost ready to hatch. If she was going to turn pink all over, later in the year when the need for hiding her young was past, that would be a magnificent sight.

I looked at Sut again. He was still watching her, looking now bemused, now excited as a child. It is truly a thrill to see one of these dragons in the wild ... really, to see any large and impressive animal.

This one was not a danger to people. She lived on ferns. Probably would taste good if we were to kill one, being that they are, more than anything, like a cow. This one might taste like cow, or perhaps like duck or chicken. But we had no thought of making an attempt on her life. You don't kill an animal that has young, and anyway, with the complicated shape of that skull, you'd be unlikely to kill on the first shot, even if you were lucky enough to hit the eye.

I was fairly certain that the father was far away, but not positive. Time to move on.

We made our very leisurely way back down the hill. At one point on this slow journey, we saw the shape of a leopard pass over the extreme edges of our vision. It must not have seen us, nor smelled us neither, or possibly it did but took no interest, for it did not turn aside.

Sut and I got close to the ravine finally, and felt free to stand up and walk downhill. Got to the ravine, and felt free to stretch, take a drink, and so on, and bemoan the fact we had no food. Discussed taking a monkey, and decided things were not that desperate. So we decided to start heading back, but keep our eyes open on the way … it would be several days' journey. I don't mind spending time with Sut. He's a good man. Charming and chattery sometimes – especially with women – but knows when not to burden a man with talk.

It took us a full day of hiking to get toward the edge of the hills again. And then, just as we were about to leave the hills for the open plain, what should come running down the now shallow ravine from behind us but our wild boar after all, the one we had been waiting for! It crashed past us and we both shot at it as it went. Sut's arrow stuck in the rump, but I had good hope that my shot had got the liver. It didn't turn in anger and charge us; no, it kept on running, like a wounded deer.

We started laughing and talking and began to follow it, not hurrying much, for we knew we could follow the trail of blood, and that eventually it would get tired and fall. And we didn't suspect any danger other than from the boar itself, because boars do have a habit of running about as if crazed.

But then, down the ravine came what it was running *from*.

We had only a few crashes to give us warning, and then I grabbed Sut and we both dived into the bracken, which here was getting rather thin. And past our heads thundered the legs of *another* dragon, this one definitely not a fern eater. It was small and light as dragons go, maybe not much bigger than a man, but running with a huge, long stride, on two legs like an ostrich.

It was obviously a predator, and you don't attract the attention of big predators when they are hunting something. I thought this was obvious, so I didn't repeat the lesson to my companion. That was a mistake, because to my surprise Sut

suddenly gave a cry of dismay and stood up out of the
bracken.

"That dragon's going to get *our* boar!" he yelled
indignantly.

And that had been true, until a second ago.

It turned out the dragon was distractible. And alert, like
all predators, for someone else coming in on his prey. He
whipped around and changed direction almost before I knew
it. Once he was facing us, we could see, all in a second, that
he had huge yellow eyes, a bald narrow head like a vulture's,
with a sort of mane of feathers behind it, and a narrow
muzzle lined with blood-chilling teeth.

What saved us was that changing direction slowed him
down a little. I was able to get off a shaft, which glanced off
his neck. That would have been bad, but he turned and
snapped at it, and while he was doing that, I strung another
and, as he turned back, sent it through his eye. Yet even an
arrow in the brain didn't stop him dead – we would hope it
would, but it didn't – and he came charging at us, furious.

By that time Sut had out his short spear, which he had
brought in case we encountered this situation with a boar. He
braced it, and as the dragon reached us, the spear grated on
its pointy breastbone, then slipped off and pierced the gut

below … and by that time the arrow had caught up with it, and it was dead.

Sut ended up with the dead dragon's head resting on top of his head and shoulders. Luckily, it didn't go into death throes – I suppose its charge *was* its death throe – instead, it stopped moving suddenly and completely. I helped Sut pull his spear out and get the weight of the thing off him, and then he got up and walked around bent double, with his hands on his thighs, saying *hoo* for a time.

It turned out he had a wrenched right arm and a bruised shoulder from the spear butt, and the wind knocked out of him. I approached the dragon – cautiously – got my arrow out of his eye – broke on the way out, the arrow did – and cleaned it and the spear off as best I could. The dragon's blood smelled like offal, and like a chicken's blood.

Finally, Sut stood up, went over to the stream, and retched a little. He took a drink, staggered as if dizzy, and finally sat down to rest with his back to a tree.

I came over to him when he was breathing better.

"You saved our boar," I said.

"What a fool I was," he said. "I guess that's the last time you'll bring me out on a hunt."

I shrugged. "I bet that's the last time you'll do that."

"I don't know … I didn't know I was going to do it at the time, so how can I know, I might do the same thing again," he replied, distressed. I saw his dark eyes flick about a bit as he reviewed the scene and what he wished he had done. Then he grinned and added, "… But I certainly don't think I will!" And then, suddenly, he embraced me about the shoulders, pressing our foreheads together. "You saved me from that dragon," he said. "I know it. I owe you my life."

I disengaged myself.

"I have saved you many other times, son of Golgal."

"No, but I was stupid. You saved me." And then suddenly, in a rush of inspiration, he added, "It's ridiculous that you should go on being a slave. You should be a warrior – our brother."

"I have a surprise for you," I told him, lowering myself down to sit beside him, for we were both very tired. "I *am* your brother."

I saw the shock in his eyes, paused to let that sink in, then continued, "Your brother Enmer and I made a covenant some time ago. He agreed to free me, but we thought it best not to tell everyone until you could see that it made sense."

It was a bit risky to tell him the truth like that, but I have always believed in seizing the moment.

Sut arched his eyebrows and blinked a few times, clearly a bit offended. But then he offered me his hand, and we clasped forearms.

Later, when we had recovered, we examined the dragon more closely. Flies were already buzzing about it. Though not much bigger than a man, it was stronger and heavier than one, with huge, long clawed legs, jointed like a bird's, and massive leg muscles. Its tail, now curled pitifully, evidently was held out behind it when it ran, for balance. It looked to us like it could run all day. Its largest teeth were as long as my little finger.

We took some of the meat from one of the massive thighs. I didn't expect it to taste very good – predators usually don't – but we thought we would cook it up for the folks at home and make them guess which was boar and which was dragon.

Then we tracked down our boar, which had indeed fallen from his wounds. We butchered him there in the twilight, built a fire, and cooked a little of the meat from each creature, wrapping the rest to bring home. Sure enough, the dragon tasted disgusting. Just as its blood had smelled ... like chicken and offal. I suggested we give up on bringing home the dragon meat, but Sut seemed to think that serving it would be a good joke on Endu, the middle brother.

We walked through the night, not wanting to have to sleep in the forest with fresh meat on us. When we returned home, Sut roasted the meat himself and served it to the others. He would not let them taste it until he'd told the story of our hunt. He didn't sing it, or tell it in a poem, for our language has no poetry yet. But he told it like a saga. Made it funny, too … he found humor in places I would never have looked. And he made me sound like quite the mighty hunter. I'd have been embarrassed to have them all looking at me, but thanks to Sut being so funny, they weren't … we were all holding our sides laughing.

Only my wife Shulgi was angry with me, and that was because she was frightened.

Then we had them try the meats, though none of the women dared taste the dragon. Princess Ninna was fastidious, Shulgi was still angry, and the older women were, I think, still leery of eating meat at all, and were put off by the bloody tale Sut had told. None of us who tried it liked the dragon meat, so Enmer decreed we give the rest of it to the Cushite prisoner. Perhaps it will make him strong, he said.

I wasn't aware that was something we wanted.

Nimri

It rained constantly that winter.

Of course, we need the winter rains, but surely, they need not be so *long*. I have always felt that way, even before my fall. Rains are for crops, and the growing of crops I was content to leave to slaves and women, while we Great Ones concentrated on matters of high culture, such as the Tower, the Tower, and the Tower. Rain threatened the Tower, and every year we were in haste to coat in pitch the bits we had completed and cover our bricks-in-progress with oiled goatskins before the rains started. Every year, I had chafed at the delay. If only there were a little less rain. I was certain the slaves and women, whose job agriculture was, with less rain could still find a way to feed us.

Now I am completely helpless, trapped indoors, and all day long there is the sound of the rain, and all night long the sound of the river rushing.

And all night long I lie awake and can think of little but the Tower, the Tower, the Tower.

I do not see how it could survive such a winter. If these rains do not bring it down, then next year's will, or the year's after that. Unless, by chance, someone has contrived to salvage it. But that is not possible; it was a project so large that it could only be finished by all of humanity, great and small, each doing his part. It was designed to be just that.

These waters are not ordinary winter-rain waters. They are a follow-up to the blow that was struck us last spring. They are the waters of judgment.

The river I cannot see, being a prisoner in this cursed wooden hut. But I can hear it, a sound very deep, as of waters running wide and high. The waters of judgment may well be approaching the under-pillars of this wooden lodge, perhaps even swirling around them. But I have felt no creakings or shiftings in the house, in all my lonely watches. I expect it will withstand the waters, rather like the Ark, and so bring us, for better or worse, alive into next summer. They did a fine job, these fools, when they sank the pillars deep into the earth, and far back from the river. We were all outdoors then, in the still-fine weather, and I watched them do it. That much they can do.

Their rude wooden lodge, the work of a summer, is going to withstand what my Tower cannot. Where is the justice in that, I ask you?

Floodwaters are dangerous for children, and so the babies have not been allowed outside in many weeks. They, and their noise, are trapped in here. When I was still a man, we did not allow babies to cry in the house with their fathers. They were kept with the wet-nurses until they could be silent. They were never allowed to disturb us Great Ones. But now, they steal from me whatever small amount of peace my thoughts of the Tower might leave me. There are two of them; I have become familiar enough to recognize their cries. One is fussy, and one is quieter. Both are little brats.

And when it is not the babies, it is the women – chattering, arguing, singing like birds. Again, noises that were not allowed around me in my former days, noises that I find most annoying.

They never allow me outdoors now, not even on sunny days. Not even out the doors of this room. How I have come to know and hate it: the imperfectly smoothed log posts, the high ceiling giving a view of dark rafters … the ugly weavings hung for warmth, the wall-panels that do not reach all the way up and so don't block noise, the narrow, cockeyed floor plan.

This little room is my punishment for what I did. And, surprisingly, it is my only punishment. Well … my only sanctioned one. I had a little visit, not long after the incident, from one of the sons of the house. Not the eldest, not the one they all defer to. This, I think, was a second son. There are the signs on him of a second son's frustrated lust for power. He is handsome enough for a Japhethite, with wavy black hair, white teeth; very young, and carries himself like a young cock. How well I know those signs.

I was a second son myself, and I dealt with it by having my elder brother assassinated. Not immediately, and not until he had proven by many trials that he was going to be difficult … by the gods, it is long since I thought of that. It was more than a century ago. It was driven from my mind by all the doings that came after – all my good deeds associated with the Tower. It crosses my mind now to wonder how, if he had lived, my brother would have fared in this great disaster.

We Great Ones are second sons as well. I have said that we were the first people, but that is not quite true. There were those who came before us, but they were overpowered by the gods. They did not take charge of the situation, when the gods came down. They interacted with them, but they could not control them. So we had gods abducting human women and human women spawning giants, and then we had gods mingling with animals as well and spawning monsters. By the time people learned to be as ruthless as the gods, it was too late; the chaos had been unleashed. And then the great Flood came and washed it all away.

But people remembered.

We Cushites are second sons, for we come from Ham. There were three sons of Noah: Shem, Ham, and Japheth. Well, Shem learned from the Flood that the gods are off limits completely. Humans are not to mingle with them, nor talk to them, nor try to call on them, and we are not to respond if they should try to communicate with us. We are only to worship, says Shem, the One who made all things.

That would be the One who tried to destroy us.

Ham, my grandfather, learned a different lesson. This time it will be different, says Ham. We are going to learn about these gods before they descend on us. We are going to build a Tower, and it will be the gateway, the only gateway, between heaven and earth. And we will control all the traffic. We will meet and mingle with the gods, but only a few of us, and on our own terms. We will learn ways to limit the power of the gods, and increase the power of the people. And we will build a civilization, one that makes sense, and this time we will not be terrified, we will not be scattered over the face of the whole earth.

This was the thinking that I was heir to. It led to human wisdom and insight, it led to cleverness, and self-discipline, and long planning. It led to the greatest city the world had ever seen, since the Flood.

But to do this, we had to usurp. We had to push ahead and do all in defiance of Father Noah and in spite of the warnings of certain Shemites, since Shem, the older brother, refused to take the lead. And Japheth hung back, unsure, and could be bullied into going along. He didn't know his own mind about the Tower, and he didn't know his own place in the world, just as these fools don't. That is how I know they are Japhethites, that and the way they look.

This second son, then, comes to see me, handsome and empty. He did not bring a lamp. I knew he had plans for me. I thought he might even kill … and it would have been interesting, if he had, to remain as a ghost and see how the consequences of that played out.

I had been lying down, as if for sleep. I wanted to meet this with a modicum of dignity, so I quickly used my arms to lever myself upright. But I did not have time to scoot back against the wooden wall before the young jackass was upon me.

He thrust his face into mine, saying something very sternly in his gabble. I had no way to understand it, but I could guess the content, something along the lines of *"This is your punishment, swine, for getting above your station. Do you think you have a right to my ...."* Sister, cousin, or whatever she was to him. I did not know or care.

Well, of course I had a right to her, or would have, if things had been as they were before. But as it happened, I had not been trying that evening to assert my rights. I had wanted to find out if a certain part of me was working any better than my useless legs. And the answer was: No, it was not. After that discovery, it did not really matter what torture they devised for me. The mental suffering would not compare.

So this second son – this puny cock – this pile of offal, this jackass, this sprinkler of ashes – I am comforting myself by writing insults about him, as I cannot regain my former strength and visit him in wrath – cast a glance at the blankets that covered my lap, as if he considered ripping off the very part in question. But then it must have dawned upon his dim little mind that I was numb below. Instead, he took his long, sharp fingernails and grabbed my nipple, twisting cruelly.

I stared at him without expression. It would take more than this to move me; we Great Ones are trained to endure pain, as well as to inflict it. How could this bring a tear to my eye, when with all my grim night watches, I had not even wept for the Tower!

With great effort of will I did not even wince. But he must have seen something in my expression, for after a moment he released me, satisfied. He spoke a few more nonsense words and departed abruptly.

He had broken the skin and given me a small scar, that was all. I wondered for a time afterward if he would make a habit of these little nighttime visits, feeding a growing lust for vengeance, but he did not. Apparently, he was a man of "principle," just like his older brother. He had taken his due and departed. One squeeze on her breast, for one scar on mine. And that night, though I burned with rage and humiliation, I also found that he had done me a favor. My body had felt nothing sharp for a long time, neither pain nor pleasure. It was weary, as was my mind. After that rush of pain, a sense of well-being flooded me. I lay back down, and felt myself become sleepy more quickly than I had in months.

If he returns? my mind whispered, just before I slept. And my mind answered, *I will use my arms to fight him. Perhaps we will strangle each other.*

That was a comforting thought. I fell into a deep, sweet slumber.

I often have troubles with my bowels since the world changed. I do not know whether it is because of my injury, or because my jailors – curse them! – seldom feed me meat, only barley. One day that winter I had such trouble. It was the middle of the day, no one was nearby, and I, to keep a shred of dignity, attempted to manage things on my own. I used my arms to heft myself from the pallet and walked them like stilts urgently across the wooden floor, backwards, dragging my legs in front of me, toward the clay chamber-pot.

The logistics, when I arrived, were more complex than expected, and despite my best efforts I was soon befouled.

There was a small pitcher of water near the head of the pallet. Burning with shame I tracked back the way I had come, leaving a horrifying trail. By the time I arrived, my arms were shaking with fatigue. I tried to handle the pitcher in order to wash myself, but only succeeded in spilling it.

In the midst of this miniature disaster there suddenly appeared one of the women of the house. She had in her hands the inevitable bowl of barley. No sooner had she entered – and probably smelled the stink – than she turned around and left again. Then she reappeared, without barley and with a large jar of water, which she gracefully slung down from her head.

I could see now that she was not the servant who usually cared for me. This was a woman of more status … I was confused what her status might be, for in addition to giving orders she also often did menial tasks. From the resemblance I thought her possibly the mother of the Young Peacock. Perhaps she did menial tasks because these barbarians had no idea of how a lady ought to behave. For all that, she carried herself as if highborn. She was tall, straight-backed, with a not very voluptuous figure; golden-skinned and clear-eyed, with long dark hair held back in a great low bun. Not one of the younger women, but far from a crone either. I am 130 years old, and I judged her to be about sixty or seventy years my junior.

She did not fuss nor flinch nor even curl her nose as one might expect from a highborn lady who intends to clean up excrement, but simply and calmly set about setting things right. The chamber pot was righted and removed. The floor was scrubbed. Soap appeared, which they had made earlier that fall from ashes and the fat of slaughtered animals. She worked her way across the floor toward me, and then she stood and looked at me for a moment, and said something, from the tone of which I took to be, "Now, you are not going to fight me, are you?"

And then … oh, the humiliation! I kept my eyes closed through the entire process, denying God or whoever it was the satisfaction of my being there. I kept my face impassive. This was worse than pain.

And when she had me clean, we boosted me back onto the pallet and I was settled there. I opened my eyes briefly at that point, but quickly closed them again, and kept them closed for a very long time. I can usually conceal my emotions, but that time I am sure my bronzy skin, of which I am so proud, was several shades darker, it glowed so hot. The gold rings sizzled in my ears. I ate no meal – why should it all come out again? – and took only a little water.

This is my life now. This sort of thing happens nearly every day. Verily, God could not have brought me lower if He had tried.

When at last I opened my eyes, there was another chamber pot, closer to the pallet, and a fresh pitcher of water, and the next person I saw was the usual servant, and this was so for several days. The servant lady was gone.

She returned within the week, however, coming just after I'd had a bath. Like her son, she brought no lamp with her. She approached, and in the dark placed a finger on *my* lips, if you please, to indicate silence. But I overlooked the insult because I was intrigued. And then – well.

She gave me what I was due.

Her sense of what sort of treatment I deserve seemed to be very different from his. Opposite to it, you might say. And give her credit, she seemed to know a thing or two.

My problem is solved. At least, it has been solved once. That is very heartening.

CHAPTER 5

THE ENEMY

Zillah

Tiras. Tiras is here. He is my father-in-law, my uncle as well. He came with a great throng, a group of about two hundred, all of them descendants of himself or at least of our father Japheth.

I am sitting with my feet crossed modestly under me, leaning back against a wall. Sleeping with my eyes open as Tiras and my son Enmer talk and talk. I am very weary. We made a great feast for them. Used their sheep, and a good bit of their hand-labor too, but still it was Shufer and I who were directing it all, and we were still seasoning and preparing and presenting it after the Tirasite women had all run out of tasks to do and had run off to go and be our guests.

It is strange to be among a large crowd of people who speak our tongue. It is strangely un-strange. It is just the like the old days. It makes a person feel as if all the tongues were never confused. We only imagined it, and here we are waking up in our home in Shinar. Except that now, instead of the talk being about marrying and getting children and the Tower, the talk is all of the harvests, the animals, the dangers, the routes East, and who is moving where.

I have never seen my son so happy as when he realized the leader of the strange group was Tiras. Tiras! We had never thought we'd see anyone from that generation again. And for it to be Tiras, our own grandfather ...!

The meeting was tense at first. We could tell from the behavior of the birds that there was a large group coming from the south. They were following the River. Enmer sent his scout, whose name is Hur, to observe them without being seen. He came back saying that it was a large caravan, with women, children, warriors, and livestock. And a great man, riding in the midst of them on a camel. A king, then! Oh, we were worried. But my Enmer, sensible as always, sent Endu and Hur out to meet them, with gifts. There was no way we could have hidden from them, for our homestead stands out nearly as much as their caravan.

At first, they were talking by signs, but then they heard the enemy talking among themselves and realized that far from being the enemy, they were family. It is enough to make me laugh, if everything were not so deadly serious. How often do things happen that way! And how often do they happen the other way round. Family can turn out to be enemy, too.

Well, when they realized they had a common language, they began to formally introduce themselves. And when they realized the great man on the camel was Tiras, Endu begged his leave and took off running for our homestead as fast as he could, to tell his brother Enmer. Leaving Hur standing there, as always. He did not mind. Hur is a good young man.

So, such a reunion there was, there by the bank of the river! And such a perfect day for it too – a bright, fresh spring day. Enmer and I came out – Ninna too, my dark-haired daughter, arm in arm with me. The house emptied except for our prisoner. And Tiras first parted the curtains atop his camel and showed us his face. And it was indeed Tiras, still black-haired even, with his small, golden features and his wispy beard. Enmer and I recognized him, though I am not sure Endu would have known him on sight, being younger. Then – down he came, and oh, the bowing and the kissing and the embracing!

The Tirasite women are chatting around me. I love to hear their happy, young voices, without a trace of any accent or strangeness. But I am listening through their voices, training my ears on the voices of Tiras and my son.

They have been here three days now. Three days of talking and feasting, three days of labor for the women –

labor unending, but happy too. Not the kind of labor that brings a child. That is hardest, even deadly, at the end. This kind is hardest at the beginning, and gets easier as we go.

Perhaps this meeting *will* bring a child. A husband for Ninna, wives for my sons. Oh, joy!

Yes, they have been talking for three days. It was assumed at first that we would join our group with theirs. Now it is less certain. There are things that Tiras does not like. He was unhappy to remember that our family had been working on the Tower. And, of course, he does not care for our – guest.

No one likes the guest. Enmer told how we saved him, how we felt we could not let him die, how he is a human being just like us. Tiras asked to see him, and so the two of them poked their heads into the guestroom, or prison, whichever you like to call it. I did not go with them. I felt that the guest might be a little too glad to see me. Or too angry. One never knows. At any rate, I did not want Tiras to read more on his face than need be. So, I was not there at that first meeting. But I can well imagine it … the golden lamplight; the flat, inscrutable face of Tiras, shadowed by his wispy beard and his turban, staring curiously down at this fellow human being whom we have tied like a stone to our heel. Tiras would show nothing on his face, however much he might feel – puzzlement, frustration, disgust. And the Cushite, staring back at him, bareheaded. His great nose cleaving the still air, he would turn the full beam of his wide, black glare onto my father-in-law, hiding nothing, apologizing for nothing. His black curls hanging in a horror of tangles behind him. It was humility meeting arrogance, and no one with any wisdom could doubt who was the greater man.

This Cushite is nothing to my husband Golgal. He is attractive, it is true, with a splendor of body that we Japhethites will probably never achieve. And he has the charisma that comes with utter and complete arrogance, somewhat diminished by his status as a cripple. Somewhat increased by it, too, as his injuries have not dimmed his phenomenal pride, but they have (thankfully!) rendered him harmless to us. If he were able-bodied, he might have done us great, great harm.

Golgal was different. Always quiet, humble, and self-controlled. And I never doubted that he was my superior. He had authority, and when he spoke, it was of what he knew. He knew more about building than anyone ever will, probably, now. My respect for him was based upon knowledge – his knowledge of the world, my knowledge of him.

I had my doubts about the Tower even while he and Enmer were working on it. Even when Enmer was yet a child. There were rumors that it was meant to be more than just a place of rule and refuge. It was to be a temple, of course ... but more than a place for people to pray. Some said it was meant to invite the gods to come down, as they had done one disastrous day in very distant memory.

"All I can say," said Golgal carefully, "is that I have heard nothing of this directly, of my own knowledge."

"But is it not wise," said I, "To listen to rumors, husband? If such a terrible thing were true, it would not come to our ears *directly*, would it? Aren't evil mysteries like this always known only through rumors?"

"That does not mean that every rumor of an evil mystery is true," he said stiffly. He was a bit larger man than his father Tiras, though like Tiras, he was straight, slim, and keen as a sword-blade. He had dark golden skin, regular features, and a long, rich beard.

We talked it over at length – always at night, when our children were sleeping. Golgal, for all his integrity, was unwilling to admit that the Tower might be used for dark rites. I think he believed that, good or evil, it was our only hope in this world. The project was going on, there was none other to join. It was bringing much good. It was, furthermore, the greatest building of which he could ever hope to be a part. And I, when I could not convince him, ended by not being fully convinced myself. Naturally, I chose him over my doubts about the tower.

These are the rumors and doubts that are being discussed now. Tiras has not stated them outright. Enmer has not caught on. Tiras is probing my son, listening to his grief, trying to find out what the tower meant to him. Civilization. Only that, my father. It was, to Enmer, only education, adulthood, hierarchy, honor. Only everything that marked his accomplishments in life.

They have been here a week. How I enjoy talking and working with these women ... women of my own age, and younger women, like daughters. I love Ninna, and I would have loved to have had another daughter.

Ninna is falling for a young man of Tiras' camp. I wonder what will happen. If only we can join our fates with theirs and live as a nation. Then Ninna could have her young man.

Besides, living in a large group is safer. Easier to survive.

It is a beautiful spring. We have harvested the grain. The spring rains have come. Now we are shearing sheep. We have no sheep of our own, so we are trading them labor for wool. Not all their flock have the right kind of wool for spinning, but a few have long wool that will give us garments. The men wash the sheep in the river and shear them; the women card, spin, and weave. As we spin, we talk. Many of us lost loved ones in this second great disaster. All of us lost homes. We talk of them. We discover mutual acquaintances, friends, enemies. Shufer had a sister who was among Tiras' group, and now they are hardly ever apart.

Ordinarily, the wool could be saved and spun during the winter months. But Tiras is talking of crossing the mountains. There may be little time to spin in the months ahead, and then winter will come and the woolen garments will be needed. We will make such as we can before Tiras feels they must move on.

Our babies are delighted with the attention they're getting. So many beautiful teenaged strangers to hold them, play with them, splash in the river! Hur-Kar is not quite a year old, and my grandson, Angki, is almost three. His feet have pounded our wooden floors all winter, and now he can run on the grass again. I must tell Ninshi to cut his hair. It is obvious he has survived the winter.

We women do not talk of the future. We hope we will be together, but it is not decided. They are having councils. I have sat in on many of the meetings, have indeed been consulted, but I will not tell what was said. Tiras says there is war coming, horrors from the West and the South. In the West there are giants, just as in the days before the Flood – no one knows how they came to return, but there are rumors – and in the South, great kings ready to sweep all before them. Human, but bloodthirsty. Already beginning again their games of power. My father-in-law is eager to get as far to the east as possible while the summer lasts. They have sent men on hunting parties – Hur is in his element – and have caught much game and are drying the meat for the lean times, for the journey.

Enmer is not certain that he wants to move our family. He is capable of decisive action, but he must be convinced first that the danger is real. This place where we have landed has good hunting, good farming, wood, and a river. Why should we move?

The women sit on the porch, enjoying the sun. Wool is drying, wool is being spun, washed clothes and linens are hung to dry. Cakes are being baked and then dried out for the journey. Ninna is laughing. They are teasing her about Hari; everyone has seen the two of them watching each other.

Ordinarily we would have our guest out here as well. No one, idiot, child or prisoner, should be denied the sun. But I have not even mentioned it. The young girls would love it – I have been asked about him daily – but it would not do to have him out here ogling them in his superior way. He is as lustful as one of the wickeder gods. Human, but not to be trusted. Only cared for.

The decision has been made. Enmer and I made it between us – decided, really, not to decide just yet. We will leave our homestead and journey north with Tiras. Enmer is unwilling to plunge into the mountains, but Tiras is willing to go north first, for he thinks there might be an easier passage there. At midsummer, if we have found no passage, we will take a decision about whether to risk it or to return here and plant our next year's crop. I think Enmer would prefer to return. As for me, I have a feeling there is death in the mountains. But there could also be death on this plain. After all, doesn't death sweep down when we least expect it? And aren't we like a fat nest full of quails and eggs, just sitting by this river waiting to be devoured? Without Tiras' army, that is. If they were to stay, we might have a chance. But he does not want to build a city here. He says there are good lands to the East that will not be so torn by war as this plain looks likely to be, probably for the rest of time or at least until there is another disaster.

We are starting to realize that the disasters may come in cycles.

Tiras, like everyone with a grain of reason, does not like our Cushite guest. But he agrees with me that it is far too late to do anything about him. We are human beings, and we must find value in others just because they are human. We cannot abandon anyone simply because he cannot contribute anything, or because he is a foreigner. If we do that, soon we will find ourselves abandoning our own children if they are born wrong; or, God forbid, neglecting our elders when they can no longer walk down to the river. In the image of God has God made man.

So our guest is coming, and I'm sure it will make a nice change for him. But not dragged on a litter this time; not at first, anyway. We are setting out to make a sort of camel-top car in which he can be slung on one side, opposite some stores. More dignified, if not more comfortable. But he has strengthened his arms, and he is intelligent enough to know to keep his balance and not to agitate the camel. We must leave him some dignity, even if he does not deserve it. I hate to see anything so humiliated as he has sometimes been, even an animal.

Enmer fears that the reason I have taken our guest's part is that I am somehow besotted with him, because we became lovers. Well, yes, we did, and I do not regret it. I am disappointed I got no daughter from him. Such a daughter would not have harmed us, for daughters generally take after their mothers, not their fathers. But now that Tiras' people are here, it is not so urgent. It appears there will be more children, after all.

I am at an age when a woman knows and enjoys her power over a man. I did enjoy our guest, for all that it took work and patience, his condition being what it is. He is attractive. But I am not besotted. Have no fear, O my son. He is nothing compared to your father.

Your father. Golgal. A man of integrity, but so taken up with his precious tower. Now that I think of it, that tower *was* his death, in a way. And it was not my death, though I was the one who had doubts about it. Oh, ye gods! Ye wicked false gods! Why must you kill your most ardent worshippers?

But he died nobly, defending his family. We had our door barred, but – God help us – we had a window that looked out on the street. A little light, a little air, it doesn't seem like much to ask, but we paid a heavy price for it. I'll never forget the way he held that window against the mob. We had shuttered it, but they broke through. At length a spear came in and stabbed his face. He had strength enough to bash back. They gave up not long after that, but within the hour my husband was dead.

O my husband, our son thinks that I do not mourn you. He is wrong. I mourn you every day.

CHAPTER 6
THE OLD DAYS

Enmer

I was delighted to meet Tiras. The old ones are treasures to us. I asked him many questions about this country (for I thought he might know more of it than I did), and of building; crops; animal husbandry; indeed, everything about how to live in this new world. I also asked him about what had happened to the city and the Tower. He said that his group had tried for a time to live in the West. But there were giants there; indeed, it appeared they were returning to Hermon, their ancient home.

Giants had been abroad in the old days, we knew. There was a great mountain in the West, called Hermon, where one day in ancient memory, gods – they called them The Watchers – had, somehow, come down. They had run wild about the Earth in those days, and – well. It was hard to know which of the old tales to believe. There was talk of their shape-shifting, of taking on the forms of animals or even of natural elements such as water. Of setting up little kingdoms of their own and demanding to be worshipped. Of saving people, sometimes, but more often of ruining them. Oh, there were many, many stories. But touching on the matter of giants … it was said that they were the offspring of the gods and of human women. How this could be, I don't know, but all the tales agree. We had it directly from our fathers, who saw it with their own eyes, before the Flood. They whispered reports of all manner of horrors ... not only giants but monsters, part man and part animal, for example. In short, the world they told of was one composed of nothing but rape, possession, chaos, horror, and war.

As for the giants, they were the heroes of old, yet their reputation as a group was not good. Being the unnatural creatures that they were, they seemed unable to perceive the natural order of things, or to see a reason not to violate it. So in addition to abducting human women, some of them would, whenever the mood took them, assault the men and even the animals ... and they taught the children of Adam to do the same. Also, they were known for eating blood, either from a carcass not properly butchered and bled out, or yet directly, from a freshly killed or even a live creature.

They were called heroes in their day, but not in Father Noah's telling. However well-known this or that one might have been before the Flood, in his mind heroism was measured not by exploits good or bad, nor yet by how great a – thing's – reputation had been, but only by how closely he, or she, or it had obeyed God. And since all of the so-called "powerful ones" had broken the ancient laws with impunity, when Father Noah told his stories he did not dwell on them. He would talk of how God had spoken to him, and of how he and his sons had done as He said.

It was all so different from the world that we, his grandchildren, found when we walked out upon the earth. All that had been wiped away. It was hard to believe in it, even.

Yet now, according to Tiras, these giants were back again in the West. Everyone – all the people, that is – were building walled cities so as not to become a target. But these were mostly Shemites and Hamites. They did not want Tiras in their territory. So Tiras had taken his group, circled far south of the Tower, and so come to our river and to the edge of the mountains.

"My brother Javan," said Tiras, "has gone to the Sea. There are a great many islands, I understand. I have not seen them."

He paused. Tiras spoke slowly and softly, and was not afraid of silences. I had not known him well enough before the fall of the Tower to discern whether this habit of speech was a natural feature of his character, or whether it was because of the horrors that he had recently seen. Later I learned that he was slow and quiet by nature; but still I gathered that things were getting very bad already in the West, and that sometimes when he fell silent, these things were parading past behind his eyes.

"I let him have the islands," he continued at last. "Let him have the West. Very few people are going east. Very well, I will go east. The mountains are perhaps less dangerous than our own former kinsmen." He adjusted his turban, a determined motion rather like girding his loins, and then added, "And the giants."

"My father," I ventured, "How can there be giants? Were not they – and all the monsters, and even the gods – destroyed in the Flood?"

Tiras wagged his head slowly. "Not the gods, I believe, my son. Not the Watchers. I do not think they could be destroyed by water. But the giants, yes. No one knows."

He gathered his thoughts again. While he thought, I delighted my eyes by looking at his face. He was not Golgal, but yet it was like having a father again. For almost a year I had been the oldest living man in our household.

"There are rumors," said my grandfather at last. "Only rumors. There is a young man, a very young man named Nimrod. A Cushite."

My head snapped up, and Tiras nodded.

"A Cushite. Younger than yours. One who was very much invested in the tower, and who showed great talent for building."

I felt a twinge of jealousy, but Tiras' face was flat. He did not say "great talent for building" as if it were good – nor indeed as if he were sure it was bad.

"This Nimrod," he said again neutrally, "some say, has found ways to alter his body. And those of others."

I was bursting with curiosity, but I kept silent through another long pause. And my patience bore fruit, for Tiras said at last, almost inaudibly, "Altered his body, perhaps, to make himself a giant."

I thought about this. This Nimrod, whoever he was, must have been starting on his project before the confusion of the languages. Had he even, perhaps ... *brought about* the confusion of the languages? Was the Tower's fall a judgment, not primarily on all of us, but mostly on him, to put a stop to him?

I was not sure how I felt about it.

"It is a terrible thing," said my grandfather, delivering his opinion. "I feel that we must get away from it, as far away as possible. It cannot lead to good. Either he will fail

…." (long pause) "… and that most likely by means of a judgment … or he will succeed, and bring back the world of monsters from which our father Noah was saved."

I asked him what had become of Noah. Had he heard any news? He had not.

Then I could not resist and I asked him, at last, whether on their way back from the West he and his party had come by way of the Tower.

"The Tower is gone," said my grandfather simply.

"*Gone*?"

"Gone, my son."

I felt as if icy water had run down my back, and was now loosening all my limbs. This was the most shocking thing he had yet told me. I did not really believe.

"How … my father … I mean, how can it be …"

Tiras told me his story. On their way back from the Western sea, they had passed very near the Tower. The center as it had been of looting and atrocities, they did not care to approach near to it with their whole party, women and children and all. But there were those among them who, like me, could not resist taking one more look at the work of their hands. So they camped in a place about two days to the south of the Tower, fortified their camp, and then sent a party of spies.

The spies, it transpired, had trouble finding the site of the Tower, because they were counting on looking at it from afar. Unable to find it, they began to quarrel among themselves. Then one of them took charge and made the group find it by ordinary means, by remembering the lay of the land. And when they finally did approach the site, they found that nearly all of it was gone. It appeared that the heavy winter rains had done most of the work, dissolving the bricks, but also that scrap-hunters had stolen many of the bricks as they were uncovered, and also nearly all of the scaffolding. All that was left was an ugly stump, and that was visibly crumbling.

The city, which had surrounded the Tower, had become a warren of horrors. Much of it had burned, and then crumbled in the winter rains, but certain parts were fortified by the few miserable bands of men that still lived there, and these, it seemed, had become completely savage. These were not kings or leaders, founding new peoples; only the crazed and the completely hopeless had stayed in the Tower city. Tiras' spies were not foolish enough to venture in to this labyrinth, but during the few hours that they spent there, they found themselves being hunted, apparently for food, by a group of desperate men. They saw no women nor children among them. The spies did not stay the night – needless to say – but made all speed back to Tiras and told him that the Tower was no more.

We had been talking of the confusion of languages as "the Tower's fall," but now it was fallen in truth. The quickness of the judgment stopped me. Then came grief, and I shed a few tears, doing my best to hide them so I would not be like a child crying in front of his elders at the loss of some toy.

Grandfather Tiras did not have much more to say after that. Soon he left me for the night, and behind him lingered only the numb repeating thought *Gone ... gone ... gone*, and the feeling of cold fingers on my spine.

I sat for a long time, letting my mind get accustomed to its new surroundings.

Then at length I got up went in to the little prison room, which was still lit, and looked for a long moment at our Cushite – or as Ninna would say, "the camel's ass."

Had you *a hand in this?* I thought, staring at him. *Did you want to be a giant, ruling humankind from your Tower?*

And perhaps (I thought with a shudder), *I would have wanted to rule with you in the same way.*

Even now I could feel the tug of desire for it. Could man really alter himself in any way he pleased? Would that not be a good thing? The city-dwelling Enmer would have welcomed it without question. But the riverside Enmer was not as certain. Living in reduced circumstances, far from the city, and hearing the certainty of my mother and grandfather, had made such machinations seem repulsive to me, though I could not think of a clear reason to reject them. Indeed, it seemed, at that moment, that I could not think clearly at all.

I looked again at the Cushite. He stared back at me with a full face, a look that was inscrutable, but might have been hate. He had gone from an irritation, to an inconvenience, to a thing of revulsion, to now a reminder of our terrible and glorious past and even a temptation to return to it. I looked at his noble features, and my eyes almost tricked me into seeing gold on his brow. I could see why he had been so attractive to my mother.

I shuddered and turned away.

I would take him far away from his Tower.

If I could have told him that it was fallen —nay, perhaps not. Perhaps I would not have told him, even if I'd had the power. Why should he feel the simple, foolish grief that I was now feeling, when his fangs were already pulled, and he already knew that he would never see his precious Tower again? Let him go on thinking it stood – where was the harm? Perhaps he would find out some day. Or perhaps he would die first. He belonged to an old, wicked world, a world that was now, even in the wake of this judgment, trying to surge back over the land.

But I would not join in that dark tide. I would throw in my lot with Tiras, with all that was humble and wholesome and right. With men who did not aspire to be giants, with men and women who were perfect in their generations.

I had almost left the guestroom, but then I returned for a moment, and with bare, hard fingers I snuffed out the lamp.

After this we continued to make preparations for about a month. We hunted, we milked the stock and made cheese, and the women prepared cakes for the journey. Hur (bless his luck) even found honey, and so we had honey-cakes. The women spun, wove and sewed; the men armed themselves. We had no way to get more metal, but there were men among Tiras' party who were skilled at seeking out stones and making weapons, of a sort, from them. Hur spent a great deal of time making arrows, hardening the tips in the fire. Also, we constructed litters for our supplies, and carriers for the weak to ride in while others walked. A great many of our deeds were things that we learned as we went, adapting old ways to fit our reduced circumstances.

And all this time, we were also learning how to rule our community together. For all my great respect for Tiras as a grandfather, I had not yet joined our community with his. We consulted together as the heads of two families. Some of his deputies, such as his sons Abijay and Melek, who were also distant cousins of mine, clearly did not like this. If we were to continue with Tiras' group, there would be trouble. The only way to avoid envy from them would be to cede all my power to Tiras, and that I was not yet ready to do, for it would limit my ability to protect my own family.

It did not occur to me at the time, but perhaps they were already thinking of succession. I was so accustomed to the elders living on for centuries that I did not think of anyone waiting for Tiras' death.

As the day drew nearer for our departure, I decreed that we men all cut our hair. We had shaved our heads in mourning when we buried my Father, but it had come back over the winter and we were shaggy again. Long hair is hard to care for when we travel; and in any case, we were leaving our riverside home, and that was a little like a death. So we shaved our heads, Hur and Sut and Endu and I, and sprinkled the hair in a little pile beside the river that had given us so much. Sut and Endu contributed blue-black hair to the pile, Sut's straight and Endu's wavy; mine was nearly black but not quite, more the color of my mother's hair; and Hur added hair that was a paler brown, almost like oak wood. Our hair mingled on the wet bank. The hair of four brothers. Anyway, kin.

Then I told them we must cut the Cushite's hair as well. We were all bracing for a fight. Endu and Sut were actually laughing about it. We knew he was likely to resist, he was so like a tiny child, and perhaps two of us would have to hold him down while a third did the deed. I believe my brothers were rather looking forward to this humiliation.

But the Cushite disappointed them. When he saw Endu approaching with the razor and the bowl, he became very still, and sat there like that, straight as a statue, staring stonelike toward the western wall of his little prison. I left them while Endu was still shearing his long black locks, well before he had got to the shaving part.

On the morning of the last day, literally as we were loading the last camels, we made a bad discovery. We had contrived to move the Cushite to his seat in a camel's saddle-bag. It took longer than expected – he is heavy as a boulder, that one, and the camel did not take to him – and while Sut and I were busy with that, Shufer was taking up the Cushite's bed linens. There she found, hidden somehow within the bed itself, a mass of filthy scribblings.

She was very distressed, thinking it witchcraft, and soon all the household was in an uproar. It is always a confused time, departing for a trip, and also a time when people are rubbed raw by the many things they must of think of, and the many things they are leaving. So they are quicker to excitement, sorrow, or anger.

They showed the book to me, and I was as disgusted as anyone. Apparently, this "guest" of ours had been writing on stolen cloths for some time. None of it was in pictographs; we could not make out even one word of it. We were ready to burn it – Endu and Sut because they thought it must contain spiteful things about our family; I because I feared to leave it on the riverbank lest it be some kind of communication with other Cushites, who could prove to be our enemies. Certainly we would have returned our guest to his people peacefully, if given the opportunity, but he seemed more the type to summon an army to come to his rescue.

If he were not writing to enemies, but only for himself, that seemed somehow viler. I could not explain why the thought made me feel defiled. I could not imagine what the contents of such writings could be, but I could imagine their tone well enough.

Also, I wanted all this to be done quickly, because it was now early summer and we were in a hurry to depart.

Then my mother returned from where she had been, helping Shulgi and Ninshi settle the children in their litters. And to my dismay, she would not hear of anything but that we give the Cushite back his book.

"Can you not see," she cried, "that this is what is keeping him sane?"

I had no desire to think about the inner life of our prisoner. I would not imagine myself in that man's mind, not for one moment, though that were all it took to verify my mother's words. Nor did I want to hear her arguments.

So I took her at her word.

"Keep the book, then, Mother," I said quickly. "We want no madman in our camp."

She took it and returned it to him where he waited, and I suppose he hid it among his meager effects. Soon, at any rate, the camels were swaying to their feet, and we turned our faces north and east, into the bright blue day, away from our little log home.

Who is this woman who has taken my part? What does she want with me? Am I her lord or her slave? Clearly, she is some kind of matriarch in this miserable band. Far too much power, she has, in fact, more than I would give a woman. Yet, not enough power to get me out of my little prison.

My body is my prison.

It has been many days that I have been unable to write. When first they brought me out of the cell, I had no time to hide this book in my garments. When I came out into the sun, I was dazzled by the unaccustomed light. My eyes were in pain, and I even feared for them. Also there was a great deal of noise and activity. I kept my eyes closed as I was manhandled and pushed about for what seemed like hours. When I opened them, deepest humiliation of all! – they had contrived to put me into a sort of baggage carrier slung astride a camel. Opposite me was baggage, actual baggage. This insult is worse than all the former ones, far worse than being dragged on a litter behind a horse. Then, at least, time was pressing upon them, they had to contrive what they could, no doubt, as they fled for their lives. But now...! I see that the carrier has been cleverly crafted. Probably it was days or even weeks in the making. This is a premeditated insult. But I am not even enraged by it. I am so accustomed to humiliation by now that I am numb. I have realized that they will never, never know they are in the presence of their betters. Only my ancestors, and perhaps, the gods, will look down and see. And may they remember me.

Before I had time to get used to the light, the noise, and the oddities of my new situation, the camel was made to rise, and there I was, swaying in the air like a captive impaled after war. A camel moves rather like a ship at the best of times, so imagine, reader, if you were hung off the side of the ship, dangling in the air! I am glad of all my physical training done during the long winter months. It is coming in handy now, for riding as I ride is an active sport, not a passive one. I believe it may actually do me some good. I believe I could ride a horse now, or learn to ride one, if given the opportunity.

Will I rise again?

No. I am numb.

In the days since, I have become accustomed once again to the bright sunlight, and to the wind that whistles constantly around a man's turban and tugs at his beard. (I had terrible headaches at first. With everything in me, I wanted to shout, to call on the gods, but I would not risk frightening the animals.)

I am exhausted at night. We are camping in tents again, and I hope this will not last. I will say for them that they take me out of my baggage rack, not just at night but at noon as well, and make provision for me to eat and to relieve myself. It is horrible, of course, to be like a child, but they have no compelling reason to do it. Perhaps they realize that I am royalty.

A campfire is nothing to write by, but I must add more. It may be some time before I get a chance again. They are traveling steadily north, sometimes a bit west, following the line of the mountains. Always we can see the foothills on our right, beautiful blue in the daytime, dark and sinister by night. Beyond them, glimpses of peaks. We are close enough that we could bolt into the foothills to hide, if we had need.

I think they do not want to go into the mountains. I am surprised they show such good sense! To go into the mountains is to leave all hope of civilization behind.

Ah, here comes one of my many nursemaids, to show me to bed.

We traveled north and east, bending after some days back to true north as the mountains forced us onwards. We saw many lions, coming down out of the hills, drawn by the sound and scent of our animals. It was early summer, and they were weak, thin, desperate and hungry. Hur and his bowmen saved us many times. We had not time to cure the lions' hides, or we could have worn them and looked like a troop of kings.

Almost every day, Tiras and I talked about our route. He was determined to take his party into the mountains, to get as far as possible from the now-defiled plain. I did not want to cross the mountains. They were dark and terrible, and the sight of them filled me with foreboding, as if the father part of me sensed that those mountains must hold death for the family I was charged to protect. Tiras and I could never settle our differences, and so every time we spoke, we ended by deciding to delay the decision, and travel on another day or two together.

Yet I knew that if he would cross the mountains, he must do so quickly, while it was still summer. For my part, I many times considered going back to Nimrod, to beg to serve him.

Our prisoner would be able to speak to Nimrod, being a Cushite. Perhaps he would speak to him for us, perhaps beg him to be merciful to us, just as we had been merciful to him. But as often as I considered this, I just as many times rejected it. The mountains might hold grim uncertainty, but I knew in my heart that Nimrod and his city held for us a certainty that was even grimmer.

At length we reached what seemed truly to be the end of the plain. For us it was like looking on the end of the world. The mountains now surrounded us on two sides, north and east, such that if we did not wish to enter them, we would be forced to return to the south, or follow the line of the mountains as it bent back toward the blue west. The mountains indeed seemed kindly at this moment, green and summery on their lower slopes, and some of Tiras' people were eager to take their sheep up into them, make a summer camp, and come down on the other side in the fall. The earth was so fertile in those days, and both men and animals so hearty, that this did not seem like a particularly dangerous plan.

We made a more permanent camp where we planned to stay for seven days. When traveling with such a large group, sleeping in a different place every night was very difficult, for all that each family did their own setting up and taking down, evening and morning. Now we had many tasks that must be done. The women were washing clothes and laying them to dry. Others continued with the spinning and sewing, and some tanned the skins of lions that had been more recently killed. Our warriors must practice with their bows – Hur was training a company of youths in how to shoot. And the children had been longing to stretch their legs. My Angki would run and run, with a whole group of other just-weaned little ones whom, since they are descended from Tiras, I must call his cousins. And always there was a girl by to watch that they did not fall into the river.

Our journey had taken us some time, and it was now midsummer. Though none of us knew what lay beyond the mountains, we knew that however easy the passage, it must still take us – or whatever party went – some time to break through. Tiras and some of his other sons and I sat in front of his tent, gazing south over the plain, enjoying the warmth of the sun. The river emerged from the foothills behind us, on the west side of our camp, then bent across our field of vision, though its waters were low and all that presented itself to our eyes was the bare edge of its high bank, dropping off as though over a cliff. It was not the great river, but one of its feeders, of which we had crossed many already.

All of us were feeling happy and relaxed for the moment, like a king in his own palace. We had sent out hunters, hoping to get some game and to eat that night better than we had in many days. My mother and Ninshi and Ninna and Shufer had started bread that morning, and it was rising. Our mouths watered at the thought of the meal that awaited us, and our eyes rejoiced in the sight of the clear sky, our ears in the voices of the children and the music of the river.

Yet we would not be sitting idle if there were not much to discuss. Travel had left little time for counsel. Now here we were, come to the midsummer and to the valley of decision.

Tiras told me, that day, that after taking a week of rest he would take his group into the mountains. We were welcome to come if we would, but we could never dissuade him. He must, he said, seek a portion for his people, a portion of the Earth to be their own. He was convinced in his mind that God's portion for the Tirasites lay beyond those mountains, perhaps a long way beyond but not farther than a man could travel in a lifetime. He meant to enter the mountains this very year, and to lead his people as far toward their portion as he could before his life's end. (He did not say, "Before I am laid with my fathers," because since mankind had been scattered, wherever he would be laid it would not be with his fathers.)

"I believe there is good land there, Enmer my son," he said in his usual quiet way. "Come with us and you will see it."

I looked about me, and what I saw was that there was good land here. Nor was there any sign of people, other than ourselves. This should have struck me as strange, for reckoning as the eagle flies, we were not yet that distant from the Tower. But I did not see strangeness, I only saw good land, unguarded, near the foothills where we might build a fortified city, near a river large enough to water many, near farmland on the flat and grazing in the hills.

I said none of this to my grandfather, but he saw where I was looking and asked what I was thinking, and I told him.

"Nimrod's ungodly kingdom may yet extend here before many years have passed," said Tiras. "Or if not his, then someone else's."

We regretted that we had no maps. Maps had been made, we had heard, in the years before the great flood. Men had sailed around the world, drawing the coastlines as they went, settling everywhere. They had mapped the stars. Some of these maps had survived the flood, but no one in our present party had one of them, nor even a detailed verbal description other than rumors of distant islands. And even a very detailed description would likely not have told us whether and where these mountains ended, what was beyond them, and in how many days' journey. This was information that I wished I had. I did not like feeling as I did now, lost as the first man when he was first cast out.

I gave Tiras no answer that evening, but I thought to myself that unless the gods gave me some very great sign, I would settle my family here. If we planted now, we could still have some things come to harvest before the winter. Furthermore, the river had many rocks. On these very hills we could build a city, and then let Nimrod come if he would. If he waited fifteen years, Angki would be a man. If he waited twenty or thirty years, we'd have raised an army of men. Let him come.

As for what kind of sign would turn me aside, I did not think very deeply. A firm refusal from my mother, perhaps, or some other sign that I had not yet imagined.

We had our feast that night. The hunters had got only one deer, for they had all withdrawn far up into the hills, but we slaughtered a few cows and we had many fish from the river. It was too early for apples, but there was bread, and tea made from mint, and beer that we had brought with us. We posted a guard and made merry around our fires, even singing and telling stories while the women rocked the little ones to sleep.

And that night, I went in to my wife Ninshi, which I had not been able to do for a very long time. Before I came to her, I lifted up Angki from her side and carried him to the tent of his grandmother, where he snuggled up gratefully.

CHAPTER 7
HERE IS EXACTLY WHAT HAPPENED

Enmer

Firelight flickers on the walls of our cave. Yes, in a cave we are living, like the people in ancient times who were driven from their cities by the bastard sons of gods and women. Like fugitives. For fugitives we are.

I have not slept for several days. The flaring fire is making the cave-walls seem to breathe; the scene is ever leaving me, then returning for a moment. My mind is beginning to blend ancient times and dream and reality.

I must sleep.

Now that the terror, the chaos, and the sleepless labor is over – for the moment – I can tell what happened on our last night in the lowlands. Indeed, it has taken us some time to piece it together. There was, at the time, much confusion, and afterward all of us were too busy rounding up the stock, and tending to the lost and wounded.

What is certain is that we were attacked. It happened in the deepest part of night, when those who slept were sleeping deeply, the deep sleep that comes after a feast. Fortunately, we had posted a guard at the river, and their cries gave a few minutes of warning.

My first word of it was Endu shaking me awake. He had been among the guard, and he had sped back to the tent to alert me.

A very great force, it turned out, had stealthily crossed the river. Only their vanguard was able to surprise our watchmen, for there were too many of them to sneak across in silence. Thus, the river saved us. The vanguard crossed very quietly, and seeing our men outlined upon the high bank they portioned them out and attacked and killed them one by one. Some were able to cry out before dying; a few, like Endu, made shift to escape and give warning.

We men roused ourselves, bidding our women to stay where they were for the moment –for we had nowhere we could immediately send them – and gathered ourselves on the west side of the camp, sleepy and disheveled, with our various weapons and tools of the hunt. Some had armor, most had not, for we were not primarily an army. Tiras did have a small militia, but these had barely time to gather before we saw, with a shock, the enemy coming toward us.

They ran forward with a yell in a great wave of muscle and ferocity, brandishing their fearsome weapons (short spears and swinging clubs, mostly, though we did not see clearly at the time), *naked*, their hair standing up like peacocks' feathers, their bodies smeared with a whitish mud that seemed to make them glow. They looked and sounded like demons out of hell.

They were Scythians, we later determined. Those of us that lived.

Some of our men wavered but none, I am proud to say, fled. We met them with a crash and that was when we discovered the nature of their weapons. Our archers had had no chance to shoot. Except for Tiras' small army, we were reduced to fighting those savages hand to hand, most of us armed with nothing better than staves or hunting knives. It was a bloody slaughter.

One's mind is not one's own in battle, at least not if one is untrained, as I am (an engineer!). Yet in part of my mind I was worrying for the women, for as far as I knew, no one was helping them to organize and flee. At one point, I had a chance to glance their way, but my eyes could discern nothing but a confusion of lights and moving figures of people and animals. Meanwhile, it was obvious that we were being overpowered and that the demons would soon flow around our edges toward the camp.

I had known grief in the loss of the Tower, but now it seemed that not until this battle had I known true despair –

despairing even of life, not just for myself but for my entire family.

I do not remember much of it, at least not in an orderly fashion; at the same time, I remember many details, as if it had lasted years. They tell me that I fought bravely – at least, I came out mostly unscathed – but I know that I fought in despair.

Sut distinguished himself in that battle. Though not trained for war beyond what was usual for a nobleman's son, he fought in a way that did credit to our family. And he died – smashed in the face with a club, stabbed in the belly with a spear. Dead twice over.

But to return to the facts of the night. Although I did not know it, Tiras had sensibly kept himself out of the battle and had organized the older men of his household to aid the women in their flight. Most of the stock, luckily, was east of the camp. They brought the women and children out, so that while our battle was taking place, a great number were running, carrying sleeping little ones, to where the cows and camels were pastured. Those that arrived first were put on camels and sent up further into the hills, with a man or two to guard them. A second group arrived and was sent, partly by camel and partly on foot. A third group did not make it to

the stock before they were overtaken by the Scyths who by
now had made it past us.

My mother – I write this with shame – had no one
organizing her, for Tiras was taking care of his household,
but I had not thought to direct mine. When she heard the
cries and realized the camp was under attack, she scooped up
Angki, still asleep, and brought him quickly and quietly to
the adjoining, very small tent, where she laid him at the side
of the Cushite prisoner. Returning to her own tent, she
picked up the nearest weapon to hand (a weaver's shaft, for
she had been planning to set up her loom), and dashing back,
thrust it into the hand of the Cushite, who was wide awake
and seemed to realize there was danger. All this happened in
the time it took me to wake and arm myself.

By this time my wife Ninshi had waked and, though not
yet realizing what was befalling us, had begun to call for
Angki. My mother grabbed her arm with one hand, shushed
her mouth with the other, and told her firmly, "Angki is safe
for the moment. Help me to get the horses."

The two women then went to get two of our horses,
which were pastured not with the camels and cows but south
of our camp, near the river. The horses were frightened and
beginning to mill, but the women calmed them and led them

back toward the camp, where the horses very much did not want to go. By now the sounds and smells of battle were unmistakable.

Returning to the Cushite's tent, the women found a dead Scyth at the door, and terror overtook Ninshi.

But my mother entered the tent (which was still standing), and there were the Cushite and Angki, both unharmed, but Angki awake and staring. They had not time to search for saddles, so they mounted the horses bareback but for a hastily thrown blanket. How my mother got the Cushite on a horse, and herself up behind him, in the dark, I'll never know. But the Scythians were on foot, and though they were pursued, my little family made it well east of the camp and eventually caught up with the other fugitives in the hills. The horses were glad to go in the direction of safety.

What saved us in the fight was that the enemy were nearly as inexperienced as we. There had not been a great deal of war since the Flood; there had been no large armies. Everyone was to be together working on the great project, the tower. On that night our attackers had worked themselves into a frenzy, and they had the initiative in the fight, but luckily for us, most of them had not years of training behind them.

We made an agonizingly slow retreat across our former campsite, fighting all the way; and they, as if they had no commander or overseer, began to stop and pick up plunder one by one, and flee back the way they had come. Eventually we made it to the small hill on which I had dreamed of building a city. When they saw that we had the high ground, and were prepared to defend it with spears (some of which we had wrested from them or from their corpses), they were satisfied. They broke and returned to our camp, and began to plunder in earnest.

We took account of ourselves and of our wounded. Many were missing, including my brother Sut. (I was not surprised by this. I had seen the blows he took.) Endu was barely scratched, for my second brother always manages to avoid having harm come to himself, though I know that he fought alongside the rest of us. We were in a sorry state, many of us not even dressed; I myself was naked.

Our next concern was our women. Some from Tiras' party knew that many had been fleeing, and one of these had a rough idea where. We went to the pasture, knowing they had started from there, and found to our astonishment that some of the enemy were raiding our cattle. But we were so enraged by this that we charged them with spears, like madmen, and they gave way and fled. But the cows were scattered.

We found the trail the fugitives had taken. It was not hard to follow, marked as it was by camel dung and the occasional spots of blood. Hur, who was with us, led the way as we followed it into the mountains. One of his eyes was a gory mess, and he stumbled along covering it with his hand, seeking the trail with the other.

We found our women, and it seemed also that they had found each other. Many were missing, and we could not immediately tell whether they had become separated in their flight, or whether all the missing were lying dead. Hur was frantic to find Shulgi. I was relieved to see my mother and Ninshi and Ninna. Tiras had led them to a narrow, defensible valley, with a stream. We posted a guard; it was a good enough place to spend the night. The little ones were crying and their mothers were shushing them.

One difficulty – one of many – owing to its being a feast night, was that not all family members had been in their expected places when we were attacked. My sister Ninna, it transpired, had been staying with the family of young Hari the Tirasite, who – it transpired – had spoken on the night of the feast, asking her to be his wife. So much may happen at a feast! But being a highborn girl, and not a temple prostitute, she had been sleeping not actually with him, but in the tent of his sisters. Hence, she was with the second group that made it out to safety.

My mother's old maidservant Shufer had been staying with her sister, had gone with the third group, and was killed. It took us some time to sort all this out. Certainly we did not sort it all out on that very night.

We spent the night crying, counting ourselves, vomiting, drinking from the stream. There was a little rivulet, and the healers used its clean waters to tend as best they could to those who had been wounded. Still we could hear all night the suppressed groans of the suffering.

The next morning, we sent out scouts. I was among them. We crept up the hill of our last stand and saw, below us, that a very great part of the enemy was picking over what remained of our camp. Apparently they had a whole village-worth nearby, larger than the fighting force they had sent, and this they were intending to support with our spoils. We had not the numbers or the strength to stop them.

If Hur had been with the scouting party, he would have wanted to pick off a few of them with his bow, even if this gave away our position. Luckily, he was not. He was feverish from his injury, and I went in his place, even borrowing his tunic. He was mad to go, for we still had not found Shulgi.

In the afternoon, Tiras led a group to find a more secure place, and we spent several hours ferrying our party to this present ledge with its cave. Then, certain women ferried up much water, while those of us men who had strength went along as a guard. Our valley of the previous night seemed unacceptably dangerous as soon as we had left it.

Then came another night of suffering.

After nightfall, I and some others who were unwounded returned to the camp to find such stores as we could. We found that the Scythians, for all their interest in cattle, had not touched our goats, who had scattered but had since returned. These we herded to our hiding place, going by a roundabout eastward route that took most of the night to traverse. Some fished in the river and brought back food for the suffering ones.

The morning after was when all our questions were answered, and a bitter morning it was. The enemy had removed west. Tiras and I and his surviving sons and leaders went out to the camp to make ourselves look upon it. We walked through it, located our tents, and step by step we re-constructed what had happened. He showed me where he had led the fugitives, tent to tent, and we showed him, as best we could remember, the course of the battle. We concluded that by our fighting, ineffectual as it was, we had indeed bought the women time to get away.

We found a few bodies of the enemy that had been left, why we could not tell. That was how we discovered that they had red hair, and it was then that Tiras from his knowledge concluded that they must be Scythians. They are from the line of Japheth, as we are, though clearly, now as foreign to us as the children of Ham. Their red hair, which had been spiked up with mud, looked shockingly odd, obscene in the morning sun. Yet I am told that this color, along with black, was very common in elder days, and that you might even see brothers born, one red, one black.

We also found the bodies of our loved ones, and then we made the terrible discovery that in the case of the warriors, the Scythians had taken their heads. I can only guess they meant them as trophies. Yet another barbaric custom from the elder days that is being brought back since the destruction of the Tower.

So we could not make a proper burial for Sut, having only his body not his head. But we knew him by his hands and markings, as we also knew many others.

We made a mass grave and covered them with great stones taken from the river. Some of the women ventured out to help us with this. Ninna was among them. She was in great distress, having lost not only Sut but young Hari who had spoken for her. When the mound was made, she stood before it and wailed for a long time. At last we had to make her stop and come with us, thinking it was not safe to continue.

Then began the work of salvaging what could be salvaged of our food and other stores. This we did in small, guarded, inefficient bands, always bringing spears with us, ready to fight for our food. We glanced about to the left and to the right like mice venturing out after the shadow of the hawk has passed … I suppose we might have looked funny, to some. I suppose we ourselves would once have laughed to see people behave this way. But now, we were not laughing. Never again would we find merriment in the spectacle of suffering.

We did have one thing to be glad for, that was that the Scythians had not managed to carry away much of our dry

stores. They had gone for the obvious ... the cattle, the
cheese, the fruits both fresh and dried, the tools and clothing
and spices ... and they had trampled and befouled most of
our things, both with the battle and with the plundering that
came after. But they had not carried away much at all of the
seed ... wheat, barley, millet, or rice. Perhaps they did not
have the organized manpower or wagons to haul away great
sacks of it, or perhaps they were uninterested, having already
abandoned farming, choosing instead to prey on farmers.

We managed to bring a few sacks of grain up to the cave,
using litters, hammocks, or whatever we could devise. But
this was a difficult thing, as there was a climb involved. By
now it was late in the day. Some of us, who had not slept at
all, could see the hills expanding and contracting in a red
haze around us. At last, after much blurred and futile
discussion, we agreed to find a place intermediate between
our ravaged camp and our new home. It was to be in the
hills, easier to approach than the cave but still defensible. We
would transport the precious grains to there, and there post a
guard until we could think of a safer storage place.

As this decision was made, darkness was upon and us we
had to return to our eyrie. We could not think of seeking a
storage place or of transporting more grain tonight. We

would have to leave it on the field of battle yet again and trust to our gods – such as they were – to keep it safe until we were in a condition to attend to it.

CHAPTER 8

IN THE CAVE OF SORROWS

Zillah

Well, here we are. Reduced to this, as now it seems my heart always told me we would be, perhaps from the very moment we started building the tower. All this loss started the moment I saw the tower-madness in my husband's dark eyes … and now I sit with his son, trying to comfort him.

You need to sleep, my son. You are wounded.

Enmer came back from the battle naked as the day he was born, pierced by a spear through the bicep, left forearm nearly broken, and with numerous lesser scrapes and bruises. He was nearly unable to use his arm, but he has been unflagging in leading his men and hauling supplies. He has not bathed, except the bathing of his wound which we did the first night. Now he is sitting before me in Hur's borrowed tunic, eyes unfocused, raving, yet he seems unable to sleep unless I can relieve his mind.

You must sleep, my son. We are under guard. It is morning. In the light of the morning you may sleep.

I bathe his forehead, push his shoulder to make him recline, and listen to him rave.

He is sorry that he was not there to direct me and Ninshi, and to protect Angki. You did what was right, my son. Your place was in the battle, and you took it. So did your brothers. I am proud of you all. Not trained as warriors, yet you gave your blood to protect us weaker ones.

And Sut gave his life.

Sut, little Sut, my sunny, sweet, youngest son! How I miss you! How I regret not getting to thank you, or even say goodbye. I am glad that my last memories of you are happy ones. I remember you in the firelight, your white teeth flashing, your dark hair shining. You were happier than you ever had been: laughing, dancing, and flirting with the young women from the other camp. Showing off and walking on your hands. And all that strength was not just show or vanity, my son, because they tell me that you put it to good use at the end.

We don't have a single scrap to remember you by. Not a fingerbone, not a lock of hair even. You are clean removed from me, just as your father was. It will take me a long time to believe in the fact that you are gone.

Enmer tells me that your sister gave you a good mourning, there at your grave. Well, I will mourn you from here, and I will give you a good mourning as well. Loss, mixed with love, mixed with a heavy measure of what we all feel, which is guilt and responsibility.

Enmer, as always, carries this for everyone. He says we should have anticipated, we should have set a better guard. Well, that is certainly true, but you are hardly the only one to blame, are you?

Enmer does not blame only himself, of course. His sense of shame is too burning, he must toss it to others like trying to get a hot coal off his own hands. For me, he finds fault with the way I handled the guest and Ninshi and Angki. I should not have tried to save our guest, he says. What is that cursed Cushite – is he my child? I owe him nothing, says Enmer. Certainly I don't owe it to him to put my own grandchild in danger. Why did I not flee with Angki in my arms, bringing Ninshi with me? It was madness to bring the horses back into the camp.

And how did I manage it anyway? How did I get mounted onto a horse a crippled man who weighs more than I do?

Ah, my son. Thereby hangs a tale.

I will not tell it to him now, though. Sleep is finally winning, and this is the best thing that I could wish for Enmer, at this moment. At last he has allowed himself to be laid on his back. I bathe his face with a wet rag, and I tell him that – no doubt he is right. I, like everyone, had to act in haste. I acted without thinking. No doubt my actions were madness. No doubt, God forgive me, I endangered our grandson. But thank God, my foolish, impulsive choice worked out. Can he accept that, for now, and simply sleep? He needs his rest, I tell him. Sleep, my son, let your body heal, give your mind a few hours' peace, the better to care for your family when you wake. We are not yet completely destitute. We have the goats, and the seed, and we have the summer before us in which to find a safe place and fortify it. We have not infinite time, but we have a little time. Certainly enough time for you to take a little sleep.

The tale I will tell to myself alone, for I do not think that my son would believe it.

When Ninshi and I returned to the tent, there lay the dead Scythian. It was obvious that he had tried to get in to where Angki and the Cushite were, and we were afraid. I even thought I might find another Scythian in the tent, and I was preparing myself to fight. But when I entered, there was Angki, and there our guest in a protective stance. He even made as if to lunge at me, until he realized who I was.

I gave Angki to his mother and settled them on one of the horses. Then (and yes, this was a risk), I returned to our guest. I had never lifted him by myself before. But when I put my shoulder under his, to my surprise he stood with me and helped a great deal as we left the tent and traversed a few steps over the ruin outside it. And – I whisper this in your ear – when we reached the horse, *he stood*. He stood on his own, for an instant, long enough to reach up with his great ape's arms and grasp the horse's mane. And thank God, the animal did not dance to the side, and he hauled himself up onto it with me boosting him. And he helped a bit to haul me up, and then we were off. But he stood – for an instant.

And there is this little bit more. Angki, who like many of the children has not spoken much since the attack, has once or twice called the Cushite Grandfather. And yesterday, the precious little one crawled up on to my lap and whispered his deepest secret in my ear.

"Grandfather, stand-up," he said, "Grandfather stand up."

It is true that Grandfather stood up when getting on the horse, but I think that Angki saw a bit more. There is no way to be certain, because in the chaos and confusion of that night, many pieces of evidence were overlooked. I had no interest in examining the Scythian's death-wound. Nor did I stoop in the dark to pick up my weaver's rod where it lay on the floor, to see if perhaps the end of it were bloody. It is possible that our guest, the Cushite, my sometime lover, repelled the enemy with a throw, and that as the enemy reeled backward, someone outside the tent finished him off. We cannot be certain, so I will say nothing.

But in my heart, I am certain.

I believe that he stood, when defending my Angki. He seems to have struck one blow, possibly two. A jab to the throat, perhaps, and then an overhand blow the head? We cannot know. We cannot know what our Angki's wide eyes saw. But we know that the Cushite did something to save him. And that Angki was trying to tell me so, with his whispered "Grandfather stand-up."

Nimri

Well, I have become one of them now. I tried to resist it, by all the gods, I did. But now we are bound to each other by cords of obligation, of life-saving. It is all that woman's doing. That Zillah. That is what they call her. (I am beginning to understand now, which names go with which of them. That much I can pick out of their gabble.) She put the child beside me, she armed me with a tool of her own making, and she left me alone with the assignment to guard him. What else could I do? Could I let her child die? I defended him as I defended myself. She gave me a gift, trusting that child to me. At that moment he became my son. And then she saved my life, leading me from the field of battle, not as a piece of baggage but as a man. She gave me back my manhood when she led me to that horse.

I *can* ride a horse, as it turns out. Not very securely – more a matter of shifting my weight than of pressure from the legs – but I stayed on it for more than an hour. The gift of the mounting of it may not be given to me again. That was a dispensation of a moment … the battle muse gave it me, as he gives battle madness to uncrippled men. But the riding. If these people see fit to treat me as a man, if they think to offer me a mount again, I believe I could develop a way to ride it. And then I might prove myself useful.

Proving myself useful. I have faced death with them. Because I was in their camp, their enemy were my enemy. (And truthfully, compared to those spike-haired brutes, my captors seem very far from barbarians.) Our lives have become intertwined, so now I am proving myself useful. There is not much I can do at this moment. Many are sick or injured, many are grieving. Those who are whole are run off their feet with the tending of wounds, the finding and cleaning and mending of clothes, the cooking of food. Some keep going away. I believe some are exploring for a new home, others keep going back to the field of battle.

Most of the tasks that need doing in this cave are women's work. I cannot wash clothes, I will not bake or sift or grind. I cannot walk to move from sickbed to sickbed with herbs and comfort, as some are doing. Please God, for some needs of my own I must still be tended to like a baby. But there are a few things I can do. I spend much time holding the little child. He is frightened, he wants a strong pair of arms to comfort him. His father lies sick. His mother seems glad of the relief. Often now she will hand him to me and then jump up to tend to this or that urgent thing. (Truly, I have never seen the women's side of what happens after a battle. In their way, they must show as much stamina after the fact as we men show in the defense or taking of a city.) And the little child – Ki, I believe they call him – I will hold him like my son. Nay, not my son. His father yet lives. I will not be his father, but his teacher. The things I could teach him, if we could speak!

I wish I could talk to you, Grandmother Zillah. You lost a son to the barbarians; you must be grieving. I would give you my condolences.

Also, I would ask to be stationed on guard at the mouth of the cave. I cannot sleep, many nights, and have I not proved myself useful? Letting your menfolk sleep, that is one thing that poor Nimri could still do.

And there is one other thing. Many are wakeful in the night, many are sad, many are tossing in pain. For them I can sing. The gods have taken my legs, my lineage, my very words, but one thing I have left to me ... my voice. So I sing, in the bad hours of the evening when the torment of mind and body is greatest, when the infants will not be consoled. I will sing a lullaby to Ki-Ki, a slow sad peaceful song that may give the wounded something to listen to even if they do not understand its meaning. I will sing.

Ninna

It seems that all I am able to do anymore is hold a child.

There is comfort in a holding a child, in knowing that, though you can do nothing else, you can bring this little one comfort. There is comfort in knowing this is almost your only duty.

I used to be a young, adventurous girl, of the line of Japheth, adept at weaving and tanning and riding, an aristocrat, a lady, a warrior maiden. Now I am none of those

things. I feel that I have aged one hundred years in a single
night. The night I lost Hari, the night we lost Shufer and
Shulgi and Sut, we lost our future as well. I was going to
marry Hari, I was going to be a mother of the new line of
Japheth, I was going to raise a household of princes in an
estate perhaps here and perhaps beyond the mountains. I was
ready for anything.

Now all is death and pain, and I can do nothing about it.
Hur is laid out, raging with fever from an infection where his
eye is missing, and I can do nothing to heal him. It is not
safe to gather food or go to the river. Our trips are furtive
and quick. We have not yet re-made our tools for sewing and
weaving. All the womanly arts are lost to me. There is
nothing I can do except hold this child.

Hur-Kar, I mean. He is the son of Hur and Shulgi. His
mother was killed, but he was saved. He is one year old. He
had begun to walk, and even to try to track animals like his
father. He would take a stick and follow after a chicken as if
it were a dragon! Now he has stopped walking. He has
become like a much younger baby, clinging and fussing and
wishing to nurse. I can hold him and soothe him. I feed him
goat's milk from a twisted rag, keeping the rag clean,
making sure I get to the goat at the same time each day,

rocking Hur-Kar throughout the night, keeping myself fed somehow.

This is the extent of my work.

I had thought that this narrowed, concentrated life would come when I had a child of my own. I looked forward to long days and weeks spent in a tent with my new baby. It looked peaceful and easy when I saw other women do it. I saw how they would barely stir from their bed. I did not know that was because this is as exhausting as climbing a great mountain. Getting through each night, you are as desperately tired as when you walk into camp at the end of the day, still needing to set up the tents, your arms liquid and your legs shaking.

Strangely, the hateful Cushite seems to have made the same discovery. I always make sure I am well away from him, yet I can't help but notice that my nephew Angki is seldom out of his arms. Sometimes he and I will glance at each other across the cave, our eyes meeting briefly as we cuddle our respective children. At those moments, he is almost like another woman.

When Hur-Kar sleeps, sometimes I take the opportunity to sleep as well. Sometimes, if it is the right time of day, I will creep up from our bed and tend to Hur. I feel that he is

my responsibility too, since I am caring for his son and I
have a free moment. Hur has been very good to our family.
In fact, we would not have survived those horrible early days
if it were not for him. Mother cares for him sometimes, but if
she has brought the food and I have a moment, I will spoon
the lentils into his mouth, or give him a bit of willow-bark to
chew for the pain, or raise the cool mint tea to his lips. He is
no longer raving with fever. He looks at me clear-eyed and
no longer calls me Shulgi. If only he could! There is sadness
in his eyes, the sadness that is in all our eyes now; he looks
at me but I know he is seeing her.

I return to bed and settle down beside Hur-Kar. He is still
almost bald. Only a few long strands of black hair lie across
his smooth, dry little brown head. He feels me near him and
cuddles up to me with his skinny arms and legs and his little
protruding belly. He gives a sweet baby sigh.

Faintly – for the shape of the cave does not allow it to
carry – I can hear the song of the Cushite. We will have to
name him, I think, or find out his name, if he is to be with us
for very much longer. Why was he spared and Hari was not?
My body is relaxing, drifting off as if in a boat over swaying
waters. The Cushite's song is rocking me to sleep. It is
foreign, yet not foreign. Obviously a lament. There were

many laments they used to sing in the old days, songs commemorating the tragedy of this or that god or goddess. I suppose this song was not written for ordinary troubles such as ours, but it sounds as if it was. His voice is strong and gentle, it does not get in the way of the song, and this song was written for us, is my last thought before I am asleep.

After a few more days, Hur fought clear of the fever and he seemed to come to himself. I feel that I am coming to myself, too, or at least I am striving to. I am striving to clear the fog around my head. I will tell this story as a proper tale, talking about one day or many days at a time, seeing them from afar, not just seeing the moments close up as a child might do.

Then Hur's task was to gain back his strength. Because of his wound and his grief and his fever, he had not been eating well. Now it was his task to eat. Decimated though our camp had been, Tiras had decreed that we should kill a sheep a day, to build up the strength of the wounded. So Mother and I set about feeding Hur with mutton-and-lentil stew, into which we mixed healing spices.

Tiras was the leader now, as my brother Enmer lay in his own raving fever. Nor was this the only change.

Responsibilities were shifting to the left and to the right, as those of us who had survived stepped in to take the place of those who had not.

Hur, who was always very alert to all that took place around him, asked me formally as soon as he could.

"I see," he said, "that you have been caring for Hur-Kar. Will you continue this, daughter of Zillah? Will you continue to do it for – for as long as it is needed?"

"Of course," I answered. "I am as a younger sister to you. It is always the younger sister's job to tend the little ones, whenever –"

My voice faltered. I had been going to say, *Whenever their mother needs help.*

He gave a single nod, satisfied.

In the days that followed I found out why he had wanted to secure my help. Very quickly, as soon as he could walk, Hur was up and about. He was no longer a crack shot with an arrow, but there were many other things he wanted to do. He presented himself to Tiras, and suggested that he go on training the youths of our company to use the spear and the bow. This was urgent, they agreed, for the red-haired enemy were still at large in the area. (Endu was acting as the go-between for our family with Tiras, until Enmer should be better. But Hur was, as he had always been, in charge of security.)

At first, these activities truly took all of Hur's strength. He still was in daily pain from his ruined eye, and this pain drained the strength from his body. In time, however, he began to lead hunting parties to bring back stags or wild goats from the hills. And also, he was seeking a route further north. Our father Tiras had asked Hur, and also some of his own trackers, to seek whether we could bring the horses through the mountains.

I, meanwhile, continued my care for Hur-Kar. Frequently I was also being asked to watch Angki too, for my sister-in-law Ninshi – though she was neither wounded nor widowed in the raid – seemed to have lost her heart to get up. She would do a little, venturing timidly to the river to bathe herself or Angki, or to wash a small armful of clothes, and of course she was helping to tend to Enmer … but often she rose very late and retired early. She took little food (it took us some time to notice this, and if anything, we were all grateful), and she had a tendency to look pale, to moan and groan more than seemed warranted. So eventually it fell out that I was watching both children during the day; and at night, I would sleep with little Hur-kar while the Camel's Ass would sleep with Angki.

I remember our stay in that cave of sorrow as being many long days. Indeed, the days were long, but they were not many. They seemed long because of the newness, the soreness and hunger, the sleepless nights, and the sorrow. But while I was content, like a new mother, to inhabit these days, the great minds of our family were feeling a sense of urgency. They knew the Scythians might return, or there might be other groups and other raids. They knew the summer would not last forever. Autumn would come, and winter, and we would have no way to live if by then we had not found a way to get the livestock through the mountains. So it was not long, as the sun and stars would see it, before they were telling us it was time to move again.

CHAPTER 9
IN THE VALLEY OF PARADISE

Enmer

And so, we were on the move again. I had received my sign and then some. It was simpler than getting an omen from the flight of a bird, and far more direct than looking at an animal's entrails. It was like when a foolish man, instead of using commands and reins to turn aside his horse or donkey, strikes him a great blow on the side of the head. That was how God had dealt with me: a mighty blow.

We stayed long enough to see the wounded begin to heal. Those that were fated to die, died; the others cast off their fevers and lived. We did our best to follow the ancient rules for keeping sickness away. We burned herbs, we bathed ourselves, and women washed a great many clothes and bandages and blankets. Perhaps some of us said prayers as well; for myself, I have been too sick and tired to pray.

Hur led the family until I could get up from my bed. He cannot shoot properly, not yet (what a mighty blow, for God to take his eye!), but he has re-formed Tiras' militia that was wiped out by the Scythians. Endu, who always knows what is best for Endu, has joined as well. When we set off, we made sure to have a guard before and behind, as well as scouts riding ahead. All these hills could be alive with the enemy.

We also needed to wait a little while until clothes could be found or made for the naked. My mother has made several woolen tunics. I myself, as head of the family, am wearing one of the lion skins. Yet how unlike a lion I feel!

We set out on a fine summer day, the kind that makes the young want to skip and run. Some of the children, indeed, were running: my Angki among them. Then we picked up our pace and he was scooped up onto a horse with Ninna. Other children sat staring and silent, and had to be beaten before they would help with the packing-up. Angki was a lucky one: he did not lose a parent in the battle, though I am not sure how much carnage he may have seen. Also, he has a very wise grandmother. I think my mother has talked with him about what happened, whereas no one has talked with some of these little ones.

Despite the fineness of the day, despite the smile on Angki's face, despite that I was adequately rested and fed, had less pain in my arm, and could hear the cheerful braying of the livestock … despite all this, I felt old, older than Tiras, older than Father Noah if he still lives somewhere, unseen by us. Old and ready to die. I had done my best to provide for my clan so that we might not disappear from the face of the earth. But after what had happened, I was fairly certain that I would be unable to do it. I had little plan, and could not think how to construct one. My mind seemed to be stunned and weakened, just as the fingers of my left had still could not grasp with their full strength. "Get through the mountains" … that was my only plan. But if it were to meet the slightest obstacle, such as a clan of giants, winter, or even another attack by the same Scythians, then certainly my plan would fall down like a mud house built by a child.

Also, during this time Ninshi came to me with tears and accusations. "Why have you done this to me? I am with child – I am sick – I cannot eat – I can hardly care for Angki." And so on and so forth. How can we have another child at this time? I comforted her as best I could, reminding her that we still have Ninna to help, and plenty of livestock, and a good chance of finding a safe place before winter.

"We will help, my wife," I said. "Don't be afraid. Think how glad you will be to become a mother again."

But in my heart, I thought, she is right. We will be lucky if we don't all die along with the baby.

Of course, there is no luck. There are spirits on the one hand, and God on the other, but like a dog with a drunkard for a master, I am a bit confused about Him. He provides beautifully for us with one hand, then gives us a vicious blow with the other.

Hur

Scouting leaves the mind too free.

Not all the time, of course. We jog ahead quietly – my head pounding with every step – and during those times, our minds are fully occupied on the tasks we have set ourselves. Keep on going, make no noise. Scan the hills above and the valley below for signs of trouble: woodsmoke, noises, horse or donkey trails, people smells, strange behavior from birds. I am here with Endu and two younger men named Hirsa and Gugi. Usually we keep to a path that takes us neither across the floor of a valley nor along the top of a ridge. We stay partway up, hoping to be concealed by brush. Our elevation gives us a view of the valley below, for some distance to either side. By not being on the ridge, we avoid the howling winds and, of course, we avoid making ourselves targets. Side of the hill for us. Hour after hour, it's a bit harder on one leg than on the other. We don't go straight across, of course. Depending on the brush and other opportunities, we zigzag a bit.

We don't get to see many beasts, compared to before. Wild goats, and a few scavengers, like vultures, and predators, like lions. But as far as squirrels, hyraxes, deer … they all flee before us. The animals here have become canny. I think I know what it is. It's those Scythians. They are taking nearly the same route as we are through these mountains, always a few days or weeks ahead of us, depending on our progress and on their side trips. They have driven the animals out before us.

I'm not sure it's their whole party that we keep nearly running into. It might just be a party of their men, out having a brutal good time, on a loud careless hunt or looking for people to rob and kill. Or even, like us, seeking a homeland.

They are none too cautious. They don't send scouts backward – at least, I haven't seen any – and their hunting and camping methods are not quiet. That is very helpful to us. Every so often we come up on them from behind, but it is always just the four of us. If it's a large group of them, such as might plan an ambush, we return to Tiras, stop the caravan, and our whole party circles out of the way or finds a place for a few days to go into hiding.

If it's only a few of them, we kill.

Then we leave a false trail, pointing elsewhere.

It's when we come upon a party of them, quietly, that the time for thinking comes in.

It's at those times that we're obliged to lie on our bellies at a good vantage point and watch them for a few hours, until we know their numbers and what they're up to. And these can be tedious hours, and naturally one's mind starts to return to – things.

Things that hurt to think about, but that also feel like home.

I miss them, I do. Seemed as if the raid on our big, foolish camp by the river took, out of our immediate family, all my favorite people.

Sut. I liked him very well. We had become cautious friends on our expeditions, and he was showing promise as a scout and as a warrior. He started out a little bit behind me, but both of us were learning just as fast as we could.

I like his older brother Endu well enough – not that it's my business to have an opinion of him – but he's not the same sort. A trifle lazier, a little more of the young lord about him. Luckily, he has his pride. That keeps him going on the long jogs. He does just fine as a horse in the herd, so to speak, but – well, I miss his brother. On these scouting trips, when I raise my head to look for my companion and give a silent signal, it's Sut that I expect to see.

Shufer. I liked her as well, because she was another former slave. She was about the age of my mother, but she seemed much older, like everyone's favorite, somewhat crazy grandmother. She would get resentful about little things, as women tend to do, but that was because she *noticed* all the little things, the little details. And that was good. She could brew, spin or pound flour faster than any other woman in our tent. A strong back, clever hands, practical and funny. She'll be missed.

And then – Shulgi. My wife. She had – now that I think of it – many of the same vices and virtues as Shufer. She was quiet, cautious, resentful of any intrusion on her rights. Practical, capable. A canny freedwoman. No "lady" about her. She was not especially beautiful, but I didn't want her to be. I was a slave – and then, later, a freedman – not a nobleman, not a pretty man, not a hero, and no fool, and I wanted a partner suitable for me. And suit me she did, head to toe.

She was a solid mother to our son.

I approved of her. I did not think that I was in love with her, not the way that people are in stories, where some fool goddess will ruin her own life and lot of other people's for the sake of some beautiful mortal, or a king will do the same because he's taken with a shepherd girl. I thought I needed her, like a good piece of farm equipment, and I was set to take excellent care of her just as a man would take good care of a well-made bow or plough. I was not aware of "love." Yet, now that she is gone, it seems I must have loved her after all. She has left a gaping hole, as when a bit of one's flesh is ripped away.

At first, I was confused without her. Now, the thought of her is coming to be just a sore place, as men who have lost a leg or something will talk of a ghost of the limb.

But – I am surprised by how very sore is the place she left empty.

To this day, no one knows exactly what happened to her and to Hur-kar. There will always be unanswered questions about that night. The two of them seem to have fled on their own, for no one remembers seeing them with the first party that fled the camp. Perhaps she did not trust anyone to flee with her. Someone from the second party stumbled onto a woman's body, realized there was a child still alive with it, and scooped up the child and ran on their way to the first way-point. And that child was my Hur-kar. So he made it up to the cave, and made his way back to our family, but whoever rescued him does not know any more details about my Shulgi, or is not saying.

They found her body later, when they were finding and burying bodies. They tell me that they gave her a good mourning. They examined her; she did not seem to have been raped. None of them had, it seemed. That was good, as far as it went. A good thing on a very bad night. The red-haired enemy must have been in too great a hurry, wanting only to kill and steal. Or else they have not yet fallen so far back into ways that were common before the Flood. That will come, no doubt, in the years of the future. That's why we must get away.

When I think of her, I can see her panting and running in the dark, grasping Hur-kar. And then I find that my good eye, the one that does not hurt, is watering. Can't see, and that's not good on a scouting mission. Weeping is the only mourning I can give her, so I try to give it at night, before sleep.

It's for her that I kill, more than anything … for her and for our son. Not sure, sometimes, whether I'm doing it for vengeance or from simple calculation – to protect him and the rest of what remains. And what remains is not merely less than what we had before, but different. That attack changed us. It shattered and re-formed us in a different pattern. No one is the same.

Enmer has had the heart knocked out of him. I keep watching to see if it'll come back.

Father Tiras, though, was not surprised. He had seen a few things before then, he and his party.

Hur-kar lost his mother, almost had to start again as an infant, it seems. God knows what his little eyes saw that night.

Ninna, Golgal's daughter, had been a little lady, daughter of a great house, naïve and spoiled, and now she is a young mother, suddenly.

Me, I just feel fuzzy in the head. Not disheartened, like Enmer, for I fancy I knew before this that men could be cruel to each other. And I still know what I must do, and still am confident that with the help of God, I will be able to do it. But I am sometimes – unclear. As if I had been knocked on the head and set down amidst a bunch of strangers. I know that I need to protect them, and I know how to do it, more or less. I just have no idea who *they* are. And no memory of who I am or how we got here.

Now I have lost the thread, it seems. I was here with Hirsa and Gugi and Sut – I mean Endu. Stretched out on our bellies across a warm grassy hillside. The Scythian camp we were observing had seemed small at first, but more kept coming as night closed in. Soon it was clear that they were a big camp. Less than half the size of our force, but all of these are fighting men in their prime or close to it (a few teenagers), and none are badly injured. They could take us, probably, or at least break us, if we give them a chance. I signaled to Endu, and he to the others, and we began working our way backward very slowly. Once the ridge blocked us from their view, we moved a little more quickly, until we made it down to the trail and started on our way back home. We would tell our leaders to take a long way around. I was a bit relieved. I don't really look forward to killing.

We walked quiet, scratching gnat bites, under a brilliant white half-moon.

Enmer

We traveled another month, going from mid- to late-summer. And we were lucky – lucky, I say, meaning that God did not favor us with His attention. (Tiras would say this is blasphemy, what I am saying about God.) We found our way (greatly helped by Hur) through many hills and mountains; going slowly, but we never had to cross a high ridge. Our habit of sending scouts saved us a number of times, for it turned out that the Scythians were in these hills as well. Whether they had followed us, or whether in our flight we had actually headed toward their stronghold, was open for speculation. I expressed to Tiras the thought that perhaps going into the mountains had been a mistake, and he made a *tsk*ing sound and said, "No, my son. We would be even easier pickings on the plain. Unless we went south toward the mercy of Nimrod."

The mercy of Nimrod was not something any of us would prefer to risk.

But we survived our near-brushes with the Scythians. Our strategy was to hide, and avoid battle. It shamed us, but this was the wisest, a large company as we were with wounded and women and children. We also, by scouts and archers, avoided the wild animals. There were many in that country. There were hawks and rock badgers and wild horses, vultures and lions and wild sheep with horns of every description. There were many small rivers. Once I had to spear a lion that approached to carry off one of our sheep.

Ninna says she will tan the skin for me; then with the other, I will have a cloak. But after the first flush of relief and victory, the killing of the lion burdened rather than cheered me. There will be other lions. A lion will come one day that Enmer son of Golgal cannot fend off.

By summer's end we came out into a large place. We looked about us in disbelief: were the mountains truly over? Had we, indeed, made it through them before the winter rains? We found ourselves in a beautiful, lush valley, heavy with fruits of every kind. The air was humid and warm, as warm as it had been on the plain of Sinar and if possible, more fertile.

Our first day in the valley was paradise indeed. We camped in a defensible place, by a pleasant river. We feasted on dates and figs and apples, and on a small golden fruit, very sweet, with a single stone, which none of us had seen before. Our animals basked in delight. Nor we were alone in our enjoyment of the valley, for we spotted many other creatures, such as horses, unicorns, antelope, hind, and many of a large, ponderous, bovine type of dragon bearing showy feathers and great shields on their backs.

We were too tired to do any hunting that evening, but Hur and his pack of youths were already in great excitement, planning what they should do the next day. Everyone was relaxed and happy, but we were not as great fools as we had been, for we still had sense enough to post a heavy guard.

The next day we began, more soberly, to explore this paradise. And what we found, over the course of several days, was that it was no paradise but a beautiful trap.

Things were much worse than we had hoped. The large place, first of all, turned out to be merely a valley, a large triangular valley, beyond which was not the end of the mountains but a continuation of them, higher than ever. The triangle came to a narrow point among heights to the west of us. To the east, its large blunt end ran down into another great surprise – the sea.

Our "paradise," meanwhile, was filled with foes. There were settlements of Scythians throughout … and along the northern edge, something much worse. Our scouts swore they had seen giants. The giants appeared to be living in the hills, and some were building their customary massive fortresses along the coast of the sea. It seemed that we could not stay here.

We were still at our original camp (which, since it had not been attacked in seven days there, we took to be as secure a spot as any) when we had a conference about it: Tiras, his elders, Endu, Hur, and myself. There was an amount of shouting and arguing, for the men were frightened. Tiras gave it as his opinion that we should move along. I sat and dumbly agreed with him, unable to think how we might do this, yet unable to make a plan of my own. My mind was still numb; it seemed to have been that since the last attack. For ordinary, everyday tasks I was sufficient, but for these grand plans I had nothing.

The next day, Tiras and I set out on a journey to see the giants with our own eyes.

We felt it was important to know firsthand what it was that faced us: How many of them there were, how terrible, and approximately what area their camps covered. We needed to know them a bit in case it ever came to a fight with them. And if they were truly as terrible as we'd heard, we needed to see that it was truly worth it for our people that we leave this good place.

It was a journey of about three days: across the valley, into the outskirts of the hills. We took with us two men,

Taman and Raja, hardy warriors who had been on the first scouting party. And also with us came Tiras' son Abijay, a fierce, brave man a little younger than myself. In charge we left another son of Tiras, named Melek. He was a steady man, a good choice for the job. I of course entrusted Endu with our family, with Hur as his military captain.

It was a pleasant two and a half days' journey across the valley of paradise. We brought with us roasted grain and dried meat, and we helped ourselves to fruits from the trees. There were many springs at which to refresh ourselves. But though it was pleasant, we hurried along at a great pace (which the scouts set), often scuttling from wooded area to wooded area like hunted men. Once, in a horrible grove, we found traces of a Scythian camp. We changed our route, bending to the East to avoid them.

On the evening of the third day, we entered the foothills. We walked for some time in the dark, first through ravines which were deceptively pleasant with light winds, the scent of sages and evergreens, the sight of stars. Then climbing a bit, until finally Raja said it was too dark and he no longer knew the way. Taman concurred, and we found a high, dry hollow to huddle in. But on their instructions, we built no fire.

The fourth day was different. We were tenser than before, barely speaking. We climbed about, furtive as before, but now feeling much more exposed on the bare hillsides, on which it was difficult to anticipate both vistas and hiding places. Then at last, Taman and Raja seemed to find their stride and remember where they were. They brought us crawling on our bellies through a field of resinous bushes which towered over us when we crawled like this. It was now about noon. They would be constantly stopping and shushing us, and making us wait for a hundred heartbeats before we went on. And all the while the gnats were flying about us. At last Taman slithered back and, with our heads close together, told Tiras, Abijay and me what to expect. At the edge of this hill, he said, you will be looking down into a piney ravine. At the head of the ravine, you shall see a cave mouth where the sun falls. That is the place where, about a week ago now, we saw a giant camp, he said. If we are lucky, they will be there again, and then you can see them.

Whatever you do, don't lose your head, my fathers, he said. If you scream, it could be the end of us all. If you feel sick, bury your head in the dust and breathe slowly. Don't stand up to fight or flee.

We nodded.

Taman gave us a sharp glance. He had no grins now, as he'd had before, being in his element. Now all was deadly serious.

Forward we crawled. As promised, we found ourselves looking up a small ravine, our view somewhat blocked by many young pine trees. The ravine faced south and west, and the early afternoon sun sent dappling shadows under all the soughing pines. Beyond them, lit up as on a stage, lounging in front of a rock wall with a fissure in it, were six giants.

Seeing them gave us a queer feeling. I myself felt as if I were standing on the edge of a precipice. The blood pounded in my ears. I heard Tiras draw in a quick, appalled breath and knew that he too felt their unnaturalness rippling out through the air. But I did not look at his face to confirm this, for there was something fascinating about the giants, something that held the gaze.

They certainly made us look inferior, even contemptible. All male giants they were. Their height was about three times that of a man. In form they were like tall, well-formed and well-muscled people, with loose limbs and large, broad, well-defined joints in the knees, elbows and shoulders. It was a hot day, and some of the giants went naked, others wore breechclouts. They seemed, from the way they moved and held themselves as though for display, both aware and proud of the glorious, glistening, well-defined expanse of chest and back, calf and thigh.   Looked at longer, they seemed less beautiful and less human. Their hair was in colors too bright and pure for men. Four had blood-red hair, one blue-black, and one had hair of a yellow that was almost green. It lay on their round heads closely, like a pelt, and extended glistening and furlike down their cheeks to the jaw and down their necks almost to the shoulders. A few had darker pelts running down the middle of the back, or from chin to bellybutton.

Their faces, though beautiful, were wrong. Their eyes in particular were too round, fixed, and bright, like hawk's eyes. One felt that these eyes would hold the gaze, even the will, of little things like us. Although the giants had not seen us, I felt the beginnings of a mad urge to run out, calling and waving my arms, among the pine trees.

I pressed my face to the dust as Taman had said and counted my breaths for a space of fifty. I raised my head and scrubbed my hands over my face. Then I looked again at the giants.

They had sheep in a pen. As I watched, one giant picked one up with effortless strength. Without bothering to kill it, he seized its back legs and tore it apart as a woman tears apart the carcass of a quail. Its scream was horrible to hear. This was mixed with a gruesome ripping that I will never forget, and the bleating of all the other animals.

My stomach heaved. I pressed my face into the dust again, to no avail. I wriggled backward behind our large bush and retched as quietly as possible.

The others joined me in a moment. Abijay, warrior though he was, had given a squeak that would have become a scream had Raja not clapped a hand over his mouth. Old Tiras was shedding tears quietly.

I learned that day that I am a coward. I sat for a long time, feet braced in the dust, elbows on my knees, blood singing in my ears, while my vision stayed so narrowed, I could see only the little spot of ground at my feet. My recovery was slowed by the sounds that came from behind us, which were more animal screams and the noise of loathsome eating.

I learned this as well: what my mother meant with the words *In the image of God has God made man*. It is not the form. These giants, though in form like men, were not in the image of God. They were positively not-God. While looking at them, we had seen that which was not, and this was the source of their strangeness. When my vision cleared and I could look again at my companions, I again saw God. They were the image of God to me, and I to them.

And this is also why beasts tend to love men. We are the image of God to the beasts. The giants were not. No man could, or should, mishandle an animal the way those giants were mishandling those sheep.

"We must rescue the animals," I whispered. It was foolish, but it was the first thing that came in to my head.

Abijay nodded. But Tiras shook his head. Taman also shook his head, and that vigorously. And he gripped my arm, as if he expected me to rush off at once on a rescue expedition.

"Have you seen enough?" mouthed Raja, looking at all three of us but looking first and last at Tiras.

We nodded.

"Then let us go," he said quietly, "Before they begin to defile one another."

We crawled away on shaky limbs. Terror urged us to crawl faster, but the scouts made us pause often and these were rests we needed. We made it back to our former camp by sundown, and there they made us eat some fruit. Again, we slept without lighting a fire.

"This is but one of their camps," said Raja. "They are scattered to the east, between here and the sea. Tomorrow we will show you."

Over the next few days, he did show us. The giants were scattered, living easy lives in the hills, but they would come together to build great fortifications. We did not approach these closely, but observed them from a distance. It was strange to us to realize that they were intelligent; were, indeed, excellent builders. They did not behave like intelligent beings in their camps, simply because they did not care to. They did not enjoy self-discipline, preferring to live slovenly and engage in all kinds of abominations, of which the eating of live animals was only the beginning. But when they wished to, they could show themselves as brilliant engineers. After seeing their building site, we had no hope left that we could take them on. We could only go around them, and that would involve going far, far to the west, into the Scyth-infested hills.

At last we began the return to our home camp with very little speaking. We agreed we would tell none of the women or children what we had seen, and only those men who might need to know. The trip had filled us with horror, and filled me at least with shame at my own cowardice. This shame stayed with me a long time afterward. It, and the lingering sense of defilement, were the price I paid for having seen the giants. But seeing them also brought me a great benefit: I was firmly out of love with paradise valley. I would gladly follow Tiras wherever he wanted to lead.

CHAPTER 10

THE SEA

Enmer

We stood at the edge of the sea. It stretched before us, flat, reflective, and unnatural. It was not a place where people could live.

I looked at my family, and saw that their experience of the sea was not the same as mine. They saw the beauty. My mother's eyes were dancing. Ninna was taking great, deep breaths, her face beaming. She held the hands of Hur-Kar and Ki-Ki and let them step in the water. Farther out, big waves were breaking, unbelievably large, smooth, and powerful. I had never seen anything like this before. Farther out still, the horizon was dark blue with cloud, and the sea was bright.

My wife Ninshi just looked tired. After a moment she went to rest in the shade.

We had come here by dint of creeping along the mountain edge on the southern end of the valley, and so we had arrived safely and without attack. The giants, our scouts told us, were building their fortifications farther up to the north. And indeed, as we stood there on the beach, we saw no one. This coast, this strange flat horizon, might have belonged to a world with no people except ourselves.

The smell of it was strange to us. Most of us young ones had never seen the sea. After the flood, people were afraid of water. They loved rivers, but they tended to move inland and stay away from the coasts.

"I did not expect to find a sea here," said Tiras. In the heat and humidity, the old man had taken off his turban. The breeze stirred the thin white hairs on his brown head. "I may be wrong. I may be failing to remember the way it was before the Flood, the way my father described it to me. I thought that to the north and east was all land. Good land. Land where we could settle."

"Perhaps things have changed since the Flood," I said. "Perhaps these waters are the waters of judgment, left over."

"Perhaps," said Tiras.

The two little boys had found some odd, thin-legged birds, and they were chasing them. They ran back and forth, brown legs flashing. Their shrieks of delight seemed hardly to make a dent in the great silence.

"Over this sea," said Tiras. "Over this sea, to the east or the north, that is where I believe our direction lies."

I opened my mouth. I could think of many objections to this. We had no ships, no boatwrights. We had no knowledge of this sea. Any sea, as it was known from ancient times, was danger itself, death itself. And we did not know the extent of this sea. It could span the world. Looking across it, all that could be known with certainty was that land was not visible on the other side.

I closed my mouth. These objections would bear no weight with Tiras. Earlier he had been adamant about going through the mountains, and the attack by the Scythians had proved him right. Now he wanted to take his people to the east, and to the east he would take them. And what could I do without him? My party had been reduced to three able men, three women, and a cripple.

"How?" I asked him, like a child.

He looked at me. "I have a few people who have some experience with boats. Let us start there."

They made rafts, in the end. Tiras had some people in his party who were very skilled in their work. First they made coracles and explored the coast to the north and the south. To the north, they found a giant city being built on a great spit of land that projected out into the sea … and beyond this, the sea seemed to continue, north and east, as far as the eye could see.

To the south, they eventually found the southern coast of the sea. We decided not to go this way, for fear it would undo all our work in coming through the mountains. We might not like the Scythians, but at least they, and the mountains, were now a barrier between us and the kingdom of Nimrod. This was what our plans had come to, a series of choices between unacceptable dangers.

The scouting party came back and reported that using rafts, we could pass the giants' city in a day or two. Then we could put in at the coast on the other side, and so make a series of hops northward, until (they trusted) we should come to the end of the mountains. And this (they trusted) would happen before winter, so that we should have time to build ourselves a home. And also (we trusted) there would not yet be any people or giants so far north. Such were the series of mad gambles we were taking.

Tiras had his boat-master, who was named Raku, directing crews as they felled huge trees and made a fleet of great craft. These were not the huge and beautiful ocean-going vessels that we had heard existed in the old days. These were rude things with basic sails that could also be steered by poles. Some built them, some guarded the camp. The women fished and prepared the fish for us to eat.

Another group prepared the horses. Hur, Endu and I led this group. Horses are cowards about anything they find unfamiliar. These horses of ours had already been accustomed, before the fall of the tower, to the city, to large groups of people, to work being done. They had taken happily to our travels across the plain, and had even (mostly) been uncomplaining through the mountains. But they did not like the sea.

First we got them used to the sea itself, to its smell and feel, by walking them along the edge of it. We would take them in groups, five or six at a time, as many as the three of us could handle, for horses are calmer in the presence of other horses. Camping near the sea was helping their gradual adjustment. A few tried to drink it, and we laughed when they whuffled and found it salt.

Then we needed to find a way to load them onto the rafts. When the first one was completed and sitting on the dry land, we tried making them to go up on it. A few refused for hours, and of those that did ascend, none liked it. We had them stand on a raft for an hour every day, putting feed there to tempt them. Finally, we had them spend a night on the raft.

After this, we went and spoke to Tiras and his engineers about arrangements. We wanted to bring the great bulk of the horses on just one or two rafts, separate from the women and supplies. The reason for this, besides the comfort that horses find in other horses, was that if one of them should panic, we should not lose any human lives.

"It will need to be a very strong and stable raft," said Tiras, "to carry all that horse-weight."

His engineers looked about, considering it.

I remembered my training.

"I am good at making things strong," I said.

"But not at making them float," said Raku sharply.

"Let us not fight, my sons," said Tiras. "Enmer may offer his help in making the horse-rafts, but Raku will be in command." I bowed my head. "And meanwhile, Hur, my son, will you continue to get the horses accustomed?"

Hur agreed to this.

"May I also help with the rafts?" said Endu.

"Hur may need you for some things," said Tiras after consulting Hur with his eyes. "You will divide your time."

"That's what I'm best at," said Endu ruefully.

So I was back to engineering – of a sort – and Hur and Endu continued with the horses.

Ninna told me later how she and Hur-Kar and Ki-Ki
watched every step of the horse training. Angki was very
worried that the horses would be lost in the passage, and
Ninna allowed him to watch so that he would be reassured.
He loved the horses, anyway, my son.

Hur, she reported, was as gentle with the animals as a
mother with her child. The loss of his wife and eye had, if
anything, made him even slower and more patient of manner,
as if he felt a kinship with any creature that was afraid or
suffering. Many times, when something went wrong with the
training, he had first to calm Endu, then calm the animals.
They were training the horses for the whole party.

The day that they tried to bring some horses, standing on
the small first raft, actually out into the water nearly brought
us disaster. With help from other young men of our party,
they maneuvered the raft until it was in the very edge of the
sea. Then they led some of the bravest horses up their
accustomed ramp (sitting now at an unaccustomed angle),
and on to the raft. The horses whickered and stamped
nervously, but Hur and Endu ascended to the raft and calmed
them.

Perhaps they should have stopped there, but they had it
in their minds to tow the raft out into a few feet of water. Hur

stayed on the raft with the horses, stroking their noses and talking to them, and Endu descended and began pulling, helped by some pushes from the young men.

Endu proceeded, pulling until he was waist-deep in water, and the horses were getting more and more anxious. Hur told him quietly to bring the raft about. This proved more difficult than they had expected; in the course of trying, Endu first towed it farther, until he was chest-deep in water.

It was then that the horses panicked and began to bolt.

Hur, after only a few seconds of trying to hold them, realized he could not. He jumped into the water on one side.

Endu, realizing he was about to crushed, dove and swam out of range in the opposite direction.

Then the whole herd, joining each other in panic, came down like an avalanche, landing on their hooves in the shallow water. The raft rocked, tipped up high on its side, balanced, and came down as it had been before, hitting the water with a loud crash. The horses churned their feet for an instant in the soft bottom (and in that instant, Hur later told me, he thought he might be going to lose them); then they gained purchase and ran screaming for the shore.

As they did so, there was a large belch and a huge bubble of foul air came up from beneath the water.

Ninna swept the two little boys to safety, as other mothers were doing with their children. The audience on the beach cleared a path for the horses as they came up out of the water, bolting, but only as far as the stakes where their brothers were tied, where they slowed, stopped, and stood trembling with relief and began nosing each other.

Ninna was never so relieved as when Endu surfaced from the water. Hur was thankful to see that the horses had not continued running; they were well-trained after all. Furthermore, not one of them had broken a leg, as could easily have happened in the fall from the raft. He quickly came up on the land and began drying, brushing and calming them, while a shaken Endu retrieved the raft.

Angki and Hur-Kar had been delighted with the whole performance. They had watched in horror as they saw the horses beginning to panic, screamed when the men bailed out, and laughed when the raft made its great splash. Then they exclaimed in delight and disgust over the unexplained smell.

Now they both wanted to run to Hur and hug him about the knees. Hur-Kar clung to his father, and my Ki-Ki, brave fellow, waded into the water to "help" Uncle Endu.

Ninna expressed her relief that the two men were unhurt. "But," she asked, "What was that smell?"

"What smell?" they responded. Endu had still been underwater. Hur had been too concerned about his charges to notice it, though he found the memory within himself when Ninna described it.

"Perhaps," he said, "There is rotting matter below the floor of the sea."

"Rotting matter!" exclaimed the two little boys, with disgust and delight. Ki-Ki wanted to dig for it, but Ninna forbade him. The adults, meanwhile, looked at each other with dismay. They could guess where the rotting matter had come from.

But there was work to be done. They examined the horses, and amazingly, not one was injured. Then, when they had got everyone dried, calmed, and fed, Hur insisted that they do the exercise again, *that very day.*

Endu, with his lazy streak, was dismayed by this, but everyone saw the sense in it. Once again, they loaded the horses onto the raft as it sat in shallow water. Once again, they pulled it out, only a very little ways this time, and this time they got it successfully back to shore and got the horses down the ramp.

By the end of the day, Hur was bursting with ideas about eye-covers he would make for the horses to keep them calm, and about teaching them to swim in deeper water in case it should become necessary. Angki and Hur-Kar were bursting with hero-worship and a love for animals which they would never get over. Endu sank down beside the campfire and declared that he was aching in every bone of his body. And my sister Ninna, she was looking at Hur, our former slave and adopted brother, in an entirely different way.

"This is madness," Endu said to me later. "We are certain to lose horses. What if they had broken their legs in the stampede?"

"You are right, brother," I told him. "But our horses would fare much worse at the hands of the giants. Have you forgotten the scene I described to you?"

He pressed his lips together and shook his head.

Nimri

Now I must write of the mad expedition that the leaders of
our little clan have undertaken. I saw them preparing for it,
but I could hardly credit it. How did they propose to bring
over the water a group this size, flocks and herds and all?
And I wondered if they would bother to take a crippled man.

Well, they have done it. It was more work – for them of
course, I could not help much – more work than I imagined
existed in the world. I had been involved in the building of
the tower, but a tower tends to stay where you put it. As do
loads of bricks. As do, mostly, slaves. If the work must be
stopped, the stopping does not undo all that came before.
Not so with a boat journey. One mistake, and all could be
lost. Our leader, Tiras –

I must say a word about this Tiras before I proceed. He is
the closest among them to my equal, or to an equal of the
man I used to be. He is actually from an older generation
than mine, though perhaps not older than me in years … he
is the son of their forefather Japheth. So, if I were in their
clan, he would be my superior.

He does not have the air of command as I and all my
family had. He does not carry his authority out in front of
him, as it were, nor does he command a room. In mien he

carries himself more like a beggar, or like a lonely shepherd. But like a shepherd, he seems to have gentle and invisible control over his sheep. I have seen them defer to him as if he had great wisdom as well as power. Were my body not broken, I would never submit to this Tiras, never, never. But now, because of my situation, I am forced to do so.

This Tiras, then, as I was saying … I should call him Father Tiras. Father Tiras, then, is clearly the one who made the decision to go by raft. He has been the driving force behind all the preparations. If I had not watched it happen, but only heard about his decision, I would have said that it was the move of a coward. He would rather take on an insane project, very likely to fail and fail in a ridiculous way, than simply stand and fight for his people against the enemies when they come. Before my fall I would have taken this as final – that Tiras is one of those inferior people who are always giving in and running away. But now, I have just the seed of doubt.

The insane project, then, is to load a hundred people and as much livestock on to a series of rude rafts and strike out across a sea that is clearly poisonous, only to come back to shore each night and make camp, thus making ourselves just as vulnerable as if we had traveled by land.

They do some things well. For the sheep and horses, they have made sides on their rafts, and they have blindfolded some animals that are more likely to panic.

On our first day, we struck out as if to go across the ocean – truly mad that would be! – and I surrendered myself to the certainty of dying before the day was over. I do not object to death, of course, but I can think of nobler deaths than drowning in a sea that smells like a manure pile. Also, I knew that death would not come immediately, but there would probably be many hours of confusion and terror, and if we did sink, I should be obligated to try to swim with one arm and with the other, save the little boy, whom they call Ki-Ki.

But after all these grim speculations, we swung about and moved parallel to the shore, going north. This was not done quickly or easily, for the supposed experts were still learning to handle their craft. Clumsily we bumbled on our way north. It was maddening to watch, for a man like me who could do nothing to help or direct it. It must have been equally maddening for Father Tiras, but as far as I know he never showed it.

After the first hour, a demon of headache had taken up residence in my skull. It was, no doubt, because of the sun glaring off the water and the many unaccustomed movements that it took to be loaded on to, and then to keep one's balance on, a raft. I was to spend many of the next few days curled up on my side, my hand pinched over my eyes, my face pressed to the boards.

But on that first day, there was one moment at least when I sat up and opened my eyes. The family had been chattering a bit, and the sound carried over the water, but now I could hear them hushing each other. Then I felt a gentle touch from Grandmother Zillah on my shoulder. I raised my miserable head, and she pointed where they were all looking.

Far away, projecting from the shore, we were gliding past a promontory. On the promontory was what looked at first like a second Tower. And on it were human figures, working. My first impulse was to forget where I was and hail them, as if I had found our Tower again, and these were my brother Cushites, and in another moment I should find my body healed. But Zillah stilled me with another touch. Then she said something, to me or to Angki, the sense of which I took to be, "They are giants."

We had found a giant city. It was this that we had gone out onto the sea to avoid.

It was a long, tense hour as we glided with all silence past the giants and their city. They could not help but notice us. We had not quieted our chatter until we were within sight and hence earshot of their labors. Nor could our long string of boats be hidden, out on that mirror sea. The sailors made all the haste they could, and meanwhile all of us were praying that they would not take it into their heads to pursue us. They could hardly build their own boats in time, but they might have them already, or they might employ war-machines or arrows. But they did not. We were then left to hope they would not follow us up the coast and attack our camp and make their feast. (I did not know at that point that we would put in to shore to camp that night, but I imagine this worry was much in the mind of Father Tiras and the others.)

So we proceeded with painful slowness up the coast ... myself with the headache demon nearly every single day until my eyes became accustomed, and everyone tense and silent and giddy with the uncertainty and danger and boredom of our undertaking. We saw no more giants after that first day, and every day that the coast continued uninhabited, our hopes rose.

At long last, Tiras judged that the land seemed safe, and that risks were now greater if we continued by sea. At least, I imagine that he so judged, and that it was his mind that made the decision. I was not on his raft, nor could I understand his speech if I had been there to hear it. In any event, carried along like an idiot child, I found my helpless carcass being pulled to the shore in the middle of the day rather than as evening was drawing on. And that day we made a very elaborate camp, as if to stay for many days, and the next day we put to sea no more. We had come out of the sea stage of our journey.

CHAPTER 11

THE HEART OF THE WORLD

Enmer

We had come ashore at the mouth of a great river. We paddled upriver a way, and camped on the north side, for Tiras felt that we must head north before long. The sea had become shallow, and there were a great many reeds, willows, water birds, and fish, and we feasted on fish, for they seemed never to have encountered people before … which encouraged us.

The terrible mountains we had left far behind us. The land had become a plain, though not as friendly a plain as we remembered from Si Nar. The days were very hot, but the nights were chill, and we could tell that when the cold came, it would be bitter. But even with this dim guess, we did not realize how bitter it would be, nor how quickly it would come.

Thus began our years of wandering over the plain. North and east lay our way, so said Tiras, and I had not the strength to refuse him, nor any plan to substitute for his. His idea was to get away from the other peoples … the Scythians, the giants, and all who might mean war. And indeed, in those days we found plenty to run from, and plenty of space to run to.

As for the people, we discovered that we had not escaped the Scythians forever. They too were moving north, as were tribes like them. We would travel, camp, set up a settlement, and spend a year or two planting crops and growing our children. Then would come war or the threat of it, and we would move again. It did not take much, by this time, to make us decide to move on. If our scouts or our hunters saw distant horsemen, in numbers enough to mean a settlement or an army, that was enough. Sometimes it was obvious they were Scythians. Others seemed to have yellow hair, which also made us uneasy. But even for those that looked dark-haired and familiar, those who might have shared our language, we did not often stop. Sometimes we wanted news, but the news was always the same: the violent were building themselves cities and kingdoms, and the less strong were moving out, pushing out the very weakest. So, for many years, we chose to pass up the chance for news rather than risk that news of us should be carried back to Nimrod and his kind.

As for the land, it appeared that we had found the center of the world, the place where all land came from. It gave the appearance of going on forever, extending in all directions, north and west and east, never giving way to sea. It seemed like a place far from even the memory of the Flood. Surely such a land could accommodate our family, and many more like it.

Tiras felt strongly that this was a place God had given us to flee to, far from the waters of judgment and the evils of men. He could hear God's voice audibly in those days, though according to Tiras, God would speak only occasionally, sometimes remaining silent for many years.

As for the land, it was a strange land. The soil was very fertile, friendly to our wheat and barley, perfect for planting. Some years we could produce a lush crop. But it was also dry, and racked by winds, and – this was the hardest for us to accept – prone to sudden spells of cold. In between the good years, we had years when nothing grew at all, the weather being too cold or too dry. Between this and the constant moving away, we never settled into the yearly rhythm of farmers. Yet somehow the land fed us. There were always grasses for our livestock, that was of first importance. There were also a great variety of other plants, some of which we remembered from the plain of Si Nar far to the south, others such as we had never seen before. We set about learning them, their dangers and virtues. And we were constantly finding new ones. All it would take was a little hollow or stream, or a low range of mountains, and we would find ferns, say, or evergreen trees, where none had been before. And often they were of a kind we never encountered again.

There was much game. There were wild horses; wild goats of every kind (especially in the mountains); a great variety of antelope including some with pendulous noses; and in some places, shaggy wild elephants and cattle. Further north, there were mighty deer. With all these came the hunters: wolves, bears, lions with and without manes, and the occasional dragon. We, the men especially, Tiras and Hur and Endu and myself and many others, spent much of our time talking about these beasts: their habits, their directions, their paths, and how we could use or befriend or outwit them. It never occurred to us that their presence might detract from the virtues of this harsh paradise into which we were fleeing. We had been given the means to deal with them, in Hur's bow and in our own experience with flocks and herds. We felt, to a man, that we would rather deal with the beasts (even the blood-thirstiest among them), than with our fellow men or with the giants.

We came to live mostly on meat and on milk from our herds, eating grain only when we could get it. A person living on game can never look as kingly as one who lives on grain, even if he is a descendant of engineers. Our bodies became lean and hewn compared to when we lived near the Tower. My son Ki-Ki would have been considered quite ugly back on Si Nar, yet I could not be prouder of him. You never saw a man who speaks to horses as if he were one of them, who hunts like Hur, and rides for days without rest.

Ninna

There are many tasks in a woman's world which are undertaken while seated. Because seated, they look easy. Yet they require as much fortitude, in their way, as a grueling day spent on horseback.

One of these tasks is that of suckling a child. I am nursing my daughter Ai Li. Despite having seen many women do it and hearing their talk, despite the great honor given to pregnant women and nursing mothers, I did not imagine that this task would be painful. From the outside, after all, it looks sleepy and comfortable. I did not imagine how much it could drain the body and the mind.

Nevertheless, I am glad to do it. I am grateful beyond measure to have a husband and a child. I am delighted that everything it takes to satisfy her, in this world of hunger, is produced by my body. I am honored to have given my husband this greatest gift, of bearing his child and keeping it alive and healthy until it can contribute.

Ai Li is my daughter by Hur. Yes, Hur and I were married, during that first winter after the crossing of the sea. We married because he needed me and I adored him. Enmer and my mother approved the match; Endu, with his residual snobbery, tolerated it. But I could think of no finer man to marry. Hur has been our protector and provider ever since we left Si Nar. He does not lead, like Enmer; yet quietly, he has been the very engine of our forward motion as well as our safety. All he asks in return is the chance to do as he sees fit in the field when riding, shooting, or hunting. And of course, while he is doing so, someone had to care for his child. And since I was doing that, I began to care for Hur as well. And so, little by little, I proved myself to him until he was willing to consider me as a wife.

His eye is recovered … not seeing, but no longer infected. He keeps it hidden behind a headband which I wove for him. His skill at archery came back completely, with practice. So now we have our best bowman restored to us. He divides his time between hunting, bow-making, and teaching the young men to hunt and shoot, and lately they are beginning to learn to shoot from horseback. I care for the tents, the children, the food, the clothing, and the livestock.

It is strange. I no longer think of myself as being of an age with the young men that Hur teaches. Married and with a baby, I am a woman grown.

We were married, as I said, that first winter after the sea-crossing. It is bad luck to marry during the winter, or it used to be considered so. But we saw many practical reasons for it. The many dangers urged that we should marry as soon as possible; there was little else to do; the excitement of a wedding was a welcome distraction to all of us who were shut up in our rude new home by the snow.

We had dug ourselves a village that consisted of a series of pits covered over, as it were, with houses, which we built using wood from the river and plenty of mud for plaster. This was not ideal, perhaps, but we knew that winter was coming, and there did not seem to be a more livable, or more easily defensible, place nearby, though they had sent out scouts to seek one. Winter came with an unexpected quickness and ferocity. Some of the family homes were not finished, consisting only of hides stretched over wood. Even those that were solidly chinked turned out to be cold and smoky and, in short, miserable with a misery which we had never known in the South.

A few times there came a great snowfall, and we would be trapped in our little burrows for days until we could tunnel out and find each other again. We took our livestock in with us; we moved multiple families into some homes and put the horses into others. But for the most part, there was not much snow, only an incessant wind and a merciless cold.

It was in these conditions, then, that Hur and I were married. But let me back up a bit and tell how it came about.

It happened that first autumn on the great plain … but there is not really an autumn in that rather harsh land, so let us say it happened in the fierce heat of summer, yet on the very cusp of winter. The nights were cold, warning us of a winter such as we had never experienced or imagined. The wind, as the weather changed, was also fierce. It was obvious that travel was going to be difficult, and that if we were to stay in this place, mere tents were not going to do. My brother Enmer had just announced his and Grandfather Tiras' decision that this good place by the river would be our camp, and that a village should be built, as quickly as possible. They were talking about the best way to do this. Engineers such as my brothers had already thought of building the family dwellings half-underground. It was clear that there was going to be a lot of work in the near future. There was the also the matter, while we were building, of keeping guard.

I hardly saw Hur, for he was gone all day. The work had begun in earnest. The men would dig, miserable with scraps of cloth wrapped about their faces to keep out the grit that the wind blew in, streaming with sweat one moment and shivering with cold the next, and then they would break for a meal and in a matter of moments they would eat like lions. I, like all the other women, was helping make the huge feasts to sustain all this labor; weaving tents and blankets that it was obvious we were going to need; constantly washing everything, which seemed to get dusty so quickly. And, of course, watching Hur-Kar, always.

Hur was constantly on his feet and seemed to do the work of three men. He would ride out, far to the east, to the limit of the horizon, looking out for enemies. This was done twice a day. In between, he was helping to dig floors and raise posts, and sometimes bringing home an antelope for us as well. I watched out of the corner of my eye all day for his comings and goings. He always came back, always

embraced Hur-Kar at least once a day, and when he
appeared, I would feel my heart lift and my pulse quicken.
And that moment of seeing him was all I got, more often
than not. But oh, how I looked forward to it!

All this changed one bright, windy afternoon. I had gone
down to fetch water for the evening's feast. I had left Hur-
Kar behind. He was napping in the tent, watched over by the
Cushite.

Hur approached on his horse. I believe he was just about
to depart for evening patrol. He rode right up to me where I
stood at the edge of the water.

I was very excited. I sensed that this was important, and
by that time I had it very badly for Hur.

Looking back, I must not have looked very pretty,
standing there in an old linen garment, one hip thrust out to
balance the water jar, my hair tied back and whipping like
strings, my eyes, as I looked up at him, squinting against the
wind and sun

But I was not thinking of how I looked. I was drinking in
the sight of him. He did not look like any of the men I was
used to, in the days before. My ideal of male beauty had
been shaped beneath the Tower, where we wanted them to

look mature and kingly, with dark hair like my brothers;
curly and well-kempt, with a beard. Hur, by contrast, kept
himself clean-shaven. His hair was short, straight, of a light,
almost golden brown, and in the sun and wind it was
standing out like a gilt corona around his head. He was not
much taller than me, when standing, and was built rather
along small, square lines than along tall, dark ones. Yet at
that moment, I was looking at my ideal. I thought him the
most beautiful man I'd ever seen.

He looked at me gravely for a moment and then drew
breath, and then his horse, which was a small red mare, put
her head down and started pulling toward the water. Hur
chuckled and dismounted and led her there, slapping her
neck affectionately, and then she bent her head and took a
long drink, and there we were looking at one another over
her back.

"You have been a good aunt to Hur-Kar," he said. "You
take good care of him."

I should have bent my head at this, but I don't think I
did. For at his next words, my heart gave a great leap and I
am sure I was as bright-eyed and open-mouthed – and
clumsy – as a stupid little foal.

"I would like to make an agreement," said Hur carefully. "I would like to make that arrangement permanent."

And I said – and I still don't know if it was in a squeak or in a husky voice – "I would only make it permanent if it meant becoming your wife."

"Of course," he said. "That is what I meant. Do you agree to it, then?"

And I made some sort of sound of assent.

He nodded, pressed his lips together, and gave the faintest, pleased smile. "Let it take place in winter," he said, "After the town is built. Will that suit you?"

"I – yes," I said, struggling not to drop the water jar. "I will speak to my mother."

Hur glanced around him as if looking for something, then laughed at himself like a dazed man, and said, "I've brought no token to give you. Wait a moment," -- And he pulled a small blade out of the pouch at his belt and cut off a few strands of his mount's tail. They were long, black, and coarse. The mare snorted and danced a bit, then lowered her head huffily to finish her drink. Hur stepped delicately around behind her, and came and wrapped the coarse hairs around my neck beneath my bundle of hair, and knotted them loosely over my collarbone.

"That'll have to do," he said. "I'll be out on patrol for the next few hours, but you can show that to your mother."

No kiss. Not at that time. But his voice was tender. And he looked at me, just for a moment, very intensely out of his one remaining eye, which was a golden, greyish color. Later there would be kisses, and later I would raise my hand to stroke the woven headband that angled down over his ruined eye, mourning.

Then the mare was finished with her drink and Hur had remounted and was gone, leaving me with my head and heart full of speculation and excitement.

I spoke to my mother and she told me that she could not have been more pleased. We were tempted to begin thoughts of wedding preparations immediately, but that had to be put off a bit, for the houses were not finished yet. Then we spoke to Enmer and he reacted as Enmer did to nearly everything in those days, not making trouble but offering no new ideas either. Putting on his stamp of approval with passive assent. Things were not good with Enmer, but I was too happy and excited at that time to bother about it. I was only glad that he hadn't taken it in to his head to forbid us.

But Endu said, when he heard about it at the meal that night (for I was having trouble keeping my news to myself), "How can you be so happy about marrying our former slave? How far you have fallen, sister!"

And I said, shaking with anger, but rather enjoying the anger as well – as I was enjoying the intensity of everything that day – "How can you *say* so, Endu? Our former slave? Hur has saved our lives many times, and well you know it! He may have come from a slave family, but he is actually a great warrior. I don't think I could marry any better!"

"Well, it's true there are not many fellows around here –"

"I couldn't marry any better *even if there were!* Hur was a gem always, but we didn't know it. It took all of our troubles to show him to us for what he is." And then I added, for I was swept away by emotion, "It's *lucky* for me that all these troubles have happened to us, or I would never have had the chance to marry Hur."

When I said it was lucky, something changed in Endu's face, and I saw that he would never see what I meant. So I shrugged it off, too happy to go on being angry.

"Times have changed, brother," I said in a less heated voice. Before I moved on, I poured him more wine, stepping rather quickly and spilling a little. "It is too bad for you that you have not changed with them."

"Times *have* changed," Endu muttered, raising the cup to his lips as I moved away. "That much is true."

After that, there were many days in which work on the houses continued, and all of it seemed to me to go very quickly – there was so much to be done – and at the same time very slowly. Now that Hur had been promised I was eager to have him securely.

Then there was a great, unexpected snowfall when the village was only half finished and we were still in the tents. We had several days of panic while we moved into the houses that were built and thought of ways to shelter the livestock. Also, many of us fell sick. Then after about a week, the snow melted and we worked like mad things on the houses that remained and on the paths between the houses. And then, winter came again and that time it had come to stay. So for a while we were entirely miserable, resting, nursing our sick ones, and shuffling and arranging ourselves among the shelter that there was. And going, whenever we could, to the river to get firewood. It was that winter that we realized also that we could burn animal dung, after it had been prepared.

But at last, we got ourselves all sorted, and then there was little but the misery we had never experienced before: the misery of surviving a true northern winter: hunkering in our little shelters, eating through our stores, trying as best we could to keep ourselves and especially the children warm, to clean things with no water and to dry things with no sunlight, and to keep from going mad. And then, *at last*, we had plenty of time on our hands and it was time to make preparations for a wedding.

By that time, I had almost forgotten whose wedding it was we were making preparations for. The panic of the early arrival of the snow, being cold all the time, and especially being sick, had taken the heart out of me temporarily. Also, Angki had been sick and it was all we could do to pull him through. So I prepared for my own wedding with a sense of calm anticipation, but without quite the edge of excitement that I had experienced when warmed by the heat of the late summer days.

We women made a great celebration of it, sensing that this was exactly what our clan needed to distract us from the winter and all that came with it. We spent plenty of time weaving wedding garments for Hur and me, working in designs of the things we had seen on our journeys, down to the little plants we had encountered, on entering this country, for the first time in our lives. We had not had time to preserve much fruit, but we made dishes with milk and the grains left over from our civilized days.

We feasted for five days, at the end of which Hur and I were given our own, somewhat private corner of the family burrow, surrounded by weavings to protect us from eyes, and by cheering, music, and the baying of animals to cover any noise we might make.

The conditions were not ideal, but that did not matter. Marriage to Hur was all that I had hoped. He did not disappoint me.

He devoted himself entirely to me for several weeks that winter. (There was little else to do.) Others covered our chores. We enjoyed each other, rather like a couple falling in love in a prison.

It was also during that winter that the Cushite first picked up a lute. We did not realize it then, but this was to become important later. At the time, it only seemed like another half-useful thing that our odious prisoner could do, to only half-

lessen the burden of having him there. (He *had* been
entertaining the children quite often, especially around the
time of the wedding, and though we all kept a close eye on
him, he seemed genuinely to bear them good will – at least,
he did them no harm.)

We were not very musical as a group, but we did have a
few lutes and such things about, and one day, not long after
Hur and I were married, the Cushite saw someone carrying
one and contrived to make it understood that he wanted to
hold it. Then he spent a long while tuning and stroking it,
and then he began to pick at it with his fingers. And then,
after finding some chords that he liked and could repeat, he
began to accompany himself and sing.

It was not a song that we understood, of course. But we
were enchanted. We all looked at him with blank faces,
giving no sign of our pleasure lest he become shy – or
perverse – and stop.

He sang a great deal after that. Eventually he realized
that we liked it, that this was a way he could earn his bread.
As he began to learn our language, he would sometimes
weave in a word or two of ours, usually something easily
recognizable such as "horse" or "barley," which made the
children giggle. It was funny to hear such words in songs

that were obviously about loss. But how *could* he learn the more abstract words, such as "loss" or "gods" or "sky," or the words for things that were no longer with us? Anyway, this adding of words came a bit later; I am now telling about our first year after the crossing of the sea.

Early that spring, I fell pregnant. It was around the same time that Ninshi had her baby.

Yes, my sister in law was with child … that had been the reason for her bad temper around the time of our flight from the Scythians. She had a difficult pregnancy, made worse perhaps by grief, fear, uncertainty, and travel. She had a long birth. I assisted at it, and this gave me plenty of nightmares about how my own labor might go.

But my little Ai Li gave me much less trouble than expected. She was born in the autumn, and we are now on our second winter here. Perhaps getting married in the wintertime was not so unlucky after all. Ninshi's child, meanwhile, was also a girl. Ninshi has called her Lina. Ninshi is a good deal better now that her pregnancy is over and she has seen her daughter safely through birth and through those first few months.

But now I must say a word about my brother Enmer. Of the things women do while seated – spinning, weaving, cooking, suckling – listening to him talk is yet another deceptively difficult, though seated, task.

Enmer has quite changed since we settled here. He is listless and irritable, and I do not mean from hunger, for our food has been adequate. Even at a feast or a successful hunt or at another time when most other people are happy and content, he finds reasons to be morose. Nothing is good enough for Enmer. He does not like hunting ... it is cold, uncomfortable, dangerous, and uncertain, and he spends the whole hunt, he says, worried about the safety of his men, and is unable to concentrate on finding the game ... and then he worries about being unable to contribute to the hunt. It all takes many hours, he says, and where the other men seem to enjoy those hours almost as a kind of leisure, to Enmer they are nothing but hours that might be spent in vain. He is gifted at the war-arts they are practicing ... excellent on horseback, and becoming passable with the bow ... but he hates the training. It reminds him of the possibility that we will be attacked, and the unlikeliness that he will be able to defend all of us.

Building is his area of expertise, but although we did much building again this summer, putting up houses and sheds, digging canals and latrines, anyone could see that his heart was not in it. He told me later that this was because he knows we will likely have to flee again, and the work will be wasted. Also, it is frustrating not to have the same materials and knowledge at our disposable that he had at Si Nar. Also, it is maddening when he sees that his lethargy undermines his authority with those who work for him, so that half the time he leaves Endu in charge. Also ... well, no one really knows why he cannot stand anything, not even Enmer himself.

That is the tenor of his thoughts, and it is wearying beyond belief to sit and listen to them, though I have done so many times. His talk is one endless outpouring of complaints – when he is not simply silent. Certainly there is much to complain about, especially if we compare our camp here to our former life in Si Nar. But what is the use of raging against smoky fires, leaky tents, endless wind, runaway animals, disobedient children? We have homes here, fresh water, a wheat crop that has just been harvested, and we have men like Hur to help us prepare for war. Surely there is much to be thankful for as well as many problems. But even good things are a burden to Enmer. He is even annoyed by the horses, which is surely the lowest point a person can reach!

Life is simply too much for him. I do not know what has happened to my brother. He was once my hero, the one I looked up to – that is, after Father died.

Grating as it is to listen to him, I try. I listen as well to Ninshi, who has nearly been dragged to the grave by Enmer's helplessness, coming so soon after her hard pregnancy and labor. It is vital that I listen to them, for when we live as close as our family does here, everyone must respect everyone else. Family relationships must be kept as harmonious as possible. If we let grudges and irritation grow, it could get very bad indeed.

Nevertheless, my irritation is growing.

When I need a respite, I go to the edge of the pastures and pick the long grasses and watch the flocks and herds. Or I go to get water at the river. At least, that is how it was this summer. Now it is winter and I get out less often. Enmer's blackness seems to be pressing down on him like a great cloud. Everything is pressing down on all of us.

It will be better in the spring. I suppose that next summer, I shall have to take Ai Li with me. I'll tie her to my back or to my belly while I work or roam outdoors. And the summer after that, she will play in the shallows of the river and come up with names for the sheep and cows.

We had a grand time of it this past spring, when it was shearing time. We took the fleeces to the river to wash them, and then this winter there was the task of processing the wool. I was not able to do as much, having a new baby ... but there will be more next year, and the year after that, and every year after. And Hur and I are married – married! We have two children, Hur-kar and Ai Li, we have the sheep and horses and the other stock, and we have our snug little holes in the ground. I know it's foolish to feel this way, but I can't help feeling that with all this, if God smiles on us as He has been doing, we can face anything.

Nimri

I know what has beset him. It is that malady that sometimes comes upon men, when all things seem to them meaningless, flat, and tasteless; when even pain seems like a ghost rather than a creature. Men in that condition have no spirit in them; they are useless for anything.

I should despise him for it, I should hold him in contempt – that is, my old self would have, I would have back in the days of my greatness. But now, how can I look

on him with such pity? I myself am in his very condition.
My body is useless, my mind silent – or if not silent, then
trapped as it were behind a wall of ice. My mind may still
churn, it may still produce thoughts, but these thoughts are
of no profit to anyone around me, and so indeed it is to them
as though I were silent. I cannot speak to them to do more
than make my needs known. Of their plans, designs, fears
and gods I can discover nothing. I might, with great labor,
learn their language – indeed I am beginning to learn it – but
that will be the work of long years, and in the meantime I
will still contribute little. I am as a child, an infant. A dog.
Nay, a dog understands the speech of his master.

So no, I can neither blame nor condemn this man who
leads our little party.

And neither can I help him.

But what will happen in the future, that is the question?
If this malady does not leave him, then the day is coming –
not far off – when he will be unable to lead, or indeed to do
anything more than what he does now – what I do – which is
to sit and stare into the fire.

And what then?

Have they a leader in mind?

At this moment, the father of Ki-Ki can get away with doing and thinking as little as he does, because they have put systems in place for the daily running of the family, and because the larger group is led by Tiras. At this moment. But any of these things could change at any time. As we have learned to our sorrow.

Nay, if this continues, we may all freeze, or starve; or, failing that, I foresee a family at war.

At one time, this might have made me merely curious. But now I feel an obligation to see into the future as much as possible … to protect the little child either with or from his family.

With all this, there is one thing I can do. I have continued to sing.

Once in the very blackest part of winter – it was so black and dreary that it seemed like the very grave – they had had a feast of some sort … all right, I know of what sort. That young nubile girl (I believe she is Grandmother Zillah's own daughter) has married that little fair-haired, deceptively small and light, warrior fellow. She seemed thrilled with the arrangement, while he gave no sign of appreciating that he had got himself a princess. I don't mind giving her up to you, sir, I have a queen of my own age now. But what I do mind is listening to their so-called wedding "music" … I call it painful, like the yowling of hyenas. I was already on edge (and I was not the only one) from living in that smelly little hole, but having to listen to their untutored singing nearly drove me over. At last I decided that if I was not to go mad, I must myself find a way to sing.

Yes, I want to sing. I will sing a song to Istra, Dawn-Maiden, from before the Flood, she of the lovely evening star. I will sing of her ascent into Heaven, and of the tragedy that befell her … she, for whom I never gave a fig, before everything else was taken from me. I will sing to her now. It is a song I know, a song that shall remind me who I am and from what stock I have come. Lovely goddess, I hoped to meet with you – once – but the tower will never be built now.

I will sing. Give me a lute.

You – there – passing by me just now – yes, the lute, or the crude lute-like thing that is in your hand. Give it to me – give me the lute –

By all the gods …! Give it to me!

I must sing, though none around me can understand my words. I must sing or go mad.

… And so, I obtained the lute, somehow, and I played and sang my hymn to Istra, and hymns and ballads to many, many others, who in the short time since everything died are already being forgotten.

And they stared at me, hostile, uncomprehending. Yet I found out very quickly that this was the loveliest music they had ever heard … or, had heard in a good long while. It did not sound very fair to me, for the lute was not like the lutes that we had in the old days (by which I mean a handful of years ago) … it was a copy, or not exactly a copy, made in haste, with materials they had to hand; not with great skill and long years of work such as we used to take for granted. Nevertheless, it was serviceable enough, and playing it was water to my soul.

My voice and hands were worn with singing before my heart was.

CHAPTER 12

AN INCREASE OF EVERYTHING

Enmer

And so it began again during the second spring after we had crossed the sea. I had known it would come … our little village was too appealing, too accessible, sitting there just beside a major river, with fields and fish within reach. I had known that those giant-haunted mountains would not hold back the Scythians forever. Father Tiras agreed with me, though the way he would put it was that we were not yet nearly far enough east or north. Ah well, at least we had a year and half of peace. We did not waste our time that year, either: we had one good harvest, from which we kept the seed; got Hur safely married to my sister Ninna; and two babies born in our immediate family and several others in the greater camp. Angki and Hur-kar, once known as the babies, were both healthy children of three, my Angki being slightly older and larger. They loved to play at bows and sit on ponies.

All this lovely increasing and growing was rudely interrupted – as we had known it would be – by an attack early one spring morning. We knew it was spring because the sun was rising earlier than it had, though everything was still wet and bitterly cold.

Ninshi had risen early to go and get water with the other women – waking me, for in those days I was dull and stupid and found it hard to wake myself. And no sooner had they left than we heard, carried on the wind, approaching horses. I threw on wool tunic and trousers and a fur vest (for I will never be caught fighting naked again!), and scrambled upward out of our house and into the village courtyard. And next door, from Mother's house, I saw Endu doing the same.

"Is it only a patrol?" I asked him quickly. "Is it only Hur returning?"

And he shook his head and said, "Hur is *here*!"

At that very moment Hur emerged from *his* burrow. And then we were all grabbing our bows: myself and Endu and Hur, soon joined by the young men Hirsa and Gugi. And then, as we rushed to the west end of the camp, Abijay, Melek, Taman, and others of their party also joined in, many of whom were eager young teenaged boys. I cast a glance back over my shoulder, wondering who would fetch the women from the river, and there was Tiras, waving us away and calling, "Go! Go! You do this – I'll take care of them."

They had made it easy for us, in a way. They were all coming from the same direction, west of our camp. Our village was in a slight hollow so as to be near the river. We ran up the low rise to the west of the village, our boots crunching on the frozen grass, and there they were spread out before us beautifully, strung out in a line as neat as you please, easily visible as they approached from the flat horizon. And as if this were not already enough like an archery exercise, just as we topped the rise, the sun came up behind us and illuminated them all.

We spread ourselves out, having just seconds now, and knowing that if we failed – and even if we didn't – some of us were likely to be run over. All of us were shaking, I believe, but the young ones were excited, and Endu and I were determined not to be made fools of again.

Hur yelled, "If you can't hit the man, hit the horse!" All of us were slightly shocked at his ruthlessness – horses were so precious to us, and not responsible for the behavior of their masters – but at that moment, they came into Hur's range, and he sent off one shaft that missed and another that felled a man by hitting him in the shoulder. And then a third that hit his victim's forehead.

And then they were in all of our range, and we were shooting madly, though not very skillfully, in my case. Hur was right, it *was* easier to hit the horses, except that now the horses were panicking and swerving, and crashing in to each other. The riders realized what was happening, and began to turn their mounts and wheel away. Only their leader was too far along, or too battle-mad, to turn his horse in time, and he came flying through us as we dived out of the way, and horse and man fell down the slope toward our village, the horse with a few pitiful shafts barely piercing its muscle, the man with Abijay's arrow in his throat. He was dying from that already, and then badly broken by being rolled over by his horse – an awful sight. Abijay gave him the mercy-stroke while the rest of us were still on top of the rise, staring into the distance, the better to assure ourselves that the enemy had indeed retreated. And then, as it turned out, the horse was so badly broken that we had to kill it too. A horrible business. It brought tears to my eyes, having to kill such a fine animal, and I was not the only one.

One of the youths, a boy named Rumi, had had his right leg very badly bruised by the horse as it plowed through our group. At first we could not tell whether it was broken, and we took him back to the village and tended him accordingly.

But that was all. None of us had suffered any other injury. We were even able to retrieve some of our arrows.

It did not seem this way to me, but everyone else seemed to consider it a great and glorious victory. They were delighted with how easy it had been. Hur was the hero of the day for his work as master bowman, as was Abijay, for his killing of the lead horseman. Hur did not seem to care much for the adulation he was receiving, but my sister Ninna basked in his reflected glory. She kept looking at Endu as if to say, "You see?" And Endu was so pleased with his own part in the battle that he did not mind indulging her. He even clasped Hur's hand and called him Brother, which had never happened before.

There is never much food about in spring, but as best they could, the women even made a sort of feast, as if we had something to celebrate. Feasts always make me nervous – they seem like tempting God. However, we kept a careful watch for the rest of that day, and the enemy did not return.

I ate my fill – and I was so sick at heart that it did not take much to fill me – and then I went out and stood on the edge of the hollow where the battle had taken place, watching. The sun had wheeled around to the west, so that soon I was looking straight into it. The day was already losing what little warmth it had gained, and the wind scraped cruelly, bringing tears to my eyes. Then Ninshi came out and with a wheedling voice pleaded with me to go back in to the feast.

"Why don't you come and eat with us, husband? Everyone thinks you are angry. We miss you in there ... they all want to honor you."

And I said shortly, "I've got to keep watch, woman. What if they return?"

They *would* return, this we agreed when the ten or so leaders sat together and discussed it. We had examined the dead enemy before we unceremoniously buried his and his horse's body (reasoning that he would want his mount in the afterlife). Although he was well kitted out, wearing a felted hat and a vest and so on, when we removed his hat we saw that he was indeed one of the same kind that had attacked us before, with that stupid red hair that, by now, really makes me sick to have to look at. His horse was hung with all sorts of bags for storing booty. Apparently, during the time we had continued to build and farm, they had continued to raid and steal.

"They have improved their methods," said Tiras, as all of us sat in grim and weary silence around his hearth-fire. He was flanked by his sons Abijay and Melek, and by Taman and Raja, while I sat with all the men – all the actual *Japhethite* men – from our family.

"They come to us on horses now," Tiras went on. "They don't dismount in order to attack. They can get away easily if we resist. And," he added with a twinkle, "They have adjusted to the climate. Now they come to us in *clothes*."

Everyone laughed feebly.

"They weren't expecting the welcome we gave them!" said Endu triumphantly. He looked over at Hur and cuffed his shoulder in approval. "They ran as soon as they started getting shot! Eh? I only wish they hadn't run so quickly … we could have killed *all* of them."

"You are talking like a foolish man," said Tiras, not unkindly. "If they had not retreated, they could have run you down."

"Let them come!" said Abijay, and Endu nodded fiercely.

"They will come back," I said woodenly. "Either they will bring a much larger force, or bows of their own. We will have to leave this place eventually."

There was much objection to this, but I was right, in the end. They returned, in fact, only a few nights later, when they judged that our alarm would have subsided and we'd have stopped setting a guard. They were wrong, however; we had guards stationed all around our perimeter, and when they heard hoofbeats they raised the alarm. So, by the time the enemy drew close, they were met by men shooting arrows – rather randomly, in the dark, but we thought it would deter them. Whether we got any of them or not I don't know, I only know that no one fell and they left no horses behind. But this time, as they turned to wheel away, some of them apparently turned around in the saddle and began *shooting back*. My brother Endu took an arrow on the outer edge of his upper arm, in the tricep. We removed it and saved the arm, although it has never been quite the same since then. I was beside him when it happened. The first I knew of it was that he was knocked to the side, and then I heard him cursing fervently in the dark. And then, filled with the energy that a bad wound sometimes gives us, he stood up and began shouting after the fleeing riders, angrier than I have ever seen him:

"Come *on*! You sons of jackals! Grow your *own* grain! Breed your *own* horses!"

And then he went on to call them many other uncomplimentary things.

His admonition was futile, of course. They would never grow or make anything of their own. Throughout that spring and summer, they carried out a series of clever raids. They would wheel into our camp with very small numbers, then ride away having stolen some of our horses, cattle, or later, our grain. They usually came by night. It was quite inconvenient always to be keeping guard, for it was now the season of planting, when we were putting all our energy into the work. And we never knew what time of day they would strike, or at what pen or field, and this was wearisome. They would keep pestering us like a fly on a cow, until we either killed them or made ourselves harder to reach. And we could not kill them all, for they would not stay put.

Eventually it became a bad drain on our resources always to be keeping a guard. We began preparations for leaving, and this meant scouting parties to seek a better place, and much work of packing up and making our camp mobile. At the same time, we hoped to stay long enough to get a decent harvest. We called on all our half-men to guard the fields while the rest of us were elsewhere ... by half-men I mean all those men who, for whatever reason, did not have full strength or skill or ability: the aged, the young boys, the injured. At the very least they could raise the alarm. We equipped them with trumpets. I even pulled that Cushite out of his useless niche in my mother's tent and set him beside a field of barley. If the raiders come and kill him, at least he can do a good deed before he dies by warning the rest of us.

It turns out he can sit on a pony, and stay on it decently too, using his balance and his great ropey arms, and apparently his confidence with the animal. He was so clearly pleased about being brought outdoors and helped to ride that I almost repented of asking him for his services. I hate to bring any joy to the person my sister has rightly nicknamed The Camel's Ass. But we needed him, and a pony was the easiest way of getting him to his post. I was pleased to see that the sun and wind seemed to bother him, especially at first.

The fall of the Tower, and all the disasters and inconveniences that followed it, has turned everything upside down. Misery and incompetence for me, confidence and – momentary – happiness for the crippled foreigner.

The final blow came when one of the raiders (no doubt their village idiot) *set fire* to one of our fields. These fellows have so little self-control, and their impulse for destruction often undercuts their desire for loot ... but still, I cannot conceive of the stupidity it takes to set a fire out on the dry, windy plains. We contained it by setting a backfire, which we extinguished as quickly as it was set, and ended by losing only one field, and that rather far from our village ... but it was a long, exhausting, black and dirty day of labor, all for nothing, all for the privilege of losing only one field. That was when we realized that perhaps we could not wait for the harvest. Much as it broke our hearts, we would have to harvest was what ready, leave the rest, and depart right now, immediately.

It was the Cushite who first saw and warned us of the fire-starter, by the way. He saw the man and knew him for a Scythian before he had even set the fire. Tried to get to him, himself, ended by falling from his pony, *then* blew his trumpet, so that we knew of the fire almost as soon as it had started. I find some fault with him; if he had blown the trumpet immediately, perhaps the fellow would have run off without doing any damage. Still, he was brave enough I suppose, and managed to keep his head and stay conscious even after his fall, and he did us some service by the early warning.

We know his name now. Mother has found it out and is trying to get the rest of us to use it. It is the unbearably high and aristocratic name of Nimri.

CHAPTER 13

NEW BEGINNINGS

Nimri

Well, here I am on horseback. Almost as if I were a man
again. Almost as if none of this had ever happened.

We are traveling, and they need a convenient way to
move me. That is the only reason they are allowing me this
concession. They do not do it to please me; I have no
illusions.

But they cannot stop me, now I am here, from enjoying
the day, the wind, the clean new smells, the sensation of
being up on a pony; level, at least, with their boys and
women, and able to look straight at, and no longer up to,
men. The only way they could do that would be to kill me,
and I have finally realized that no one is going to do that.

It is uncomfortable, mind. The overwhelming misery is
the heat. This affects not only me, but everyone, the little
ones and women, and most of all the horses. Wherever we
go, the heat goes with us. We have traveled for many days
over grassy plains filled with wildflowers. Now we are
coming in to great, hunched, grassy hills, the ravines
between them filled with little, stunted trees, and with
fragrant bushes and evergreens. And from these, little
streams and rivers feed the plain. But at this time of year

many of them are low or even dry, not nearly enough to slake the thirst of all our party. And soon, there will be mountains.

Riding wears me out. At the end of the day I verily fall off my mount, and lie, barely moving. But at least I have no more headaches. My body has again become accustomed to the outdoors. That is a consequence of our way of life for the last few months before our departure.

King Enmer hated, it was clear, to give me any responsibility. That is his name, I gather, and I am almost certain that he is Grandmother Zillah's son. I call him "king" because he is the king of their family, while Tiras is the high king, the patriarch. And that would make Zillah a queen. It is good to know, to observe the lines of authority. A man likes to know where he is.

As I said, a foreigner – a hated foreigner – a cripple … well, I would not give me any important tasks to do, were I in his place. But they were being harder and harder pressed by some enemy, even I could see that, and in war, every man must pull his weight, so to speak. So, to shorten matters, they assigned me some low, foolish slave's beast – the one I am on now, in fact – a little, old nag that could bear my withered weight and onto which it was not too difficult to hoist me.

They looked carefully, at first, to make sure I understood what was going on and would not fight them.

Then they brought me out of doors where there were a lot of other low and useless people like myself (half-grown youths and so on), and gave us to understand that we were to keep a watch for the enemy ... and, well, you know the rest.

When I first saw that redhaired fellow I was reminded of my relative Mizra. He had red –gold hair and bright burnished skin like my own – only even more ruddy, just a shade darker than his hair. He was tall and thin, with a long, thin, arrogant face. Between that and his unusual coloring, he was a very striking-looking man. He used to stalk around the architects' complex like a very god ... how we all admired him, and wanted to be like him! But no one could compare to Mizra.

He had a great mind as well. He was always the one going over things with a plumb line, sextant and other tools, blistering the architects' ears if everything was not exactly perfect, which it never was, of course. He was a brilliant mathematician, and he didn't want the slightest margin of error.

I wonder, now, what ever happened to Mizra when the tongues were turned. He survived, I imagine; he was not the sort to lose his head, nor to die in a stupid accident. Though seeing that I have been brought so low, perhaps anyone could be.

So when I saw the redheaded fool, my first thought was Mizra. My second was to realize exactly what he was doing, and that, perhaps, I could prevent disaster, if I were just near enough to stop him. So I slapped the pony's flank with my hand and gave it a sharp command, and it galloped obediently enough, but it had a clumsy gait and it took off rather quickly, and then … well, everything went to stupidity and futility, as it usually does. When I fell, I even dropped my trumpet, and there was a moment of mad clawing and hauling myself over the grass to get near enough to use it. And then the pony took fright at the fire and bolted back to the camp, leaving me to greet the warriors flat on my back and, of course, with no words to explain my failure. It was not as bad as being covered in shit, but nearly. Someone came and got me and dragged me out of way while they were all busy starting and extinguishing a back fire. I lay there for a while watching them work, and then after a bit someone else showed up, leading my pony. And that person was the only person who I've ever known to rush into a fracas specifically to remember and rescue a useless cripple

… namely, the Lady Zillah. Once she had brought the beast, everything became easy, as least as far as getting me back to camp was concerned.

Later – much later, when king Enmer finally came back to camp all covered in soot with tears cutting through it – they all gabbled at me a good deal. I gathered they were asking what had happened. I didn't know their word for "red" or "enemy," so I at first I tried telling them, "Mizra." I thought they might remember him from before. What a hope! Eventually, with a great deal of what seemed to me to be unnecessary raising of voices, they got through to me with the word Scyth. And yes, yes, I nodded, Scyth is the word for those people, those barbarians. Yes, yes. I repeated Scyth many times. Really, did they think it was I who had set that fire?

Later still, I tried again to comment on the fact of the stranger's red hair by saying "Mizra." I am struck, you see, from time to time by these futile impulses to communicate.

It was to Lady Zillah that I said it, being as she is the one who brings me my meals, generally bathes me, and usually is the only one who comes near enough to hear anything I might have to say. Unfortunately, she thought I was trying to communicate my own name. For a few moments, I was in

serious danger of being called "Mizra" for the rest of my
life. I was tempted to take on my relative's identity, but only
for a moment. It would be a foolish, pointless joke, one that
would amuse no one else but me, and that not for very long.

Besides, I realized that I wanted her to know my actual
name. I decided to stick to the truth. It took a few moments
of perseverance, but finally she was repeating, albeit with a
very odd accent, "Nimri." And then she told me her name,
which I had already discerned some time ago, but as there
was no way to say this either, I acted duly pleased. After all,
the woman had just saved my life for, at the lowest estimate,
the third time. The least I could do was to pretend a little.

Despite saving my life, I am sad to report that she has
not given herself to me a second time. Long as I might, I
may not have her. That's as it should be; she is a queen. She
makes sure that I have what I need to care for myself as
much as possible, and for the rest, she cares for me matter-
of-factly but not tenderly, like a – like I know not what. Of
course, who needs affection, when living as a stranger in
their house, they feed me regularly and know my name? And
save my life, let's not forget, in her case. Although if it were
a choice between that and another night with her, I'd have a
hard time choosing.

I have never been a fool for anyone before.

I wonder how you say *that* in their language.

Ah, here we are coming in to our camp for the night. It is time to fall off the pony.

Ninna

We are in the mountains. These are not high, rugged, and giant-haunted; they are gentle, understanding mountains. We withdrew here because we suffered another attack by Scythians, in the second spring of our camp by the Sea. Apparently certain groups of Scythians were moving north, just as we had. I am told that later they veered off west. At any rate, I never did get to take little Ai Li wading in that particular river, for we were driven from it before she was old enough to walk. But she survived, we all survived, that is the important thing.

We were much better prepared this time. As soon as they heard approaching horses, all the young men grabbed their bows, and were out to meet the enemy with arrows on the string. And they proved capable of hitting moving targets. When the raiders realized that we would not be easy pickings, they quickly withdrew. My Hur, being the leader of the bowmen, gained much praise for this easy victory. His name is growing in our camp.

They returned, however, at night, raiding our cattle and grain. So none of us thought it was bad counsel when Tiras and his sons Abijay and Melek, and Enmer and the leaders of a few other families, agreed together that we would decamp. We chose these mountains as a more defensible spot. We crossed another river, even greater than the one by which we had camped, which flowed from the north into the northernmost end of the Stinking Sea. Then we traveled east for several miserable weeks, and there was our new home. The days were horribly hot for travel, and we arrived without much of a growing season left.

Then it was building, building, madly building. There was much more timber here than there had been at the last place, and they have been able to build several great wooden barn-like things. Here in the north, we don't put them up on stilts as before, and to shed the snow they have given the roofs a steep pitch. Perhaps in future years, each family will have their own dwelling, but for this winter, we are crammed into just four large halls. Livestock at one end, people at the other. Trench in the floor to sweep the filth into. And then on the people side, rows and rows of wall bunks covered with curtains. I'm grateful for the shelter, but it is not ideal. There is little privacy for us married couples … little privacy for anyone. We hear every spat, unless we choose to ignore it. And in the deadest part of winter, it is almost true that we do nothing but sit around and look at each other.

Tensions are higher this winter than I can ever remember. Endu has nearly come to blows with any number of people. Then he retreats into a horrible ironical sort of smugness.

"This is a cursed country," he said the other day. "This cursed white stuff falls from the sky."

"It is the land of our sojourn, my son," Mother murmured. She was either concealing her impatience or she was not feeling it. I wonder to myself whether she ever hates her sons. I cannot imagine feeling toward my own children someday as I now feel toward my brothers. But everyone feels a bit hateful in the winter, I must remember that.

As for Enmer, he had become somewhat better during the frenzy of work that constituted our spring and summer, but with the long dark days, his own darkness has again descended. I think he realizes, at last, that his complaints and criticisms were becoming wearing on his family … and unfair as well, hard as we all were working, especially Hur.

Hur is no longer a slave – indeed, that seems like a distant memory – but Enmer's manner to him has sometimes made him feel like one.

We are starting to realize that a family lodge, in the dead of winter, with people snapping and complaining at each other, is a dangerous place to be. Enmer sees that, I think, more clearly than any of us. He knows that as the leader, it's his job to keep the family together, not to destroy it with bitter words. He realized, I imagine, that he must make himself stop.

And his way of doing this was to cease altogether from speaking.

It is early spring now. Enmer stopped speaking a few weeks after the snows began … so it has been months now that he has barely uttered a word.

I so feel for my sister-in-law Ninshi. After her hard pregnancy and our many moves, I have no doubt she would like a chance to be weak for a while, and be comforted by someone. During the difficult days I find a refuge in Hur, who is always calm and fair. Ninshi has no such refuge. Mind you, I do think that like the rest of us, she felt a measure of relief. But behind the relief, you can see she feels fear. If Enmer ceases to work and hunt? If he speaks never again?

Of course, the rest of us go on providing for Ninshi and her children (Angki and Lina and now one on the way), sharing our meat and so on, but I think she fears whether we would do this forever, if my brother were to die. I don't want to raise the specter of Enmer's complete collapse out loud, or I would tell her that she need not worry. Enmer's children are our children, and my mother is always there to make sure that no one neglects or punishes the helpless. Still, in days when food is uncertain, no one wants to be seen to take more than their family contributes. It's not safe, even with someone like Mother to speak up for you.

It was during those dark, early winter days that Enmer took to sitting by the Camel's Ass for hours at a time. At first, he would just sit and stare … hating him, I think, to be honest. Sometimes, my mother told me, Enmer had murder in his eyes.

(Mother saw more of the Camel's Ass than any of us did, since she was responsible for his care. By this time, she had figured out his name, and was trying to get us to use it, rather than just calling him "the Cushite." Apparently, it had once been a very high and aristocratic name, something like

Nimri. But whether from difficulties of language, or whether he was ashamed to claim a lordly name in front of us, we all ended by calling him Nirri.)

As I said, Enmer would sit and stare at our – patient, prisoner, guest – the one whom we women once thought so lordly and beautiful, the one who had screamed nonstop for a day and a night when we first rescued him, the one who had once assaulted me – this creature, my brother would stare at him for hours as if to kill him with his gaze. I believe he saw the wretch as bad luck. He was blaming him for all our misfortunes that loomed so heavily in Enmer's mind despite the many good turns that we had also had. And, in truth, Nirri *could* perhaps be blamed for the judgment that had fallen, since from his appearance he had been heavily involved in the planning of the Tower. But so were all of us, all. I think Enmer had forgotten this.

Nirri *had* been a very bad drain on our resources, especially at the beginning. No one could deny it. We all just bowed to my mother's pleas that we not become like a pack of animals who cast out their injured or sick. But already, even by that fourth winter, he was beginning to find small ways to make himself useful. Transporting him was less of a trial with each move we made, for he went with us willingly and had even shown that he knew how to handle a horse, if helped to mount. I don't believe he could apply much pressure with his legs, and would perhaps have fallen off at a gallop, but he knew how to show the animal who was master. Indeed, I had never seen him look happier than when up on horseback. But that was only during our moves and at other times of great need; there was no need for him to ride a horse once we were settled. This is no doubt a bit of a trial to him, but he has become diligent, willingly caring for Angki or Hur-Kar or the other babies when we mothers need help, doing any number of humble tasks such as carding wool or rolling bowstrings. He is also beginning to learn to speak our language, making an effort to learn people's names and the names of objects. He is always looking about with his great, alert eyes, trying to understand what is happening.

Nirri has also made some conciliatory gestures towards us. I do not often go near him, for obvious reasons, but once when I was forced to, he saw me looking at him, and meeting my eyes, I swear he deliberately thrust his hands behind his back.

Whenever Enmer came and sat by him, the Cushite would stop whatever he was doing – arm exercises, child care, scribbling, whatever it might be – and look steadily back at him as if pinned by my brother's hate and misery. He seemed to realize that his full attention was required by such a powerful flow of meaning ... even if the meaning were muddy and turgid. Sometimes this was too much for Enmer (who found it hard to meet anyone's eye) and he would look resentfully at his feet. But as time went on, I saw them looking at each other more and more.

It was a strange thing. But it was not a frightening thing. For some reason, none of us were worried by it. We were frightened by Enmer's moving about in silence, but not by this. It had a peaceful feeling to it. It was as if – I say this now for the first time, not having realized it before – as if something long due were happening. As if those two were finally having the court case, or even the duel, that two enemies wait long to have, and that makes them then rest easy.

I am not sure whether they mean to have this silent struggle every winter. That would be wearing. It would also take Nirri from us unnecessarily: after all, he cannot sing a song or entertain the children if he is sitting staring at Enmer.

At any rate, now that spring is here, Enmer has seemed to wake up a bit, and it appears that all that staring has done him some good. There is more to be done outdoors, not to mention that Grandfather Tiras, sad to say, is talking of moving us again. So Enmer has begun speaking again when he deems it is called for. He will come in from a long, wet day outdoors, not happy certainly, but pink-cheeked from the cold and with little beads of water on his fur cap, and he will stop by the Cushite's bunk and just look at him gravely for a moment, and then go about his business.

I forgot to say, I am with child again, just as Ninshi is. Again, we get to bear children together, and that is companionable. Our food is adequate. Not much grain, unfortunately, but there is a lot of game. The stock eat a lot of acorns and pine needles and truffles and such things, so the milk is small and sour, but whenever there is good amount, it is given to us. And sometimes … sometimes someone will make us a milk-and-blood pudding. It sounds disgusting, and to be sure the eating of blood used to be forbidden in the old days … but when you are pregnant and ravenous and haven't had any meat in a while, it is so, so good!

My first encounter with this … substance … came actually not when I was pregnant, but shortly after Ai Li was born, when I was having to nurse her every hour or two. I was so ravenous, all the time, that I was miserable from it.

Nothing that I ate ever seemed able to keep me full. And though it was autumn and was harvest time, so there was plenty of food about, everyone was busy; no one had time to cook for me. During one period, I was in tears nearly every day just because I was so hungry.

It was during this time that Hur came to me one day, bearing a sheepish grin and a boiled bag made from a sheep's bladder.

"I know you may not like this," he said shyly, "But if you can get it down …"

He slit the bag and spooned a little into a wooden bowl for me. It was black, made of mixed blood and milk, with a little barley boiled in. I found out later that in order to make this pudding, Hur had a method where he would slightly nick a beast's (usually a cow's) artery and catch the trickle of blood. The nick would later seal, not even harming the beast. So in this way you could get sustenance from an animal without even slaughtering it. That was typical of Hur – it was at once earthy, initially shocking, but in the end, clever and resourceful and provident. Life with him was full of such surprises.

But to return to the first time he brought me a blood pudding. I took a few hesitant bites – because at that point I would try *anything* – and almost as soon as I started eating, I knew this was exactly what I needed. The barley was pleasantly chewy, there was a slight metallic taste but nothing offensive, and I really felt I could eat the whole thing.

"Hur, this is *wonderful*!" I exclaimed as I poured myself some more. "Is this all for me?"

Hur laughed in a surprised way, and said, "Yes, wife, if you want it." And then in a rush he started explaining why he had thought of it for me: it was easy to make a great batch of it; I could serve it to myself whenever I wished; I needed to eat milk in order to make breast milk; I had lost blood during the birth and eating blood would make me strong. He seemed relieved.

"Do you really like it?" he asked in disbelief as I took my third helping.

I gestured toward the bowl, for that was answer enough. Then I swallowed and said, "Thank you, husband. But why do you keep asking me …?"

"I wanted to help you," he said shyly. "But I was afraid … you would be a fussy eater."

I stiffened at this. I wanted very badly to be good enough for Hur, to impress him, but in those days, I was always afraid that I wouldn't measure up to Shulgi. She, as a slave woman, no doubt had eaten whatever was set before her.

"Well, I'm not," I said, making a mental note never to complain about food. "But ... well ... was I before?"

He blushed up to his eye patch. "You wouldn't eat that dragon that Sut and I killed, once," he muttered.

I laughed. I had forgotten the incident – this was before I'd even noticed Hur – but now that he mentioned it, it came back.

"As I recall," I said, "No one else would either!"

"But you wouldn't even *try* it ..."

"Well, yes," I said, getting a little teary, "I was a spoiled city girl, I admit it. But I have changed since then. All of us have changed. And I promise you, husband, from now on I will eat whatever you bring me ..."

Then he said he was sorry. I was right, none of us were the same people we had been even a year ago; too much had happened. He apologized for bringing it up.

We often had painful little misunderstandings like that during the first year we were married, because I was thinking of Shulgi. I had already resolved that I would do my best to be just as strong as she had been. (As she had *probably* been, for I'd never paid much attention to Shulgi when she was alive.) I would work harder than I had ever worked in my life. I would be quiet and uncomplaining and bear many children, and be a worthy wife for Hur.

It was hard for me to be quiet, though, because that is not in my nature. Also, I kept asking him about her, and he hated that. It took me a while to realize it, but he honestly did not want to talk about Shulgi. At last I realized that I was only harming the both of us by my curiosity, and I stopped. And Hur, at some point, seemed to understand I was comparing myself, and he told me (awkwardly, never having been trained in eloquence), something along the following lines:

True, he had never imagined or hoped to marry his former master's daughter. He was a simple man and he had been content with a simple woman. But now that circumstances had brought us to this point, he had indeed married me willingly, without hesitation. And that he did indeed find me beautiful and, in fact, now couldn't believe his good fortune. Furthermore, that he was not concerned that I do everything in the household exactly as Shulgi would have done it. He had been content with my care for himself and Hur-kar before we were married, and he was still content with it now. And finally, that for most everyday tasks he was not sure, nor did he bother to ask himself, what

Shulgi would have done, seeing as our lifestyle had changed so much since the time we lived in the city.

He said all these things seriously and ploddingly, and nervously too, almost as though laying out a court case, or dictating a covenant. I was not put off by his serious, and put-upon manner, because I could see that it was almost physically painful for him to drag all these words out of himself, but that he had put plenty of thought into them, meant them, and was forcing himself to say them because he wanted me to know where we stood.

So I believed him, and stopped doubting myself.

I am lively and chattery; Hur does not mind this. I now believe that. I sing at my work; and though Shulgi never did, he does not mind that either.

This last year has been much better than the first two. We are settling in to a happy rhythm of married life. I believe our tribe is going to move again soon; but Hur and I can survive it.

CHAPTER 14

THE BEAR AND THE SPINDLE

Zillah

Well, my relative Tiras has got his way at last, again. He had been saying that we were still not nearly far enough north or east to have found the land God was giving us. Meanwhile there was really no reason at all to uproot the family, as far as anyone else could see.

Then something happened that seemed to confirm his belief that this was not the place for us. It was a horrible, gruesome bear attack. One of the young men from Tiras' group, quite a nice young man named Imsag, had gone out to check traps when he somehow ran afoul of the beast. No one else witnessed the horror, but it must have been quite a huge animal – we have seen such in these mountains – and it tore him until, they tell me, there were only scraps left. Hur was the one who found him, and he was left white and shaky for days afterward. He knew it was Imsag only because of where the young man had said he was going, and because of recognizing a few of the remains of his clothing.

After that, nearly everyone was afraid to venture into the woods at all – certainly no one would go out alone – and everyone was afraid even to whisper the word "bear." We have started calling it "the bad one." Mothers didn't want their children to play outside, even though by then spring had begun in earnest. Women were afraid even to go and get water.

Hur had mentioned, cautiously, that he might take a group to find the beast and kill it. The problem was that no one knew its distinguishing marks, nor did they know if this *bad one* was an exceptional individual. They might be faced with having to kill every bear for miles.

Meanwhile, Imsag had a young wife, no children yet, and she was utterly destroyed. So with all this, Tiras came out looking like he has knowledge of the future, like a seer. Although really, a bear attack might happen anywhere, however far over the land we go. Moreover, bad things happen regularly in this world in which we live. Something is always bound to happen, sooner or later, that will seem to prove right those who prophesy disaster – which Tiras does not, actually – or who even call for a change. I myself have trouble seeing this attack as a sign of anything, other than of the general judgment that is the fate of the children of men living in this present world.

But I have kept that opinion to myself, both out of respect and because … because actually, I do think that my uncle hears from God. Not so much because events prove him right (for events can prove many things), but more because of his motives – he has the good of the clan at heart – and his manner. His manner is quiet, never showy like the priests used to be in the old days, and yet this quietness is natural to him, it is not itself an act. He simply delivers the message, and we must take it or leave it. And I do take it. Not because it makes sense, nor yet because it appeals – quite the contrary – but in spite of these things.

I do not hear from God myself, but I can recognize His words when they are spoken.

Anyway, where is the harm in dragging ourselves all over the face of the earth in obedience to Tiras' visions? Perhaps God does have a special land for us … but perhaps He just wants us to plod here and there and all about. I imagine that we will continue to do this until eventually Uncle Tiras dies, and then we will drop, exhausted, and settle wherever we land up, unless of course that place is occupied by some enemy.

So after the bear attack, in the midst of a period of fear and grief, we again packed ourselves up to depart. The timing was good. It was a bit early for planting – nights were still freezing occasionally – and moreover, we had far from settled among ourselves about where, if we'd stayed, our fields were going to be. This gave us plenty of time to strike out before the horrible heat of the summer settled in. We moved swiftly, drinking a lot of milk and eating a lot of antelope. And by the true summer, we were here ... back on the vast, fertile plain, but a good way north of our former home by the sea. An excellent place for planting huge swathes of land, also for hunting. And also, with swamps beginning to the north of us, with creatures such as water birds, otters and minks, and great cow-like things that love to stand knee-deep in the water.

We are in tents again, which is not going to be pleasant if we are still here come winter. I think we had better build some earth-mounds to burrow in. And we are busy catching and tanning furs just as fast as we can.

My daughter, Ninna, has had her second baby, a coppery-dark little girl she has called Magya. The dear little thing has a great thatch of shiny black hair, just as my Ninna had when she was first born. She has been very good for her father. Hur will often sit cradling her in his arms – and with Ai Li on his other knee, as often as not – just drinking in the sight of her and, I hope, using it to drive out the sight of Imsag's mangled body. And, I think, fearing for her too, for one can sometimes see his lips moving as if in prayer. At these moments, little Hur-kar is usually climbing all over Ninna, enjoying a rare chance at his mother's full attention … for by now, she is the only mother he remembers.

Ninna is in that hard, that very demanding, stage of life, the years of childbearing. I think she is doing beautifully. She has plenty of help, of course, not from servants as I had in the old days, but from relatives: teenaged cousins from Tiras' side; her sister in law Ninshi (though in this case, Ninshi has a new baby of her own – a boy named Gorman); and myself and Nirri. It is clear she loves the little girls and Hur-kar too, and does not feel the weight of caring for them as a burden. As long as we keep her safe, warm, reasonably clean and adequately fed, she does the rest for the children and for her husband, and she seems to glow while she does it.

Sometimes when I see them and they have all fallen asleep in a heap together, it brings tears to my eyes.

When we lived in the city, I had haughty, though vague, hopes for how and when she might marry. All that seems a bit unreal now, mercifully. She is every bit as happy here, in these tents, as I ever hoped marriage might make her … happier, actually, than it was realistic to hope for there in the city. Food here is more uncertain, but love is more certain. Not completely certain; nothing is, in this life; but the chances are better, here, far from the Tower.

I, after all, married well. Golgal was not just a "great" man in the sense of intelligent and aristocratic, but a good man, which in that time and place was rare. But his goodness was pressed and squeezed by the pressure of the Tower, until it was a small, compacted thing. I cannot blame him. Even a very great goodness on his part could not have saved me and his children from the evil that surrounded us on all sides, and ended by piercing all of us with many griefs.

These plains are lonely. They can be hungry. They promise to be deadly in winter, and they are overrun with wild beasts. But – I cannot help it – I like them. Out here there is *room* at least; room for things to grow. Fear could grow, and madness as well, no doubt … but also virtue, bravery, the willingness to sacrifice the self for the family, the urge to explore. All the things for which there was little room in Si Nar. Whereas violence, it seems, out here might lose itself, might not spread so fast and deadly, like a plague through a city. People here are few and far between. In the worst case, when once the victim was dead, the violence would spread itself out and sink into the bare ground like water. Where could the violent man go to find his next victim? Would it be a ride of days, of weeks, of months, even?

Yet there is a great sadness in these grasses. Is it only because the world is broken? Or is it the dreadful shadow of some past or future evil? We have no way of knowing, in any given place, exactly what happened there before the Flood. And no one, not even Tiras, can see more than an occasional glimpse of what is to come.

My son Endu has married Sari, she who was the widow of Imsag. It was his own idea, rather to our surprise. So, in this way, Endu's "I want" coincided with our family's greater needs. It is not good to let a widow go too long unprovided for, and worse, unslotted into the family. For an older woman, we would find her a place quickly in someone's household, as a cook, weaver, beloved mother, grandmother, or aunt. Young widows – they are dangerous.

Sari was indeed a prize, leaving aside her widowhood: beautiful, hardworking, only a few years older than Ninna. My Endu swooped down rather like an eagle on a hare, and snatched her up – over the heads, I might add, of some slightly more eligible young women from Tiras' group …

perfectly marriageable women a little younger, a little plainer, and without Sari's tragic history.

I thought, at that time, that he was only trying to be kind and helpful. Moved perhaps by her beauty, wishing to dry her tears. And truly, he *was* trying to help the family. But I wonder, now … did he perhaps wish to marry a woman who would *owe* him something.

Hard as it is to credit it, I can see him already wondering whether he made a mistake, any time she seems to him insufficiently grateful.

Endu does like to see gratitude – or at least, knowing their place – from any who, in his view, have arrived late to the family. Most of the time he goes quietly about his duties, but every once in a while, the young prince of Si Nar that he once was comes out in a spiteful little gesture.

Earlier this summer, he thought he had found a clever and amusing way for our crippled guest to earn his keep. We were all sitting outside in the long twilight. It was no very special night; we had just stopped after some days of travel, and we had just cooked and eaten some very ordinary food, I believe it was greens and prairie fowl. Sari had a spindle in her hand – we must always be spinning and such against the winter, whenever there is a spare moment – and was about to begin her work.

This is the way we spin. We have the fiber on the left side, wrapped loosely around our left arm usually. On the right we have a spindle. It is a simple spike of wood, with a clay weight fastened on the end, which we call the whorl. We fasten a bit of fiber in a groove just below the whorl, then turn the spindle with our wrist. This twists the fiber into thread. Then we feed out a little more fiber and twist again, stopping often to wind the made thread about the spindle between the whorl and our hand. In Si Nar the fiber was always flax, but we have not had flax for a few years now. Some of our sheep have wool that can be spun into thread, and we have begun using that. It weaves up into a much warmer fabric, and it comes covered in its own oil, which is nice because we do not have to be constantly wetting it, as we did with flax.

Sari, then, had a bit of wool wound round her left arm, and was just about to fasten a bit of this into the groove when Endu strode by, plucked the spindle from her to her surprised squawk, and suddenly he had tossed it into the Cushite's lap.

"Here," he said, laughing. "Make yourself useful."

Nirri reacted as any grown man might when given such a command. He huffed, held the object out at the end of a stiffened arm, and from the look he gave Endu, it was clear what he would do with the spindle at that moment, if he could.

Now many people were laughing. My son was shocked, and more amused than ever, yet a little irritated too, that his power play had turned into a joke.

"Mother," he said to me, "Help me, help me make him obey."

"I am not going to help you, my son," I said, still laughing along with everyone else. "You must untangle the knot your own hands have tied."

Endu, perfectly aware that he could do no such thing, turned and walked away.

Nirri looked after him with gleaming eyes, and for a moment it looked like he was about to throw the spindle. Then a little wisdom came to him, and instead he dropped it onto the blanket on which he sat. A few moments later, moved by curiosity, he was examining it idly. Sari meanwhile had pulled out another and begun to get on with her work.

I waited for a double handful of days, so that the spindle incident should have no connection to what I was about to do. I awaited a day when a hunting party had drawn off many of the men, an evening when the mothers were busy bedding down their children – for once the child is asleep in her arms, the mother tends not to want to rise – a evening that was still full of light, for these summer evenings tended to have a very long, bright twilight, and the more so the farther north we traveled. On this evening, then, when tired families were bedding down though light still shone strongly where it was admitted through open smoke-flaps, I went to him.

Sometimes it really seems that I have learned nothing in all my years, but one thing I *have* learned is how to undress gracefully. That, if you like, is what marks out an older woman from a young one … knowing how to pull a woolen or flaxen shift over your head without looking awkward.

As I was doing this, I looked at the Cushite and he looked at me. At first with a great, white smile (for he still has all his teeth) … then his large, dark eyes developed a dark furrow between them, and I knew it was not anger but puzzlement. He could not ask his question, but I understood it. *Why?* he might ask, if he could speak. *Why are you doing this? What do you hope to accomplish?*

He has begun to learn a few words, such as our names, and the names of objects, but he could not hope to frame such a complex question. It must be very difficult for him to tease out the meanings of subtler words, such as *why.*

It was lucky that, even if I had replied, he could not have understood me. For I did not *know* why, apart from the faint hope for a child, and that he is handsome. And there was no answer, in words, that I could give which he would not find insulting. Best to leave it, and speak a language that needs no words. I make you smile, Guest, because I can.

Meanwhile the evening sun warmed the tent, and the wind outside rattled it pleasantly.

The next day he was looking smug, but doing an excellent job of hiding it. Reigning in that dazzling smile. Bowing his head over his work whenever anyone, especially I, passed. He was using the spindle Endu had given him, learning to work it slowly and clumsily, like a little girl just starting out with her spinning. It is uncommonly slow and tedious work, especially when one is just beginning. And it is always women's work, so I suppose he has never seen it done before. In our old home in the city it was always women and girls who would spin, each for her own household.

I take that back. If a garment was to be very prestigious, then perhaps a man might spin it. That was always how it was in Si Nar. If any job was very highly honored, you could be sure it would be given to a man, regardless of whether it was difficult or easy. So, in some cases, for very important robes or hangings, you might see a famous man do the spinning. Which means that Nirri may have had a chance to observe the process, if he ever commissioned some important piece of cloth and watched to make sure that it was done properly.

He did seem familiar enough with it to get on. His ears as he worked were dark with humiliation, but he seemed to welcome it too, perhaps as a sort of puzzle to avoid lassitude. He certainly has the sparkling eye, the ability to learn quickly, that is required for the task, not to mention the strong and well-developed wrists and fingers.

I suppose I must know him pretty well, if I can see the smugness in all of that. But I can. He is no fool. We must hide this. I can only imagine Endu's reaction.

Easy to hide, when it happens less than once a year.

It does nothing for him, by the way, the sight of me taking off my shift. His body is no longer connected to his mind, it must be ministered to with more direct methods. Yet I do nothing of that kind without his permission. I am not about asserting power, as if to crush him further. He has been as mangled, in his way, as Imsag … mangled in the soul, and I believe this happened well before the fall of the Tower. Yet this is one case where the mangled man may be knit back together again. But if we find a bloody ruin, and if by some mysterious power we are able to command it to re-make itself and have it obey, the scattered pieces will surely come together not in a shape that we design or expect, but in a pattern foreknown only by God. It is only by watching, with appreciation, the bits as they are assembled that we come to the slow revelation of what it was first designed to be.

CHAPTER 15

FRESH MEAT

Hur

It has been a bad couple of winters.

That first winter, it was the wolves. Our first winter in the far north, I mean. We had heard from pre-Flood legends about how things were here: how it is light for half the year and dark for the other half, how the cold goes beyond what could be imagined, how there was no food and how there were actual spirits visible in the sky. We had heard, but we didn't fully believe. At least, I didn't. These were rumors. And we guessed that we were, by now, pretty skilled at building shelters, hunting, and surviving a snowy winter. So we built, as before, shelters partially under the ground – grave-pits, basically – and timbered them over, ready to go, using evergreens from the great forest. We dug a lot of swamp-sod, once the edges of the swamp dried out, in blocks to be burnt, and we laid in a lot of firewood.

We figured that between the dried fish and game we had, the barley we had grown, and the hunts we would make, there would be enough food to last us the winter.

We didn't figure on the wolves. We had seen them, of course, happily hunting elk or aurochs on the plains. But their range was wide, they only came into sight every so often, and we reckoned – I reckoned, at least, and Enmer took my word for it – that there would be enough meat for us all.

But when winter came, some of the beasts – such as the aurochs – left. Others stayed, such as the reindeer, which at that time we were calling "the great deer," but the fish were all frozen. The wolves kept their large range, but they increased the speed of their patrols, so that they were cycling over their whole range more quickly. For all that there was plenty of meat, they seemed to be very concerned about us taking any. They were clever and crafty. We could not chase the prey – we had not yet learned to use the horses to do that, and the great deer were as fast or faster – but we could lie in wait to shoot some, even perhaps some that were driven our way by a wolf-hunt. But when we did this, the wolves would take offense and sometimes actually fight us for the fallen animal.

They then began to come and encircle our village at night. Great huge packs of them. They could smell us and smell our cooking, and they realized that here was prey that preferred to hunker down rather than run. They watched us as they might watch a rabbit-hole. It got to the point, finally, where every night they were out there – and the nights were long – calling to one another, for re-enforcements. It didn't work to drive them away with a torch. There were too many, and the winds generally blew the torch out anyway. The only thing one could do, was to go out and shoot one. I did not resent them for their behavior. They were only being the beasts that they were. It's their nature. I never resent predators, except those that kill from spite. But malice or no malice, we had landed up on opposite sides. They were the enemies of man, and I – I was their enemy, yes and a bitter one.

The winds, the darkness, the wolf-howls affected everyone, especially our more vulnerable women and children. I didn't take it personally – from the wolves – but some did. When you are a little frightened child, you can't help it. Nearly everyone had seen, at that point, a wolf pack hunt and bring down an animal, or had seen the results. Our horses were occasionally taken, for example. And we all remembered the fate of Imsag.

Enmer got very bad again, and he showed it by taking foolish risks. He would go out on his own, in an ill-planned way, to drive off the animals, or he would stand "guard" outside until his nose and ears and toes were frozen. Then

Ninshi and Ninna would be pleading me, with tears, to bring him in, almost as soon as he had gone out.

It *was* hard to avoid frostbite, mind you. I remember many an afternoon when several of us would come in from a hunt, and the first thing we would do was to unwrap our feet and rub them down with snow, to bring back the blood. It might seem cold, but it burned like fire in comparison to our cold, nearly dead flesh. We did this diligently, and no one lost any flesh that winter.

One night, I went out to fetch my brother Enmer and found him staring angrily at the sky.

"Look, brother," he said. "It's the messengers of God. They have come to demand an accounting of us."

I looked, and saw lights – veils of light, tonight they were blue and green – such as we had sometimes seen in the sky since the autumn. Sometimes, if there was no wind, you could hear them singing.

"Those aren't the messengers of God, brother," I soothed. "They are only spirits. Sky spirits, that imitate what they see on Earth – red for fire, blue for water, green for forest."

"Yellow for death," said Enmer.

"I do not think," I said carefully, "That they want anything with us. My own thought is that they stay in the sky. I have never seen one come down to the ground. Never."

"But they have some ill effect," he urged again. "They might make us sick, or insane."

I looked at him hard. The green light was on his face. But he did not yet look insane to me … only frightened, and troubled.

"It's possible," I agreed. "But I don't think that is their design. I am not certain that they think, brother. They have a nature, and act according to that nature … that is all."

"It's God's design," said Enmer. (By this time food rations were getting short, and all of us were getting nervous and desperate.)

"Come inside, brother, and stop looking at the spirits. You need to see a human face."

"I cannot face Ninshi," he said.

"Talk to Grandfather Nirri then. He will listen." Everyone knew that their stare-downs did something good for Enmer. Seemed to clear his head.

"He *has* to listen," snorted Enmer, but he came.

Nirri was called Grandfather Nirri, by that time, not only by Angki but by all the children. He was the oldest man in our immediate clan ... although of course they loved Grandfather Tiras as well, and clambered all over him, whenever he made an appearance. But Nirri was right there for them, every day, in our low, round earthen communal hall. Despite his constant presence, he was a mysterious figure to them. My little girl Ai Li found him frightening, but to Angki and Hur-Kar, he was endlessly entertaining. He, the old rogue, encouraged the fear and mystery the boys held him in, by alternately smiling and glaring; growling at them; and singing them endless songs that had only one word. (Hur-Kar's favorite song was "Wolf, Go Away." Angki's favorite was "Horse.")

Nirri that winter made a beginning at learning to spin and weave, and he proved to be a quick study. His long, fine fingers were nearly as clever as a woman's, and he would work for hours with great concentration, getting done what seemed to be huge amounts of work, compared to the women who were always having to stop and attend to such things as cooking.

With the scraps, he made little toys for the children. A horse for Angki, of course, and a lion – as requested – for

Hur-Kar. He made a little soft sheep for two-year-old Ai Li, which made her thaw towards him a bit. Then for Enmer's daughter Lina, whose toy was to be next, I saw him winding wool around a frame of twigs, with a long, swaying neck and a great stone in the middle for a hump on the back. He saw me puzzling over it, and held it up, pronouncing, "*Gote,*" with a proud grin.

"You mean a camel, Uncle," I said, cracking a smile of my own. And when I told Ninna, later, she laughed and laughed.

Spring came at last. At first it meant no lessening of the cold, but only that the days were once again day. Then, while there was still plenty of snow, the creatures became more active, and I went out to set traps and, later, check them. I wasn't afraid to do this, but it frightened Ninna.

"Wife," I said to her, "Predators will do what they will do. But we people need to live as well. We must be as wise as we can, but take risks also, so that we can live."

I hated to see her nearly cry every time I came back, but I was getting food, and many furs as well. I would give them to Sari to tan, or sometimes to the Cushite.

Then there would be a thaw; the streams would rise, the game trails would change, and I would have to go out and change my traps.

On one such trip I saw something that I have not spoken to anyone of, until today. I saw a stranger.

I had come into a little clearing – this forest is so different from the warm, wet ones near Si Nar, I can hardly call it the same Earth – and he was standing on the other side of it, watching and waiting quietly, just as I had intended to watch and wait. I did not see his tracks before I saw him. He had come from the east, I from the northwest.

When he saw me – at the same moment that I spotted him – he took a single step out of his hiding place and stood. And I stood likewise, each letting the other see that we were alone.

He was dressed very much as I was. Leather and furs and things. I did not see any wool on him. He had on a fur hat, and I think black hair underneath it, for his eyes were dark black, and his round, smooth face was dark as well, even a bit darker than Grandfather Nirri. He was clean-shaven, or perhaps was unable to grow a beard, as are some of our people also.

Neither one of us tried to speak. I was waiting to see if he would be friendly. He, it seemed, was doing the same. For long moments we looked at one another. For my part, I liked what I saw. Then at length I drew back, raising both my hands, as if to say, *Very well, this is the border of your hunting-grounds. So shall it be.*

And both of us drew away. Neither had gone for his weapon. Neither had cried out for help. Nor had we exchanged any gifts, except each leaving the other the pinecone-strewn clearing.

I never told Enmer about this, for he was just beginning to come out of his own winter, and I was not sure what he might do. I never told Father Tiras either. If it had become necessary, I would have, but it never did become necessary. I had a feeling that this man did not have a very large group behind him. Perhaps it was just himself, his wife and children. I never saw him again, but from the fact that he was out trapping, I surmised a great deal. He had become a friend, of a sort.

We had looked at each other.

I worked a great deal with Tiras' people that spring. We all came out of our burrows, so sick of being trapped, cold, hungry and wet, and sick of looking at our immediate relatives' faces. Never talked much about it, but we all sort of broke apart and re-formed into different groups for a while.

First of all, when spring came and the wolves did not seem to be stopping their siege, we set out to teach them a lesson. That was mostly the younger men: Melek and Taman and Raja, Raku and Rumi and a few others from the other camp; and from our side, myself and my two brothers, Enmer looking very grim. We built a ring of huge bonfires, for it was now possible to do this, and yet wet enough still that prairie fire was not a great danger. And we went out and shot as many wolves as we possibly could. They did not stay long that night, and though we posted a few bonfires after that, they stopped returning in numbers.

They left behind one very small pup, too young to be hunting with its elders. It must have been an early birth, for they usually have litters later in the spring, and keep them in a den until the summer. This one was large enough to eat meat, but barely. It must have come along to see the camp of the men. Or perhaps they really hoped they would get to eat *our* pups (our children, I mean), and so they brought this adventurous little one, so sure they were of a feast. At any rate, I am sure they would not have left the pup if it were not for the confusion we created by killing so many of them and driving the others away.

Enmer saw the thing moving in the firelight and drew a bit closer to kill it, and then found himself unable to kill so young a thing. He picked it up, far more gently that I would have expected, and brought it to the rest of us to examine. As he approached, the scent of the wolves grew stronger and surrounded us. The pup was skinny, with large paws, rounded ears, a good deal of red color in its coat – which we consider lucky – and a slightly curling tail. It was licking and nipping at Enmer's chin as if it expected him to produce some meat for it.

"I will give it to Ki-Ki," he said, meaning his son, who was now five years old. "He wants some animal to care for."

I saw some of the others raising their eyebrows, and I quickly backed him up by saying, "It is spring now. I think we can find enough milk and meat."

Our approach to animals was not the same in those days as it is now. Perhaps we remembered the Garden. If we had an interest in an animal, we would approach it, and, more often than not, it responded to us to some extent. Wolves, for example, were more fluid in their kind at that time and, depending on the individual, more trainable. Even after such a thing as a bear attack, it did not seem strange for a man to bring home a wolf pup to his five-year-old child. Animals since then have become more distant from us and from each other. I would not now bring home a wolf. But this pup that Enmer rescued, it was nearly a dog, and we had no troubles with it all throughout its lifetime.

Ki-Ki loved it on sight. He has a great capacity for love, that one. (My Hur-Kar is more reserved.) He is deeply attached to his father and his mother, and his cousins, and to each and every one of our camp's livestock. And also, to "Grandfather" Nirri, which might have caused Enmer some jealousy, except that Ki-Ki spreads his love so lavishly and (especially come spring) spends much more time outside, with his father and with the animals, than he does indoors near the grand old man. When Enmer brought him the pup he at once named it Reddy and was soon stroking its fur, hugging it nearly to death, getting nipped on his hands and even feeding it morsels from his mouth. Reddy was exactly what he needed to spread out his joy. Hur-kar enjoyed the benefits of all this, for he too got to play with the pup, but could leave when he became tired of it.

The women agreed they would not have it sleeping in the family quarters, at least in the summer, so Angki began the habit of sleeping, curled up with his dog, just inside the entrance of the door. I believe he will still sleep that way after he marries, unless, as seems likely, Reddy has died by then. Eventually he and Enmer managed to give the creature a bath, which lessened its wild smell somewhat and drowned a great number of fleas.

We traveled very, very far that summer. It was as if a madness came over us, the madness that comes on people when they are nearly at the upper edge of the world. Nothing seemed real as it had seemed real when we started our journey. First there had been the endless winter, during which it was so cold that it actually hurt to go outside, not to mention the eerie lights, the howling and smell of the wolves, who had been our enemies, but one of which we had now taken in. Then, suddenly, instead of the bitter cold and constant dark, the world opened up and became sweet and fragrant, and ... if not warm, then at least pleasant ... and there were swamps and water-birds everywhere, and everything coming out and feeding itself after the winter. And, above all this, the long, long days. Eventually with almost no night at all. The change was not really instant, but it seemed sudden to us. To me and Ninna anyway. We felt as if we'd spent the last five years of our lives in the cold and dark, instead of only five months.

All these extremes tend to make a person a little crazy.

We opened up our camp, turning everything inside out, washing everything, shearing, milking, setting the animals and the babies out in the sun. Setting the Cushite out in the sun, too. He would sit on the south of the tent, leaning back on his hands, eyes closed, his face turned directly toward the great day-star. How he had hated the cold, that one.

We men starting taking long trips. Grandfather Tiras wanted to keep going north. It was as if this had become his only thought. He seemed to think we would find something, something important. The world beyond the world, perhaps. Perhaps God. We were willing to go with him, not only because he was our father but because we too wanted to spend time away from the little circle of faces that, during the winter, had become our hell. We wanted to stretch our legs. Make the most of this energy and these long hours of daylight. Find fresh meat.

I was happy to spend time with Tiras' sons, Abijay and Melek, and with the younger men from his group; Taman,

Raja, Raku, and Rumi, and others. We went in search of food. The grasses sprouted, the waters rose, and there were wild cows, both the huge aurochs and the skinnier kind with branching horns; rabbits; as the swamps and rivers rose, the fish increased; and the ducks and geese were coming back. We never killed the young or the mothers, being crazy but not complete fools. We would take the big males. The challenge of doing this added fun to the hunt. There were so many of everything that we did not need to worry about diminishing their numbers (though the wolves might think otherwise). We would do a big hunt, bring back plenty of meat, have a feast and give it to the women to cure against the winter … and then off we'd go on another ramble.

On one of these, we were gone several weeks. Not all of us went, of course – again, we were not complete fools – but we had along myself and Enmer, Grandfather Tiras, Abijay, Taman, and Rumi. We went on foot, because the terrain was uncertain for horses. Often there were swamps that would have been difficult to cross with them. But we were strong, walking much, sleeping little. At last, we reached the edge of the sea.

"The sea! Here!" said Abijay, surprised and dismayed, when we saw it from a half a day's distance.

But Father Tiras nodded, unsurprised, and said, "We were bound to reach it eventually, my son. We are told that there is a sea that runs around all the edges of the world."

Enmer looked a bit relieved, I think, that we would be able to go no farther.

"And now we have seen two of the edges!" breathed Rumi.

I was not certain that he was right. We had certainly been on the Stinking Sea, but we had not properly crossed it. We had traveled along the west coast of it, I remembered. Meanwhile we had approached it from the south. And in the years since, we had gone far east of our landing-point, and yet had found no more traces of the Stinking Sea. It seemed to me that we had gone nearly all around it. And this meant it must be a very … bounded sea, not one that encircled all the edges of the world. But Tiras, if he had noticed this, did not correct Rumi. Even if we had not truly seen two edges, yet we had seen wonders. And another wonder was in store for us, shortly.

The coast was very cold. There were no friendly dunes to block the wind, no acres of reeds. We came out on to the beach, and then we had not to pick but to climb our way across it. It was a confusing jumble of things we did not understand. At first, they came before us only as things in our way, which roused a bit of irritation. Not only Tiras but all of us were eager to get to the world-edging water. But it was impossible to climb quickly over these obstacles, so before long we were forced to look at them. And what we saw was bones.

The beach was a boneyard.

Looking closer, we saw that some of the bones were those of trees. Great trunks had been overthrown, cast about as if by a child, and now they were decaying very slowly, with their roots sticking up like huge many-fingered hands, being scoured by the wind. But mostly, there were animal bones. Not small ones, either. It was all so jumbled together that we could hardly tell what was what. A lot of it had been smashed to bits. But the skulls were huge. The ribs were huge. There were great curving sword-like things that we finally determined had been teeth. Finally we found some still attached to a skull, and decided between us that these dead had once been some sort of elephant.

There were no trees on this coast, now. But there had once been. There were no beasts, other than fishes and birds. But there had once been a multitude.

We stood in the never-failing light, shivering in the wind off the sea, and looked around us at the evidence of death and destruction.

"This must've been worse than when the Tower fell," said Taman at last.

"Wish I could've hunted it, before," said Rumi.

"I do not think there were people here to do any hunting," said Tiras. It was true that we had seen no human bones – not that they'd have been easy to find, if present – and besides, we knew that people had not normally eaten meat before the Flood. At least, good people had not.

"Maybe we can find their descendants, though, cousin," I said to Rumi with a grin.

We made it to the water eventually and paddled our hands in it … the Sea of Death, we by now were calling it. I looked out over it for some time, and though my eyes are not accustomed to looking at water, at length I could see that there were many creatures living in the sea. Some of them were very large. I thought there would be good eating on them, if a man had a way to get to them, and if he were desperate.

Enmer had a haunted look on his face as he stared out over the silver-grey water, to where the clouds lay scraped into the form of fish's scales on the sky.

"Imagine being here in winter," he murmured. "All these bones ... and endless night above them ..." Then he added, so softly that I almost did not hear, "... I am sick of death."

We traveled east on the beach for a day, Enmer clearly hating every moment. We made the most uncomfortable camp I've ever experienced, before or since, hunkered down on the leeward side of a pile of bones, trying to sleep in the merciless wind and the merciless light. The next day, we walked back. No matter how far we went, nothing seemed to change. Sometimes there were more bones, sometimes fewer. That was all.

"Did you find what you were looking for, my father?" asked Tiras' son Abijay.

The old man was silent. After a long moment, he said softly, almost as if he were ashamed, "It is not here anymore."

"What was it?" Abijay pressed.

Tiras was again silent, and at last he murmured, so quietly we could barely hear it, "Death."

Death, of course, was not what he had been looking for. He had been looking precisely for life … life for us as a people, that we might carry on. But death was what we had found instead. If not death for ourselves, then at least the death of a lot of other things.

It discouraged us to see so many bones beside the sea. It was, as they say, a sobering sight. But for myself, at least, it was not crushing. We had known already that nearly everything had perished in the flood, that when we walked on the earth we were walking on a floor of bones. This had not stopped us before from bringing, and enjoying, life from that very earth.

Also, I had seen the creatures in the sea. Birds swooped down and skimmed up little creatures; armies of ordinary-sized fish came to the surface, turned as one, and made the water appear to pucker; every once in a while, a huge, dark-colored fish would rise out of the water like a distant but formidable hill, and spew water into the glittering air. The sea creatures were alive and well, and ready to feed one another for generations to come. We would go back, I was sure, to our own families, to our comparatively warm, dry, and safe forests and plains. Meanwhile they would swim about in their vast grey wilderness, hidden from our view,

but just as happy as we were, probably more so. The thought
of this made me smile.

On the way back, we found an even greater wonder. As we
moved inland, we came upon a shallow valley, an old
riverbed. We approached it from its downstream side as it
issued from a low cliff and we saw that it was full of what at
first appeared to be rocks. But a second look showed it was
packed with splintered wood, frozen mud, rocks, and a great
many things we could not recognize, and all this was
encased in dirty, opaque ice. And looking closer still, we saw
what looked to be more bones. And more than bones … we
saw something made of leather and fur, as if a creature had
just recently been buried. We were curious.

Abijay and I approached it and hacked at it rudely with
rocks until we could use our knives to saw off a piece and
pry it away from the rest. As we'd hacked, it had become
obvious that the creature was a very large one.

"Why, I believe it's meat," said Abijay, holding it
cautiously in his hand and poking, then sniffing at it. "Frozen
meat." At that moment his belly gave a growl. Unlike his
father, he was a big man, built narrow but deep, with a long,

creased face and his father's golden-brown skin, and long
ropey arms. He needed his food, Abijay.

And so ... well, it sounds a little odd to tell it, but we
were hungry. It had been a while since we'd had more than
our preserved food, which was cured meat from last fall, and
rancid fat mixed with barley and berries. And like every day,
we had been walking all the day out of doors, and we had
recently tried and failed to shoot a goose. So, with all this ...

I will just say it. We cooked and ate some of the meat.

And yes, it was still fresh.

When we put it over the coals, it first thawed, smelling a
bit musty but not rotten, and then it cooked. And then – well,
it tasted like beef. We had pulled food out of the rock and
eaten our fill.

I should add, we did not make our camp and our fire
right there within sight of the ice-filled gully. It was a bit too
much for us to consume the meat right there where, as it
were, the rest of the animal would be watching us. Although,
in fact, the ice was so cracked, so dirty, so flatly white, that
really we could not see the rest of the animal, let alone its
face. Nor could we tell whether, as we suspected, there were
others in there. And we did not know for certain what kind of
creature it was, but based on the taste, and on the texture of

the bits of hair, we guessed that it was either a shaggy sort of ox creature, or a great elephant like those whose bones we'd found on our last adventure.

Rumi was the first to try it. He was short and skinny, with a square face, a round nose, and big hands and feet that promised more growth. He was only eighteen years old, and would have been just a boy when the Tower fell. He didn't have the grim grieving spirit of Enmer, nor the horror of things left over from a judgment that the older ones had. His memories even of the legends of the days before meat were dim. Also, he was young and eager to learn and try everything in the world. And further, his body was young and still growing, and so, hungry.

When the meat had been steaming for a long time, when its edges were black and the smell was bringing the water into the mouths of all of us, young Rumi stepped forward, bent, and then looked over at Tiras and said, "May I, Grandfather?"

Tiras gave him a nod and a little smile, and Rumi speared the meat, held it up before his face and began blowing and nibbling.

"It's still good!" he said, with a delight that made the rest of us smile. "D'you realize what this means … we might be able to *dig* for our meat and find it in the *ground*!"

It was an intriguing thought, especially when one was hungry. But it didn't sit well with the rest of us, at least not as a way of life. The meat was oddly tender, for one thing, so much that we did not know whether to be enraptured or revolted. And the process of taking it out and then thawing it took nearly as long as hunting and butchering an animal, and was far less pleasant. It was fine when one was desperate. It was not, like cannibalism, something we would sooner die than do.

But there was also the problem of the … fitness of the thing. Eating an animal that had probably lived before the Flood, in the days when people were not allowed to hunt them, an animal that had never been meant to be eaten … well, it gave all of us an uneasy feeling. It was as if we'd reached our hands through the veil and taken something from the other place … and then *eaten* it, made it part of ourselves. We felt … I cannot describe it. We felt different, doing things that were the same things we had always done, but yet were not the same. Just as men always had, we walked, we ate, we slept. But eating *such* meat, sleeping beside such a sea, walking under such a sky …!

Were we now to go back to our familiar camp, to our families with their loved faces, to familiar smells, familiar food, familiar tasks? It did not seem, at that moment, like a thing that was possible. Perhaps, as we walked south, there would be sort of curtain, like a huge tent flap, that we would walk through without seeing it, and then we would be back in our own world. Or perhaps there would be no such curtain, and we would find that we were stuck forever in this other place.

That, at least, was what I sensed as we sat there, eating. I say *sensed* because I did not really *think* it – not to believe it. I knew, I mean, that we would certainly walk back to our camp, and that as we walked, we would feel no sense of shock as of a curtain parting or of a tent flap brushing our faces. Instead, things would gradually come to seem more usual. Our old selves would seep back into the shells of us as a deep, narrow vessel slowly fills with water, and soon we would find ourselves doubting the strangeness of this distant meat and sky.

That is what I expected to happen, and that is exactly what did happen. I was never truly lost in the strangeness, because I am a practical man. Enmer is not a practical man. I fancy he felt it much more strongly than I. Perhaps he feared its power. He ate the meat, but he seemed hesitant, revolted. As if eating a curse. We all know – and Enmer is the sort to remember such things – that the world can change forever because someone has eaten the wrong thing. But I, a former slave, remember something else as well: you can die because you did not eat it.

We made it back home, our old selves after all, just as I said. Everything seemed to have changed while we were gone. Everyone was windblown and happy from being outdoors. The goats and horses were thriving. Old Nirri was turned so brown, from sitting out in the sun, that I would hardly have recognized him ... except that there is only one Nirri. My Ninna, always dark, was browner as well. The children all seemed to have grown since we'd left. They were so happy to see us, and we to see them. The happiness of the summer was on us; it seemed that everything was right. To crown everything, that evening Ninna took me aside and told me that while I was away, she'd discovered that she was with child again. Now we would have four.

We did a barley harvest. We sat in council with Tiras' son Melek and with Raja and the others who had not been as far as the Sea of Death … and with those of us who had, as well, for we six had far from sorted out our own thoughts about it.

We discussed whether we should approach the Sea of Death and accustom ourselves to living there, at least in the summertime. If we were pressed back by some human enemy, we could retreat to the eerie beach, where we would know how to live and the enemy would not. We would have to learn to make decent fishing boats, of course. (Raku liked this idea.) We could dig for meat … no one else would think of that! If all else failed, the place itself, the sea and the boneyard and so on, would be a formidable defense against any human foe. So said Melek and Endu, who had never seen the place, and so said Abijay, who is a very fierce and warlike man, apparently ready to do anything at all in order that we might not be wiped out as a people. Even live in a huge, alien graveyard.

Luckily for the sanity of everyone, Tiras was not yet so visionary or so mad that he thought this a good plan. He gave our trip what was, I believe, the correct interpretation: that we had already discovered the edge of where the world was habitable. That the farthest north held no promise for us, nor for any other people. That whatever he had hoped to find by going continually north, he had not found it, and now it was time to seek a home elsewhere.

We considered moving a ways farther south before the winter, but decided against it. If we did nothing else but preserve food from now until the first snows, we should be comfortable. We had our burrows already built; we could re-chink them against the cold, even piling up additional earth for better insulation. We had the barley already in. We could milk the goats and make various sour things from the milk that would keep well. What we needed to be doing now, rather than dragging ourselves across the country, was to start harvesting grass for the goats to eat this winter, and start hunting the animals – the *normal* animals – now that they were plump for autumn, and preserving their meat. So we did all this. We felt that we were ready for whatever might come. Fools.

But that winter turned out far worse than the one before it, because Ninna …

I cannot tell of it.

CHAPTER 16

DEATH WAS IN THE WORLD

Enmer

We should have known better. I, at least, should have known.
I do not blame my relative Tiras, for I do not trust Tiras
anymore. I don't mean that I doubt his character. He is still
as solid and good and, in his way, as wise a man as you
could hope to find. He still has integrity that is glistening and
whole, like unmixed metal, just like Golgal my father. But I
no longer trust him to see things as they are.

We should not have stayed in this place after all those
very bad omens. No, not even with winter coming on. In
fact, the approach of winter should have been a warning to
me, that the death we had seen slumbering, as it were, in the
summer was about to awake and swoop down from the top
of the world to ravage us. I cannot think why I did not pick
up my family and flee from there as we had fled from the
giants, from the red-haired Scyths, and from the Tower. I
really cannot think of a reason. The reason, of course, was
my cursed lassitude, my trembling stillness like that of a hare
before a wildcat … but still that is no excuse. After all, the
omens could not have been clearer. We had walked openly
on a great pile of bones. We had eaten the dead things and

found that we liked them, and what could be a worse omen than that?

To me, this seemed like a very clear revelation that the world was, at its core, death. We had got past the hide or hair of city, fertile land, and forest that covered the world, and had managed to peek under the world's skirts, as it were, and what we saw was death. Death had first poked out through its covering at the Tower, and we had run, thinking we could escape it. But there is no escape when death is under all and behind all and is all. Still, even if there is no escape over the course of a long life, yet we might by running have escaped it for a time … fifteen or twenty years, say, or thirty or fifty, enough time for our children to have children, who would in their turn, run. And because we did not do this quickly enough, one child at least will never get a chance to marry and have little runners of his own.

Tiras does not see any of this. He looks at the world and sees promise, even glory. He knows that all things die, of course, but what his eye sees is overflowing life, constantly renewed, there for the taking like a ripe fruit. Conditions that have not been present since even before his time. When, I ask you, was the last time that the children of Adam found safety anywhere? Or found feeding themselves as easy as …

as reaching out your hand to pick a grape? (Grapes! What I would give for even one grape! We have not seen grapes in years.)

But I am better now. I am awake, aware, and I see clearly that if anyone is to save this family, these children, it will have to be me. Mother helps a great deal, of course. She keeps the heart in everyone. But she cannot be everywhere at once, nor see everything. She did not see those huge heaps of bones.

Here, then, is how that winter – the sixth since we fled from Si Nar – fell out. It started out with a whacking great storm, which brought days and days of darkness that had nothing to do with the sun's going away, but only with the clouds. Though we thought we had done a fairly good job of preparing our little houses for winter, this storm tore up two of them to such a degree that nearly everyone was forced to move in together, into the great (but still inadequate) hall that had previously been occupied only by Mother, the Cushite prisoner, and my children, and Ninshi and me.

The storm also brought a great deal of snow, more than I remembered from the previous year, or at least, more at one time. This made it difficult to get out and fix the huts that were broken; and as it turned out, we never did end up fixing them. It did give us unlimited water as long as we had fuel to melt it and boil it. But I couldn't help thinking that these snow clouds had probably come straight from the sea we had lately seen, the Sea of Death. Meaning that they carried fragments of dead things in them. Therefore, we were drinking death. Death was piled around our house, keeping us warm. We were living by the death of the old world. Of course, I did not speak these thoughts to anyone. I dealt with all this death by not thinking about it, which is how I deal with many things in these latter days. I think of what is immediately necessary in order to make plans, and nothing else.

And when with all this not thinking I become weary, as a last resort I go and sit and stare at Nirri, and allow myself to think, very hard, about how much I despise him. And after this, I find that I am refreshed.

Living with him is another matter. Imagine the person you most despise in this world, and then imagine yourself forced to spend an entire winter living only a few cubits from this person, and you will have an idea of my feelings. I begrudge him every mouthful of food, every little pleasure. In the summer, for example, or even when the day is not bitterly cold, if I see him sitting and sunning himself like a great damned bronze dragon, I think how he does not deserve to be living, sitting there enjoying the sun. The one in the sun ought to be another: my brother Sut, or else my father. This Cushite should be indoors, in the tent, or better yet in the grave. He should not be here.

He cannot contribute much to earn his meat (not that he eats more than a child, usually), except for one thing. Much as I despise him, all that is forgotten as soon as he picks up his lute.

We were unlucky in that among our family when we fled from Si Nar there were no professional singers. My brothers Endu and Sut were a bit gifted in music, but dabblers only. They had participated in temple worship, back in the old days, but they were never ones to lead the sacred hymns or to compose ballads. And then we lost Sut, and with him a great deal of music, dance, playfulness, and laughter.

A few in Tiras' party were musical, but in the winter, we saw them seldom, and winter was when we were in our direst need to have our hearts lifted.

So we were in a very unfortunate situation when it came to music. Not only did we have no one with the inclination, but for several years, our minds had been occupied mainly with the struggle to survive. We had no time to practice, let alone invent a new music to go with the new language God had given us. Nor did we have the heart. Our story as a tribe was just beginning. It seemed at that point to be mere chaos, with very little meaning, not anything that anyone would sing about. The old legends too seemed to have little bearing on our life today. We had no need for the invented or half-remembered tragedy of some hero or goddess, when there was so much tragedy of our own to be had. For myself, I confess I did not even feel the loss of music, until that … Nirri … re-awakened it. But he must have felt the loss. Else he would not have gone to such trouble to begin filling it.

I cannot account for what happens when he sings. His music is not in the grand, palace style I would have expected. It has almost no worship it in, and absolutely no swelling choral effects like there used to be in the old temples. It is mostly the style of one voice and a lute, or at most call-and-response, which he is teaching the children. Many of his songs consist only of humming, or they are built around a single word. And if they do happen to have words, of course we cannot understand what he is saying, or rather, singing.

Yet despite all this.

Despite all this, when he sings, he seems to be telling us our own story, but telling it as something that does, contrary to what I have said, have meaning. When sung in his deep, round voice, all our scattered running, hiding, hunting, and arguing seems to become something noble. The animals are there in his songs – I cannot describe it, really – as are the stars. Even the heap of bones seems to be there, though I cannot tell how he might know of it. Perhaps he got it from his own flood legends, or simply from the experience of the winter.

I have said that nothing that has happened to us is anything that anyone would sing about. Perhaps that is simply because I am a non-singer. Nirri has certainly found plenty to sing about, and what he is singing back to us, is us. Even death, in his laments, seems to become something that may have a mysterious meaning.

That lasts as long as the song does, perhaps a few heartbeats more. After that, I am unable to reconcile any of it again. But it helps, for the space of a song.

One winter night I woke and thought I heard him stirring. But when I listened, there was nothing. I felt about in the darkness with my hands, making sure that my family were still snuggled around me. And there they all were:

Ninshi, Ki-Ki, Lina, and Gorman, the one-year-old baby. All there and safe. I turned and went back to sleep.

The winter had seemed to be going … if not well, then at least not disastrously … when my sister Ninna began having cramps. I should add that she was pregnant by Hur, her third pregnancy and her third child with him, not counting Hurkar, who had been born to her sour-faced predecessor, Shulgi.

Such things as pregnancy and childbirth once used to be considered women's mysteries. They would barely be mentioned in our chronicles, which would usually only say that a father begat a child, the rest of the process being assumed, and being played out mostly hidden from men's eyes and ears. We used to have a dim idea that sometimes there was discomfort involved, but that was all. And in fact, birth, though painful, usually went more or less as expected in the days before the fall of the Tower. A woman could have ten or more children with no adverse effects, always providing the children's father was an ordinary human man and not, as in the ancient days, a god or a giant.

All this had changed when we fled for our lives from the Tower, and that on two counts. First of all, pregnancy

became more difficult and birth more perilous. The troubles
my Ninshi had with her second child, Lina, in the days when
we were fleeing the Scyths and then the giants, those
comprised the first difficult pregnancy I had ever witnessed.
Then besides becoming more difficult, birth and all that
attends it became less private. After a few winters in a
communal tent and a number of children born in the winter,
we men were no longer ignorant about what our wives went
through, either during the birth or during the days
immediately before and after. We had even helped
sometimes. Even the children, if they kept their ears open,
knew a great deal about the whole process, from conception
to birth to weaning.

So when Ninna started having birth pains, all of us
together felt the panic, not only the women. We knew how to
calculate, and we knew it was nowhere nearly time for her to
deliver. We immediately laid her flat on her back and piled
her about with furs to keep her as warm as possible. Our hall
had subsided about a cubit in one corner, making a natural
depression in the floor, and we bedded her in this, as if to get
below the baby and, as it were, catch and scoop it up, and
keep it within her body. This was probably a bad decision,
looking back on it. The hut subsided again in the spring,

which meant that we had put her on unstable ground, ground that encouraged movement. But it is so hard to make decisions that are wise all the time, especially when things are desperate. We do what is right in our own eyes, and it nearly always turns out to be a mistake, but what else can we do?

Mother had some herbs, some calming and others healing, that she had lovingly saved – in some cases for a very long time. These she administered to Ninna. In particular, I know she gave her some now-precious mint tea, to help with the pain and anxiety, and that she made her drink an infusion made from the bark of a bush that grew along the streams when we lived by the Stinking Sea … a tall, white-flowered bush with tart red berries. I remember we used to make love potions from these berries, and unless memory fails me, they were even used in the sweets at Hur and Ninna's wedding. Those berries were long gone, but Mother had saved the bark. Made into a tea, it was supposed to relax the muscles, and to stop cramping and bleeding.

It did no good. Ninna continued with her before-time birth. The worst of it was, she herself knew what was happening. One could see her trying to fight it, trying and having no more success than those of us who did not have the child within us.

Then she looked up at the circle of faces ringed around her – Hur, myself, Sari, and Mother, all sick with worry (Ninshi was occupying the children) – and said, as if to a group of stubborn donkeys, "A *sacrifice*. We must offer a sacrifice."

Hur and I looked at each other, and both muttered, "A sacrifice. Of course."

I had very little hope that it would accomplish anything, and looked at coldly, it was foolish to slaughter one of our animals. But I could not deny my sister this request, and for all its futility, it seemed like the right thing to do.

We went out to the sheltered animal pens. Almost none of our cows had survived, and not all the horses. Those that had, had begun growing extraordinarily thick fur every fall, and burrowing their heads down through the snows to get to the tough grasses, besides what we had harvested and saved to give to them. Likewise, certain of our goats had done well, by dint of turning nearly into different creatures.

It was one of those days so cold that the snow squeaked beneath our booths, our skin immediately stung, and our breath at once became icy clouds. Furthermore, the spirit curtains were hanging red in the sky, and they were singing. As soon as I saw that, I knew this sacrifice was in vain. It would be useless except for the roasted meat we would all eat.

But Hur looked at it and said, "That's the veil to the place my dad has gone … and your father, too, son of Golgal. They are both grandfathers to this baby. Perhaps they can save it."

I had never met Hur's father, but I doubted he could speak our language. Nor was I certain that we could be heard through such a veil by our own dead, or indeed by anything at all that would bear us good will. But this man's child, and perhaps his wife, were dying. I kept my questions to myself.

We selected a young male goat, one that had been born the previous spring. Hur held it up in his arms toward the sky, and then, because our hands were already too numb to be of much use, we brought it in to the antechamber of the great hut and did the slaughtering there. Red, my son's wolf pup, came and pranced about us with great interest, and we gave her some of the entrails, but forbade her to go into the main body of the house with them.

Then we brought the hairy little body of the goat to the main fire and there did the ceremony and then roasted it, a

pleasing aroma, in a corner of the fire on a bed of coals.
Ninna hobbled over and knelt there for the entire time it took
us to do the ceremony, and by the time the rite was finished,
the cramps had become so fierce that she was doubled over
on her hands and knees, weeping. And we waited for the
moment to come when she was able to rise, and then took
her by the arms and assisted her back to her bed of birth or
death. And there, not two hours later, her child was born. It
was a baby girl, perfect in face and limbs and body, born
dead. It never drew one breath.

Then there was a great rush to save the life of Ninna.
Mother was concerned that nothing of the birth be left inside
her, and that she not be allowed to bleed without limit. And
then, that evening descended into horrors such as I can
hardly tell of. But Mother saved her – Mother, and Sari
assisting her, not Hur's father nor my father Golgal (what
would they know of birth?), and certainly not the angry
spirits nor yet God. Mother told me later that it was
essentially a normal birth, except that it came too early.
Ninna was never in any great danger during the birth, she
said.

But my sister had carried, however briefly, something
dead inside her, and Mother took great care in the days that

followed that Ninna not fall ill. We gave her the best food and drink, and many concoctions. She did not fall ill – at least not in body – and Hur was so relieved that she was well, he had an easy time grieving for the lost child.

Ninna did not have an easy time. She held the baby for a few hours, wrapping it in the skin of the sacrificed goat. Then we told her to say goodbye to it, that we would take it outdoors and bury it. We did not tell her that with the ground so frozen, the most we could do was put it outside, allow it to freeze, and wait for warmer weather to bury it properly. And she did not seem to realize this, for she was hardly aware of such things as the weather.

But perhaps she sensed it with her spirit, for she began asking to hold her baby, again and again in the days that followed. We gave her a doll – I can hardly write of this – and she would hold it, content. Then she began to laugh, and sing, and talk to and about her baby. Then she was talking, with great joy, to people we had not seen in years. She apologized to Shulgi for allowing the baby to die, saying that perhaps we should have offered more sacrifices. Then she explained to Shulgi that she, Ninna, had married Hur, and hoped to have many more dead babies by him. And she seemed to be seeing Sut, and Golgal, and even Hur's father and mother, whom in life she had never met.

We kept her own children away from her, of course. Hur-kar was five years old at that time, Ai Li was three (old enough to understand madness), and little Magya had turned one in the summer and was just learning to walk. We left Ninna right in the very room where she had delivered (another mistake, perhaps ... we were making them by the handful), curtained it off, and kept the children well at the other end of the tent, with their cousins, Ki-Ki's puppy, their grandmother, and the Cushite. He had made the doll that we gave Ninna, and now he kept the children jumping and dancing to any number of little skippy tunes, and all the while his eyes, and Mother's, kept stealing tragically to the low end of the tent, the end where madness lay.

Sari, my brother Endu's wife, took the death of the baby very hard. She was newly pregnant by Endu, and she had helped, as I said, my mother with the aftermath of the birth. She would sit silently crying during the middle of the day. Endu made some attempts to comfort her, but they were futile. It seemed as if my family was falling apart before my eyes, like a badly made doll that had been given one too many rough embraces.

Ninna's madness progressed to the point where she was no longer talking or singing. She would just sit holding the doll, stroking it, humming. Hur and Mother were frightened about what was going on in her mind. I was frightened by how little she was willing to eat.

As Ninna drifted farther and farther away from us, Hur also became more and more distressed. Indeed, I have not seen him so dismayed before or since, not even when his first wife was killed by Scythians and he himself lost an eye. He would sit by my sister's bedside, trying to feed her, sweating, staring, not himself eating. Their children were for a time left with, essentially, no parents at all.

At times like this it is helpful to have extended family, and for a while they became Ninshi's and my children. Ninna had, after all, done the same for us before, during Ninshi's darker days.

One day, after another of his long watches, Hur suddenly gave a loud sort of belly-sob (very unusual for him), and jumped up and ran, just as he was, out of the tent. I threw on a fur cloak, snatched a second one to give to him, and ran out after him, not only for his own sake but because if Hur ever dies, our family will truly not take long to follow.

He was running steadily north. Even in his pained state he was a good runner, quick and graceful on his short legs. I caught up to him and threw the cloak about him and threw the hood over his head, and then I actually embraced him, to stop his wild motion.

"She is gone beyond the curtain," he said. "I have to go through it. Then she will be able to see me, and I can talk to her."

"Your children are not going beyond the curtain," I said. "They need you here. Don't leave them as orphans."

"I cannot reach her," he said.

"She may yet come back to us." I was not sure I believed this, but I didn't disbelieve it either. I had, at that moment, very few ideas about the future. "You asked your father, and he spared her life. Maybe he will give us back her mind as well. Your children need you," I said. "Come in."

Thank God, Hur is more sensible than his talk would sometimes make one think. He came in. But now that I had calmed him, I was the one who felt I couldn't stand it anymore. I set Mother to watching Hur and Ninna, then put my own cloak back on and went back outside. I had to talk to Father Tiras.

I am not now sure why it seemed so urgent to me that I tell him, right at that moment, that we would no longer follow him into the North. Nothing could be done until spring in any case, and taking a decision now was unlikely to save Hur or Ninna. But the mind of man despises uncertainty, and often, when we are twisting on a bed of pain, taking a firm decision can give a kind of relief. I think this may be the reason my father first threw in his lot with the Tower.

I blundered into Tiras' tent, not acting at all respectful because my face was numb with the cold. They received me kindly, setting me beside Tiras, who was sitting very close to a glowing hot bed of coals. Almost nothing else in the room was visible. I sat beside the heat and bent my face over it. As soon as my face thawed, I realized that I was weeping.

"What is the matter, my son?" said my grandfather.

"O my father ... I cannot follow you anymore," I said. But I choked it out, with weeping. "You have led us here, and you have said you were led by God. You have said that God has a place for us in the East or in the North. But we have been two years now in the North, and it is not a place my people can live, my father. With every month that passes,

life becomes harder to cling to, and there comes upon us …
more and more trouble and death …"

At this point, I had to stop speaking, for I was weeping
too hard to go on. I had given nearly the whole speech that
I'd planned to give my grandfather, but not in the manner I
had planned to give it. I had imagined myself hard and firm,
declaring that for the good of my family I must separate
from him. Instead it had come out like a string of a child's
fears and complaints, punctuated with sobs and choking.

Tiras sat in perfect silence, resting a leathery hand on my
back. I drew up my knees, put my head in my arms, and
gave myself over to grief. I had no choice but to do so. This
was an irresistible force, like the cold. I curled on my side
beside the deliciously warm coal pit, hugging my knees,
keening like an animal.

After many hours – so it seemed – he said quietly, "What
has happened?"

I sat up and I told him. I also reviewed the fact that we
had found a beach full of bones and had eaten dead meat
there. He had of course already heard this tale from his son
Abijay, but the meat did not bother Abijay and he may not
have told the tale as clearly.

When I was finished, I said, "I am very grieved, father, as you have seen. But that does not mean that I am not thinking clearly. I have truly made up my mind that I can no longer follow you and your sons wherever you go. This land is killing my family. I must lead them to a safer place, one where we have some chance to live as people should."

Tiras did not argue with this, although he did ask me again, much later when the weather became agreeable, whether my decision was still the same and whether I gotten the consent of all my party.

But at that moment, he only said, "It is your decision to make, together with your people. You are a true king, my son. That is why you have sat beside my fire grieving. You feel their griefs as if they were your own. That is what a king must do. Most of the time he must feel without feeling, so that he can still stand up and move about and speak and think. But in a dark time like this, when griefs come thick and fast, a king who has no wish to become hard and cold must take a little time to weep. He must seek out another king who feels that same burden."

And again he placed his slim brown hand, light as a bird, on my shoulder.

Then we sat there, feeling the warmth from the fire. At length he said,

"Your sister will come through this and live, probably. She has a good chance of coming back to herself as well. What she needs is to cry over her baby, as you have just done. But maybe she won't be able to do this until the spring, when she can go outdoors and have some privacy. Encourage her to cry, but wait for the spring. It is not far away, and many things may come right."

I stayed with him until the dawn, which was only a few hours away by then. When I returned to the tent of my own family, they had arrived at the solution on their own. Not that getting Ninna to cry mended all, it is not for this that I call it a solution, but that for her it was the beginning of new life again.

They had taken a smoking brand and held it close to her eyes, so that her eyes of their own began to water. And with this forced water, along came the true tears. And then Hur held her and they had a proper mourning, the two of them weeping as I had wept before Tiras. And it was not many days later that she set down her doll, looked about her, and said, "Where's my Magya?" And then for the first time in many weeks, she cuddled her one-year-old daughter.

CHAPTER 17
SMALL COMFORTS

Zillah

Summer again. Moving again. And here we are.

We had a horrible winter, one where it seemed that all of us had died inside. This seems to happen every year. In the winter, it seems that spring will never come, or that if it does, we will remain frozen. And then, in the warmth of summer, we find it hard to believe in the reality of the cold months. We tell ourselves that this time it will be different. It cannot really get that cold, we reason; it will not really last two and a half months past the best part of our food. Surely it was all in our minds, and this time we will resist it, this time we will keep our spirits up.

Well, it *is* all in our minds, but no less dangerous for that. It turns out that the human mind cannot stand its ground against relentless dark and cold and hunger. At least, normal minds cannot. A few, like Tiras' son Abijay, seem to be unaffected, but I think he was perhaps always dark and cold on the inside.

This winter was worse than many. My little girl lost her little girl, and we might have lost Ninna herself as well, if we had not happened to know the right things to do. It makes me fear for future winters. And all of us had been so excited for that baby. How many days were Nirri and I forced to inhabit our outer selves as puppets, playing games with the little ones while we struggled not to weep! But a few good things have come out of that horrible winter. For one thing, if I ever doubted it before, I am now absolutely assured of Hur's love for my Ninna. I had thought he married her as a glorified nursemaid. And because he was so clearly hesitant about marrying a highborn girl, and because she was clearly so besotted with him, I feared for my daughter's heart. I have grown easier in my mind with each year they are together, but this, this was the final proof … when Ninna went mad and Hur nearly joined her. Enmer said Hur wanted to go "beyond the curtain" to reach her. Surely that is the ultimate proof of love. Also that he did not blame her for the death of the baby. Many husbands would, but it did not seem even to occur to him. I have said it before, and now I say it again with even more conviction: Hur is a good young man.

If only Golgal were here to see what a good man Ninna has got for herself. I think he would be pleased … yes, even though he only knew Hur as a slave. Hur has been in our household almost from childhood, so we knew him quite well, at least Golgal did. (And if Golgal could see us now, you ask … what would he think of the way I am handling our guest? Well … were he here, I would not be having an affair with Nirri. Ah, you say, but what if Golgal can see us only … well, I do not think he can, for we buried him in the earth of his own farmstead, untold miles from here. But on the off chance that he can, he has, sadly, no longer any say in that. Death changes many things. We may bemoan it, but we cannot ignore it.)

The other good result from the awful winter was that Enmer determined we would not come this way again. He made the decision in the darkest moment, and he made it firmly, swearing he would not be swayed by the kindness of the summer, when the land wakes up again, when the birds fly, the grasses sway and the biting flies rise from the swamps in clouds. He communicated his decision to Tiras immediately – before even consulting us – but all of us were of one mind. Nirri, I believe, thought that all of us were mad ever to have come this way in the first place (not that we would consult him). But really, we were all of us ready to flee this northern plain as warriors flee a rout.

Then when spring came – well, a number of things happened, which I will tell about, but in the end, Enmer confirmed his decision with Tiras again. Having decided seems to have eased my son's mind. It is Enmer's nature to carry all the responsibility on his shoulders. He is, after all, the oldest son of Golgal. For a time he found it too heavy, or found himself too weak, and tried – at least in his own mind – to let Father Tiras shoulder all. But this, it turned out, he was unable to do. He still felt responsible, and felt that he was shirking. And when anything went wrong, he would tend to blame Tiras and to think that he could have avoided it by handling things differently. Perhaps he could not have, though, and he will find that out now. And then I must help him see that we live in a broken world, and that not all evil comes as a result of his mistakes.

I do my best to keep everyone's spirits up. It is not something I can do absolutely. I have no power that can stand against cold, darkness, attacks by wild beasts, or any of the thousand other things that might strike our group at any time and cause one or all to drop into an abyss of the mind. I can stop none of this, nor give any reason for it. But I do have a great deal of influence over the daily atmosphere in our little chain of interlocking households. My daily presence, the way I comport myself, the manner in which I attend to their sorrows or fail to do so, all will have an effect for good or ill. So I try to make sure, as far as I am able, that my presence is one that brings warmth, industry, order, rest, and peace.

Enmer is the hardest, frankly. He will not be comforted by any small thing, and I have no comforts to offer him that are not small, poor, halfway comforts. Hur keeps his own spirits up, for the most part. He is content that in this northern country we have seen wonders. He realizes that it was perhaps bad luck, and not the spirits or the cold, that made his baby die. For the young children, if we keep them fed and clothed and clean, and cuddled and listened to, they are happy. As for my son Endu, he tends to be moody, but most of the time, if you flatter his vanity, all is well.

And then there is Nirri. He also is surprisingly easy to keep content. In a way a man is easier to please if he has few expectations and few real pleasures.

I risked going to him but once this winter, when all were sleeping. (This was before Ninna had her tragedy.) I crept over and found that I did not need to wake him. He seems to be often wakeful in the night ... perhaps, I think, from pain. I felt about in the dark and put a finger on his lips to indicate *absolute silence*, and what did he do but seize my finger and begin sucking on it. And then with his other hand he began groping about my buttocks. Grinning in the dark, the rogue.

He knew it was I. But, the next day ... respectful, sober, even surly as ever.

With the women it is trickier. I must spend a great deal of time and energy talking with my daughters, working with them, ensuring that they feel appreciated and that they do not fight one another. This morning, for example, in the matter of cooking breakfast. Today it is a fine summer day and, though we are farther south than we were and hence the days are shorter, still it has been light outside for over an hour. We are cooking outdoors. On mornings like this, one's spirit seems just to expand. Except that is not true for my girls, for Ninna is still grieving and the other two are worried about what to think of each other.

Sari, Endu's wife, is very fond of cooking. But she is shy in her new place in the family and doesn't like to push herself forward. So I haven't given her charge of the cooking fire. Instead, I direct things. I set her to making the barley-cakes. Even middling pregnant as she is, no one has faster hands than she does as she shapes the cakes and then slaps them down on the hot stones. She has a round, flat, pretty face of a pleasant shade of milky brown. She does not turn this face toward me as she works, but I can see she is eager for my approval. I praise her quickness, and her plump mouth tucks back in a tiny smile.

Ninna follows her around the fire, scooping up the sizzling cakes with a flat bit of horn, flipping them over, then stacking them in a large serving-basket woven of swamp reeds. Ninna still has black periods when she finds it very hard to smile or to be present with the rest of us, but she is at that stage where she appreciates being set to a task, to take her out of herself. And the cakes are smelling so good, and this does the heart good as well. Small things. Small comforts.

Enmer's wife Ninshi would like, really, to be in charge of the cooking fire. Or else not to have to do anything at all but let the others cook her breakfast. Were I not here, she would be the senior woman in our group. She is still very young, but she doesn't realize it: after all, she started having children *ages* before the others!

Ninshi had "married down" – much as I hate that phrase – when she married my son Enmer. One would think that we would not have had class distinctions among us, being only one generation out from the Flood. Indeed, we were all kin, even back there in the city, and if you wanted to find out who someone was, it was not difficult to search and trace their family right back to Noah. It was only a matter of asking a few people a few questions. People tended to do this, and to marry within their clan. But even though we were all cousins, still people set about creating distinctions of high and low just as quickly as they could, and the way they did this was through the tower.

So, though Ninshi was a Japhethite and indeed a Tirasite, her father had been a priest of the great God, and her mother's brothers had all been very high up in the work of the tower. She came from a "good" family (much as I hate that distinction). She married Enmer because he was the oldest son of a Tirasite family and was a rising engineer, and because Golgal had known and worked with her uncles. So, when the tower ended, it was as big a loss for her as for any of us. She lost her maidservant Gia too, and not too long after they had both just given birth.

It has indeed been an adjustment for Ninshi, going from aristocratic city life, back to being essentially a simple farming family as we now are. All that business about good and less-good families was reversed again when the languages were stirred, bringing us each back to our own clan. All of which tells me that, though it was very hard on us, God knew exactly what He was doing.

I have set Ninshi to rendering a gravy out of the fat of some ducks that we roasted last night. It's a tedious job, with a lot of uncomfortable bending over the heat, but it's also one that takes some skill, and this pleases her. We will drizzle the barley-cakes with this gravy. There are also dried berries, that we found in the early summer as we passed through the great forests. Barley and berries and duck gravy, it is a feast! We will add goat's milk for the children and for Sari, who has a child within her. We will live like kings.

It is good to be back in a wholesome place, eating normal food again. We had a very odd experience earlier this year, with some very odd people.

Spring was coming and the animals were beginning to return, including vast herds of very great deer, some of which had the longest and oddest-shaped horns we had ever seen, even including our few sightings of unicorns and dragons. These deer did not seem to be familiar with people – we had not seen them the previous summer – and they would let us wander right up to them, as long as we did it slowly and in a meandering way. The children, especially Ki-Ki and Hur-kar, would delight in getting very close indeed, and they would watch them for hours. (We had forbidden them to approach within touching distance, for we had observed that the deer had very sharp hooves.) But we had to keep Ki-Ki's dog Red tied up at times like these, for should the herd catch one glimpse of her, and they would all be off. "Wolf! Wolf!" you could almost hear them bellowing.

On one almost miraculous day, Hur with his characteristic gentleness and love of beasts approached one of these creatures, stroked its fur (which he reported was like many northern animals' – rough on the outside, thick and soft beneath), and actually managed to milk it. Then we all had some of the milk – sweet, frothy, warm. Endu laughed, clapped him on the back, and said, "Hur, it's true … you can find food *anywhere*!" But Hur paid a price: he came back from that grazing ground with his little square face completely covered in insect bites. The rest of us were suffering too, from the insects, especially at night.

We discussed trying to tame one of these creatures and use them to replace our cows, which were all completely gone. But we already knew we were to be moving south, and these deer were headed north for the summer. We did not know how we would feed it, or keep it from running off to follow the herd. Let's save the idea for another year, said Hur. We need to know more about their range and so on.

Still, it was good to know there might be cows of a sort
waiting for us if ever we were forced to go north again.

But before all of this about the deer, I was saying that
spring was coming, and the food was beginning to return,
but we were not yet quite ready to depart. We were making
preparations. The younger men made trips to the distant
forest for young straight pine trees, that we might make
sledges and litters and the like. We hunted, and smoked and
preserved the meat on fires that were now, mercifully,
outside of our tents. We washed clothes and cut hair and
shook out blankets, turning the houses inside out and getting
rid of all the stink of winter.

Tiras' party, who were now so easy to visit, were doing
the same. All that separated our two camps now was some
soggy ground, chilly winds, and occasional unpredictable
showers – not blinding dark, as before, and killing blizzards.
In a few weeks it would be warmer for travel, and the ground
perhaps would be drier. Then, Enmer said, we would go.

It was on just such a breezy, wet, exhilarating day that
we observed a party of people approaching from the east.
Hur was no longer making extremely long, mounted patrols
as he used to do farther south, but he and my sons still took it
in turns to keep an eye out, once the snowstorms were no

longer our guard. We would guard the east side, and Tiras' people took the west, as they were camped to the west of us.

So it was that Endu came back from an east side circuit, running hard, and reporting, "There's a large herd coming, with banners!" And then, when we looked at him blankly, he stammered and said, "I mean, a group – a herd of – of people."

All our men grabbed their bows and hastened to go and see, and Ninna took off running to Tiras to warn them as well. And I could not restrain myself … I went with the warriors to see what I could see.

Though this plain and these swamps appear completely flat, yet there are gentle slopes in it, and if you get on one of these, you may see a fair distance. It was hard to judge distances in that flat country, but we had gotten better at this after several years of traveling with the herds, observing deer, and so on. What we saw was a group about as large as our own, which seemed to include women and children just as ours did. They had horses with them, but many of them were on foot, so they were advancing at a very slow pace.

The most striking thing was what Endu had called the banners. They had very long poles, and on these were mounted things that, as they drew closer, we could see were the skulls of beasts. These skulls had narrow strips of stuff dangling from them, not wide enough to be proper banners (which would be hard to control, anyway, in that wind). And some of these skulls seemed to be wearing some sort of shabby crowns. They had two of these poles stationed at the front of their party, two at the middle, and two at the back; six altogether.

By this time Tiras had arrived at the low hill east of the camp. The younger men helped him forward to a place where he could see well, standing on either side of him, ready to shield him if the need should arise. He squinted at the approaching force, and immediately smiled and said, "They are not here for war. Let us try and talk to them."

Indeed, it was obvious they were not coming to attack. They were coming by day; they had all their weakest people with them; their men were on foot; and there were those standards. In those days, immediately after the fall of the Tower, armies did not ride out with banners or standards as – we were told – they had sometimes done before. War was all about stealth and speed. I am not sure what those strange skull-poles were intended to mean. Later we speculated that maybe they stood for each of the families within the strangers' tribe. Or perhaps they were merely meant to

announce their group, or perhaps to invoke their gods.
Certainly we found them very intimidating when we saw
them up close, a few hours later.

"If we are to talk with them," said Abijay, "We should go
out to meet them. Do it a bit farther from the camp, in case
things get ugly."

"And we should do it quickly," said Melek. Indeed, they
were coming closer and closer. "We should ride out to them,
so that we can pick the point of meeting."

"But if we *ride* out," said Tiras, who had been nodding at
his sons' suggestions, "They may think they are under attack.
And then it could become war indeed. Let us send out a
woman, along with whoever else goes to meet them, to show
that we mean peace."

"I will go," I said.

My uncle inclined his head.

We had all been peering very hard at the group of
strangers, for we were eaten up, of course, by curiosity. Now
all our peering had borne fruit. We could see that they were,
in general, taller than we were, including the women. This
we judged from their size relative to the horses. Moreover,
many of them had very pale-colored hair. The women's hair,
and the men's too, was long, and in some cases unbound, not

in buns like those worn by our women. Nearly all the men had long beards, some dark, some red, some yellow. They seemed to be a very *hairy* lot of people. It would have made me smile, except that we were all so nervous.

"Oh my father," said a very nervous voice suddenly. I turned and saw that Hur was addressing Tiras, with a shamefaced deference I had not seen him use in a long time.

"Yes, my son?" said our patriarch.

Hur's face beneath his eye patch was flushed as he said, "My Mom had yellow hair like that. My Dad ... he was pretty hairy too. Please let me go with those who go out to meet them. Perhaps I'll be able to talk to them."

He stopped there, but Tiras heard the unspoken hope and voiced it: "And maybe, one of them will be your mother?"

Hur looked at the ground, and all of us stayed respectfully silent. We all knew – Hur included – that there was very little chance that one of this strange group would be his mother. Yet each of us knew that, in his position, we would do the same. We would want to find out, even if there was only a slim chance.

I looked over at that young man – still very young, for all we had lived through – and felt a pang of guilt. I didn't remember ever hearing him speak about his family. Nor did any of us ever ask him, before this. But now he was my son-in-law, and that yellow-haired woman, if she still lived, would be to me a sort of sister. Grandmother to my grandchildren. I wished we had thought to help him search for her, back at Si Nar.

In the end, we left it that the greeting party would consist of Tiras and his son Melek, and from our family, Hur and myself. Ninna was not happy to hear this. "Why does it always have to be Hur?" she wailed, in a voice much higher than usual. But I said to her, "My daughter, we will do our best to keep him safe. And you know that if anyone can get through to a pack of strangers, it is Hur."

We prepared ourselves and mounted. I was wearing loose leather trousers and was riding astride the horse like a man, but I had unbound my long, blue-black hair and pulled it forward over my shoulder, so that they could see what I was. We rode out of the camp, and the eyes of everyone followed us. Even those of Nirri, who had dragged himself out of the tent to enjoy the sunshine. We left, of course, a great number of warriors back at the camp ready to defend the little ones if things went wrong. And the horses were nearby with some provisions so that, in the worst case, the survivors might make a getaway.

It was strangely like a procession, riding out at a walk,
the four of us keeping in formation as best we could over
that pathless ground, me with my hair unbound and
fluttering. I had not been in a procession since my girlhood,
in the city. We hoped that this was not one of those
processions that would end in human sacrifice.

Just before we came within hailing distance, a small
swamp intervened between us, and both parties came to a
standstill. It was now about an hour or two after noon. The
light was hard and clear; we could see the individual reeds in
the swamp, and the pale sky reflected between them. The
party of strangers drew and up spread out along the other
side of the swamp. The skulls were lowered a bit and then
were evenly distributed along this line. And now we could
see the people quite clearly. They were a fierce-looking
people. They had bones not only on their standards, but bits
of bone bored through their ears, and even some noses, and
bones or teeth or claws were bound about their wrists and
waists, fastened as beads around braids, and hung about their
necks.

We had made a bit of an effort at color in our clothing
over the years, dying wool as best we could with various
plants and things, but these strangers' clothing seemed to be

all fur and leather, with bones their only decoration. Furthermore, with their hard, knobby faces and generally pink skin, the sun and wind had not been kind to them. Many had raw-looking red patches on their cheeks and noses, or even bits that were black with frostbite. Some of their womenfolk looked like warriors, and I began to wonder if my presence would really signal peace after all.

Still, despite their ugliness, our eyes devoured them hungrily, because it had been a long time since we'd gotten a good look at a different kind of human being. And they of course were doing the same to us.

Grandfather Tiras dismounted from his horse. He took a few strides forward, wearing his grey-white turban, robes flapping about his legs, with both hands raised and held, palms forward, up beside his ears.

In response, one detached from their party. He was very tall, with a long red nose and startling blue eyes visible even at this distance. Though he had been on foot, he now mounted a stallion, and advanced, at a slow walk, straight into the middle of the swamp.

Tiras withdrew, looked up at Hur, and gently slapped his horse's shoulder. Hur then imitated the stranger, advancing at a slow walk into the water. His mount was not happy about this, but he had her well in hand and helped her pick her way along a few steps of soggy bottom. Since she did not take fright, I can only imagine that Hur was exercising that almost supernatural calm that he seems able to summon from time to time.

Looking back upon it, this might have been a sort of test on the part of the stranger. He wanted to see if we had any horsemen among us who could make a horse walk into the water. If only we could have told him how, only a few years ago, we had crossed a sea with them!

Finally, the two of them came as close to the center as their two horses were willing to go. All of those present, on both sides of this middle ground, were watching with bated breath. Hur looked comically short beside the other, but I saw several of their people catch sight of the eye-patch and give little starts, realizing, I suppose, that here was a small but dangerous man.

Then Hur spoke, and the other answered, but alas, I understood Hur perfectly and understood the stranger not at all. Hur had said, "We are sons of Japheth through Tiras. Who are you?"

And the stranger had said – well, I cannot remember even one word of it, nor could I tell the words apart, for they blended in to each other.

Hur sat very still for a moment. He bowed his head, and then spoke a single word that I did not catch. He was trying, we found out later, to bring back even a word or two of that language we had before, the speech that all men had shared, the only one he had ever spoken with his mother. But he was unable.

The stranger did not respond to his single, half-remembered word. They went on for a while speaking to one another each in his own language, and then they fell to making gestures. Meanwhile, Hur was looking all the while at the faces that had so conveniently lined themselves up along the shore opposite. And what he discovered was what we had all expected. His mother was not among them.

We managed, somehow, to invite them all to a feast, without saying one word they could understand. Once it became clear we were not going to kill one another, Tiras had someone run back to the camp for a bit of food to offer their leader. And then he made inviting gestures with his arms.

All of us were looking at him doubtfully, as if to say, "Truly, my father? You want to bring them back to our camp?" But he was right that eating together is the quickest and clearest way of forming a friendship – or, at least, an agreement not to be enemies – and they had women and children with them who were surely hungry. And rather than cooking for them some ways outside of camp, which might have sent mixed signals and would also have been inconvenient, it did make more sense just to bring them and seat them around our central fire.

But I could not ride ahead and warn my daughters to start cooking on a much larger scale, because the strangers were picking their way cautiously about the swamp, and we had to escort them. It might have frightened them if different ones of us had suddenly starting riding off in a hurry.

Thus, it was quite exciting when we all got back to camp and Ninna came rushing out to meet us, and I told her we were going to have to do some butchering and roasting. She raced back and told Sari and Ninshi and the children. "Why? Why?" they all asked.

A surprise guest for a feast. That has really not happened for a very long time.

Fortunately for us, we are quick and efficient at butchering by now. To take a number of goats, to kill and bleed them, and get them cut up and roasting, with everyone working, takes us only about the fifth part of an hour.

Then we made some precious bread, which turned out almost to have been wasted effort as the guests barely knew what to do with it. The younger ones among them seemed never to have seen it before. But we also made a stew – more familiar to everyone – with root vegetables and green plants and the tasty bits from the meat, to add flavor. And we were not the only ones contributing. They brought out from their skin bags milk, and when we tasted it, we knew at once they also had tried to tame the herds of great deer.

I wished we had some fruits to serve them. When I was a girl, fresh fruits were always an important part of a feast. But this was before we had found the berries. We did have beer, however – sour and of bad quality, but it was beer – and we offered that. And it did have a little effect on them, for they had been sitting very stiff-looking on the ground, with a few of their warriors standing by, and after drinking a little beer they relaxed visibly and began to smile.

So we had our strange feast. The strangers sat in the inner ring around the main fire, our head men were there with them, serving the meat and watching them eat, and rest of us darted in from behind, attending to needs. Their children began by looking around in wonder. Then, when they got a little in their bellies and got happier, they began to sneak off and play with our children. The little girls wove little houses out of grass, and the boys were petting and wrestling with my grandson's pet dog, Red.

Tiras tried to speak to them, and you can believe I was paying attention while that was happening. We had not tried to speak to any foreigner since the languages were confused, which was when there began to be such things as foreigners. Well, save for Nirri, but I was the only one who ever spoke much to him, and that was usually one-way; I did not learn his words.

I had not realized how difficult it would be with our guests. Even after an hour of listening, it was impossible to pick out the individual words from a solid stream of their speech. The only way we – or they – could even *hear* a word to learn it, was if it was spoken singly and clearly, left to stand by itself. Any added explanation, and the word would go right out of one's head.

I learned exactly one word from them, and that was their word for "west." Evidently, they were going west, and it was repeated, with pointing, many times. I believe Tiras tried to get their words for the other directions as well.

After eating, their men got up and did a dance. Someone produced a bone flute (which Ki-Ki studied very hard in order to copy later), and someone else brought out a hide drum. The dance worried us at first because it seemed very warlike. After a little while, we guessed that they were re-telling their escape from the Tower. Their story seemed, like ours, to have included plenty of cowering, and plenty of running and falling down. Then the dance moved on to other things. We could not tell all that they were saying to us, but we gathered at the very least that they must be hunters of some extraordinarily large kind of animal.

We had no such narrative dance to offer. But Tiras beckoned me and said quietly in my ear, "Now we must give them some music and, if possible, we must dance together. That will make us even better friends."

He is right that dancing together makes people friends. But none of us have any gift for it and we haven't really danced in ages – or ever, that I could remember, except for the children capering about when Nirri plays something lively.

"Go to your prisoner," said my uncle. "Tell him to play something lively."

Nirri was sitting, as always, well out of the action, near the hut door. I went in and brought his lute out, and handed it to him. Then I bent to place my shoulder under his arm, that I might help him closer to the fire. But he did not immediately rise.

"Why?" he said.

I stood up, stunned. Indeed, if I had lifted him already, I would probably have dropped him. I had no idea that he knew that word. I suppose he must have learned it from the children. We have several little ones now who are at that age when they are forever asking why.

"Because," I stammered, not certain of how much he would understand, "Father Tiras wants you to play something lively so that we can dance with the strangers."

"Why?" he said again.

I found myself feeling annoyed. I did not really know what he was asking (about the dance itself? or the whole feast?), nor did I fully know why we were doing either. And the small amount that I did know would take some time to explain, even to a native speaker of our language. I was not sure he had a right to make such a demand on my time, especially since he was unlikely to understand my answer. Also, everyone was waiting for him to play us some music.

I looked at him to see if he were asking it on purpose to annoy me, but saw no trace of a grin.

"Are you asking why you must play music?" I said.

He paused for a moment, as if thinking, and then said, "No."

"Are you asking why we have feasted these strangers?"

Pause. "Yes."

"Because we are being kind to them," I answered shortly, "Just as we were kind to you." And then I added, as I again hefted him with his long ropey arm over my shoulder, "And Father Tiras does not mean you to play one of your sad songs, that were written just for us. He wants a quick one, so we can all dance."

I am not sure how much of this he caught, but I didn't want him trotting out one of his carefully crafted laments for these people we had just met. Some of those are treasures.

Endu came and helped me, and we got him close in, where everyone could hear him. We made him understand that we wanted a dance tune by clapping out a rapid beat. Like a true musician, he gave us what we asked and more, taking some of the lighthearted tunes he'd made for the little ones and picking them up, and alternating with slower passages so the dancers could catch their breaths. And before very long, the strangers' drummer picked up on it and began to keep time.

At first it was only the children dancing around the outer ring. Then some of our young people – we have a few from Tiras' side – joined in, and then, many, many people, though not all, began to dance as best they could. I was among them, I don't mind admitting. Even if you are not a dancer, the music gets into you. What we did, I believe, was mostly stomping. That was the best we could do.

Afterward, I found myself missing my son Sut with a sharpness that it had been long since I'd felt. This was the sort of thing we he was good at, the sort of thing he enjoyed. He'd have been doing leaps and tumbling, right across the fire as likely as not. He would have gotten everyone dancing. But at the time, I was not missing him, because I was caught up in the joy of the music and of the fellowship that we feel when we enjoy music together and when we move our bodies in time – even in clumsy, error-ridden time – with others.

By the end of the feast, we had done this. We, strangers, had moved in time together, and would now find it hard to kill one another. And then we all laughed when Red, and some of their dogs who had crept close to steal the food-scraps, heard something in the music that seemed to call to them, and they began to howl.

Unfitting as it may sound, all this happened in broad daylight. Our feast was a mid-day meal. Thus there came, eventually, an hour of confusion when the feast was clearly over, but we had still many hours of daylight left, and we did not know what to do. Most of us (Tiras, perhaps, excepted) did not want to invite these strange, bone-covered people and their skulls on sticks to spend the night anywhere near by, let alone within, our tents. But it is impossible for us to say to a guest with whom we have feasted, "Now you must be on your way." Even if we would prefer that the guest be on his way, we could no more say so than defy nature by floating straight up into the air.

It is hard to read people who are so different from yourself, but it did seem to me that they also did not want to stay in our camp. Finally, they solved this problem by standing up and giving us gifts. My son Enmer was given the bone flute that his son had coveted, and I was proud of how well he hid his disgust. Tiras was given a spear. We acquired a number of lovely necklaces made out of large teeth, and things like that.

Then we had a mad scramble to find things to give them that we could part with. It was not too difficult, for in the case of some of our winter gear, we had all summer ahead of us in which to make it again. We gave away a spare bow, a number of lovely horse-blankets, and Nirri's old, rather crude lute (he had just crafted himself a new one).

Then there were a few gestured lessons in how to use the gifts. Ki-Ki made sure to get a bit of instruction from the player of the flute, and Nirri actually put his arms around one of the skinny strangers' shoulders, to show him the right finger positions for picking.

Then, much to our relief, they picked up and moved themselves off to the west. They were gone well before the sun set. They did not actually make it out of sight before they stopped to set up their camp, for these plains are wide. Observing them from a distance, their tents looked only like little dark humps, but Hur had seen some of the stores they were dragging, and he said he thought their tents were made of hide and very large bones or tusks.

Dusk fell, and we lit our cooking fires. The strangers did not light any – I suppose they were still full from the feast –

but it was not difficult to imagine them standing before their tent flaps, raising a hand toward our fires, and saying to one another, "You can see it right over there. The camp of our friends."

CHAPTER 18
SAYING GOODBYE

Enmer

We said goodbye, late this past spring, to Grandfather Tiras and most of his people.

It was a strange experience, saying goodbye. In the – hard as it is to believe – *seven years* since judgment fell and scattered the peoples, we have not once had the experience of saying goodbye to friends or family, of being able to wave at their tiny figures dwindling in the distance, knowing they were going on a long journey, knowing that we would probably never see them again. People have left on trips for hunting and scouting, of course, but we generally don't say goodbye when they do. Fear of bad luck seals our lips. And there have been many deaths these years, and then we may stand by a pyre and bid their spirit farewell, but that also is not really a proper goodbye.

Yes, it has been seven years. It happened in the spring, so we have just passed the seven-year mark.

Tiras is as much a prophet as ever. He now believes there is a place for him and his people in the West. He gathered from our strange visitors that to the west lay great forests, full of timber, fresh water, and game. However, it seems that many people are heading that way, so in order to find a place of their own, they will almost certainly have to fight. He brought with him Abijay and his sons, for they love war. Also, they are planning to stay well to the north on their journey, and I have vowed not to do that for another winter.

We are planning to head south, but not back to Si Nar. South and east. We may have to fight – probably will – but it is not as certain. And now we know that when we meet other people, it is possible to make friends.

They were ugly, the strangers, as shockingly ugly as anyone I've ever seen, and they were so much bigger than we; I wondered if they had perhaps interbred with giants. My mother thinks it is because they have been living on game. Meat makes people tall. Also, though Mother is tall for a woman, as a group we have always been on the shorter side, compared to the bulk of men, even among those at Si Nar.

These strangers were also built differently from us. They were loose-limbed, big-featured, and almost all their men were hairy. We have a few beards in our group, but they are thin as a rule. My father, when he was alive, had a long, straight, smooth, lush black beard, but almost no hair on his upper lip, and Tiras is the same way. Now in our late thirties, Endu and I still have trouble growing hair on our faces. We generally pluck out the few that do grow. Even our Cushite, though he is from a different stock and has a curly black beard to be proud of, has an upper lip with only a few neat black lines. But these bone men ...! Every one of them, over the age of about eighteen, seemed to have a bush sprouting not just from chin, but from upper lip, to the point of obscuring their mouths, and sometimes from the neck as well. Some had hair that came so far up their cheeks, and brows that hung so shaggily down, that their little bright eyes appeared to be peeping out from a cave covered, as it were, by a thicket, reminding us of the eyes of that animal that we do not name. Endu swears he saw one of their women with a beard as well.

It does seem that all that hair might protect a man's face, when the harsh wind blows. I prefer to cover up with a woven scarf, myself.

The strangers mostly had light-colored eyes, as yellow, green, or more commonly, pale blue, looking out from faces that were white, pink, or sometimes dark brown. As for their clothing and their gear, I can hardly describe it. It was hard to believe that these people, or at least their elders, must have been city dwellers like us only seven years ago. They looked to me and Endu as if they'd crawled out of the very earth, and that on emerging, their first stop had been the Sea of Death. Whether they loved death or were trying to ward against it I do not know, but the entire time we were eating, those animal skulls were rocking gently on their poles, with their strings of dried grasses and flowers fluttering down from them like a grim bride's veil. If those were their gods, they did their job well: we were rattled. At least, I was rattled.

Yes, I know. I am a coward, afraid of everything in heaven and on earth, whether it's lights in the sky or skulls on a stick. My aged mother is braver than I am. I don't need anyone to tell me. Endu was rattled too; he kept mocking them to me out of the corner of his mouth.

We had a little practice farewell, there at the edge our camp, when we said goodbye to the strangers. I clasped arms with the tall one – for our leaders and their leaders did each other honor – and as I grasped his brown forearm, I looked down and saw a white scar there that was very clearly a human bite mark. And the hair stood up all along my own arm at the thought of what they'd been through.

Yes, I know. Coward again.

We kept a good watch that night, believe me, just in case they changed their minds and decided to come back and raid us after all. But they did not, and the next day we saw them moving on again.

One thing we did discover from them is that it's possible for people to learn each other's languages. We were not sure about this, previously. It had been impossible to communicate with anyone else at Si Nar. Any kind of shouted greeting or question only seemed to provoke an attack. We had thought that perhaps the curse was permanent. But now it appears that people can reverse it, if they wish to, albeit only with slow, hard work.

Tiras got a great many words from them. He learned their words for sun, west, north, bone, meat, milk, and their word for *great deer*. Also, Ki-Ki taught one of their little boys to say "dog" and my Ninshi got the word for *baby*. The great deer seem to be very important to them; they came up many times in "conversation." We would signify them to one another by putting hands to our heads like antlers.

We gathered that the strangers live mostly by these deer, and that they were following them west. In fact, that is what we now call them among ourselves. When it is not "the bone people," we call them "the people of the great deer." And we talk of them a great deal, because they are the most sensational thing that has happened to us as a whole group, in a long while. We have suffered – though our sufferings have been fewer than they could have been – and we have seen wonders, most of them rather horrible at the same time: the stinking sea, the great plains, the bone beach, the spirit lights, the long winters that feel as if they belong to another world. But none of this has given us as much to talk about as the visit of the deer people. However repugnant we may have found them, we still found them interesting, more interesting, for my part, than anything in nature. They were men like us, unmistakably made in the image of God.

The appearance of the deer people seemed to give Father Tiras courage to go through with his plan of moving west. He gave his sons and the other members of his family free choice to go with him or to go with me as they preferred. This was lucky, for in this way we gained a number of families, including Melek with his wife and his half-grown children. Melek, though slightly older than I am, joined on the understanding that he would be only an equal with Hur and Endu and me. We also gained Damai, a solid man, heavily scarred about the face, who is much older than his second wife, having lost to the Scythians his first wife and two teenaged daughters. He is a quiet man, and seems to be a natural farmer. Indeed, it seems as if the quieter, more peace-loving families sorted themselves to come with us, while the bolder ones went with Tiras. I am not certain this is a good thing. I am not certain that I will be able to give them the peaceful life they hope for.

We did a leaving ceremony on a heartbreakingly beautiful late spring day, a day when the gentle sun, breezes, and smells of wildflowers made it seem as if we were mad to go our separate ways, for surely this was a world in which nothing bad would ever happen. I hardened myself, thinking of the winter we had just passed, of death snowing down on us, death singing prettily in the skies, and of the little, smelly tent in which were housed horror and madness.

We sacrificed some animals, had a feast, and then made up a ceremony to represent our leave-taking. We broke a number of clay cooking pots and things of that sort, showing that, though we would not forget one another, we were no longer one household, and we could not be held accursed for failing to carry out household duties to those from whom we'd severed, who would, by the end of the summer, be very, very far away. We asked God to witness our parting, to make it a good one, like a clean break in a bone that heals well. We even asked that we might not meet again soon, for if we did that, it would mean that something had gone very wrong.

"But perhaps we will meet again, far in the future," said Tiras, as he embraced me, "In a hundred years or so, on the other side of the world."

We were still accustomed to a world in which people lived hundreds of years and were able to accomplish many things in that time, such as the founding of nations or cities.

So now we have been traveling south again, trying to see how far we can get before it is time to stop and build and plant barley. We have been going through the great forests – and they are very great, with endless evergreen trees (good for building), much game, many wolves and bears, and also many biting flies.

Speaking of people being able to reverse the curse by learning each other's languages, that has finally been proved to us in another way as well. After seven years with us, our Cushite prisoner Nirri has finally reached the speaking level of a two-year-old child. He has learned the word "why."

He does not use it often, at least not with me. I believe he realizes it's an impertinent question, as likely to earn him a slap on the cheek as anything else. Some people enjoy being teased with "Why?" But, I am not one of them. Occasionally, though, there really is a need for him to know something, and then we do answer, and when we do, he listens intently, just like a two-year-old child would.

Someone says, "We have got no game today," and Nirri asks, "Why?"

"Oh," they laugh, and say, "that's a funny story …."

And soon we are all hearing about the misadventures on the hunt.

"Grandfather Nirri …" (everyone calls him that now), "… I need you to hold Hur-Kar for a moment while I tend to his bruised foot."

"Why?"

"A horse stepped on him."

"Ah."

"Grandfather Nirri, can you weave pictures of a pack of wolves into a blanket?"

"Why?"

"It's for Ki-Ki. He loves wolves now because of Red."

And then we see a number of grey woven wolves and one red one.

At times like this, you can see him paying attention to all the words. His face is a bit more guarded than a child's would be, but the eyes glitter with curiosity. So he is not quite the great fool that I thought him. I wonder, since he now appears able to learn our language, why it has taken him so long to do it. Perhaps the confusion remained in the air for some years after the fall of the tower, or maybe he just had to get over his donkey-like stubbornness first.

As always, it is the children who are the most patient to answer his questions, which are so inconvenient for everyone else. Indeed, they delight to do it. It is the only time they know more than somebody, especially some older person, and they love to flaunt their knowledge. They will even tell him the words for items. And, though one moment they are afraid of him (as well they should be, and I encourage this), the next moment they are giggling because he needs something and they are making him say "please" before they will fetch it.

It was Mother who first taught him weaving. She would set up the loom (we don't have a great huge loom, of course; he couldn't work at such a one, and anyway it would be no good for travel), guide his hands, answer his occasional "Why?" (which in this case means "How?") with a demonstration.

I thought she was wasting her time. After all, we have plenty of women around who know how to spin and weave. But she said, "My son, this may be very useful to us later." And I believe it will be. It is a way for him to contribute a little something. Though he is still an awful drain on our resources, Mother is right that we cannot simply toss out anyone who isn't strong enough to contribute a full adult's share of the work all the time. After all, nearly everyone goes through periods when they must be cared for. If we demanded perfect productivity, what would become of our little ones? What would have become of Ninna last winter? Or even, from time to time, of me?

There are other problems that any leader has to deal with, and one of them came up in the autumn, after we had settled and built (we'd left planting too late, except for a few vegetables). Sari, my brother Endu's wife, had had her baby, and after a woman has had a baby, she is entitled to a complete rest for several months. At least, as much of a rest as it is possible to give her. Her job is to keep the baby and herself alive, which means mostly just sleeping, eating, and frequent trips to the river. The other women generally cover her duties, and they make her special food to build up her strength again.

So, Sari had had a baby, her first, a son, and she had named it Jai. It had a lot of black hair which was already very long, and a face that Mother said looked just like Endu when he was born. On a cold grey day, I found her sitting near the fire, nursing Jai, and weeping quietly. I didn't think she would have anything to weep about. No one had died recently, her baby had been born healthy, and as far as I knew she had been taking her rest.

I thought perhaps she was weeping for no reason, as women sometimes do in the early days after their baby, especially while they are feeding it. That's a thing that depends on the woman. Ninshi always gets sad, for some reason, when nursing a child. Ninna gets calm and happy and turns to look at you with power and strength like a goddess.

So I didn't think much of these tears, but then when Sari saw me passing, she quickly stiffened and wiped her face and tried to hide them. I thought that was strange.

"How are you, sister?" I asked. "Are you all right?"

And the more she insisted that she was indeed all right, the more it became obvious that something serious was wrong. I did not want to press her, for she was getting more and more distressed, but I did want to know whether there was a rift developing in my household. To be honest, I wondered if she'd had a falling out with Ninshi. If so, I would ask Mother to handle it. I put this to her, and she denied it, getting more and more panicked, and then her baby began to fuss. And she was more afraid of waking him, apparently, than she was of defying me, for at last she told me her trouble.

She peeled back the blanket, pushed up her sleeve, and showed me a great purple bruise on the soft skin of her upper arm. In the middle of it were two little cuts. Those were from my brother Endu's long fingernails.

She told me that he had been angry the other day, because she was not cooking for him. He had pinched her arm like this, and thus led her forcibly to the cooking fire.

"Please don't say anything to him," she told me, her aspect rather hard now that she had made her decision. "I know he has a right to beat me. I will be a good wife to your brother. I will get up and do more, and keep him happy. You see, older brother, I have not argued with your wife, I only showed you this to prove it was not that."

"Don't worry," I told her, "I won't make trouble between him and you."

And then I walked away quickly, with the blood rushing in my ears. I was furious with my brother. I did not doubt Sari's word. I had witnessed before now Endu becoming cruel with those fingernails. But Sari was not a dog, nor a slave, nor a careless builder nor a lazy fieldworker. She was his wife ... who, moreover, had just borne him a son. I thought he ought to be grateful for that, and give her understanding instead of cruelty.

To Sari's relief I said nothing that night, but as soon as I had the opportunity I brought the matter to my mother.

"What can I do?" I asked her. "I'm the clan chief, but I can't kick my brother out for beating his own wife."

"Can you not?" said Mother, and she looked so grim and frightening that it made me glad I had always been patient with Ninshi. "Well, *I* can."

She went and examined the evidence, which was still visible on Sari's upper arm, and then she went and had a very stern word with Endu. I believe she actually threatened to exile him. He then felt very put-upon, and came to me whining that Mother was being harsh with him, and so then it was both of us telling him that we did not find his behavior honorable. He grew more and more sulky as we spoke.

"You must not think I will side with you because you are my son," said Mother. "Sari is of our blood too" (she was a cousin, as were all in Tiras' group), "and anyway, the moment you married her, she became my daughter. It is my job to protect her."

"I would think you would side with *justice*," muttered Endu.

"Sari hasn't done you wrong, brother," I now put in. "I think you have no idea what life is really like for a married man. Women don't come back to us immediately after having a baby. Their life is consumed for a while by the child. When the child gets older, when he starts sleeping, *then* she will come back to you. If you want to have a lot of children" (as all of us did) "you will have to understand this. And," I added, "if you treat her kindly now during her time of weakness, she will feel more warmly toward you later."

Endu glared at me. Then with a visible effort he relaxed his shoulders, sighed, and even forced out a small bit of his charming white smile. "All right," he said, "perhaps I got impatient. I only – I wanted things to be good. I wanted my wife to be as good as all the others."

"She is, brother," I assured him. "She is only doing exactly what women always do. And look, she has given you a son! And she is very beautiful, Endu," I added, pointing out the obvious in order to flatter him a bit.

"*And*," said Mother severely, "I will be watching you."

And she stalked off, without any flattering words or any motherly embraces.

Endu grinned at me and gave a little shrug as if we were little boys and Mother had just beaten him for stealing fruit or something like that. But this was nothing like that. It was all I could do not to glare witheringly at him and open the conflict again. I stared at him stonily for a second and then took my leave.

We had tried to do all this quietly, but everyone knew a bit about what was going on. In a tribe, they always know. And in future years, we did watch Endu. Sometimes he would be all right with Sari, though a little breezy and perhaps not very understanding. He was always under the impression that he was doing her a great favor by being her husband. Then whenever anything put pressure on their family – someone humiliated him, or we were moving camp again, or, most often, whenever she had had another baby – he would become dissatisfied, then fed up, and would begin to practice these little cruelties. It was never a case of a loud, dramatic beating that roused everyone in the tent, but usually someone would overhear something, and we would again have to put a stop to it. Mother kept a very sharp eye on him, as she did on everyone. I did so as well … sometimes. But there were black days, even after that, when I really couldn't see beyond my own nose.

And there were many times when I felt my spirit reaching out in friendship to Endu, for we were brothers from of old. He and I hunted together, we stood guard together, we had many opportunities to build things together, just as we had been doing all our lives. I wanted to enjoy him, I wanted to be his friend. When he was not sulky, he could be so funny and charming, like Sut. This friendship was precious to me, and I didn't want to give it up for the sake of a woman (for all that Sari proved to be a sweet person, a good aunt and sister, and a perfectly decent member of the clan). At times like this I would try to drop my guard and my disapproval and let myself laugh with him, telling myself meanwhile that Mother would see to it that he treated the women well, and that for my part, he was a perfectly fine friend with us men. But usually I was unable to truly relax with him. I would feel myself checked, as a horse is checked by a rein.

Much as I wanted to, I could not forget that this one, who was so good to me when we were strong together, was cruel to the weak whenever he thought he could be. And I could not bring myself to enjoy his fellowship because of this.

CHAPTER 19
GRANDFATHER

Nirri, seven years later

I have really become one of them now. "Grandfather Nirri," I am to the young ones. They have no idea that I'm not their grandfather at all, but a stranger. I think they attribute my strangeness, my isolation, to the fact of being crippled. I am an august, mysterious figure to them, as well as a pitiful figure of fun. How these can both be true at the same time I can't understand, but they are, and this is just the tonic my heart needs to heal the wounds that are inflicted on my dignity every day by my crippled state.

After a few difficult years in the far north, we are back in the Gentle Mountains again. And now they are preparing to move again. East, always east. There is a reason for the decision. It followed days of discussions this past winter, almost all of which I could not follow. I think, frankly, they just like moving about … and frankly, I like it too, though it sometimes results in short commons for a year or so afterward. For myself, it gets me outdoors, sometimes on a horse if I am lucky. Also, moving gets easier every time we do it. Our tents are better each year, the children are older, everyone knows their place and their task.

Usually they move in the spring, as now. It can still be very cold, but not bitterly so. There may be snow, but the sun is warm during the day and we avoid the sapping heat of summer. We have a narrow window in which it's comfortable to move, so we have to make good time.

They had built a sort of village here with many wooden cabins, some large, some smaller. Enmer and his family have a larger, more visible lodge on the central clearing. It is built up on a rock foundation and you approach the porch by several steps, making it clear that this is the leader's house. In the back are kitchens and so forth; in the clearing in front of the lodge is the great fire-ring for our gathering fire. The rest have houses ringed round the edge of the clearing, or scattered back in the woods.

I am sitting in the main clearing, watching them all mill about. I am in front of my hut, so that anyone who likes can approach and give me a task.

I have been living these past few years in a comfortable hut which was built for me. When we are on the march, I usually live in the great tent with Enmer and his wife and children and with his mother Zillah. But here in the Gentle Mountains, I cannot live in the great lodge because I cannot manage the steps. So I have a hut not too far from it, oriented

(I fancy) about where my room in the tent would be. It is a little, low thing, rounded to shed the snow, barely high enough for a person to stand in the middle, and it suits me. Most importantly, its floor is flush to the ground, so that I may get in and out easily.

So here I sit in a hut in the woods, rather like a wise man, which I am definitely not.

A young woman approaches and brings me my favorite hot drink.

"There you are, Grandfather," she says.

This young woman is Zillah's daughter. I tried to attack her, once, a lifetime ago. It is hard to say who has changed more in that time, she or I. I remember her as she looked then: a chit of a girl, face still rounded, her black hair in long loose curls, for that was fashion then; everyone would curl their hair to look like us Hamites. Nowadays she, like all of them, wears her long black hair in a practical bun. (Her little daughters wear it long – "like a horse's tail," they say.) She has changed, in this time, from a child into a mother. When she calls me Grandfather, she means I am grandfather to her children. She has married, and has spent many years, interrupted by some tragedies, doing what she seems to love … which is bearing and raising children.

She has five – Hur-Kar; the little girls Ai Li, Magya, and Amal; and now an infant son, Mut. I know all their names. And I do feel as if they were my grandchildren, just as I feel, now, as if she were my daughter, for she is Zillah's daughter.

And now I even know her name. Ninna.

She approaches me with Mut balanced on one hip, holding the steaming clay bowl of leaves in her other hand, with a cloth between so she won't be burned. She still comes near me very rarely, and still looking, as now, as if she is ready to throw the tea in my face if need be. I reach out to the length of my arms and take it from her.

"Thank you, Ninna," I say. She gives a faint smile and bustles away.

I don't call her Daughter. Not sure how that would be received.

And I do not have a good enough grasp of their language to tell her, You are safe from me now. You have been for many years. I feel more like a father to you, especially since your mother and I … No, it would not do. Not at all.

The tea is made from willow bark and peppermint leaves. It has a penetrating, steamy smell. I breathe it in with pleasure, for this is early spring and though I am sitting outdoors, the ground is cold and there is still a chill in the air.

I sit, drinking it and watching everyone bustle back and forth as we prepare for leaving.

I can understand most of what they say. When they get to arguing or telling long stories, I get lost easily. Their language is horribly hard and complicated, and it is worst when something complex is being said, such as talking about the distant future, or about things that might happen but haven't happened yet. Also, I cannot go on any of the hunts, so I miss about half the hunting metaphors.

I was helped greatly in learning their language by the fact that I have almost no pride left. I had no desire to say anything; indeed, I had nothing to say. I had no desire to speak correctly. I did not care greatly if I made a language error or even an error of fact, such as getting someone's name wrong. They already viewed me as an imbecile child. I did not try, for a very long time, to make long sentences, and even now I seldom do. I confine myself to single words. I learned the words for water, barley, rest, milk, and meat; for lute, of course, and "wash" and "dirty." I learned to say "give-me" for when I needed something.

I have had to learn "willow," for I now frequently have pain in my nether parts and legs, and chewing willow bark can sometimes relieve it.

I also learned "Thank You."

I really needed this word. People do services for me every day, and I am truly grateful. They feed me, for instance, and not just the leavings, either. That is far more than I would have done for any of them, if I had found them on the day the Tower fell, lying crippled in their own offal and blood.

I do not miss Nimri, the man I once was, for all that he was a man of prestige and power. He was also a blind man, a man narrow in his own interests, a shallow little man … he was, as little Ninna would say, a camel's ass.

It is too bad that this Nirri whom I have become must be a man who is crippled and in frequent pain. But when the gods give with one hand they take with other, they say … meaning everything comes with a price.

I have found ways to repay them a little. Making a whole bow is too physical for me to manage, but I can help with the strings. I can tan hides, if someone sets up the frame for me. I cuddle the babies, of which there have been many. I am often unable to sleep at night, so I can help the mothers. Time was I would have been gruff with a baby, but now I know that their fathers will turn them into little warriors as soon as they are able to walk; there is no need for me to do it. This life of ours is still so fragile. Any baby could sicken and die, or we could suffer a famine, another attack, a bad winter. It is not a bad thing to give a night of cuddles and songs to a baby.

I have also become passable at making weavings for carpets or tent panels or horse blankets. I can use goat hair, sheep's wool, even horse hair and sometimes the hair of wild beasts, whatever they bring me. Not all of it, of course, can be spun to be woven. Some must be felted. Some is good only for hide cloth. Each has its own qualities and its own uses. It is women's work, of course, or it used to be in the days before … yet there seems to be a certain honor in it.

I have learned to work images into my weavings. Mostly I confine myself to beasts, as they are easier to recognize than people when displayed on the side of a tent. Also, beasts have become very important to us here. Everyone remembers and re-tells stories of memorable hunts … the stag that tossed Endu, the time a bear was stalking this or that one, the lion that rose on its hind paws, the omen bird that they saw just before a battle. I work these in as best I can. Once I did a whole panel full of lions for King Enmer. And for everyday use, many are the flocks and herds that have paraded across my tapestries. I have made occasional mistakes ... and let me tell you, it is far more embarrassing to get a legend wrong when woven into a piece of work than it is to make an error in speaking!

I try to work out of doors whenever possible. The light is better, and it keeps me from going mad.

I can locomote myself from place to place, but it is tedious for me and for anyone who must watch me. Usually I am transported.

Some of them still hate me, of course. I cannot blame them. I am another mouth to feed, I make a great many messes, and the truth is that none of the tasks I do are completely free of an element of make-work. Vanity, vanity, all is vanity. Sages said this before the Flood, and it is still true today.

Everything we do has been done before, and everything we think has been thought before. But still we must continue to do and think it.

With the king it is more complicated. He hates me, it is true, but he needs me as well. To him I am not so much a strain on the food supply – I think he recognizes the value of my contributions – as a symbol, or repository, for all that is wrong in the world. When out in the open, he might be able to forget where he came from, and to know himself merely as a king, a leader of men who is young and healthy, and on the hunt, or leading his brothers on a scouting expedition, and he might perhaps rest in that. (I say "might," of course, for I cannot observe him in these conditions.) When he comes back to his home and sees me, the cursed Nirri, sitting by his fire, he sees his whole life from the view he imagines I take … that of the South, the sunny fields, cities and civilization, and the Tower. Then everything seems to him rude and savage, and he is reminded of all he has lost. I can see his face darken whenever he gets near me.

He thinks my broken body is a judgment that none of them should have to share.

Well, you are right, my lord the king. What has happened to me is a judgment; I am indeed guilty. My hands are stained with the blood of countless rivals and slaves. My tower, if it still stands, stands as a fist thrust up in defiance against the Great God.

I have said that Enmer needs me. He does need me, for he needs someone to blame. For he is guilty too. Yes, all of them are guilty – the older generation, I mean. Of *course* the scattering of the peoples was a judgment. Of course it was. We knew what we were doing. We were trying to bring back the old order, the days of walking gods, of temple prostitution and monsters and demons and unchecked power. We were trying to undo the Flood.

Well, now a second flood has been sent on us and we are having to submit to it ... which is what we should have done all along.

I have changed my understanding of what it is to be human. Once I had thought it meant to be on top: to stride through the sky, to look down upon beasts and men, to exert dominion. In the events of these past years, I have had to go lower and lower. I have had literally to crawl on the ground. And then I have had to work my way up from the bottom, starting with the most menial chores. I rocked babies, I tanned hides, I progressed *(progressed!)* to spinning. And as I have come lower and lower, I have found that this too is human. I have become more a human being, the lower I go. So now it seems that both are true: to be a son of Adam, we must exercise dominion over the world, making it feed and protect us, ruling over the beasts, making others understand what we want. But we must also be under things: under the dominion of pain, of limitations, of other human beings ... and surely, if this is true, under the dominion of God.

Speaking of Enmer, there goes his oldest son. Ki-Ki is now a boy of fourteen. He is not yet tall, but is beginning to get skinnier than ever, which is usually a sign that they are about to start growing. He is strong and wiry, for all his skinniness. For years now he has been accustomed to doing chores around the goats, sheep, donkeys and horses. That gives a man strong arms and a patient spirit.

And that skinny, strong boy – whom I have just called a man – is the very baby whose life I once saved, because in a moment of crisis the Lady Zillah came and set him beside me.

He is still my best friend among the grandchildren. He gave me a little wave just now, in passing, on his way to somewhere very important. I don't see much of him now that he growing. Most of his pursuits take place outside my domain; they are the pursuits of able-bodied men. But he, bless him, will come home and chatter to me about the hunts every once in a while. King Enmer doesn't like him to come near me, except that he approves of my giving Ki-Ki music lessons. Now that he is a teenager, our "lessons" are more just opportunities to play together … and they are some of the most enjoyable hours I can pass.

Ki-Ki is gifted in music. I have no idea how he came by this gift, given that he comes from *this* family. Sometimes we will even sing while we play. His voice has not changed yet, which means that we can harmonize. He would like to be able to sing down in my range. Perhaps within the next year or two, he shall.

Now he lures his cousin under a tree, then shoots at the branches so that snow will come down on the two of them. Little scamp.

Ki-Ki had a very sad time last year, when his beloved companion died. I am talking about the she-wolf that he had named Red. I had no special love for the cur, for in the city, dogs were not considered a noble animal, certainly not one that we would keep for a pet. But out on the plains, things are different. We quite admire the predators, and if one can successfully be made a companion to humans, that is considered a fine thing. As for Ki-Ki, he had been inseparable from this animal since both were small. They slept together, hunted together, shared their food, and he would even bathe her, to get rid of the fleas. She had number of litters of pups ... not every year, but every once in a while, when a wolf came about in the right season. Some of these pups were wild and would run away to join a pack as soon as she had raised them. But about half were more doglike, and would stay, and now they have been distributed among the younger members of the clan. And they keep finding new uses for them. It appears that we are now going to be a dog-having people. I can't say that I welcome the doggy smell, but then, there are so many other smells about the camp, good and bad: daily smells of lanolin, woodsmoke and cooking; horse smells and smells of people's bodies; and, depending the work that is being done, the fresh smell of split wood or the stronger smells of tanning and slaughtering. These are the smells that we live by, and seeing that I contribute to them myself, I suppose I cannot complain.

As for Red, last spring – it would be a little less than a year ago – she had a litter, and then when they got a bit bigger, she got into some sort of fight with a deer over one of them, and was kicked or tossed, perhaps both … I never got that part of the story entirely clear, and of course I wasn't there to observe it. Ki-Ki brought her back to the camp injured, nearly disemboweled, carrying her in his arms like a person. She died within a few hours, and everyone felt so badly for him. I petted her to please him, even sang her a song in farewell, though when she was alive, I had never cared for it when the dog tagged along on his visits to me, always out with her filthy tongue and wanting to lick my mangled legs. But I gladly embraced that dog, for that young man, on the day she died. It was clear his heart was broken.

It is strange to think that Ki-Ki has walked untouched through so many disasters that have horrified and nearly broken his elders: the fall of a city; slaughter by the Scythians; dangers of giants; killing winters, and so on and so forth … and yet this, the death of a dog, this is his first real experience of grief. He was so placed that none of the other things affected him like this has. Not unlike myself, come to think of it, as a young man. I had no real griefs before the Tower fell, but then in my case that was because there was nobody that I loved.

In Ki-Ki's case, he loves much, but life has been gentle to him so far. That is a strange thing, indeed I can hardly believe I just said it, for it seems that in this harsh world it cannot be true. But yet it is true. His elders have done a fine job of protecting him, in keeping with his age, as he grows into a man.

There is the lady Zillah, moving about the settlement, solving a crisis here and settling a fight there, speaking at least a word of command or encouragement to everyone. I watch her go one way carrying an armful of furs perhaps, until she disappears from my sight. Then back she comes, this time hauling an unruly child by the ear.

I think of her as a quiet woman, and she is not given to chatter, but at times like this, she is talking almost constantly. Her greatest tool is her voice. With it she asserts her authority, calms frayed tempers, sets the sluggards back to their tasks. It is a pleasure to watch the way she quietly keeps the preparations humming, though of course it is her sons who give the greater orders. She is a very great lady. I have come to admire her deeply.

I am her opposite, I suppose ... I am like dark black dust which forms a background that shows off the brightness of a flower. She, speaking often and always to useful purpose; I, speaking seldom and often ineptly. She, quiet and fading in to the background; I, sticking out like a maimed cock among chickens even when I sit silent and still.

Yet for all this, she seems to put up with me. More than puts up. She is quite friendly.

We have been occasional lovers these fourteen years.

She does not come to me often. Seldom is there a good chance. Seldom are both of us clean enough. Sometimes my body will not co-operate ... but we have found ways around that. Indeed, it was from her that I first learned a word I have never used outside my hut: their word for "tower."

It's disgusting to think now of the early days, because I am disgusted with the man I once was.

I have no idea why she selected me. I do not think it was pity, though she had plenty of that at first. I think, rather, she had a need, and I was the only man there who was not of her immediate kin. That is not true now, of course. But she and I are among the oldest people in our clan. She must be nearing eighty, and I am older than that. Both of us are still dark-haired and well-preserved. I do not know how long we can expect to live; the world has changed a great deal; but people were expected to live two or three hundred years, before the fall of the Tower. At any rate, sometimes it can be a comfort to be around someone who remembers things as they were before. Perhaps she feels the same way. Also (oddly), we now have a history together.

It has been a new thing to me, this, this ... I suppose we must call it friendship. I have had lovers before, of course ... though "lovers" is not really the right word. Nor is "I," come to think of it. There was no actual love involved, and nor was that man I, but rather haughty Nimri, crafty and cruel and, it now seems, rather stupid for all my clever machinations. I was married, rather young, to my half-sister; that was for the getting of pure Cushite children. But in those days a man had no need to even *like* his wife, and we had concubines and temple prostitutes and so forth, always thinking of them more like slaves than like friends or family. And of course, there was always the hope of someday coupling with a goddess. That was the fervent but unstated hope of the Tower. It was what everyone, at least everyone in my circles, considered the ultimate experience.

All of us Great Ones thought ourselves too good for ordinary human marriage. Now I wonder if that was because we had never really experienced it. But whether high or low, goddess or slave, it was always a relation of one higher, one lower. There was never this … love between equals.

Lady Zillah has made me an equal.

Talking of friendship, I sometimes wonder what would happen if I were suddenly to find myself face to face again with one of my men friends – or perhaps I should say, allies – from the old days. Nearly all of them were Hamites, so perhaps we would share a language … but leaving that aside, with the Tower gone I think we would have nothing to say to each other.

Now that the peoples have been scattered and we find ourselves living in the wilderness, that old, aristocratic way of life, I mean concubines and such, is no longer possible. Now what is possible is this new sort of arrangement, where a man and his wife must work together and live in the same tent, and be married to the same person for many years. And eventually, if all goes well, they may even become friends.

Even if all does not go well, a man has nowhere else to turn and must be content. I have seen this less than ideal, but still long-lasting, kind of marriage among the other men and women of our party. I have even seen them chide a man when they think he is not treating his wife well. It's incredible – a man is held to account by his own family! In this new life that God has forced on us, having a concubine would be difficult, to say the least, and temple prostitution would be unthinkable. It takes a city for that.

I have seen true marriage-with-love-and-friendship in the case of little Ninna and her husband, who is a former slave, a quiet, standoffish, but good man. And I have experienced it, to some extent, with Zillah, though of course we are not married and I cannot work by her side. We are friends only. Secret lovers only. And, given the limitations on my time and energy, for me that is enough. She may not be quite a goddess, but … well. Close enough.

Lady Zillah, witch-woman that you are, high priestess that you are!

CHAPTER 20

THE CREATURES OF THE DESERT

Hur, later that Fall

This bow has been months in the making. I found the mulberry, carved and fitted it together in jointed sections. Then the long strip of cow's horn glued to it. This was last winter. Let it dry two months. Then, during our journey from the mountains, I took deer tendons and pounded them, and soaked them in glue. Hur-Kar helped me apply this mixture to the back of the bow, on a warm day. Twice this was done. Then, we tied it like a prisoner, bending the opposite of the way it will bend in its later life. We let it sit like that another two months, while our party traveled, and then I inserted the bone shim at the center, where the horn plates separate. Finally, now, we are settled as fall is again coming on. And I am about to tiller it ready for use. Gods of archery, smile upon this bow.

I draw it. I observe the arms. If I find stiffness, I file that arm slightly. Then I draw it a little farther, and file again. I will continue this until it bends perfectly at full draw. Then it will be a good bow, please God. I will give it to my son Hur-Kar, my oldest. He is thirteen years old. He does not have his full strength yet, so this bow will not have as heavy a draw as my own. But it should serve him between now and when he comes into his full manhood. Then it will go to another boy, if it is still intact.

We have come out of the mountains now. We had lived there for several years, catching our breath, as it were. We took the time to build a really nice village out of wood. I was sorry to leave that. Perhaps we will build another, some day, when we find a place to settle, but I have a feeling it will be many years of living in tents before we are ready to settle again. It will be hard to find as nice a place as the Gentle Mountains.

We had to modify our methods of building. That was one reason it took us so long. Here in the North – not the far North, but still a long way north of Si Nar – you get snows and such, and the ground tends to subside. Also you have huge amounts of mud in the spring to reckon with. We have started learning to account for these things. The other problem is that our tools have started to give out. The axe, for instance, the one all of us were so glad to have when we fled the city … it had become thinner and thinner, and finally broken from overuse.

And we have no way to find, or mine, or extract, or forge any kind of metal. So, although we had a forest full of beautiful, useful trees that had been growing since the Flood, we were forced to use very slow methods, such as slow burning, to fell them. Then for shaping them, we had either to use them whole, or to use wooden or stone wedges with mallets. These we had been beginning to use before, but for a large project like a village, many more of them had to be made, and we are not experts. And even when they were made, and well used, not every tree would break cleanly into boards. We were learning as we went. That was why it took us two years to build Enmer's great hall.

On the day we finally finished getting the roof on, we all stood around looking at it. We felt proud of it, because we all knew the amount of work that had gone in. Also, we knew it was well made ... a solid stone retaining wall around the foundation ... the walls well chinked with mud against the wind ... the roof nice and waterproof but with vents where needed for fire smoke. It was useful. I was satisfied with it. But I could see that the princes, Endu and Enmer, hurt to look at it. All could see that despite being well-built, it was ugly. Or, rather, plain. We had no good metal tools to carve with, so it was unornamented. We'd left the bark on in some places, which extended the hall's life, but made it look shaggy. The mud we had used gave it a half-plastered appearance. There was no way to paint it without a lot more work. There was no way to make it acceptable to Enmer.

Of course, when the winter came and the hall was often seen with white snow blanketing the roof and lining the porch, contrasting with the dark wood, it did look beautiful. All the more so when you knew there was light and warmth inside. Also, we got the women to take a nut extract that they use for a dark brown dye for wool, and paint over the dried white mud with it, so that the plastered patches were less visible against the logs. That was the best we could do.

Once Enmer's family started living in the hall, and it became our winter meeting place, it seemed just fine to me. More than fine. In the eyes of the little ones, it was a palace. But it was a long way from a gilded, high-as-a-horse-can-run tower. And Enmer never forgot that. When it was time to leave that place, he wanted to burn it down. I tell you truly. We had to talk him out of making us all burn our family homes, and the hall.

"We will never come this way again," he said bitterly. "We should not keep these hovels to give ourselves a place to retreat to."

Others pointed out that the family homes would rot soon enough, and that the hall, if it did last a few more years on account of being well-made, might provide a one or two-night haven for travelers. ("Or for wild beasts," said Endu.) In the end, the only thing that dissuaded Enmer from his lust to destroy, was the thought of causing a destructive fire in the forest.

Those years in our wooden village in the Gentle Mountains were good ones for Ninna and me. Not easy years, but good ones. We had two more children, Amal and Mut, so that now our family consists of a son, three daughters, and another son. We were busy during those years with getting and bearing and raising small children, and that is what made the years both hard, and also good. Before we married, I used to think of Ninna as a princess, but now she is something even better: a mother, and my wife. She had gotten curvier with her years of childbearing, though still strong as a steppe pony. Just as strong as Shulgi, God keep her, ever was.

Our daughters are all growing out the same way: square-built like my family, curvy like Ninna, short like both of us. Ninna spends time making sure they have the skills, and the wrist and arm strength, for things like kneading, spinning, tanning, milking. I think a lot about how to protect them from their boy cousins until they're safely married.

One thing we all kept looking for, after we landed back in the Gentle Mountains, was for the bear that had killed Imsag. Our village then was not in the same place where he had been killed earlier. We had moved a bit farther east, which seems to be our fate. Still we were in the same general part of the country, and large predators have a wide range – if they're not killed by other predators – and this one, I thought, would be crafty and clever and might have developed a taste for human blood. I wished he had shown up sooner, so that I could have had some peace.

But that bear stayed away for almost the entire six years we were there. I kept one eye out for him, and for others like him, especially as we were building the great lodge, believe me. And we made it as strong as we could, given the poor state of our tools, because I had it in my mind that he might try to enter.

It wasn't until the winter before we left that he made his appearance. Something started springing my traps and taking the prey. I wasn't sure what it was. Could have been a lion, could even have been a dragon, for though they don't generally like the cold and snow, still occasionally one would come through. Whatever it was, it was clever, and big enough to smash a log trap, *and* it didn't want to do its own hunting, apparently. And problems with the traps had been the early signs of the bear that took Imsag.

I spoke to Enmer, told him there was something about, possibly a *bad one*. Possibly *the* bad one. I advised him to have everyone stay in their homes. He did me one better, and brought everyone into his lodge, where Ninna insisted they offer sacrifices for those us of who were going out.

I took with me Rumi, who had grown into his large hands and feet and was now a powerful man, and Damai, and I made sure I invited Endu, for I thought his grudge with this bear might be personal, just as it was for me. He was glad to come.

We made a large log trap across the tail end of a little gorge, with a roof and a sort of door that would come down when the animal entered. We brought spears, hoping we could stand on the sides of the gorge and stab down into the animal's back through the roof. We had never done this before, and were nervous and unsure whether it would work. We laid the trap with a goat and some milk – since we'd come east we had been unable to find any honey – and then we got up in some trees. We knew our scent would still be on it, but didn't think that would matter to this creature. The biggest danger was that he would turn out to be cleverer than we were, and know it was a trap.

He didn't, though. He *was* the bad one, and I am sure it was the same one, based on things that we later found in his stomach. He came after only a few hours – which was lucky for us, all stiff in our trees – and thrust his head into the trap and began drinking the milk noisily. The trap worked, but it came down on his hindquarters and back legs, with a bit of him still sticking out. This did not seem to concern him, for he started on the goat. Damai and I came down from our trees and ran over and tried to tug the back of the trap down over him, but we couldn't do it. So we scrambled in a panic up to the snow-covered sides of the gorge and began spearing him through the top. But he backed out in a fury and came after us, luckily through a smattering of arrows from Endu and Rumi. Rumi is, as I said, a powerful man, and his arrows can punch through a thick surface, perhaps including the hide of a bear. But their arrows did nothing at first.

The bear came up to the top of the gorge after Damai and me. He put one foot on the top of the trap – *and it held* – and his foot was caught between the logs for an instant, and in that instant, we scrambled down on the other side of the little gorge. Then, knowing we could not outrun him, and because there was nowhere else to hide, we threw ourselves inside the trap, and closed the door. We managed to bring one of the spears with us, but not the other. And the bad one whirled round and came to the door, trying to smash in to us through the trap.

Damai and I looked at each other with that look that men give when they know they are probably about to die together. And besides terror, my only thought about dying was that if the two of us got mauled, how angry Ninna was going to be with me!

Endu and Rumi shinnied down from their trees and approached the bad one from either side, shooting at him from much closer range, until they ran out of arrows. Some of the arrows went in fairly deep, till the bad one was prickly with them like a hedgehog. Every time one shot him, he would raise his head and snarl, but he was still focused on Damai and me. He knew we had tricked him, and that we were in there with the carcass of a goat.

Finally Endu, in desperation, ran up to the top of the gorge to try and retrieve my dropped spear. The bad one leaped to the top of the trap to go after him. So Damai and I raised our spear and got him from beneath, and at the same moment (as far as we can tell), Endu speared him through the throat.

He died then, more quickly than we expected, but maybe one of Rumi's arrows had also done its work. But in death he almost killed Damai and me, for the roof of the trap suddenly gave way. We'd have been crushed if the near end hadn't held an instant longer, such that the whole thing tipped, rolling the bad one away from us and on to the rocky ground.

Then we heard the sounds of Rumi and Endu approaching and stabbing the thing again and again through the throat, through the eyes and into the brain, until they were sure it would not rise. The air was smelling like slaughtering-time, but worse.

Then we heard Rumi's shaky voice calling, "Are you all right?"

We assured him that we were, in voices higher than we had meant them to be. "Are you all right, boy?" we added. "Is Endu?"

"Endu's here ..." he replied, sounding very young. "He's ... uh ... *Endu!*"

It seemed my brother was still tearing at the bear.

Rumi got my brother's attention, pried him away from his prey, and then the two of them set about pulling apart the collapsed roof that had trapped us in the gorge. We worked from the inside, and heard them heaving and lifting, and when the battered cage was finally pulled free enough that we could emerge, we at last got our first look at the being that had freed us. It appeared to be a demon out of hell.

It was Endu, but an Endu whose hat had fallen off, whose head was so covered with the spurting bear's blood that his black hair was lank, his face red and gleaming, and his eyes and teeth flashed out crazily from amidst all that gore like the eyes and teeth of a mad thing. The killing madness had been upon him. It had worn off a bit while he and Rumi were tearing at our prison, but when he saw the shocked looks on our faces he laughed wildly.

Endu had always been a cool, calm man when it came to violence. On a hunt he uses his mind, not his instincts, and Enmer tells me that it was the same during that horrible first battle with the Scyths. I don't remember how Endu handled himself in that battle, for my memories of it are not clear, but I believe Enmer. All this means that Endu learns well when you teach him hunting skills, and he often makes better decisions than some others who might lose their heads. But he gets meat less often than I do, because he doesn't know how to relax and let time flow over him when sitting in the forest. Everything has to go through his *mind*.

This was his first experience of flowing with anything, and he seemed to have liked it.

He had nearly decapitated the bear, which is not easy to do. We helped him finish the job, and then for the sake of drama, Rumi accompanied him back to the lodge, bloody as he was and bearing the animal's head, to show everyone how he had taken vengeance on Imsag's killer.

Meanwhile, Damai and I stayed behind to make a start on butchering the animal, so that later we could transport its meat and skin.

I am told it was a great success: Endu entered the camp like a hero, stunning everyone with the sight of him; ballads were made on the spot, and he walked on air for days. Oh, and his wife Sari was greatly relieved to see that between a bear and a man, the man could win, and her man had. And Endu took this relief for worship.

I do know that from that point he began to know what I meant about *feeling* things in the forest, probably because he began to trust his ears and not just his mind.

All in all, the killing of the bear was a good end to our time in the Gentle Mountains.

That bear had come in from outside and had been king for a while, but after he was gone, the old hierarchy started to come back. We had rid the mountains of one predator, not of them all. But we were kings at the moment, so it was as good a time as any to move. Some were not happy to leave our homestead and follow Enmer, but I was. Six years in one place makes a man restless. I was eager to see some new things.

We moved eastward through the mountains, and they became dryer and dryer until we were traveling through desolate rocky hills that were so much a desert that there was nothing on them but colorful red and white stripes of earth. Then we emerged to overlook a sort of huge basin with many grasslands and even some forests in it. And that is where we are now. We are camped near a small river, which appears to flow into a lake. It is enough for our group at this time, but I do not think it will be a good place for us to settle and grow. We need more water, more pastureland. I will wait for a moment when he is receptive, and then I will tell Enmer so.

This country has a great many grey wolves. They are large, as large as a man, and they howl to one another at night, each warning each to stay away from the prey that each is claiming. We have had to build a rock wall and create a nighttime pasture. Actually, it is several rock walls and several pastures. And we are having to take it in turns to sit up through the watches of the night, guarding our animals.

Enmer's son Ki-Ki loves it, of course. He still loves to get a glimpse of any animal, even wolves. The wolves are a disadvantage, but they are one that we can endure. It is not like the forests of the far North, where we had to contend with wolves and with everything else too.

Our dogs will help to guard the sheep. They warn us of the wolves' coming, and it is extraordinary how they will snarl and snap and treat the wolves as a definite enemy, even though they are essentially the same animal, and though our dogs would certainly die if they tried to take on the wolf pack without our help. It is clear that they have chosen a side. It is a huge advantage to a pack of people like ourselves, to have our small pack of wolves on our side, even though it does create some challenges, such as keeping them away from the young sheep.

So in these last weeks, it has been my duty to try and get to know this desert place. Hunting is good here. There are many, many gazelles, enough for us *and* the wolves if they would share.

These gazelles are odd little creatures. The first time that Ki-Ki and Hur-Kar and I went out to sneak up on a herd was several days ago. We split up and snuck in from different directions. Before one of us could shoot, they must have caught wind of Ki-Ki, because the whole herd began leaping like fat on a skillet. Then they thundered away from him, past me. Directly over me, in fact, so that I wasn't able to get one that day.

Hur-Kar came and found me. He was worried that I'd been trampled. Then we wondered why we hadn't seen Ki-Ki, so we went to where he was hiding. We found him doubled over with the laughter at the way that first gazelle had leaped straight in the air when it caught scent of him.

There are snakes in this land too. I have observed them crawl sideways, and I have seen them eat the scorpions that also haunt these parts. There are fish in the lakes, and these are eaten by eagles. And though I have not confirmed it myself, some of our men who have hunted farther south and east have sworn they've seen dragons.

There are some odd, bushy trees here. They tend to grow twisted and warped – their wood not good for making much – and they have tiny leaves, as if they are stingy with how much flesh they'll present to the wind and sun. We have sometimes seen rodents emerging from burrows beneath them. Even rodents all covered in prickles, as if for armor.

Armor against what, I ask myself? And I answer, against wolves, eagles and snakes. And please God, let there be nothing else to armor against.

Could we make such prickly armor? Answer: we could indeed, but it would be hell on the horses. And what for? Our long-established stratagem is to run, not to stand and fight. Like these wise little gazelles … only we do it without popping up into the air first.

Tiny sparrows have nests in the middle of these dryland-trees. They make them round, like a wasp's nest buried deep within the branches. While guarding I have watched one make many trips back and forth, repairing her nest. Hur-Kar says he has even caught them stealing sheep's wool from the bushes to line their little homes. So whether we move on or stay long, a part of our flocks will remain with these small creatures here.

The boys and I had gotten a gazelle. We had dressed it in the field and were carrying it home between us, excited about fresh venison. We returned, dust-covered, from our hunt to find the household in turmoil. I can't remember when, but I somehow felt this had happened before, but a long time ago. As the years have gone by, we've gotten better at living with one another. Usually if I come home to fighting, it's just a matter of some of the women having a spat among themselves, limited to one or two households, and settled without a great conference.

This was nothing like that. It all started with one woman, apparently, but she by herself was enough to set the whole tribe on its ear.

The woman was Ninshi, wife of my older brother Enmer. She was contending that mother Zillah and Nirri the Cushite were lovers. She was determined not to allow this.

The odd thing, the really odd thing, was that though Ninshi was causing a huge scene, practically a trial, for which everyone else was standing, she was doing all this from a seated, almost reclining position as she sat on a blanket, cradling her sleeping baby. She had recently had a child, Peres; indeed, she had given birth to him while we were traveling, and I wonder if she was exhausted from all of this, and if that was the reason she reacted so strongly to what she had just discovered.

It might also have been the reason that, home alone during the day when everyone else was out, she had discovered it.

"I've heard them myself," she was saying. Nearly shrieking. "She gives him a bath," (her voice shook with disgust) "… and then they make love, or do something that sounds exactly like it. It's disgusting. I won't allow it in my tent."

I looked at the two boys. They did not need to hear this. The family were gathered in the space between our tents. My sister-in-law's shrill voice seemed to be bouncing off the very hills beyond. Most of the adults were there. Even those who were supposed to be guarding the perimeter of the camp had wandered in, goggling. Everyone was reacting. Ninshi's news seemed to be new to everyone else too, and no one seemed to like it. Mother Zillah stood there in the midst of it all, her face flaming, but with her chin up and clearly not taking on any of the shame that Ninshi intended. Skinny old Nirri was sitting in front of his tent, beside a fleece he'd been combing. He was not red at all and his face betrayed nothing.

"Come on," I said to the two boys. "Let's get this carcass cooking." They followed me quickly, used to obedience. I led them to one of the firepits that was a distance from our circle of tents. There we would be upwind from the camp and couldn't hear as well. We set to work getting a fire going and hung the gazelle to bleed out until it was time to roast it. They were both looking at me blankly, more confused than shocked.

"What's wrong, Uncle?" said Ki-Ki. "What's Mother saying about Grandfather?"

"And why shouldn't they make love?" muttered Hur-Kar. "They're Grandfather and Grandmother, after all."

I did not answer. I set them to guard gazelle and fire, and returned to the family, who were still in full fury.

"Come on," I said to my wife Ninna. "Let's get the little ones out of here."

Silently, with one eye over her shoulder, she gathered Ai Li and Magya and some of the other older girls, and had them take the little ones to the river for their evening baths. But she drifted back to the tents as soon as this was done. She couldn't tear herself away. I knew she wouldn't be helping us with any cooking.

She hadn't been able to tear away Lina, either. Lina was eleven years old, Ninshi's daughter. She was clearly fully on the side of her mother. She stood by her shoulder, face tear-streaked, not moving for anything.

I sent most of the guards back to their places, those that would go. I wanted to pace the perimeter myself, but I needed to hear what was happening. It looked to be the end of our clan.

Ninna sidled up and took my hand, and whispered to me, "Isn't this awful? I had no idea."

I nodded, but I didn't agree. The charge was true, clearly. That was on both their faces, and neither had denied it. I didn't think it was so terrible, though. Why should Zillah, being an old woman, be denied her little bit of pleasure? This Cushite was doing us a service. I was surprised he was up to it, and felt a rising bit of respect for him. He couldn't hunt or fight – no fault of his own – but he was far from useless, he'd proven that. And now he was making our matriarch happy.

So I spoke up and said so. "Why shouldn't they be allowed to marry?" I added. "They're of the same generation. All the kids call them Grandmother and Grandfather."

Everyone was speaking up. But Enmer had hardly spoken. He looked very bad – ashen grey, like a dead man. His eyes were on me when I spoke, but he seemed confused by my words.

He turned to his mother.

"You told me," he began. "You lied to me. You said …"

Ninshi, whose voice was already strained, sucked in a breath that seemed would break it.

"You *knew*?" she said to her husband. "You mean you *knew* about this? How long has it been going *on*? How could you *allow* it? How could …" Then her voice grew so thin it couldn't be heard above the babble.

A riot was ready to start, and at the worst possible time. It was sundown, the time for wolves. None of us had eaten. The children were coming back in a straggled line from the river. Enmer should have called us to order, but he was standing in the center of the camp, facing down his mother, still looking helpless as a dead man.

I ran into the tent, got my spear and shield, and banged them together. Everyone fell silent.

"We mustn't fight like this," I said. "We are hungry, and the children are hungry. Ki-Ki and Hur-Kar are roasting a deer," (I could smell it now) "and whatever happens we all need to eat. Let the women gather grain and things, and let us eat together as a family. Then we will put the children to bed, and then when he understands the situation, Enmer will render a decision."

Luckily, I'm thought of as something of a big man. Second to Enmer, actually. They listened.

CHAPTER 21

PAYING

Zillah

Enmer would not eat. He was angrier than I have ever seen him. His anger was like a living force that lifted him up and bore him along, filling him with a hot, restless energy. He was Enmer still, but a different Enmer, one who instead of being able to do nothing, could not help but take action.

He paced impatiently while the children were fed and the adults ate in subdued silence – for whatever else is going on, we must eat. I could not get anything down and did not even try; my stomach was sour. Nirri had a nervous stomach too, but he ate, greedily, defiantly, far more than I had ever seen him get down, putting away great heaps of venison as long as we would bring it to him … and then he had indigestion later.

The entire time, Enmer was either looking daggers at us or staring blankly as if inward, speechifying in his head. Clearly he was preparing what he would like to say to us. And once the children were in bed (as well as many of the adults not directly related to us), and the hour's delay had completely failed even to begin to quench the blazing coals in his stomach, he said all of it.

He had much to say to me. I need not repeat it all. It seemed he felt compelled to go over every incident of the years of our exile, re-visiting each in the light of this newfound truth, that I was now a villain. Of course, the things he said about Nirri were even worse, but those were not designed to hurt. They were incidental insults that my son offered to one whom he believed disgusting, useless, helpless; in function like an intestinal worm (which we were beginning to learn about, as the world grew older and sickness became more common), and viler than vomit. A taker, but a little, inconsequential taker, like a flea. Enmer could not believe that I would take up with a flea. It seemed to him a betrayal of all that he'd thought I was, of all that our family was or had ever been. It seemed I was not the great lady – or even the halfway competent housekeeper – he had thought me. I was a little, vile taker, too. It was my good luck, and the family's bad luck, that I had ever happened to be married to his father.

I remember these things so clearly. I tried to feel myself above them, but I was not. They were coming from my son. I will remember them to my dying day.

The bits that made me angriest were his insults to Nirri. One would never know, listening to Enmer, that this man had

lived with us for fourteen years. One would never know
about the changes he had undergone, about the objects his
hands had made, or the songs he had sung to us. Or that he
had learned to speak. Or his name. Indeed, one would never
know that he was human. Most of all, one would never know
that he had contributed to our family at all. Enmer made him
sound of less use than our herd animals.

"You told us that a guest was sacred," he raved ... not
shouting, but in his quiet, suffused ranting voice. "You said
all men are brothers, that we must save any human life we
can. You *quoted our father Noah*. And it was all for this ...
so you could gratify yourself ... and *I let you*. I risked our
family's life because I thought you meant it. We shared our
food with him. We risked his people coming after us. We
dragged him along – exposed ourselves to danger – we built
special equipment, we wasted water on bathing him, we gave
him his own room in our dwellings, and all for nothing."
(Enmer has long believed that *everything* is "for nothing.")
"All to serve this selfish whim of yours. I thought you were
doing it for the sake of our family – to make us obey God
whether we would or not – to keep us from turning into
animals – yet you dressed your desires up as this, you

represented – my God, you even *told* me the first time it was
for the sake of having a child .... "

And on and on and on.

By the time he was finished there were no secrets. Any
who had stayed to hear knew everything there was to know
about the history of Nirri and Enmer and me. And this itself
was significant. Living together closely as we do, it is not
wise to tell all. Secrets can allow us to live together in
harmony. Now Enmer had exposed them all ... and his bare
facts were true, though not the telling of them. After he had
done that, intending it or not, he had effectively sealed our
deaths. With everything exposed, he could no longer keep us
in the family. At least, not do that and still keep the rest of
the family intact.

He wore us all out in the end. He poured out his words
until nearly dawn, swarming over us like stinging ants, like
scorpions. Most others had gone to bed, even Hur, who had
tried a number of times to dissuade him. He knew he must
get a few hours of sleep to keep the household running on
the morrow.

Endu eventually went to bed as well. He was as
disgusted as his brother, but he dismissed me more easily. He
had not the energy that came from Enmer's shock and anger

and especially his disbelief. By the end of the night (when we had moved the whole operation indoors), the only ones left were Enmer, Nirri and myself, and my daughter Ninna. She was in disbelief too, but it took her differently; she was crying. She stayed, I think, because she wanted to understand me; she wanted to find that it was not that bad. But I could not explain to her. Enmer's anger had flooded everything like a tide and given everything its color.

I, too, was crying by the end … crying with anger, with frustration at not being able to explain, crying for how Ninna's heart was being wrung, and with weariness, and with shame at my tears.

And by the end I was very worried. I knew Enmer would have to put us out. I was worried about what this would do to the little ones. They depended on me (though physically they could survive without me; no one is indispensable), and Nirri, they loved. For them, too, I was grieving. I had thought it harmless, this matter of being lovers, but it was not. It was not. It was going to do great harm to the children and the grandchildren.

While I wept, Nirri sat silent, sometimes reaching to comfort me. I had stood in front of him at first, as if to protect him. Then at some point I moved beside him, as it was clear we were of the same kind and would share the same fate. Now I was leaning on his shoulder.

Before dawn, Enmer gave us his decision, which surprised us not at all. We were to be put out of the camp. I wondered how the loss of two grandparents would be explained to the littlest children.

I tried once more.

"He cured your madness," I rasped. "Your son loves him."

These things seemed to Enmer the sickest things of all. It was as if I were reminding him that we'd eaten feces for our survival. That it was still in our bloodstream.

He did not hit me, not with his hands. He is a well-brought-up young man who respects the order of heaven and earth. The very universe would rise up and kill the one who struck his father or mother. But he left us soon after. And the look on his face had been as good as a blow delivered to mine.

Finally, when we were at last alone, Nirri spoke.

"I've brought death to you," he muttered, the words humming through his shoulder.

"No, no," said I, still weeping. "Life. I brought life to you, and you have ... you have repaid me. I am well paid."

He paused, then: "But would you ... choose ... me over your family?"

"Enmer is wrong," I said. "You are part of this family."

He sighed. He knew it was true. His roots were deep in our soil, and they wouldn't be torn out without loosening it. Enmer was damaging his own.

"You are a grafted-on branch," I said. "You have grown in to us."

"If they let us marry."

"That would have been better," I said.

Then I believe I fell asleep. And I believe that Nirri, who often had trouble sleeping, sat up, holding me, until they came to take us away.

CHAPTER 22

LEAVING

Nirri

This Enmer was determined. He was still leader of his family, and now to his rather empty status he had added an iron determination born of anger before which none of them could stand. At last, he was a leader I could respect.

As they were all breakfasting, he announced that he was sending us away. He did not make a great speech out of it, probably feeling that he had done his explaining the night before. It was all done very quickly. We had not much time to say goodbye. I don't know how it was for Zillah, but for myself, there were barely a few minutes to look about the camp, watch them all arguing, and realize it was the last time I would ever see them do so. To bid goodbye to the familiar smells, the voices, the faces. I did get embraces from many of the children, especially Ki-Ki (which Enmer quickly broke up). The boy was now wearing the same stunned, confused look which his father had worn the night before. I must say I did not expect anything like this to be his second experience of grief.

"Take my lute," I muttered in his ear as his father pulled him away from me. "I give it you." But he looked so confused that I am not sure whether he understood me.

Many of the children clung to Zillah. Others treated her as a stranger. I remember causing events like this, myself, back in the bad old days of the Tower. It's peculiar how, though a few people will resist (the troublemakers, I once called them), most will surprisingly fall into line. They will even be vicious with the exile, though they don't understand the reason why.

They bound us (yes!) and put us on two donkeys, she seated, me flung over the back of mine for greatest indignity. I had eaten a great deal the night before, realizing it might be my last meal, and when they threw me on my stomach over the donkey, I vomited. Not the dignified exit I would have hoped to make in front of the children. Endu came and threw water over my head and over the side of the beast, and cuffed me a bit. I was expecting no less ... after all, I had robbed them of their mother.

But she spoke to him sharply and made him stop. And then she said, "At least give me a spear so I can keep the wolves away."

And they gave her that as well ... that is, brought a spare one along to give her when her hands should be untied.

So that was how we left the camp ... Zillah looking back over her shoulder, sad with the goodbyes, but struggling not to weep in front of her sons. Me, sick with gritted teeth, bouncing along, unable to look back for trying not to fall on my head.

They did not take us very far, a ride of perhaps an hour or two. They took us down into the valley, away from the fertile part, to an area of salt flats. Put us atop a little rise with a very fine view, dumped us, cut our bonds, made it clear we were not to come back (as if we could). I am not lying when I say that even before we got there, buzzards were circling.

Endu took a little trouble to make me a sort of palette on the ground, because, after all, it won't be long, so why not? He would not look at either of us.

Enmer, on the other hand, couldn't look away. He was still staring at us both with his eyes big and blazing. I tried to stare him down, and I won, too. He had to turn away at some point, otherwise they couldn't leave us there. Had to get back to his camp which he had now purified. It gave me some comfort to know he probably wouldn't sleep that night.

Then they were gone and Zillah and I were alone with each other, the glaring sun, and the salty wind.

Vomiting.

Again.

My stomach is empty, but my body will not stop voiding itself. We both know this isn't good. I am exhausted from it.

She grows more worried every time I shake or vomit. There is a little water nearby, a pitiful salty marsh, but we have nothing to carry water in. Zillah has made a number of trips down the ridge, trying to make a bucket of her cloak, but the water soaks through before she reaches me, and she ends by wringing it out, mad with frustration.

"I'm sorry, I'm sorry," I keep saying. And, "Thank you."

And she says, "Stop."

It is not really that bad, my friend, my love. I am growing weak quickly. That is a good thing. Even for you it is good. When I am not here to care for, you can walk on your own and find water. You can walk back, even, and make them take you in again. But if I linger very long, you may grow too thirsty to do this. You have that spear, but I won't ask you to kill me. I know you would not do it. And to tell the truth, I don't want to die by your hand. All the years I have known you, you have given life to others. It would cost too much to reverse that now.

Night came. Very cold. We heard wolves, but they didn't approach us. Possibly didn't like the way we smelled. I certainly didn't.

Morning, very cold. All day I did not warm up, except to burn with fever a little. By that time, too far gone to know whether she was also ill. Hoped not.

It is not clear to me what was dreaming, of that time, and what was real, but I *believe* that we were approached by the buzzards. Have a sort of memory of them ranging around us, waiting, hopping a bit. An image of something sliding sideways, poking them away. Must have been the Lady Zillah with the spear.

I know that at one point, I came to a clear patch and opened my eyes, and saw the round yellow eye of one of those fellows looking hungrily at me. And I remember thinking, I have not come so very far after all, from when I first woke beneath the Tower.

Another night. "Don't speak," she says. Leaning against her.

When I closed my eyes, I'd dream that I was back on the Tower, falling off it again, leaning in to the fall, shaking and fearing but never quite toppling.

In my dreams, the wind up there was very, very cold.

Sometimes I'd look down and see the Japhethites crawling like ants, looking up at me with faces I recognized. "There's Nirri," they'd say in their funny gabble, which somehow, I understood. "How did he get above us again?"

I would turn to Zira, intending to say, "I know those people. They shouldn't be slaves," but when I turned to tell him, I'd feel the impact of the ground and wake up on my back, twitching like a dying animal, my limbs shaking and shaking with the cold.

Near dawn on the third day, I woke up feeling very clear-headed. No longer shaking, but with my legs hurting badly, so much that I had to breathe quickly so as not to cry out. Zillah was sleeping, eye sockets sunken. Not good, that.

Then, with a fresh breeze blowing up from the west, a sense of God came over me, so palpable it raised the hackles on my arms.

He had found me at last, the One I had long tried to forestall. The One who had broken and humbled me, and then left me completely, so it seemed, for a very long time, and Who had then slowly, slowly come stealing back, so slowly I had not known when He arrived. Now that my body was dying, He revealed Himself to me. And may He stay in this valley long enough to be known by the grandchildren.

My eyes were beginning to fail by this time. I could see things on the ground, such as her face, from my peripheral vision. But if I looked directly at anything, I saw white circling things, like vultures. I looked up into the dawn-grey sky, and the white vultures melded into bright white light.

I shook with it. Holy dread all around me, and the sun about to rise.

I couldn't see, but I reached out and touched the Lady Zillah's cheek. She woke, and then I rose up into the cold, white spaces of the skies above us.

And I was singing as I rose.

CHAPTER 23

RETURNING

Ninna

God curse us for the murderers we are.

It took us a day and a night to change Enmer's mind.

It started with the children. We had all gamely given the explanation that we'd agreed upon, namely that Grandfather and Grandmother had done something forbidden, and when someone does something that is really, truly forbidden, the penalty is that they are put out of the camp. But then they asked what, and of course, for the younger ones, we were not willing to tell them. All we could say was, "It was nothing you would ever do," which did not comfort them.

And for the older ones – most of them – Lina being an exception – they were baffled about what the problem was. It turned out that most of them had assumed Mother and Nirri were married already, when they thought about it at all. After all, she cared for him night and day, and they had adjacent quarters in the family tent.

So we had two days of little ones crying and saying, "When is Grandfather coming back? Who will sing us his songs? Who will teach us the things Grandmother taught us?" and so on.

It did not endear Enmer to the absent Nirri, to see how beloved he'd become in the clan.

But the adults were unhappy as well. It had happened so suddenly, with so little counsel. And this was not the sort of thing that people were meant to be exiled for, such as bestiality, or cannibalism, or incest. Enmer seemed to think it was all those things and more, but no one else did. Even his wife Ninshi was rather shaken by what she had done. She had sometimes had her differences with my mother, but still I believed her when she told me later, dismayed but still defensive too, that she hadn't imagined that Enmer would turn out Zillah. Perhaps Nirri, but not Zillah. She had only wanted to shame them, really. She hadn't known how Enmer would react.

And Mother, to be honest, left a gaping hole. Endu's wife Sari missed her especially, for mother had often been very firm with Endu when he was prone to beat his wife.

I at first was of one mind with Enmer. I didn't like it, but I did feel that what with the deceit that Mother and the Cushite had carried out, we had no choice. By the second day, I was over the shock of that and moving on to the shock of losing the two of them. Finally, I threw in my voice with the others.

At last, on the morning of the third day, Enmer said with a bad grace to my husband, "You can go and get them if you like, Hur. I am not going myself. We'll see whether the desert has judged them."

I suppose he felt that if the Camel's Ass could survive two days and nights alone in the desert, he couldn't be the burden on our family that we'd thought he was. Apparently, my brother was hoping he'd be vindicated ... somehow. At any rate, he could hardly continue as chief while holding stubbornly to such an unpopular decision.

It is the greatest shame of my life that I for a time colluded in killing my mother. If she was weak for loving the Camel's Ass, I was a thousand times weaker.

So Hur led out some of the other mature men (this was no sight for youngsters), taking with them the same two, thrice-cursed donkeys. They took plenty of water, and food, and so on. Endu went along on this trip. Enmer did not.

When they saw my mother from a distance, she did not look like herself. She was a mad witch woman, for she was standing up – in a feeble tottering way – holding her spear in both hands and lunging, nearly falling, as she drove away the vultures from the body of Nirri which lay at her feet. Her hair was unbound ... it was her hair that made her look so

different, for it had turned from black to white, and it was
flying about her.

Then as they watched, she sat – nearly collapsed – and
sprinkled dust in her hair and began keening for the dead in a
pitiful feeble voice, for she was nearly dead from thirst. And
she stroked the Cushite's curls as she keened.

When they approached, Endu said to her, "Mother, we
will have a funeral."

And she creaked out, bitterly, "Why would you ever do
that?"

"… And *that* is our Mother," Endu said to me, proudly,
later. "Even when she's weak and half dead herself, she is
holding a spear, fighting off death to the last. … Even," he
added softly, "when death has already occurred."

"Fighting off death from the ones she loves, you mean,"
I reminded him fiercely. My brother had overlooked the fact
that we had taken from Mother someone she truly loved, just
as she loves the rest of us. He was only proud of her on
account of the spear.

They brought her back on a donkey and him on a litter
behind the second donkey, exactly as we had first transported
him fourteen years ago. And in all that time, most of us had

hardly needed to be bothered by his malady, for mother saw to nearly all his care.

Enmer, to his credit, was waiting for them when they returned. He stood outside the camp, partway along the trail, staring at the approaching party. His arms were folded and every line in his body said, "not repentant." When they approached him, he stepped up and looked at mother. They spoke to one another privately, and what was said we shall never know.

We found out later that we had missed rescuing Nirri by only a few hours. Apparently he died on the morning of the third day, perhaps at the very moment that Enmer was agreeing to send a party to bring him and Mother back.

This, like so many other things in life, raises a host of "if-onlies." Sometimes these can only be dealt with by simply banishing them from the mind.

We did have a funeral, even sacrificing a horse to see our guest off. We had done many different things with bodies over the years, but our favorite thing in time of crisis was a pyre. We made a pyre for our guest, the longest guest we'd ever had.

Endu (who was now very solicitous), said, "Mother, do you want to keep his bones?" And Mother said, "No. His spirit is gone, so should the rest of him be." And she added, "He will not be wanting *this* again." By *this* I take it she meant his broken body, and no doubt he was glad to be quit of it.

But it was difficult, watching those curls catch flame.

So the children got to grieve, and understand that Grandfather was dead. I think the younger ones concluded that Grandfather had gone out into the desert on purpose to die. Overlooking that he had gone out bound on a donkey, for of course they themselves were often carried places they did not want to go, for things such as bedtime, as a matter of daily necessity. The older ones learned a different lesson. They learned there were forbidden actions, not always ones that were obviously wrong, but if undertaken they had grave consequences. Not a bad lesson either.

We learned something different, we men and women. A few things, really, things far less satisfying. We learned of our own weakness. How we did not, at any given moment, know what was right. How when cast adrift in this cursed world, if a clan-chief takes it into his head to ruin someone, nothing can stop him.

Mother made it through the funeral, and then she collapsed. We had been giving her sips of water, but now we put her to bed and nursed her just as … well, "just as" what should be obvious.

She remained sick for a long time. We nursed her through the autumn and the first part of the winter. She began to get better, oddly, in the middle of winter, right around the time that most people begin to get sick and crazy. I was glad of this, for often when someone has been fighting an illness they will die in the spring. Her hair regained some streaks of dark grey, but she would never again show the glossy black head of a young woman.

Ki-Ki had somehow got hold of the Camel's Ass's lute. He would play it, in secret, whenever Enmer was out, which he often found excuses to be, the coward, while I was nursing Mother. I spent much of my time in their tent that winter. In fact, I was nearly run off my feet between my usual duties to Hur and my children, plus running over to Enmer's tent several times a day to care for Mother, plus of course, although that came farther down the list, my own confused and perhaps broken heart.

I would be tending to Mother, and suddenly her eyes would get bright and she'd turn her head as if she had recognized something. And the cause of this was the series of plucked or strummed notes filtering in to us from the next room, through the paneled inner wall of the tent. And I would have to say to her, "No, Mother, it's not Grandfather, it is only Ki-Ki." But she would continue to look as if something wonderful was about to happen. And I would feel a surge of mad irritation toward Ki-Ki, but I hadn't the heart to go and stop him. I knew that he was on the other side of the panel, with his body curved miserably around that lute, picking and picking at the tunes exactly as Nirri had played them, over and over again. When I think of that horrible winter, that is always the music that stays with me.

Eventually Mother came back to herself enough to realize that the music was not coming from her lover, although there was an awful period when she had to realize this afresh, every day. When her head was clearer, she also, like me, could hardly stand that cursed lute. But still we knew enough not to stop Ki-Ki from playing it. It seemed to be the young man's only refuge. He was sad and angry, as were all of us that winter.

He finally brought it out about three months later, openly playing it in front of his father. We were expecting an explosion from Enmer – at least I was – but he only blinked and said, "Did he give that to you, then?"

"Yes, Father," said Ki-Ki, with a firm chin. Any other young man would have said it sulkily, but sulkiness was not in Ki-Ki. "He wanted me to have it."

"Well, you'd better play it, then," said Enmer. "Those songs of his were the only thing of value he ever gave us."

Ki-Ki's eyes flashed at this, but he was pleased too, and glad to see that his father actually wanted him to play the lute. After that he began to go out as usual, and when he was home in the evenings he would play at the normal times and would sing many of the songs that Nirri had sung, albeit in his own reedy boy's voice, which made them sound quite different.

I begged my mother's forgiveness for my role in her exile as soon as she was well enough to hear it. It was a reconciliation such as any daughter could dream of, with tears and embraces.

"We were wrong, we were all so wrong," I said. "I have Hur, why should you not have the Ca – have Nirri?"

To my surprise, she did not blame me.

"I was at fault too," she said, in her deep rich voice which was still rather faint. "I had a hand in … in all of it. I asked Enmer to accept too much. I could have reckoned with Enmer, if I'd ever taken the trouble to think about it. I should have done … something differently."

She was not sure what she should have done differently, though. Neither one of us were. Held herself in continence, I suppose. Or approached Enmer sooner with the truth. But when was she meant to have done this? What would have been an opportune moment? … Yet surely, in fourteen years, it seems she could have found one. Perhaps, great lady though she is, her vice was not lust, but passivity and cowardice after all.

"But I saw him die, Ninna." Here her eyes filled with tears. "He was happy to go. He is happy."

And then I had to give her some gruel and tell her to rest.

It was not until much later, nearly a year later, that I got a chance to ask her the questions that had been bothering me ever since Enmer, in his long, horrible, but horribly truthful rant, first raised them. By that time, she was strong enough – in fact, we were on the move again – and she seemed open to being asked, for we had settled, as a family, into a habit of not talking about any of the bigger things, just so that we might live together in peace.

I could sense that it was hard for her, as a grieving person, to have nobody ask her about Nirri, barely to be allowed to speak his name. So I sought opportunities. These were short, for with my husband and children I had many demands on me. My chances to speak to her usually occurred while we were cooking together or going to get water.

Was it true what Enmer said, I asked her, that she had only insisted on saving the Cushite because she fancied him? No, of course not, she replied, she would have saved any wretch we had found still living at the base of the Tower, whether man, woman or child.

But was it true, though, that this affair had been going on for the entire fourteen years? She was afraid so. She explained further, in answer to my horrified but hesitant pressing, that it had seemed urgent, at the time, that we have many children. This was before Tiras had joined us, and frankly, she had never dreamed that God would bless us so richly, with so many little ones, as He has since done. At that time, it did not look as though our tribe would survive two years.

But why, then, did she continue the affair, after the coming of Tiras and his people, after my marriage to Hur? She did not know. Habit, she supposed. Habits could be harder than expected to break. Also, for the sake of keeping Nirri happy. Also, at some point, as all of us were gradually becoming different people, she found she had come to love him. And, again, habit.

The answers to these questions, as it turned out, were not what mattered to me the most. It was merely the act of asking them and of hearing her answer. She would tip her head, giving each one careful thought, then answer with measured tones, just as she always had. She was the same person I had always known. That was the belief that Enmer's words had shaken, and that was the belief that talking with her restored. She had indeed done all, or nearly all, the things that Enmer had said she'd done. But she was not the person that he had made her out to be.

"Don't *you* take a lover," she said to me, half seriously. "That Hur of yours is still alive, and he is a treasure."

"Oh, I would not do that, Mother," said I, shocked. Setting aside that for her it had caused death, I had no desire to. Though in one way I understood her, still I could not imagine doing as she had done. I was a grown woman, no longer a little girl copying and worshipping her mother. We were two different women, not exactly the same, and now, as two different women, we could be friends.

CHAPTER 24

ONLY ONE END

Enmer

We did not try to plant any crops there, at the edge of the desert, where our camp was bounded by green fields and then pale salt flats to the south; and to the north, dry, red-striped, perilous hills.

The winter had turned out to be very bitter, and the spring was not showing many signs of rain. We needed a better place for our livestock, and everyone knew it. Also, many (the rumors came to my ears) were left with a bad feeling about the place, after the horror that was revealed last fall. They wanted to get away, to a happier, fresher land.

I was willing to move them – for reasons of water and such – but as for wanting to leave the bad place behind, I thought they were acting like children. It is foolish to think we can leave a bad thing behind by running from the place where it happened. *It* will still go with you. I knew it would with me. It would be a part of me always. In my case, it was not so much an evil presence with me, as an absence of something that should be there, like a missing limb, or like Hur's eye. I had been living with such absences for many years now. Cut it off, burn it up, leave it behind. Thus we had done with the Tower, then with the broad and fertile South, then with our loved ones who were killed by the Scythians. Then with many other, smaller things along the way. And now, with my mother's pretended, foolish ideals, which came from the ages before the exile, when people could still hear from God. Perhaps she half meant these rules, even, when she espoused them, but we could not keep them, that was obvious.

None of this was what we would prefer perhaps, but that was the only way to live. It let one save one's body, which was all there was to save. There was no saving anything else, not when a judgment came. By the time of the occurrence of the judgment, one had already lost the other things, the invisible things that, given a choice, one would rather have kept.

If, that is, they were real things at all. I know that I felt their presence once. Most of the younger ones seem to sense them still. But it has been harder and harder for me to believe in those things, since I lost them.

Yet there must be rules – unseen, and now, less and less known to us – rules by which this universe is governed. I knew this because the judgments did not stop after we fled the Tower. Rather, they kept coming. We were to be fruitful and multiply and fill the Earth and subdue it, and now, at long last, our clan was doing so. We were not spending ourselves on a useless, presumptuous tower of our own making, but rather were venturing farther, far farther out into the Earth than any person had ever gone since the time before the Flood. Yet because we were doing this as refugees, fleeing from a previous judgment, it seemed we had started out behind in our debts and could not make headway. Thus every time a disaster overtook us (a river rose while we were trying to cross it; a grassfire, blown by the wind, swept over our camp; an infant was born dead, poisoning its mother; one of our hunters was taken by a bear), I knew it was a judgment. But I never knew what offense had caused it. Had one of us done something deceptive and disgusting, as my mother had? Or had someone simply been thoughtless? Or was the offense simply our being there?

The young men Ki-Ki and Hur-kar, who have reached a serious, questioning age, still think there are rules that can be discovered. They have set about studying each new land we come into, observing the animals and trying to discern the spirits, discovering the rules. Or making them up, as I see it. I pretend not to notice, I allow it, I even nod along. My spirit may be blinded and limbless, a crippled stump of a thing, but theirs are not – yet. Such spirits need something to grasp in their young hands, even if it's only a rock that they are playing is a live thing. Until one day, they grasp at something real at last, and it burns their tender hand.

Hur and I rode with a scouting party to find our way onward, east and north. We found much more of the same, hills and desert, but this gave way gradually to great, rolling plains, which at this time of year were green. They were drier, hillier, and a good deal colder than the plains that we older ones remembered from the South, but after our time in the desert, they looked to us like paradise. Perfect for our stock.

Hur and I sat on our horses on a hilltop, watching the young ones gallop down before us and then commence running and grazing. The sky was wide and pale above us, the light very bright and sharp; a strong, persistent wind stirred the braids down our backs. (We men generally wear our hair in a single or double braid these days, as the married women wear theirs in buns.)

We sat on our mounts for a moment and talked, our eyes the whole time scanning the landscape for lions, catamounts, dragons – and for giant and human predators. One could see very, very far in this landscape, but it was deceptive: we could not see detail. Only, on the other side of this valley, there were giant hills with their dark heads in shadow and their green feet in the sun, and the sight of them would cause a little, useless lifting of the heart.

"They are all afraid," said Hur without preamble, turning to me with his serious manner.

I blinked at him. *I* was afraid, all the time, and had been for many years, but I had not gotten that impression from the young ones. Indeed, it was my job to spare them as much fear as possible.

"Since you exiled your mother and Nirri," he added, and I flinched as I always did when I heard that name spoken. "They are all afraid that they will do something wrong and that you will do the same thing to them."

A great anger rose like a hot rock into my throat and I turned and looked again over the sunlit pastureland.

"Tell them not to be afraid," I said to him when I had mastered myself. "It took Mother years to deceive me, and she knew all along that she was doing so." Once again, my vision contracted to a bright point for a moment, and then I said again, "They need not be afraid. I am not going to exile anyone except for open rebellion. Tell them that."

"I will tell them," said Hur, and then we dismounted and rubbed down our horses and let them graze and roll. But I was still seething. How has it happened that I must use Hur as a go-between for me and my own family? This is yet another thing Nirri has taken from me. He and his cursed tower.

I had softened a bit toward Mother during the days of her illness. A man cannot witness his mother ill, drifting in and out of sleep, and his sister giving her sips of drink and the whole clan praying for her survival, and not join in hoping for her recovery. My sister Ninna did not help matters, for every time Mother had a crisis, Ninna would go about looking with fury at me, as if to say, "This is all *your* fault." It was far from my fault – I was not the one who had set events in motion – but I realized that I was the immediate cause of our mother almost dying.

One day when she was wakeful, I went to see her. I did not wish to repent, for I had done nothing wrong, but I wanted her to know that I wished her well.

Her tent seemed dark, warm, and smelly after being in the clean air outside. I sank to the floor beside her pallet and bowed my head respectfully.

"Is it Enmer," she whispered, or "Endu?" Her voice was so weak, but her mind was clear.

"It's me," I said stiffly.

"Ah … Enmer," she replied, equally stiffly. "Well?"

I told her that I was glad she had not died, and that I was not happy things had come to the point of exile. I was glad, I said, that the desert had spared her. I hoped she would fully recover.

She was silent so long that I began to be irritated. At last she began, "Are you saying that you repent of trying to kill me and N–"

"Don't say that name!" I interrupted.

"I see," she said, and subsided for a moment, actually closing her eyes. Then after another moment she opened them, saw me, and as if surprised to see me there, whispered, "There can be only one end for a woman cast out into the desert with a crippled man. You do not take responsibility, then, for what happened? Is *Nirri*" (she laid a defiant stress on the name) "instead of your mother, now to be the villain?"

"Of course he is," I said. "He always was. I wonder you didn't see it. I thought you enjoyed it, perhaps, but maybe … maybe he outsmarted you … you were fooled …."

She laughed scornfully and closed her eyes again.

"I do not think I am going to die. I do not yet want to join *Nirri*. I love this world … I love this family." She paused again, saving her strength. "You are my son, Enmer, and I will always love you. But it appears … in this matter … we are still enemies."

I stood up: angry, confused, but reassured as well.

"I am glad you are not planning to die, Mother," I told her, and left.

By the time the scouting party returned, many days later, from our trip to the grassy hills, I once again no longer much cared what they all thought of me. By God, I *will* save this family, though they hate me while I am doing it. My father Golgal tried to save us and ended up bringing about our very destruction. Well, so be it. He died doing his best for us and for humankind. But I do not have all humanity to worry about. I have only this little handful of people, and I will bring them safely to a homeland even if it kills us all.

On the way back, we swung even farther to the east. It was a pleasure to travel quickly, eating up the grassy hills on the legs of our horses. Rumi was with us, as were our teenaged sons, Hur-Kar and Ki-Ki. So was the old, scarred, leathery Damai. We had left Endu in command back home, with Melek backing him up and Mother, I suppose, keeping him from excesses.

We began to descend out of the hills, encountering another fringe of mountains, and after a few days we found ourselves coming down into the foothills of these mountains, overlooking a vast and pleasant green plain. A great river poured itself down through the hills, past cliffs, and out onto the plain where we could see it meandering. The scene reminded me a bit of Si Nar. It looked like a good place to build a civilization. And indeed, though the day was hazy, we thought we could see smoke rising from villages far out on the plain, along the river.

Before we could descend to the plain, we came upon an unexpected scene in one of the broad foothill valleys. About two dozen men were trying to capture a large beast. Again the scene seemed familiar, perhaps because of the setting. I was reminded, with a bite of longing, of the day Sut and Endu and I lassoed our bull, long ago when we were younger. These fellows seemed to be having just as much fun as we did that day, but their intended prisoner was rather bigger than ours had been.

It was a dragon.

It was about twice the size of the bull we had tried to capture, but it was still bullish in its stance and behavior. Just like a bull it had a sturdy frame, four legs, a head low to the ground with a beak obviously meant for grazing, and long bull-horns over its eyes. Actually, it was perhaps more like a giant pig, for it had a short horn on its nose that gave it a friendly, pig-like appearance. But it was much more spectacular than our bull had been. For one thing, it had a wide crest behind its head, and this was covered with fine feathers of blue and gold. It also had smooth feathers on the rest of its body, and spines or spikes running the length of its back and partway down its long, heavy, swinging tail. These spines waved with its movement, and seemed to give it a sense of when someone was behind it.

The men had surrounded it at a distance. They were trying to keep it distracted and disoriented, without making it angry. Some had rope loops or nets on long poles, with which they were trying to snag its horns or tail. Others would dart in and set down armfuls of grain, and when the dragon paused to eat, on would go another loop from the end of a pole. The men were calling excitedly to one another and even laughing a bit.

The dragon seemed to be taking all this patiently, letting out a musical grunt whenever something startled it, but never turning down food when it was dumped nearby.

Then at last while the dragon was eating, forward came the man I assumed was their leader. He was taller than I, square and broad-shouldered, with black hair and a face not unlike those in our own family. He approached the beast and stroked it on the cheek just before the widening of the crest. Then he bent down with a sort of collar attached to what looked like a chain carved of wood or stone. He tried to slip this collar onto the dragon's left front leg, which was hoofed like a pig's but nearly as broad as an elephant's.

When the beast felt itself chained, it squealed and flared out the feathers all along its crest … a startling sight that made it look twice as big. Then it took off running, dragging the men who had its horns on poles and the man who still had hold of the chain, up the valley. The other men followed, shouting.

Without consulting me, Hur, Hur-kar and Ki-Ki slipped from their horses and ran forward to help the men. We were up the valley from them, so my three were able to get out in front of the dragon. Little Hur-kar stood right in front of the beast, making clicking sounds like those we make to our horses, and to our surprise, it saw him and began to slow down. Meanwhile, Hur and Ki-Ki joined the men on the poles and added their weight to drag the creature to a halt.

The leader did not waste time on wondering who we were. He got to his feet, still holding his end of the chain, and began stroking the dragon again. Hur-kar approached from the front and soothed it as well. He looked transported as he reached out to touch its snubby nose. Presently some of the other strangers brought another armful of grass and grain, and with it they made a trail over to where they wanted the beast to be, which was in the lee of the hill. It followed; it seemed like a young beast, one that had bolted from panic, and really wished only to be left in peace.

When they got it where they wanted it, they drove a sturdy stake through the other end of the chain. Meanwhile, Damai, Rumi and I had dismounted and staked all our own horses, giving them first a quick rub down and a drink at the stream that flowed out through this valley.

When all the animals were where we wanted them, we came the rest of the way out into the mountain valley, and then we and strangers stood about and looked at each other.

Hur was already clasping the hand of the burly man who had chained the dragon. When he saw me emerge, coming along the bank of the stream, he gestured toward me as if presenting me, and the fellow came along and clasped my hand too. We bowed to one another. Then he invited us back to their camp, a little way farther down the valley from where they had first been struggling with the dragon. There we found they had set up tiny chairs with a breathtaking view of the plain below, and they had a large clay vessel from which they dipped out ... beer. *Beer!* We had not had beer in ages. Indeed, I had never expected to drink beer again, least of all with a pack of strangers.

Hur and Damai and I sat down delightedly to drink what we were offered. We were so busy exclaiming over having found beer here at the edge of the known world, that we did not immediately notice that the young men of our party, Hur-kar and Ki-Ki and even, it turned out, Rumi, did not like it. They could hardly get it down, did not care for the flavor (though it was very good beer), and drank one cup only slowly. And the next day, if you can believe it, Hur-kar and Ki-Ki both had headaches from that one cup.

Thus we sat with the dragon-catchers. It was hard not to look from face to face, searching to see if there might be one there whom we had known before the fall of the Tower. Their leader was older than I and must surely have worked

on humanity's last great project, but I did not recognize him
… and the majority of his helpers were younger, though not
as young as Ki-Ki. They would have been only children
when they left Si Nar. Still, these people felt more like
brothers than the skull-bearers had. They had beer, for one
thing. They also looked more like us, being generally
golden- or brown-skinned; their faces, with high cheekbones
and smooth chins (except a thin beard on their leader),
tended to look a bit familiar. Their hair was generally glossy,
not curly, again like ours, and was kept decently tied back in
a braid or bun with a leather thong. They were modest as
well, wearing tunics and trousers.

Hur and the young men were bursting with things they
wanted to ask them. Their curiosity went mostly unsatisfied.
We never found out how the strangers had separated this
young, peaceable dragon from its herd or parents; how many
more of these dragons lived in the hills or where they were
to be found; or whether it was meant to be a sacrifice, a
novelty, or a beast of burden.

For this last question, we did get some clue. They kept
indicating the dragon and then me (and I kept shaking my
head to say *never, no chance*), and then pointing at the
settlement down in the river valley. At last – they kept saying

some word when they indicated me, and then the same word with a glance at the valley – we gathered that they were capturing this dragon to take back to their *king*. We confirmed this, as best we could, through many repetitions of the word … though who knows what we were really confirming. All I know is that nothing we said made them turn against us, for all through that long afternoon they remained peaceful.

Ki-Ki, Hur-kar and Rumi were delighted at the chance to have such a close look at an unusual creature. They made many trips back up the valley to see and stroke the dragon, always escorted by a few of the strangers, while Hur and Damai and I sat and savored our beer.

As for Hur, between the dragon and the beer, he looked as if he had achieved perfect bliss. He pushed his headband up and scratched his forehead beneath it, and wiped some sweat out of the pit of his eye, for the day was growing warm, and then he returned the headband neatly to its place and sighed a sigh of contentment.

And once we had figured out what the dragon was for (for a king, as a pet or guard or god or talisman), he looked over at me, his one good eye dancing, and said, "What about it, brother? Should we capture some great beast and bring it back to you because you are our king?"

I was almost certain that he was joking, but I was still horrified by the idea. Bring home a large, showy beast, with unknown needs and instincts, which would slow us down in travel and which looked like it could eat as much as five horses? What could be quicker to ruin us?

"I think these people are mad," I said in a low voice. "Why would anyone want to bring a dragon into their camp? And what would possess a king to ask for such a thing? It's dangerous, it's smelly …" And influenced by the beer, I laid out every one of my complaints about the dragon. "It's mad," I finished. "It could be the death of them all."

By this time, Hur and Damai were looking at me without any laughter in their eyes.

"Don't worry, my brother," said Hur after a pause. "I was only joking. I am not planning on bringing you any such thing as a dragon." He paused again. "Or anything else that would cause trouble."

"Or that would endanger the clan, of course," said Damai fervently.

"That's right," said Hur. "Or that would slow us down in any way." He paused again. "In any way … at all." He was still watching me rather warily. "After all," he added, looking down and swishing his clay cup of beer, "We have only just got rid of a large dead weight, after a long time."

"That's right!" I said grimly. Then I realized, from the way they were both looking at me, that far from agreeing with me, Hur had just made a criticism.

"Well, he was!" I snapped. I did not want to have this conversation in front of the foreigners, for though they could not understand our words, any of them who watched would surely be able to tell that we were arguing, and this would show them weakness. Then again, perhaps they would not care, for there had already been a few scuffles, quickly snuffed out, among their younger men since the beer came out.

"What I wanted to ask, brother," pressed Hur, again perhaps encouraged by the beer, "What if one of us becomes a … dead weight … through no fault of his own? Say one of our children is born deformed, or say Damai or I are injured and can no longer walk …?"

I flinched as he mentioned these things. I hated to think of them happening, yet I knew that such things were sure to happen, especially now that they had been named.

"We would do our best for you, of course," I said, keeping my voice short and dismissive. "You are one of our own, your injury was come by honestly. His wasn't.

"And he was a wicked man, Hur!" I said suddenly, remembering. "Don't you recall how he attacked Ninna?"

Damai's eyes widened at this, for he had not heard the story. That is exactly what I mean. All this false glory has grown up around Nirri among the younger ones. The truth was never told.

Hur nodded. In truth, I am not certain he did remember. Ninna had not been his wife at the time, and he had only recently been freed and still, at that point, may have viewed our family as slaves view their masters, which is to say as unjust, inscrutable, and frequently nonsensical. Which in the case of the last, in the matter of Nirri, we, in fact were.

"But I do not think he was only using Grandmother," Hur finally said. "Did you see, at … well … at the … end, the way they protected each other?"

I had seen, and I could not bear the memory. And at that moment, my son came back from yet another trip to view the dragon and said something that made things worse.

"He spent hours and hours showing me the fingerings on the lute," he said – fondly, not at all with Hur's pointed accusations. "He always had time for me. I suppose ... he had nothing *but* time." Ki-Ki welcomed any chance to talk about his "grandfather," a topic that was usually forbidden.

I jumped up.

"*That dragon*," I said, pointing back toward the sheltered end of the valley, "Does *not* have time for human beings. It will never sing anyone any songs. It will never teach anyone to play the *lute*!"

These facts were unassailable. I hoped they would see that the rest of my thinking was as well. "And he was not your grandfather," I said to Ki-Ki.

And then I added, more quietly, the thing that was above all obvious, "Use your common sense, examine it out to the finish. There can be only one end for a tribe that chooses to take in a dragon."

Then, to cover the incident with our hosts, I pretended that I was interested in seeing the dragon again, and some of them led me back to it. I patted its flank, invited by my guard to do so, and was startled by the heat emanating from it. As I had once wept beside a fire of coals, so now I felt the heat of the dragon, with silent tears running down my cheeks. Why had my mother started all of this, when she insisted on rescuing that wretch? When would the fall of the Tower ever end? Would it never stop grieving us, breaking us apart?

I was not too concerned to be observed weeping by the foreigner who stood there with me. He was proud of the dragon, and as I was looking at it and touching it, I believe he thought I was crying tears of awe.

The dragon began stamping down a sort of nest, nearly at the extent of its chain, looking like an enormous, living jewel. It appeared that they planned to keep it there overnight, perhaps to get it accustomed to its captivity. I wished them all the luck in the world with it, but I still thought, from the little that I could see, they seemed to be undertaking a stupid and dangerous enterprise. We, indeed, got the better role: we got to see the lovely creature and enjoy it for a few hours, but we would have no need to figure out how to transport it, to live with it, and feed it.

We parted from our hosts a few hours before evening. We did not plan to go down and explore the great river; it clearly was already taken. They had tried, with their fingers, to give us some idea of numbers – of people, households, I know not what – and we gathered that it was many hundreds.

Anyway, we had already found to the north good pastureland that would last us easily another few years. We wanted to part as friends with this powerful kingdom, so we gave them what we could, as thanks for the beer. On a scouting trip, we had not brought any fine things with us, certainly none that were better than the things they had. I burned with shame as I stripped off my deerskin shoes and laid them before their leader, and he pretended to be very impressed with them, wrinkling his nose only slightly. I wished I had brought the pair with bone beads instead. Those look impressive, but they can be replaced every year. They can easily be decorated, by one of the young women or by N

—

Well, never mind about that.

Our hosts did not give us any useful gifts, beyond the beer and a very strange, but relaxing, afternoon; but they did give us something beautiful. We saved them carefully in our packs, and only got them out when we came in sight of our home camp, weeks later. And then, each of us rode proudly in among the tents wearing in his hair a brilliant dragon-feather.

CHAPTER 25

WHAT IS A TOWER?

Zillah, five years later

It is a beautiful spring day and we are having a wedding.

I have become one of those old women who cry at weddings. But it is lovely to see them happy and to know that they remember virtually nothing of the world before the fall that was experienced by my generation.

Hur-Kar is marrying Lien, a daughter of one of the cousins from Tiras' people.

She is not his close blood-cousin, of course, not in any way that we can trace. He was the son of Hur and Shulgi, so he's not really my grandson by blood. Though I feel as if he is. Cousin-marriage, when I was a girl, was popular, though not a must. Now it is a must again. Before the Flood, of course, it was the only alternative to marrying a god and birthing a monster.

That possibility is behind us now. Every time a judgment comes, we lose many great works, but we lose many horrors as well.

Yes, I am happy for them. They make a handsome couple. Hur-Kar is a fine young man, solid and steady like his father. A bit young, at nineteen, to be a-wedding, but as they say, it is better to be married than to burn. And he knows how to do all the things that a man ought to in these days. He can ride, hunt, make bows, care for the animals, slaughter, and fight in a pinch (though it has been years since we've needed to defend ourselves against other humans). And what matter if he knows nothing of brickmaking, of architectural plans, of plumb lines and masonry? All those engineers' skills of which my Enmer was once so proud, and which now take up so much useless space in his head. And which still, at times, weigh down his heart.

Hur-Kar, like his father, is not quite black-haired; his hair is brown. He has Hur's square, honest face and sweet, though rarely seen, smile. He has smiled several times today. He is a bit taller than his father. His bride is – not beautiful, exactly, but exquisite like a catamount, small and sharp and quick. Her honey-colored face is all made of triangles. Her smile is wide and straight, and has been beaming out today.

They sit, left and right wrists bound together, under a little makeshift canopy on a ridge overlooking a lake that is the biggest and bluest we have ever seen. Really, what more could one ask? It is safe to feast on this ridge … thus the determination made by Hur and his scouts, in preparation for his son's wedding. No human beings for a hundred days' travel. Perhaps a thousand. A feast is spread out before the happy couple, with more of the same set before the rest of us, on mats on the ground. We have all been several days preparing it. The meat was slaughtered this morning, as a part of the sacrifices attendant to the ceremony. The altars are still smoldering in a sheltered hollow a little way below us. Every so often the fresh wind will swirl through that hollow and whip across us with a bit of warmth and the smell of smoke and mutton.

It has been about five years since we left the cursed desert. None of us wanted to settle there after what had happened, and it was poor land in any case, and seemed to be getting poorer. We stayed the winter, and moved on in the spring (another year without planting), moving east, per the command that Tiras had given. We found a good land with great, green, rolling plains, ideal for grazing. But there seemed to be a kingdom growing far to the south of us, so we moved north little by little, encountering forests, and finally this lake. Perhaps we will not stay. I am not sure how well it fits our way of life (if we can be said to have such), but my goodness, it is stunning. So deep! So blue! So full of fish and little seals and, perhaps, yet undiscovered monsters.

Enmer has changed since he killed Nirri. It was as if that was something that he'd needed to do in order to know his own power as a man. My oldest son is still not happy, nor is he kind. But he is quicker and sterner and less afraid to lead our family. He is also a bit ruthless, more willing to be cruel is order to accomplish his ends. I still stand between him and the little ones when it's called for, but for large matters I seldom need to intervene and make him do justice. Hur, who rules with him, is always there to do that. And even Ninna will stand up to him when she feels it's necessary. She has never forgotten her role in what happened. She blames herself that I was put out of the camp, though I do not blame her. It was all, from the beginning, on my own shoulders.

Fittingly for the change in his personality, Enmer has grown a great black beard like his father's.

I might mourn this change in my son, and I might seek to manage it, but on the whole, it has been good for us. His instances of cruelty show themselves more rarely, and harm us less, than did his fits of lethargy. We need a warlord, and if he must be a bit cruel, so be it.

So, as it turns out, this is one more gift Nirri has given us. And I – I gave Enmer his excuse to get rid of him. Perhaps I was wrong in the first place to rescue a wicked foreigner, to bring into our camp a crippled, speechless, dangerous and dying man. But I do not think so.

I still miss him. Sometimes I'll be going about my business, whatever it is, and suddenly I will see him looking at me with his great, dark eyes – all of us have rather narrow eyes now; no one has eyes like that anymore – as I say, looking at me with a twinkle in his great, dark eyes ... and asking, "Why?" And, more often than not, I will find that I don't have an answer.

Yes, that is a very good question, Nirri. Why, indeed?

He is not the only one that I miss, of course. Sut and Golgal are often with me, as well as my maidservant Shufer. I still talk to Tiras, consulting with him as it were, from time to time, although for all we know he is still alive. But as Nirri was with me every day in life, so he is in death. You simply cannot rescue someone – be annoyed by them day in and day out – watch them die – and then forget.

Everyone else misses him too. Ki-Ki, for a long time, would play on his lute and pipes only the tunes exactly as Grandfather Nirri had played them. He would not allow anyone to play them differently. Now he has again started making tunes of his own, though once in a while he will play a "grandfather" and bring tears to our eyes.

On our way out of the accursed desert, in the spring after that awful winter, we encountered a herd of wild camels.

They were shaggy and two-humped, and they looked ridiculous, with their thin saggy humps flopping about, looking like teats that had got put on the wrong place. Of course there is nothing unusual about encountering camels, but Ninna and I, because of her old nickname for the Cushite, for some reason found them both significant and funny. And when the herd took fright and bolted, showing all their skinny rumps and tails, my daughter and I turned to each other and began a laugh that we found it very hard to leave off of.

It ended in tears, I recall. Our emotions were strange, changeable, and close to the surface that spring. But ever since then, my daughter and I share a private smile whenever a camel is spotted.

Ninna has continued having children. She had her most recent baby, a woman child called Emi, just a few days before the wedding. We were all laughing, because Ninna loves weddings, but in this case, she has not been able to help as much. She was quite active right up until the birth, though, cooking and so on. With every baby she seems to get stronger. Little Emi makes seven children that Ninna and Hur have together ... seven counting Hur-Kar, of course, whom everyone counts as Ninna's son, for she raised him. Hur and Ninna have nearly all girls. Their only boys are Hur-Kar, now married, and the now seven-year-old Mut. Their older girls, Ai Li, Magya, and Amal, are the perfect ages for helping with cooking, doing things for their mother while she sits with the baby, and of course for wedding preparations. They were very excited by the wedding, just as Ninna would have been at that age.

Other than that, Hur and Ninna have another little girl, Hyuna, who has just turned four. She has been my companion these last few days. Her mother is busy with the baby, and none of us want Hyuna to fall in the lake. So she and I walk about together. She follows me and imitates everything I do. She is delicate, chattery, and is a bit fair-haired like her father.

Enmer and Ninshi also have seven children now. It has become almost a joke that Ninshi and Ninna tend to have babies at the same time. They always seem to be pregnant together, or at least within a year of each other. And on a year when one is not pregnant, the other isn't either. Ninna has had a few miscarriages, sadly, that have only added to this effect. While Ninna has had mostly girls, Enmer has had mostly boys. His only daughters are the baby, Koret, and Lina, who is fifteen this year.

Sari, too, has given Endu four children, all sons. She handles them well when they are small, but ten-year-old Jai is already starting to treat her with contempt, like his father. Sometimes I want to apologize to her for allowing her to land in this family ... but that is one of those things that somehow one can never say. I content myself with pointing out to Endu how well Sari and Ninshi have done in helping to build a dynasty that Golgal would be proud of, in the hope that this will encourage him to appreciate his wife. Still, it seems a bit hard that of all my daughters, only Ninna should be truly happy. Unfortunately, I do not have magical powers over Enmer or Endu. Much as I would like to change certain things about their hearts, their hearts are closed to me, as every person is closed to every other. I am only their mother, after all, and now they are grown men; being their mother does not give me any special power. Even my nominal status has fallen a bit since my judgment was (as they see it) proved so poor in the matter of Nirri.

My status has fallen with my sons, that is ... but not with everyone. One grandchild, at least, still believes my word.

Ki-Ki came and rode beside me as we were moving last fall. He seems sometimes to look at me almost with awe, as if he thinks my white hair is his link to a distant world of secrets. Well, I am not certain that I am so wise, nor that the world I remember has so much to teach us, but I am happy to answer his questions. Sometimes he will sit with me and ask, searchingly, about the old days, and then will listen very intently, as if he is trying to imagine exactly how things were.

Angki is the exception, mind. Most of the children are not interested. They all think this wide, clean world of tall trees, wide skies and great beasts – and endless travel – began when they were born. They do not suspect that there was an older, wearier world … at least not one they have any interest in. But Angki has always been curious. He wants to find out about everything, and this includes the past.

As I said, he came up and rode beside me. I was carrying Hyuna (who was three at the time) in a sling bound to my front. She was facing me, her little head resting on my chest, the sling cradling her under her little seat, her legs sticking out on either side of my waist – fast asleep. One of my younger grandchildren. And on my right was my oldest grandchild. He has a square, handsome face, flashing dark eyes, skinny limbs, and altogether looks very much like his uncle Endu – but with a different spirit. He was nineteen that fall, only a few years younger than Endu was when the tower fell.

"No," I said in answer to his question, "Nirri was not your original grandfather." This seemed to surprise him, and his surprise in turn surprised me ... had we really spoken of Golgal so little? Yet ... Angki had been born before the fall of the tower. Golgal had known him and rejoiced in him.

I explained about Golgal, how he was my first husband, how his name meant "eagle" (this made Ki-Ki laugh, as "Golgal" sounds nothing like our current word for eagle), and how, like all the men of his day, he was deeply involved in planning and building the Tower. I told how there was a judgment, which caused wars to break out among men, and how Golgal had been killed in one of these. How he had been a brave man, and had died defending his family.

My grandson listened patiently while I gave him this history, and then he asked,

"What is a tower?"

What is a tower. I stared at my grandson, at his innocent smile and his bright clear eyes, as a thousand images crowded into my head. I saw Golgal coming home to our house in the city, flushed and excited, keeping me up late at night with talk of what they were doing with the Tower. I saw a teenaged Enmer, waving proudly to me from up on the scaffolding, and how hard Enmer and Endu had worked to understand the mathematics that would qualify them as engineers. How the Tower would keep the city in shade all the morning, and then glow upon it all afternoon, and give back the sun's heat through the hours of the evening. How strange it would look in the winter, when they had covered it with oiled cloth. I remembered seeing the Tower from a distance, dull and red in the sunset, as we fled the ruin that was Si Nar. Then I had a flash of Nirri, throwing back his head and laughing whitely in the darkness of his hut, when he finally understood I was referring to his manhood as a "tower." He had picked up on the word and repeated it immediately, even though this was not his first language, because he, like me, was of the generation that had lived with almost nothing on our minds but the Tower.

And then I saw some images that I had never actually seen with the eyes, but only imagined. I saw the Tower as it was meant to be when it was completed: solid, sheathed in gold, free of scaffolding, with a temple on the top of it. A moment later I saw it crumbling, as Tiras' people had said it had done, the city a warren of scavengers and cannibals below it. Then I imagined I saw Nirri falling, pushed perhaps by some unseen hand. He bounces from level to level of the scaffold – screams as his leg is impaled on a piece of it – the wooden pole breaks and then tips, dumping him lower – he is unconscious before he hits the ground.

What is a tower.

Ki-Ki was worried by my silence. "Grandmother, have I said something wrong?"

"Oh, no, my dear," I told him. "You have said nothing wrong. I am only trying to think how to tell you ..."

How to tell him. What is a tower, my child? It is a symbol of manliness and virility. It is a feat of human strength, pride, and power. Of intellect, too, and all our best thinking. It is a seeming way to get to heaven, but it turns out that the higher it is, the deeper our fall, and it leaves us broken on the ground, as with your grandfather Nirri, or actually buried in the ground, as with your other grandfather. A tower is a beautiful monster that devours the souls of men.

No, none of that would do. I decided I must strive to give him the simplest possible answer.

Well, how would you have answered?

I thought of the buildings Ki-Ki had seen in his lifetime. The largest would have been the great wooden lodge that we built in the Gentle Mountains. It was impressive in its way, but it was built of wood not brick, and though large for a cabin, it could not be compared to a tower.

Then I thought of the tower, or fortress, that the giants had built by the edge of the Stinking Sea. I tried to bring Ki-Ki back to that moment, to find out if he remembered it. It turned out he remembered being on the boat very vividly, with a sense of much excitement, but he did not seem to have seen, or understood, the giants or their tower, beyond a vague sense of danger. I realized then that, though this little one was born in the city, he had never actually seen a city, or a tower.

How to explain it to him. What is a tower.

"It is … it is like a mountain, Ki-Ki," I told him at last. "It is as tall as a mountain, but nowhere near as broad. It is very straight and regular, for it is built by men."

"Built by men!" he repeated, widening his eyes slightly.

I nodded. "Yes, my child. It takes … or, *that* one took … many years. It can only be done when men have plenty of food and no enemies … when they have nothing else to do but work on the tower." And I added, "It is the sort of thing that men build when they want to be like God."

His eyes widened again, and he said (but not regretfully nor yet defiantly), "We will never build one, then."

"No, my child," I agreed. "Your generation will explore and live in God's world. You will not try to escape it."

A moment later I added, with a smile, "… And I don't think you should let your father find out that you had to ask me what a tower is."

This comment did not surprise Ki-Ki. We had already observed that there were many things it was better to fix quietly first, before bringing them to Enmer's attention. That is why the chief is always the last to know.

After the wedding proper, the ceremony and the feasting, there was nothing left to do but to relax. We had a great deal of music, played by Ki-Ki and the other children whom he has taught, nearly all of it composed by Ki-Ki. I swear, that young man is able to do anything he sets his hand to. Though slightly older than his cousin Hur-kar, Ki-Ki is not yet wed.

(*Why?* I don't know why, my love, but he will make someone a real catch.)

He gave us danceable music, and little Hyuna could not resist it. She got up and she must have danced for two hours. She is never still, that one. I had to get up and dance with her, taking perhaps one step for every five or six of hers, so that I would not wear out. Her fair hair and her little smile are Hur's, but that joyful energy comes from Ninna.

When she was done dancing, she sat down on a blanket with me, cuddled for a moment, and was almost instantly asleep. Ninna looked over at me and chuckled. She too was "trapped" on a blanket with a little one, in this case her baby Emi, who had fallen asleep nursing and would probably wake if Ninna tried to rise. Ninna actually stretched out on the ground, and between dozes she went on watching the festivities. I sat cross-legged, leaning back on my hands, with the warm weight of my granddaughter on my legs, and I was still sitting like that when, across the camp, Hur-Kar and Lien were picked up bodily and carried to the private tent that had been set up for the occasion. Lien was carried, very carefully and gently, by her father-in-law Hur, whereas young Hur-Kar was swept up roughly by one Rumi, a young ox of a man who himself took a wife a few years ago. They bore them off with a lot of laughing and noise and foolishness. This was perhaps not what the shy Hur-kar would have preferred, but it has become our tradition.

(*Why?* Again, I don't know. Perhaps because ... we are so happy that life is going on.)

Then Hur came back, smiling and flushed beneath the festive eyepatch he was wearing, to where Ninna and I were spread out with our little ones.

"Well, that's done," he said with satisfaction. Then he gently lifted Hyuna, who did not wake, and brought her off to their family tent, and in another moment he came and helped my daughter to move Emi. By this time, the sky was turning a clear green color with twilight.

I got up and began to help with all the cleaning up and putting away that comes after a day of feasting. We had a few more days of feasting planned, but still we must do a minimal amount. Fires must be banked, dishes must be wiped, food must be well secured. In this case, we put the leftovers in a cache some distance from the camp.

(*Why? Because*, darling, bears.)

It wasn't until a few hours later that I crept to my little corner of Enmer and Ninshi's tent. I still live with them when we are on the road. It can be a bit tense at times, but the tension is offset for me because Ki-Ki is with them. Also,

Enmer will frequently forget himself and ask my advice about things.

Ninshi had a new baby too, who had been born earlier that winter. This one was a girl, for a wonder, named Koret. Koret was a good baby, waking only once or twice in the night. But on that night, in one of her early-morning wakings, she caught me in the midst of a bad dream.

I usually sleep well, my head full of happy thoughts of the children and grandchildren. It is rare that I find myself back in that desert place. But every once in a while, usually on nights like this when I have gotten too tired, I find that place waiting for me.

I close my eyes and I can sense that, outside their barrier, there is the terrible glare of the sun … the burning salt wind that makes the eyes water … the pain, in every part of the body, from thirst. I keep them closed desperately, knowing there is something I ought to get up and do. I must go down to that little puddle and try again to bring up some water for Nirri. He is far worse off than I am. Perhaps I can give him some relief … perhaps I can even keep him alive, until help comes.

For some reason I know that help is going to come.

But I resist opening my eyes, because when I do, I know that the first thing I see will be the soul leaving his thirst-blind eyes, while below that, his chapped lips break into a faint, happy smile.

I want to delay that moment.

Then something wakes me. In this case, the cry of a baby. Then with a great rush of relief I wake up in the warm tent, my face wet with tears. The deed is already done. I cannot save him.

These are not the memories that I will ever share with Ki-Ki.

There is a skin of water nearby. I grope toward it in the dark, and drink and drink and drink to the point of discomfort.

Why?

Oh, *Nirri* …

It's all right, he said.

CHAPTER 26

THE GREAT SEA

Hur

My name is Hur son of Seth. I am a Japhethite who once
lived in Si Nar, and am now a member of the clan of Enmer
son of Golgal, also a Japhethite. I was thirty years old when
God confused the languages and the people scattered. The
Tower itself fell in the next year, and men have been
dispersing over the world ever since. I turned fifty-two last
year, and this spring it is twenty-two years since the great
judgment.

Two years ago, we were at a large and beautiful inland
lake. It was very deep: we tried, but my sons and I could not
determine its depth. My oldest son, Hur-Kar, was married
there. We spent one winter, and then in the spring we
departed. We have a tribal habit of always going east. We
traveled east in the spring of last year, going over much land,
windswept plains and evergreen forests. And at last, in the
autumn, we found the barrier we had been seeking. We
found the great sea.

It is a cold sea, but it is not what we once called the Sea
of Death. We found no boneyards here. Instead we found
steep, green cliffs descending to black sand beaches. The
mist comes down the hills and makes a sort of high roof over

the beach. And the variety of sea animals that we found is dazzling. There are great fish, which we now call whales, and parts of whales that lie upon the beaches. There are so many different kinds that we are just now beginning to learn them. Some of the kinds look very similar to each other, like brothers; others stand out. My favorite are the large, striking black-and-white ones that come to the surface in groups, jumping and blowing out water. The contrast on their coats make each look like more than one animal.

There are numerous large birds – too many for me to name here – that live on and around the water. There are large doglike or lionlike things also, that live in the water, but breathe air and come onto the land to lie about in groups. We have been calling them sea lions because of the resemblance in the face. They look like a poorly made child's doll, their flesh stuffed lumpily into their fat brown bodies. With all that fat they look like they would be good to eat, but their flesh is not particularly tasty. However, there is plenty of food in the form of fish. Easiest and most delicious is a large, muscular, red-fleshed fish that comes up the estuaries and rivers. These can almost be caught with the hand. Indeed, the sea is so rich in food that we have taken to getting much of our meat from the sea, though we make our actual camp farther inland.

We are building more lodges like the ones we have known before, using the slow-burn method. The trees are a bit stunted here. I suppose they have been growing since the Flood, but this far north, in a given year they do not get a very long growing season. Their wood is hard and sturdy. As for the forest, it has many of the same animals we've become accustomed to, including the bad one.

It seems we have come as far as we are able. Go east, Tiras said, and east we have gone, and here is the sea. People used to talk of a great sea that laps around all the edges of the world; if such a thing exists, I believe we have found it. In fact, maybe this is our second look at it, if we are counting the Sea of Death. There was a sea south of Si Nar, men said, so this might be as much as the third time we have encountered it.

This sea is obviously no lake. It is salty; it is clearly vast. We traveled a little way north along the coast before picking a place to settle (we avoided the south because of the dragon kingdom there), and the coast seems to go on forever. We *may* find land at the north end of it, as we did with the Stinking Sea, but I doubt it. Anyway, I don't think we could go very many weeks north before we start crossing back again into perpetual night. And I don't think Enmer is willing to do that.

So I do not know what will come next. Perhaps this is the place we will settle after all. It certainly fulfills all the conditions Tiras had in mind, as isolated, defensible, full of food, and set very far east. I don't know what more a clan could ask. But Enmer is sensitive to the darkness in everything. Perhaps he will not be satisfied.

It is certainly as far from the sunny plain of the tower as one can get. I don't know whether he considers that a good or a bad thing. But I know what *I* consider it. If there are people who have stayed there – if they have not all killed each other, or turned into giants or monsters or some such thing – I suppose they are going on with their business. They are fighting wars, building cities, setting up kings and assassinating them. They are worshipping their gods and building their idols. And if they ever think at all of us, the people who after the judgment ran far away, I sure that in their view we are missing out. We are not at the center of things. And I say, good riddance. The center of things is not where I wish to be. I prefer to live like a sane man, surrounded by forest, fields, and my family.

I liked Nirri, once he stopped sulking, which is to say for most of his time with us. You couldn't help but like him, he was so bright-eyed and intelligent, so eager to learn. As I say, I liked him … but I do not like his type of man. That is a city type, a king-ish type, a type that is restless and always scheming. One such man, a Grandfather Nirri, yes. A city full of them, no. In groups they are far too much for this Japhethite.

He could surprise you with a laugh once in a while, too, but that was a trick he picked up later. I don't remember any men like him having any sense of humor, back there on the tower. They, and their project, were deadly serious. Good riddance, again.

My family, then. First let me talk about my wife. It is a pleasure for me to talk about her. To the rest of the tribe she is only Ninna, and has been here forever, but to me … well, it even gives me satisfaction to say the words, "my wife." We talk over everything, she and I. She had another baby just last fall, another girl – which is fine with me – named Tisha. That makes eight children we have together. So far, that is. Ninna is about ten years younger than I am, still strong, still dark-haired. Now that her face has thinned out with age she looks like a much darker version of her mother, but with a little less of Zillah's fierce look. She has her own sweet smile.

Shulgi and I were married two years, and I liked her. Ninna and I have now been married … let's see, coming up on twenty. And I like her, certainly, but there hasn't been a word made that can describe what it means to live for twenty years with a woman like her. For some of the words are too … well, too dramatic, and others don't reach wide enough.

Twenty years of marriage. You know, Zillah has been through this twice. Two husbands – near enough – buried each one – or, buried one and burned the other on a pyre – and she is still here with us. That makes a person think.

Zillah came down with a cough last fall, and it stayed with her all winter. She lives with us, now – with Ninna and me – and we tried to keep her as comfortable as possible. Ninna would bring her remedies, and we'd fill the tent with warm, steamy air by boiling snow on the fire, even though it meant that as soon as you stepped outside, the water would turn to ice on your lashes. We did not really think this sickness would end in death (and it didn't), for she is only eighty-one, still a relatively young and vigorous woman. But all the same, I asked her one day, knowing that death comes to us all, what sort of animal she thought she'd be, when her time did come.

I should explain that we have developed a convention of talking about people's spirits in terms of animals. This was mostly driven by Ki-Ki, who has become a kind of priest to us. He seems to view this not only as a tool for thought, but as a real connection happening in the spirit world. So that when he sees an eagle, for example, he really feels that he is seeing his grandfather.

I have a great interest in the animals myself, a practical interest. I am even an expert. Well, anyone would be, who watches them most of his waking hours. But I am more interested in their behavior, not in their spiritual nature. I grant you the two do overlap, but as far as totems and such, I leave that to Ki-Ki. No one can deny that he's a sensitive and observant boy, who really loves, not only the animals, but also his ancestors. But he's not the sort of priest who is always throwing dust in the air. He's bright and clever, as if he has the spirit of his grandfather. And funny and curious as well. And that is the kind of priest for me.

So, as I was saying, we are coming to talk about animals as if they were the expression, but also the patron, of a particular person or family. Endu, now, he and his family have taken the bear. And I have to admit it fits them well. They have had a connection to the bear since a very large one killed Sari's first husband, Imsag. Not a happy connection, but a connection nonetheless. Then a few years later, when with my help Endu slaughtered what we believe was that same bear, he got for himself revenge, experience, and the glory that he craved, and a reputation for ferocity. And it happened that in the meantime, Endu was revealing himself to be a bit cruel, so it fits when we call him "the bad one," which is the nickname of the bear. And now – it fits almost too well, enough to make a person laugh – as Sari gets older and has more children, she is becoming round and solid, beginning to look like a mother bear. And some of Endu's sons are built like bears as well, though their father is not, and nearly all of them live up to the name "the bad ones." So we see the wisdom of Ki-Ki's choice.

That's only one example. Not all of them fit as neatly. Ninna and I are known as the reindeer family, I think purely because I once milked one of them, but other than that there is no connection that I can see. We aren't especially tall, or long-legged, or noble, and we certainly don't have antlers.

Grandfather Nirri is called a reindeer as well, though Ninna tells me it is really a camel. When you live in a land without camels, you have to take the nearest animal you can get. This is not nearly as precise as tower-building.

It's more of a game than anything. But it's a game that gives us comfort, and that helps us put a name to things that we couldn't otherwise.

So it was that I came to ask Grandmother Zillah what animal she thought she would … move into, as it were, when she did eventually die: "Which one… the camel or the eagle?"

That was how it came out, and then I could've bitten off my tongue, for it sounded as if I was asking her to choose between her two husbands. I had said it because I was asking her at a relaxed moment; I felt at home with her, and so I wasn't careful with my words.

She smiled and moved a hand with a dismissive motion, as if smoothing the air, and I saw she wasn't offended by my blunder.

"Neither of those, my son," she said pleasantly, and then coughed. "I won't …" (cough cough) "… I won't take your false choice." Then she paused and grinned and said, "I don't know, and I dare say it's all nonsense … but if I had to say, I suppose I'd come back as a crow. They are just like me, always making trouble."

Of course, we laughed and insisted that she doesn't make trouble. Or at least, only makes it every twenty years or so. But by then it was too late. The animal had stuck. And it does seem to fit her, somehow. And the funny thing is, even though she is still with us, I now find that I notice it, and find some significance too, if ever I see a crow flying near an eagle, or hopping near the feet of a reindeer.

This past fall, not long after we'd arrived and settled, my daughter Magya, who is seventeen, was late one day for supper. Then eventually she and Ki-Ki came out of the forest together, and it was obvious they had been kissing. Maybe more than kissing. Maybe much more. After all, they're not children; Ki-Ki was at that time twenty-one years old, and Magya, who was then almost seventeen, was not much younger than Ninna was when she and I married.

Magya, in fact, looks very much like her mother did at that age. She is short, dark, and shapely, with a sweet round face and cascading black hair. All of which could still describe Ninna, but the young woman's mannerisms and the very young face … if I cast my mind back, I can *just* remember Ninna looking like that.

Magya did not seem distressed, so Ninna and I were not worried about her. Ninna only said, "You are late," and handed her a wooden bowl of stew, and then she looked meaningfully at me when Magya bent her head.

I waited until later that night, and then I beckoned her over to our cooking fire. We had arrived in our new site recently enough that we were still living in tents, but it was still early autumn and we were cooking outdoors, not bothering to light fires within. I wanted to talk to her away from the large ears of her little brother and sisters.

"So, is it true," I said to her, "That you and Ki-Ki will soon be married?"

She gave a quiet, womanly smile, and then she looked up at me with a face so full of both excitement and misery that my heart went out to her. I gathered her into my arms. And when I did that, she started sniffling, just a bit.

"What is wrong, daughter?"

"He likes me," she began.

"But?"

"But …" and here her voice dropped low, "I am afraid of Uncle Enmer."

"That he will forbid the match?"

"Y-yes."

I smiled. I could see no reason why this would be. "I don't think he will do that, my daughter. But do not worry. I will talk to him."

That is what the young ones fear about Enmer ... that he will be harsh. I, now one of the elders, have an older man's fear, a fear *for* Enmer. I fear from time to time, whenever something happens, that it will be too much for him. This is a heavier fear, and not one that a seventeen-year-old should have to carry.

I was happy about the match. I like Ki-Ki. I think I have already mentioned some of his good qualities. And as far as I knew, my older brother had no objection to Magya. In fact, the match seemed so good that I wondered where she had gotten this fear. I released her, patted her hair a bit, and then asked,

"Is Ki-Ki also afraid that Enmer will forbid the match?"

"He does not know. He says he doesn't know his father."

"I ... I think it will be all right," I told her. I comforted my daughter a bit more, and then we went inside and talked to Ninna, who was full of excitement and plans. Ai Li was already betrothed to Kira, who was one of the younger sons of Melek, so we began planning a double wedding.

And the very next day I spoke to my brother, and as I had expected, he had no objection to the match, and neither did Ninshi. So we began preparations, but just as in another autumn that I remember, the weddings could not be held immediately. We were too busy building and getting ready for winter. It looked as if our young couples would have to wait, and marry later after the snows had come.

Well, it had worked out all right for Ninna and me. But we remembered the frayed tempers and the inconvenience of starting our married life in a hall crammed with people, so to our plans and our building we added two small additional huts, one for each of my daughters and her husband.

That was a busy season, as is every autumn, especially after a move. But I found time to speak to Enmer about his son.

"He doesn't understand you," I said, being very blunt with him as I am sometimes able to do. "He doesn't know what you're thinking. But you have good reasons for the things you do, my brother. You should let him know what these are. You have got to tell him the whole story, from the beginning. You have got to explain yourself."

He looked at me, appalled. "The *whole story*? How can I tell him … how can I explain?"

I put a hand on his shoulder while I searched for words. "All right, maybe not the whole story, brother," I said at last. Did he think I was asking him to tell every detail of the last fifty years? "But … tell him the parts that are relevant. He is a man now. He can understand more than you think. Tell him about the tower. Tell him what it was like … in those early days."

"He won't believe me."

"He will. Tell him what you have been fearing all these years."

"How can I … it would destroy …"

"He may be chief someday. He needs to know that a chief has fears. And it will help him understand why you cast out Nirri."

"That would break his heart!"

I thought about this. I was not sure it would. Nirri was indeed a god in Ki-Ki's mind, but I didn't think a little tarnish would knock him off his pedestal.

"It will mean, brother," I said, "that he will have to hold two things in his mind at once. The hateful Cushite of your story, and the Grandfather Nirri that he knew. That would be hard for a child … but now Ki-Ki is a man. He is about to marry my daughter. He … well, he is going to be facing a lot of … complexity."

Enmer laughed at my reference to the moods of women, but then he said, "And at a time like this, when he is about to marry your daughter, you want me to burden him with all this confusion?"

"I hope it will relieve some confusion," I said. "And I'd like you to talk to him now, so that he has a little time for thinking, before the wedding."

"All right," said Enmer, making a face as if he were facing a very bitter drink, "I will … I will humble myself to him … and explain things to him as best I can. But only *if*," he added, looking up at me very sharply, "You will tell him the story of how you lost your eye!"

I laughed and agreed. As soon as I had, I realized in part why Enmer had been so reluctant. In order to tell the story straight, I was going to have to think in great detail about that terrible night, and bring myself back to it, as it were. That would be unpleasant and exhausting. But I would do it, to keep a promise.

In some measure, I agreed with my brother that the timing was not perfect. Ki-Ki's many questions should have been answered a few years before. And I was not sure he would absorb much, given the state of mind that a man is usually in as he awaits his wedding. So perhaps Ki-Ki would not gain much in clarity. But if Enmer only talked to him, as one man to another … this was my goal. I couldn't forget the words that Magya had spoken, when she said, "He says he doesn't know his father."

Enmer kept his word. Well before the snows, as they were working together on what was to be Ki-Ki's own hut, they had some sort of conversation. What Enmer chose to tell and chose to leave out I don't know, but I do know that afterward, both of them were very quiet and thoughtful.

Enmer, in fact, as soon as he got a chance, went off by himself for a long while. Eventually I went off the way he had gone, which was eastward from the camp, toward the coast. I followed his footsteps and found him near the sea.

He was standing on a rock partway down the cliff, wrapped in a blanket, watching the water. I climbed down to him. The sea was cold and tossing that day, its color grey with plenty of white foam. As I approached, I wondered whether I would find him weeping. Enmer still weeps frequently, never during a crisis but usually afterward. I like this about him. It means he is still human. I don't think I would trust him as a leader if he never wept.

He had been weeping, from the looks of it, but was now silent. I was reminded suddenly of my father. I used to go and visit him at his master's house in the last days before he died.

"I've failed," he would say to me. "I've failed you all."

And I would say, "No, Dad, you haven't failed ..."

It is strange that Enmer reminds me of my father. Actually, we are the same age, give or take a year. But he is such a different man from myself, that most of the time, he seems to be either much older or much younger. Older, when I don't know his thoughts, as now. Younger, when I have got to go and comfort him.

I remember the first time I ever approached him as he sat like this. His own father had just been killed, and he was the new leader of the family. And at that time, I was still a slave. I remember coming to him with my courage girded, ready for bargaining, nervous but also terribly excited about the opportunity for freedom that lay before me. And I had found him just as now, sitting very still with that strange inward stare, curled in on himself with grief. He had spoken to me of his grief, and I had listened briefly, but quickly moved on to what I considered the meat of the matter, namely our freedom; for the whole fate of my own little family hung on that conversation.

Now, I had the strangest feeling that the whole fate of the family was hanging on this conversation as well. But unlike that early night beside the fire, I had not come with a matter to talk about. I had no idea what I ought to say.

"We are going to have to go there, aren't we?" said my brother dully. His gaze was turned toward the coast to the north of us, where the rocks drew closer to the water, and the sea was smashing itself against them.

"Perhaps not, brother," I replied. I had to stand very close to him, practically leaning on his shoulder, so that we could hear one another through the wind. "We will have councils and then decide. Perhaps this place is good enough."

By that time, decisions were almost never made only by Enmer. We older men would sit in council and talk about whatever it was, until we were all agreed. And it wasn't just us deciding, either: whenever it was known that we were talking over a matter, the younger men and the women and even the young girls would give us their opinions, and plenty of them, and we would bear these in mind when we talked.

But Enmer was still our chief, because no matter how much in agreement a group may be, people still need a chief. And he still felt that he was responsible.

"I give up," he said to me now. "Tiras said north and east. I tried to resist it. But now I know that we've got to go that way, even though there is death that way. It is the path laid out for us."

I was again reminded of my dad. He had become very fatalistic there at the end.

"Well, what if we do, brother?" I replied heartily. "This time we have the sea. I think, if we learn how to take food from the sea, it could feed us all through the winter."

Enmer closed his eyes and shuddered slightly. He was terrified of what the young men wanted to do, which was make boats and learn to use them to hunt the whales. It was a very risky thing, but after all that's why God gives us young men … to take mad risks that no one else would ever dream of taking. It is often these mad, seemingly useless risks that end up becoming the salvation of a people.

But at that time, I saw that my words were doing Enmer no good, so I made myself be silent.

We stood like that for a while, and then he surprised me by saying, "At times like this I wish the Cushite were here to play me just one song."

I was so startled by this that I goggled at him and said nothing at all. But he rounded on me as if I had spoken and snarled, "I *do not miss* the Camel's Ass! I just … I miss his music … the way he would play us back to ourselves."

I was silent again, and he said, "Yes, yes, I know that Ki-Ki can play the very songs that he played … but that's no good … they don't work that way, they have to be played by someone who remembers … someone who knows …"

Then he said, "Leave me!" and I turned around and climbed back to the summit of the cliff, to let him have his private cry.

Eventually he came and joined me, and up there it was very windy indeed. But Enmer suddenly threw off his blanket and spread out his arms, which were bare. The wind off the sea came from behind him and whipped forward his long black hair and his beard.

I called into his ear, "What are you doing, brother?"

And he replied, still holding out his bare arms, though there was gooseflesh on them. "I hate this cursed cold," he said. "Do you remember in Si Nar, when we could go outside naked if we cared to? Even in the winters there, we never dreamed of this cold."

I let him stand like that for a moment, and then I gathered up the blanket and draped it over his shoulders, and said to him, "There, brother. Feel the warmth of Si Nar."

"I believe that is the warmth of Ninshi's weaving," he answered, but he smiled slightly.

"I am worried about your brother," I said to my wife, when we got back to the camp.

Her eyes got wide and her forehead wrinkled, but there wasn't much she could say at that time. She was busy with cleaning up after the evening meal, and with getting the young ones ready for bed. I helped with that, and then we talked about it again later that night.

This is where we usually discuss things, snuggled down under our wooly blanket, with the children sleeping or drifting towards slumber in a pile around us. I lay on my side and wrapped my body around Ninna's back, and she nestled in to me.

"You are worried about Enmer," she said quietly. "Do you think he might …?"

"Throw himself into the sea, or some such thing?" I asked, and she nodded. "No, I do not think so," I told her. "He harms himself a great deal in his mind, but I have never known him to try to harm his own body." And I could remember a time when he had run out into a cold night to stop me from harming myself. "But I think he will become … reckless," I added. "I think he may insist that we move very far north along the coast, even though there is no need for it."

Ninna gave a little exhale to show that she had heard me. "What can we do?"

"Do? I don't know. Keep talking to him, I suppose." As usual, there was not much we *could* do. Many problems don't have a solution. "But don't worry," I told her. "We will never move north unless all the elders agree to it as well." And that would mean that virtually the whole clan would have to agree.

We fell silent. Ninna's body grew warm and heavy; she was nearing sleep. But there was something I wanted to ask her. I nuzzled in her hair until she stirred.

I asked, "Is it true that Grandfather Nirri attacked you?"

My wife laughed. "Yes, it's true. Don't you remember? I was sixteen." And she told me the whole story.

When she had finished, I said, puzzling it out, "So this would be when he was still in his sulks, then?"

"Yes, exactly. It was that first year."

I remembered Nirri during that first year. He had been truly awful. "What a nasty experience for you, my love!"

"Yes, it was, at the time," she said. "It knocked some sense into me, you know. I was such a stupid little girl ... I thought he was so handsome and noble, before that ..."

"But it doesn't seem to be a bitter memory for you, now."

"You are right, it isn't. I suppose it's because of Enmer. He stood up for me," she said sleepily, "so beautifully."

"He is good at protecting his family."

"That he is."

We fell silent again. Eight-year-old Mut spoke something unintelligible in sleep, making us both chuckle, and then he rolled over.

Ninna gave a happy sigh and said, "Magya will be having children of her own soon."

"And what about you?" I put a hand on her belly and began creeping it upward. "How would it be if you were having a child at the same time as your daughter?" And then, when she held silent a moment, thinking, I added, "Or are you finished with all of that, daughter of Zillah?"

My wife gave another laugh; I love to hear her laugh. "Maybe not finished," she said. "Let's keep having children for another ten years, and then be content with what we have."

And she squirmed and rolled around to face me in the dark.

EPILOGUE

HERE IS THE WAY IT ALL STARTED

Ki-Ki, even later

It was an early autumn night, approaching the equinox. The nights were lengthening, and this night was already black, the sky-dome above full of brilliant stars. On the horizon there was a faint green glow. They knew they were seeing, from far off, the Grandfather Curtain.

The children had been allowed to stay up later than usual. Some of them had fallen asleep over their supper and had to be awakened for this special meeting. It was a night for storytelling around the embers of the cooking fire.

Ki-Ki was not old enough yet to be one of the tribal elders, but he was old enough to pass on to the children what everyone in the tribe knew to be true. He was respected because he had a special affinity with beasts, and few could play the lute or the bone-flute like he could, and he was a fine storyteller.

He was a lean, rangy man with large hands and wrists. He stirred the fire a little, using a stick to nudge the coals into a closer pile. They flared up red, lighting up his smooth brown arms and the underside of his beardless chin. The starlight shone on his sleek black hair.

He seated himself amidst the children, and swept over the group with his eyes. Most of these children were nieces and nephews to Ki-Ki; cousins or the children of cousins; or even his own younger brothers and sisters. Two of them were his own children: the girl, Reena, and the little boy, Eyli. And there sat some of the younger sons of his uncle Endu, their thick little bodies hunched and their grins glowing in the light of the fire. They were hoping for an adventure tale with plenty of action. And Ki-Ki would give it to them, in a little while, but now he needed to start with an important story, the explanation of how everything began. And it all began with a mountain.

He looked again at the children, smiling to see them. He took a breath and stilled himself within, preparing for the story. He strummed a few chords on his lute. Then he began to speak.

Listen, children:

We, the People, did not always live where we do now, in these great woods surrounded by beasts such as hares, bears, red deer, great deer, eagles, wolves, and tigers.

Our ancestors lived in a different land, a land that was almost paradise. It was a good green land. There was a harvest every year, and they seldom needed to hunt because the beasts were so plentiful. People were like the gods in those days. People did not get sick and die. They lived several hundred years, or perhaps a thousand. No one was ever weak or stupid, and no child was ever born with anything wrong.

Why did we ever leave this good land? We were driven out by a judgment.

Our ancestors did something bad. We do not know exactly what it was, but it had to do with a great mountain they had built, called a tower. This tower rose taller than the biggest mountains we see, but straighter and steeper and more beautiful than anything you can imagine. And by building this tower, our ancestors sinned. So they had to leave the good land.

Ever since then, our grandfathers have been wishing they could get back to that mountain, where there was peace and plenty. But this will never happen.

When our people came out of the Good Land, they were led by the Grandfathers. The Grandfathers were old and wise and strong. They had long black beards, such as no one can grow today. You can see something like it if you look at your grandfather Enmer. You call him Grandfather, but there were Grandfathers before him, and it was they – and the

Grandmothers – who led the people. They taught us to ride horses and make tents, to hunt and make bows, and to sing and make sacrifices. Everything we know, we learned from the Grandfathers.

Furthermore, some of them could turn into beasts. One of your grandfathers was named Golgal, which means Eagle. That is why we do not kill eagles, ever. Another of your Grandfathers was a camel. That is an ancient beast that we do not see any more. But I am told that it looks like a reindeer. That is why, when we kill a great deer or a stag, we do not eat its heart.

When our Grandfathers came out of the good land, out into the wide world, they knew we, their children, would have to survive and make our way. They protected us with their minds and bodies while they were still alive, defending us from enemies many times. And now, they watch over us in the form of animals, after death. They wanted us to go on. That is why they gave us the gifts they have given us. And that is why, when we roast meat, we throw a little ash into the air for the Grandfathers. We hope the wind will carry it to them, wherever they may be, and they can enjoy the good smell and know that we are honoring them.

That is also why, children, you must always honor the Grandfathers and Grandmothers who are still with us. They have much to teach you, children, much that is profitable for wisdom and knowledge and learning ... although they will never be able to convey to you everything that they know.

When the listeners had all been put to bed, Ki-Ki remained sitting by the fire. He drew up his legs and closed his eyes. This was not the perfect place to meditate, but he had just finished telling stories, and it was possible the door might still be open. He wanted to remain for a few moments, just in case he got a visit from anyone.

He had first sought a vision shortly before he got married, seeking to ground himself against the waves of the future and to find a firm footing amid the still-blowing gusts from the past. He had gone out for a day's journey into the woods, making sure that the family knew where he was going and that he didn't just disappear, leaving duties undone.

He had brought no food, nothing to hunt with. He had fasted to clear his mind. Fasting was a hardship, not something to be done often, not normally something that people would seek out. But when it was thrust upon them by sickness or famine, it was known to thin the veil between the world of people and the spiritual world.

He knew that when Grandmother Zillah had been sent out into the desert, that was a fast.

His vision trip had come not long after a serious conversation, the first real conversation that he could remember, with his father. Ki-Ki had wanted, partly, to find out whether those spiritual realities that he had always sensed would still seem real to him. For to Enmer, they were all no more than historical facts ... real enough at the time that they'd happened, but now forever locked in the past.

"We cannot get them back," Enmer had said, with that extremely grim look that Ki-Ki had always taken for heartlessness, but which he now knew was his father's way of fighting off grief. "They are gone, son."

It was during that conversation that Ki-Ki first realized how bitterly Enmer regretted their being gone.

It had always seemed to him, before, that Enmer was eager quickly to get rid of things or people that he thought might cause pain, often before, in Ki-Ki's opinion, they were ready to go. Now, he understood a bit better. He had thought that his father had not *tried* to get them back. Well, what was Enmer meant to have done? Meditate on a field of battle to try to feel his father or his brother? Try to settle his family in the midst of a burning city? Though Ki-Ki had never seen a city, Enmer and Zillah had said enough that he realized this would not have been possible.

And, though Ki-Ki thought of his father as ruthless, it was true that with the exception of Grandfather Nirri, he had never known Enmer to kill or cast out anyone who had the slightest claim on him. It was just that whenever they had to leave a place, he had always seemed so eager to forget.

Ki-Ki still did not fully understand what had been so terrible about Grandfather Nirri. Granted that he may have been a villain at the beginning, it seemed to Ki-Ki that he had quickly improved. And he had seemed to *fit.* It had been a shock to discover that Nirri was not his real grandfather, that none of Nirri's blood actually ran in his veins. Which probably meant, sadly, Ki-Ki reflected, that he would never be able to grow a great black beard. And it was unlikely ever to be curly, if he did.

What was wrong with Grandfather Nirri, according to Enmer, was that he was the antithesis of all Enmer's efforts to save his people, to have them live in peace and happiness. Nirri was the opposite of strength, skill, and wisdom; the opposite of providing for one's family. He was a taker. More than this, he was wicked and cruel, a bringer of chaos. Not to be trusted.

All that was manifest nonsense, of course. It was obvious to Ki-Ki that his grandfather had contributed many things to the tribe. But he had kept silent about them, having seen that it did not go well for others when they mentioned these things to Enmer. And, oddly, he still trusted his father's judgment about most things. Now that Nirri was gone, Ki-Ki had no intention of making a break with the one who remained.

Divided loyalty was hell.

But what had shaken him most about the conversation had not been any particular revelation, but the *tone* he had heard from Enmer: the unexpected but undeniable tone of regret.

Was it possible, then, for a man who truly longed to see some loved thing, to be denied it? Was it possible to seek a vision and not find it? Why then had Ki-Ki never been denied? Surely, he was not a better man than his father.

He had found a spot to meditate, and had sat there for a night and a day. It had been rather cold. And during that time – nothing. So he got a taste of the world in which his father lived, the world that is bereft of everything. On the second night, however, he fell asleep, a very deep, restless, hungry sleep. And in that sleep, he had a visitor.

It was not the person he had most longed to see, his Grandfather Nirri. So here was another denial. Yet this was satisfying. The spirit world was real, then: it did not fulfill your wishes any more than the walking world did. Just as in waking, if you got a spirit visitor you had to be content with whoever came along.

What came along was a rather shabby little donkey. Ki-Ki had not seen donkeys in a few years, but he remembered them from his childhood. It came trotting up to the little rise on which he was sitting, and it was obviously a city donkey, for it had on its back a complicated harness that allowed it to bear on either side a load of strange square rocks such as Ki-Ki had never seen. Also, it had a number of welts and sores, as if it had been ill-used.

But it trotted up to him with plenty of spunk and energy, navigating the rocky hill better than any actual horse could have, its load never catching on any of the undergrowth. Then it sat down as if stubbornly, bared its long teeth, and let out a long, ugly, bugling bray.

Ki-Ki laughed heartily, tickled but not enlightened. He was just thinking that he was sure to get no information out of *this* vision, when he saw that instead of its former load, seated on the sloping back of the donkey (and now bracing her feet on the ground) was a small, long-faced woman he did not recognize. And he knew that the woman and the donkey were the same.

"Who are you?" he said to the two of them.

And the woman said, "I am your uncle Hur's first wife Shulgi." Then she added with barely a pause, "Believe everything that your father has told you about the tower. It made my life, and your uncle's life, very bitter. Your father is right that you should not desire to go back to that. He is right that you should not try to converse with the dead."

"Why, then, can I see you?" said Ki-Ki.

"You will be able to see us, and sense us, frequently throughout your life. The other members of your family will not. They will see us, perhaps, once in a lifetime. You can help them understand the things they might see ... but don't force them. They are meant to live in the walking world."

Ki-Ki bowed his head humbly, which seemed to please Shulgi very much. She laughed – a barking laugh that sounded like it was rarely used – and said, "I like it! I never thought I'd see the son of Enmer bowing to *me*."

She stared at him beadily for a moment, and finally he ventured, "Do you have anything more to tell me?"

"I don't know everything. I only came by to say hello." And then, into his crushing disappointment, she added, "I suppose you are wondering about your Grandfather Nirri?"

Filled with awe, he nodded.

"I died by violence, so it is easier for me to come back. He did not die by violence, despite how it may have seemed to you. He went into the desert, fasted, and there he met God."

God. Ki-Ki was again speechless. He knew that God was a great spirit who had made all things and who could make himself present everywhere ... but he had never associated God with his Grandfather Nirri, who, for all his gifts of music, had been firmly in and of this earth.

"He was the last man you'd expect it of," said Shulgi, as if hearing his thoughts, "But your beloved grandfather has gone to God. And though you may not believe it, it was his last wish that you should know Him."

Ki-Ki blinked back tears. "God ... rejected us," he muttered, echoing the words of his father. "He cast us out ..."

"The earth is His," said Shulgi. "He can be present wherever you go in the earth. The sea is His, for He made it. Whatever you find to eat in the sea, that is of God."

"Still feeding us ..."

She smiled, a less bitter smile this time. "As He fed me, right up until the end, though every day I doubted He would do it. And for all the peoples on this earth, He has determined the exact times and places where they will live."

"Where is our place?" said Ki-Ki quickly.

"I can't tell you everything," said Shulgi, becoming willful again. She stood up from the donkey, which vanished, and began to brush off a pale dust which was thickly coated, with cracks, on her hands.

"What were those square things?" asked Ki-Ki, noticing.

"Bricks," the slave woman replied. "We had to make them endlessly to build that damn tower."

"It wasn't *my* tower," he said defensively.

"I know, dear," said Shulgi. Stepping forward, she kissed him on the forehead. The kiss quickly became wet and prickly, and when he looked up, she had returned to the form of the donkey. She turned and trotted off, not down the hill this time, but straight off the top of it and into the air, as if proceeding down a distant city street.

Now, at the storytelling fire, Ki-Ki sat for a few moments
with his eyes closed. He had just concluded that nobody was
coming by, and was about to rise, when a dark form swept
down out of the stars and landed, painfully, its talons digging
in, upon his knee.

It was an eagle.

Behind the eagle, or in addition to it, or forming a
backdrop to the entire scene, there was another presence.
This presence frightened Ki-Ki. He found himself unable to
look at it directly. So, because he was afraid, he ignored the
presence and instead spoke to the eagle.

"Is that you, Grandfather?"

The eagle looked at him and twisted its head around on
its neck.

Magya came out to find him a few minutes later, her long
deer-hide skirt making a snapping sound against her legs as
she strode. She was in the early months of her third
pregnancy, too fatigued to sit up for storytelling, so Zillah
had gotten her children up for the campfire and then, later,
down to bed, while Magya went to sleep early. But she had
woken needing the latrine, had then washed her hands at the

stream, and had sighted her husband still sitting by the embers of the fire.

"Who were you talking to?" she asked matter-of-factly, once she got within speaking distance.

"The eagle," said Ki-Ki, using his crossed legs to lever himself to his feet. It had swooped away, a black shape against the black sky, just as she approached, and in the process, it had gouged his knee worse than ever. He doubted she'd seen it, or could see it. As he rose, he brushed at his knee with his fingers. Just as he'd expected, there was no wound there at all.

"Grandfather Golgal, then?"

"Yes," Ki-Ki said. He brushed at his wife's hair, lifting it from the side of her sweet, round face. "Star Woman," he murmured. This was his nickname for her, his way of calling her beautiful. She was very dark, jet black of hair and eye, and nearly black of skin. On this moonless night, he could barely see her. But he knew there were stars glittering in her hair, in her teeth and eyes, and stars between her legs as well.

Magya smiled and pulled her head away, kissing his palm. On the walk back to the house, she asked him about his vision. Ki-Ki did not talk to the tribe about his visions unless there was a good reason to do so. But he couldn't help telling Magya whenever she asked about them. He was still infatuated with her, and whenever she showed interest, unless the spirits had sworn him to secrecy, he would light up and chatter like a little boy.

"He said that hard times are coming," he told her quietly. "We are going to go on a difficult journey, through death, that God has laid out for us."

"God?" she echoed fearfully. "And, death?"

"Yes, wife." Ki-Ki did not elaborate on God, nor did he mention the frightening presence that had been there during his conversation with his grandfather.

"Do not be afraid," he added. "Grandfather said that he would guide us. He would go with us all the way to the end. And he – he said that he will guide me especially, and I must help the … the rest of you."

This did not strike Magya as improbable. The mantel of inspirer, of singer, had long since finished passing from Grandfather Nirri to Ki-Ki. But Ki-Ki had added to it his father's ability to talk to people, to understand them and do something with his understanding, as well as the ordinary woodland skills that every grown man had these days, but which Nirri had not.

But one part of the message did worry her.

"That is very … encouraging, husband. But did he say … 'the end' … did he say what it will be?"

"Not exactly," said Ki-Ki. "But he … well … he didn't make it sound as if the end would be all of us dying. It sounded more like … a new life, a new place for the children. A new land, perhaps."

Magya knit her brows in puzzlement. The People had come to the last land, everyone knew that. But then, Ki-Ki's spirit visitors often talked in riddles. For whatever reason, visions were not supposed to make immediate sense.

She rubbed her belly.

"A new land. I wonder how soon this will come true. I only hope … I hope it's safe for my baby."

Ki-Ki grinned and gave her belly a sympathetic pat before he ducked down into the door that led to their half-underground home. Then he reached up and helped her descend.

"We'll make it safe for her," he said, whispering now because inside the hut the other children were sleeping. "I … and the grandfathers."

ACKNOWLEDGMENTS

Wonderful Beta readers (in alphabetical order so I don't slight anybody): Arelis, Dawn, Josh, Matt, and Rachael.

Wonderful editor: Kitty Kladstrup.

Husband, children, sources of material: M, D, JM, and A.

Inspiration: C.S. Lewis, Edith Pargeter, Ursula Le Guin, the book of Genesis.

Encouragement and prayer backup: Many beloved friends, literary and otherwise.

And Jesus Christ, whose energy works so powerfully within me.

BIBLIOGRAPHY

My main source for the book's ideas about giants, the gods, the Tower, and its probable purpose was Douglas Van Dorn's *Giants: Sons of the gods* (Waters of Creation Publishing, 2013).

This was supplemented by Graham Hancock's *Fingerprints of the Gods: The Evidence of Earth's Lost Civilization* (Three Rivers Press, 1995), and what it suggests about the advanced science and technology of the very ancient world.

I recommend both these books to anyone who is interested in further research about what life might have been like in the so-called prehistoric world. And, of course, I always recommend reading the Bible.

The names Enmer, Endu, Ninna, Nimri, Shulgi, and Imsag were adapted from the chapter about Sumerian in Nicholas Ostler's *Empires of the Word: A Language History of the World* (HarperCollins Publishers Inc., 2005). Sumerian is the oldest language for which we have a direct written record, and it was spoken in the general vicinity of Babel.

Information about the Scyths and about Hur's recurve bow came from Eric Hildinger's *Warriors of the Steppe: A Military History of Central Asia, 500 B.C. to 1700 A.D.* (Sarpedon).

Zillah's herbal remedies, especially the bark she uses to try to prevent Ninna's miscarriage, come from *Prepper's Natural Medicine: Lifesaving Herbs, Essential Oils and Natural Remedies for When There Is No Doctor* by Cat Ellis, (Ulysses Press, 2015), and the article "The kalyna in Ukrainian folk medicine and folklore" by Orysia Paszczak Tracz, printed in *The Things We Do ...*, http://www.ukrweekly.com/old/archive/2001/220115.shtml .

Along the west coast of the Caspian Sea, there are actually two large and mysterious fortresses. Derbent, in Russia, has massive walls and is said to have been crafted by giants. Sabayil Castle, in Azerbaijan, has outer walls up to two meters thick and is in the actual location where Enmer and his family saw the giants building a castle on a peninsula. This information comes from "Underwater Archeology in the Caspian: Past, Present, and Hopefully Future," by Zhenya Anichenko, printed in *Azerbaijan International*, Winter 2006 (14.4), http://www.azer.com/aiweb/categories/magazine/ai144_folder/144_articles/144_zhenya.html , and "The Strange Mysteries of the Caspian Sea," by Brent Swancer, in *Mysterious Universe*, http://mysteriousuniverse.org/2015/04/the-strange-mysteries-of-the-caspian-sea/ .

The dark-haired people who were capturing a dragon, and who gave beer to Enmer and company, were inspired by the Neolithic Hongshan culture, centered around the Liao River in northern China, which left artifacts called "pig dragons." Information about this culture came from *The Ancient Chinese World* by Terry Kleeman and Tracey Barrett, (Oxford University Press, 2005), and *Ancient Chinese Civilization*, by Todd Van Pelt and Rupert Matthews, (The Rosen Publishing Group, Inc., 2010).

Quotes from the Bible are taken from the New International Version, Zondervan, 1995, except for the translation "perfect in his generations," which comes from Douglas Van Dorn.

Obviously, these sources were only used for research. Their authors would not necessarily endorse the interpretation given these facts in *The Long Guest*. All interpretations, speculations, errors, etc., are my own.

Coming soon …

THE STRANGE LAND

SEQUEL TO *THE LONG GUEST*

10,000 B.C. As his tribe approaches the Land Bridge, 13-year-old Ikash longs for a better life than the one he has with his mother, three brothers, and abusive father. He wants to become a shaman like his adored older cousin Ki-Ki, who regularly walks in the spirit world. But when Ki-Ki consents to teach him, Ikash is not prepared for what he will find there.

ABOUT THE AUTHOR

Jennifer Mugrage spent her youth gallivanting around Southeast Asia with her husband, learning languages and crossing cultures. Now she lives in the Western United States and home schools three active boys. Her experiences with anthropology, travel, and motherhood inform her fiction.

Visit her web site: https://outofbabel.com